EXTORTIONWARE

A Hackers Tale

For information about this title or to order other books and/or electronic media,
contact the publisher:

ww.tripelix.com

ISBN 978-0-9915685-0-5

Second Printed Edtion October 2014
Second Ebook Edtion October 2014

Manufactured worldwide

Cover and Design
Eric Murphy & Chelsea Creekmore

Edited by
Patrick Nickoletti PhD & Brynn Petano BA

This book is dedicated to Karen and the countless others whose precious lives are trafficked, online and offline. I wish you freedom and the end to this world-wide evil.

The Bad Day Gets Worse

The interview did not go well.

The unit manager flashed his cheesy grin as he shook Jason's hand on his way out. "We will be in touch," he said.

Jason had heard that before, quite a few times, and usually for the same reason: he was unemployed. And when you are not working, not only do you have to find a company that is hiring, you have to show the head ego that you are not a threat to his job, yet are still smart enough to work in his presence.

The interview was still stuck in Jason's head as he entered the elevator. "He will eventually take my job," Jason could hear the hiring manager thinking. "There is no way we should hire him."

1

Now what? He thought to himself as he pressed the lobby button. He had the money for rent and his car payment, but that was about it. His savings were minimal; he had played the stock market and lost big a few years ago when the market crashed and he still hadn't recovered. *Tap into my 401(k)? No, no,* he thought. *Something is going to have to wait.*

After he exited the elevator and made his way across the lobby, he suddenly realized that he hadn't even noticed if there was anyone else on the elevator. He thought about it as he walked past the security desk.

"Car payment, rent and cell phone bills are due soon," he mumbled to himself as an older lady got into the turnstile door in front of him. He could hear her cell phone ring as he entered behind her. Suddenly, *BAM*—his face bounced off the glass.

"OW, dumbass!" Jason blasted loudly at the woman, who had stopped in the door to answer her phone. The door moved again, and she exited. He gave her a dirty look as he walked onto the sidewalk. The woman looked back in confusion. *What's his problem?* She thought to herself.

He scoffed and shook his head, getting lost in his thoughts again. Jason's last job had been great. He' a member of a talented team that could build virtually anything. The problem was not with the work. It was that the President and Vice President of Marketing had embezzled from the company. The news stories that followed claimed amounts as lofty as 500 million dollars, an all-time high for stealing investment money.

He and his co-workers found out on a Tuesday, a few

weeks before it all went down. Jason remembered that day clearly. He'd gotten to work a few minutes late, but everyone else appeared to already be there. He could see that they were all assembled in the large glass conference room at the other end of the office.

When he approached the entrance to the room, he saw Mary, the receptionist, who was in tears. He walked by her to talk to his team member, Mark, inside the doorway. Dressed in an unkempt button-down, Mark looked as if he hadn't gone home the night before. He liked to work all night when he was stuck on something.

"Hey man, what's going on?" Jason whispered in Mark's ear. "Did someone die?"

Mark's reaction was not in secret. "No, would you believe that the old guy split town with Gloria?" he exclaimed.

"He did what?" Jason asked in disbelief.

Gloria was Vice President of Sales. She was an extremely pretty, big-busted blonde. A rare beauty-and-brains combo. She had graduated from both of the "only real schools" in the country, as she called them, meaning Harvard and Yale. She got her Master's at one of them and her Bachelor's at the other, but Jason couldn't remember which was which. She looked like the average dumb blonde, but when dealing with big bankers and lawyers, she was smooth. Jason had heard that she would unbutton the top of her blouse during negotiations, fumble with the next button when things were in her favor and play with the next one until the deal was signed. This cheap trick was not commonly used in the ultrahigh finance world. It was something those in power never expected: a woman with an extremely high IQ using the dumb blonde act in business.

Gloria had been dating some jerk lawyer who owned a Jaguar convertible. At least that was the last thing Jason had heard. Douglas was a businessman through and through. He was the leader of the company. He had been CEO of five or six companies in the past, and rumor had it that he'd been hired to take the company public. So, what could have happened? He had read in the newspaper that he was divorced several times.

"That's not possible!" Jason exclaimed loudly to Mark, who was standing next to him.

Yael, the project manager, bumped Jason's arm and asked, "Do you have your cell phone on you?"

Jason nodded.

"May I have it please?" Yael asked. "The police want all our phones. They said we can have them back when they are though with us." She turned away from Jason and shouted over the crowd, "NOW EVERYONE GO BACK TO YOUR DESKS!" As she spoke, Jason pulled his cell out, flipped open the cover, restored it to the factory setting, and closed the cover. When Yael turned back to Jason, he handed the cell to her.

Jason walked out of the crowded room. It was obvious to him that not everyone was in work that day. He worked with more than 250 people and they would have never all fit in the conference room. There were other offices in London,

Madrid, LA and Bangalore. *The other offices must know what is going on,* Jason thought.

As he and Mark walked back to the end of the office, they spoke in a low voices to each other. Jason asked Mark, "Really?" Mark confirmed by shaking his head no, but saying, "Yeah, man, it's true."

Mark's cube was two over from Jason's. Terry sat between them. Terry was late this day, as usual. He often stayed later once he arrived, so no one ever minded that he was never on time. "Well, the phone is dead," Mark said. Jason tried his Internet, but it was out too. *Great,* he thought. He got up and went to the men's room. He could see a guy in a suit standing next to the door leading out of the office.

He stopped at Jordan's cube, where Jordan was packing up his stuff. Jason asked him, "Any news?" Jordan retorted a simple, "Nope." Jason could sense the anger in his voice. "Just askin'," he stated as he headed back to his own cube.

When Jason got there, he opened the bottom right drawer of his desk and pulled out a bag with the word "CISCO" written on the side. He opened his top drawer and started transferring its contents into the bag. He stopped when he picked up a USB Wi-Fi adapter. In the past, Jason and Mark had made a long-range Wi-Fi antenna using a Pringles can and that adapter.

Jason sat down in his chair and wheeled it into the hallway just as they did when they were working together on projects. Jason called out, "Hey Mark, you still have that Pringles can?" As he spoke, he ran his chair into a very tall man wearing a government-issued dark blue suit. "Could you come with me, sir?" the man asked with a frown, trying not to show pain. Jason's chair had just stabbed him in the ankle.

Jason stood up. "Sure," he agreed. The agent guided Jason to one of the smaller conference rooms. Two agents were seated at the table. The agent who came with him stood at the door. The older-looking agent asked Jason to be seated, and started asking a series of questions about Douglas the CEO, and Gloria the Vice President. They wanted to know about any rumors he may have heard or anything he may have seen. Jason told them what he had heard, which really wasn't much. The agents questioning Jason started getting very personal, asking where he used to live and work and whether or not he had a girlfriend. The question about his parents' status bothered him the most. "Do I need a lawyer?" he interjected.

The older agent stared directly into Jason's eyes. Jason had read about this interrogation technique in the past. The agent stated flatly, "This is a federal investigation; you must answer all of our questions. Any lawyer would tell you to do so. Not complying with any of our requests would be considered a violation of federal criminal law."

Jason concentrated on not blinking as the agent spoke. He looked directly back at the agent, ignoring the presence of the other two men in the room. "Can I leave now?" he asked.

Another agent at the table spoke for the first time since Jason entered the room. "Sir, we are not done with your interview."

Jason, still staring into the eyes of the first agent, asked, "Am I under arrest?"

The older agent said, "No sir, we are finished. Thank you for your time. Agent Watts will escort you to your desk to get your belongings."

Jason got up from the table and was taken back to his cube with Agent Watts, the same man who had previously escorted him. When they got back, Mark was not in his cube anymore. Jason continued emptying the contents of the other drawers into the bag. He left the candy bag on Mark's desk, all the while, still under the watchful eye of the FBI agent. The agent spoke up when Jason reached for a notepad on the top shelf of this desk. "I'm sorry, sir, all records must stay on the property." Jason put the pad down for a second, but then picked it up again.

"It's blank, see?" Jason said, flipping the empty pages in front of the agent. He said nothing as Jason put it in his bag.

Another FBI agent approached Agent Watts and handed him Jason's cell phone. "It didn't have anything on it," he told Agent Watts. Agent Watts handed the phone to Jason. Jason thought that was indeed an understatement, since he'd reset it to factory mode and erased all information.

As Agent Watts walked with Jason all the way to his car, he pulled out a small notebook and wrote down his license plate number. Jason got in his car, backed out of the space and drove out of the parking lot, watching the agent in his rearview mirror.

Well, that was then. For now, his life was just one long string of interviews.

Jason shook his head. *What now?* He thought. The coffee house he liked was on the next block, so he waited for the traffic to go by and crossed the street. He hadn't even walked two steps on the sidewalk before he heard someone call out to him loudly.

"What up Josh! …Jason!" he heard.

Jason turned and saw Willy, an older black man he knew from the neighborhood, walking quickly to catch up with him. He stopped and turned to face Willy, who was now just a couple of steps behind him. "What's up, dude?" Jason asked Willy, continuing towards the coffee shop. The entrance was just two doors down from the corner. Willy walked by his side.

Willy asked Jason, "You still into computers?" *Oh no,* Jason thought, *here comes the "do me a favor."* For some reason, everyone who doesn't understand those things thinks everyone that does, works for free. Willy was known for being bad news anyway. He had gone to prison for something when he was a kid. After he got out, he ran some sort of basketball camp for kids in the summertime. The rumor was he was shady, and someone once said that he dealt in stolen stuff. Another time he heard that he was mixed up with drug peddling. *What does he want with me?* Jason thought.

"Yes, I still do computers, why?" Jason asked, cringing slightly as he waited for the inevitable question. Actually that's all he had ever done. When he was 15, he taught himself C, a computer programming language, while still in high school.

He had hacked a little when he was younger, screwing with the AOL accounts of his classmates. After high school, he went to a two-year technical college where he learned java. He thought that it would be easy to pick up a job anywhere, but the economy turned to trash and people seemed to want bachelor degrees. He had debated going back to school, perhaps to a four-year college. What he found was that the technical college's credits were not acceptable to any other school, not in their system. So he would need to retake the first two years again at a four-year school.

As he reached the doorway, Willy stepped ahead and opened the door for him. With a smile on his face showing his teeth, "Can I buy you a coffee?" he asked.

Jason responded, "Sure you can." Willy walked in front of him to lead the way.

Willy said, "I wanna pick your brain for a few minutes. What have you been up to anyway?"

"Long story," Jason responded.

Willy walked directly to a booth in the far back of the shop. There were just a few people and the booths were near the front window. The coffee shop was obviously built in the 1940s, complete with its original furniture. It was run by an Italian family and really had the look of a Hollywood mafia movie set. The floor was worn but clean, the furniture was old, but comfortable. Willy sat down with his back towards the wall so he could watch the front door. At least that was the impression Jason had.

Jason sat down across from Willy. A waitress appeared

with a notepad in hand. Her beehive hairdo looked out of place, like she never noticed that styles had changed. She was an older woman, in her 50s or 60s, but you couldn't tell. She had obviously spent too much time in the sun in her youth: Her skin was dark and slightly wrinkled, resembling worn leather. She had lightly colored fingernails that looked like they floated from her fingertips. A really weird affect, Jason thought.

The waitress asked, "Do you boys know what you would like?"

Willy quickly answered, "Just coffee." Jason chimed in, "Me too. Could I also have milk with that, please?"

The waitress went back to the counter. When she was out of earshot, Willy asked Jason, "So whatya been doing with yourself?"

"Just looking for a job; I lost my last one unexpectedly," Jason explained. "The president of the company took off to Bolivia with all the company funds. Everyone in my company lost their job. It was that investment company that has been all over the news. You must have heard about it. You go to work one day, and think everything is fine. Then you find out you don't have a job and the police are harassing everybody that worked there, like we had anything to do with it. If I stole 500 million dollars, would I still be here?"

"WOW." Willy exclaimed, his eyes fixed on Jason's. "So you know where the millions are?"

"I wish," Jason retorted. He thought to himself how he hadn't made any money for almost a month now. "But you do not want to hear my garbage, and we are not best friends. We just know each other from around the neighborhood.

You must want something from me. I know you are not just some good guy who wants to buy a cup of coffee for a guy who is down on his luck."

Willy nodded. He whispered, "You know how to get rid of a virus?" Jason was puzzled by the hushed tone for such a simple question.

Jason replied, "Sure. Computer viruses have been a problem forever." Jason remembered when he was in school a long time ago, and had had a virus toolkit for generating computer viruses. He and his other classmates would infect each other with their homemade viruses. One of his teachers accidentally confused Jason's USB thumb drive with her own and plugged it into the school's network. One of his high school buddies at the time got blamed for the virus and got expelled. What got his friend in so much hot water was that initially he took credit for it. Jason thought maybe his name was John, or maybe Jay, he wasn't sure. He had never seen him after that incident.

It got out of hand when the grading system became infected. The principal and the school board were looking for a scapegoat, and Jason was glad it wasn't him. He felt guilty, but things happened so quickly. The other guy bragged to his classmates that he wrote the virus and it was his. It didn't help that he had a copy of the same toolkit Jason used on his computer at home.

The lesson he'd learned about viruses, though, is that the kit stuff always got found. However, if you wrote your own by hand, they were almost never found. This guy had no idea about any of this. *Just play along*, Jason decided.

"I can't get rid of that damn thing, and the computers are running like crap," Willy complained. "Do you think you could come over and clean them? I'll give you a grand, and you keep your mouth shut about anything else you see." Willy spoke softly with a serious look on his face. "Do you think you could do that for me?"

Jason was not stunned by the dollar amount. When he had a job, a grand was less than he made a week. But unemployment made it seem like a lot of money. "How many computers are there?" He asked.

Willy replied, "15 or so."

Jason said, "I guess, sure I can do that." With the money, he would be able to make the rest of his payments, buy food and even have some cash left over.

Willy said, "I just can't get rid of that stupid thing. It's probably easy for you—the kid that used to use the pay phones for free."

Wow, he realized. Someone else saw him do that. A blue box is a modified speed dialer that fools a payphone into thinking you put money into it. He didn't know how much Willy knew about blue boxes, or that he used to make them and sell them to his friends, but obviously he'd been seen using one.

"Oh that," Jason said, trying to sound convincing. "It was nothing. I used to have a speed dialer with a credit card number on it."

Willy's eyes narrowed as he looked straight at him.

"Bullshit," he said. "My cousin says you know your shit and that you could get rid of this thing. I don't care about that or any other shit in your life, I just need it gone."

They were silent as the waitress came back with the coffees.

Willy watched her every movement.

"Will there be anything else?" the waitress asked as she flashed a forced smile to both men in the booth.

"No thanks," Willy said in a way that Jason didn't feel the need to answer. The waitress went back to the counter. A man raised his arm in another booth towards the front of the restaurant and the waitress walked in that direction.

Willy turned back to Jason. "I need to get rid of this thing—it's really fucking with stuff," he said impatiently. "When can you come by?"

Jason said, "So let me get this straight…you want me to get rid of viruses from 15 computers, and you will give me a thousand dollars?" He was still puzzled. It seemed like a lot of money for the task. And while he thought something fishy must be going on, he also thought how badly he needed the immediate money. He also remembered that Willy was a known criminal who did time. Why would he have so many computers? *Maybe he is straight now.*

Jason poured milk into his coffee and took a sip. As he did, he watched as Willy opened at least eight, maybe ten sugar packets, poured them all into the cup, and stirred with the spoon. He watched as Willy took a sip. Maybe it was drug addiction, Jason thought. He looked normal, not strung out at all. His appearance was business casual and neat. He wore a polo shirt and khaki pants. He could have fit in with anyone at any of the offices that he had worked before. His hands looked like business too—no rings or other jewelry. His nails looked well-manicured. Not super short, but groomed. Maybe the rumors about this guy were wrong.

Willy said, "It should be easy work for you. It will only take you a couple of hours. I can pay you in cash if you want." Jason had never had that much money as payment for anything in cash. Then Willy's cell phone rang. He pulled it out and answered it.

"HOLD ON," he barked as soon as the phone was to his ear. It was a very a demanding tone, almost as if the person at the other end was used to taking commands from him. He got up from the table and listened attentively to what the other person was saying.

Willy turned to face Jason and said, "I'll be right back, I need to take this. Sit tight." He walked through the coffee house and out the front door with his cell phone in his hand.

Jason had known of Willy since he was a small kid in the neighborhood. He doubted his parents would have ever associated with him or ever had a coffee with him. That was Jason's way though. He liked people and accepted people for who they were. His parents had died a number of years ago, both from old age. They'd had him when they were in their late 40s. By the time he had graduated from trade school, his father had already passed. Shortly after that, his mother moved to an assisted living center, and later to a nursing home due to declining health. The house he grew up in was sold to pay for her care, which was until she died almost six years ago. There really wasn't anything left in the estate (he'd always thought what a laugh it was to call it that), since by the time his mother died, nearly everything had been sold. He'd kept a broken alarm clock he played with as a kid as his only trophy.

He pulled out his own cell phone to check if there were any new job postings. He had last checked in the morning. There was nothing new. *There is always tomorrow,* he told himself. *Maybe I will have to get a part-time job doing something else for a while. Or maybe it is time to move somewhere else to find a job.*

While he thought that the work opportunity would cover all the bills for this month, he was concerned about all of the secret shit and why this street hustler would have that many computers. Willy was a scammer. He was always up to something. That's all that Jason knew about him. The rumor that he'd been in jail was just a rumor, something kids hear when the adults talk among themselves. He wondered if anybody else remembered the phone call gadget.

While finishing his last sip of coffee, Willy came in from behind, but did not sit down. He simply threw a $10 bill on the table. He asked, "Do we have a deal?" He was looking down at him and standing in a way that blocked Jason from getting up.

"Sure, I guess," he said sheepishly.

Willy put his hand in his pocket and pulled out a business card. He held it in front of Jason to take it.

"Give me a call tomorrow," Willy told him. "I don't know

what my schedule is going to be. We'll set it up." With that, Willy turned and started walking toward the coffee shop exit. "See you tomorrow, kid," he said.

By the time Jason rose to his feet, Willy was halfway across the restaurant.

He saw the waitress looking at him and told her, "You're all set." He needed a drink. It was early in the afternoon and he felt guilty about going directly to Tony's, the bar around the corner, but he wasn't sure what else to do with himself. He always had a job. It wasn't the weekend yet. It just felt funny. He was not used to having nothing to do in the middle of day, in the middle of the week.

He decided to stop by the apartment and change his clothes before going out for something to eat. He was shocked when he got to the parking lot. His car was not in its space.

His heart was racing, and he felt sick to his stomach. *Who would want to steal a 5-year-old Nissan Sentra?* He called the police, and waited almost two and a half hours for a patrol unit to come take a report. The two police officers were nice and understanding as they explained that his car was a popular type for people to steal.

After the police left, Jason called his insurance company. They transferred him at least five times. One of them finally took his information and said they would get back to him. Since Jason did not pay for their optional "towing and disablement package," he was not eligible for getting a rental car.

After he hung up, he went back outside and walked toward Tony's.

Along the way, he stopped for Pho, a Vietnamese soup

dish. Pho was Jason's comfort food. He had it whenever something bad happened, or when he was sick. And it was the restaurant he always visited for a bowl of soup.

At the end of the bar, Jason could see Randy, already buzzed. He always drank martinis, and once he had five or six and could barely walk, he would call a cab.

April was sitting on the other side of Randy. Now in her 60s and not well preserved, it was hard to imagine that she'd been an exotic dancer in her youth. She was always at the bar, and when she wasn't, the regulars would all ask where she was. Jason had talked to her a few times about nothing particularly important. Her life was now about getting drunk every day. He wasn't sure if she had a problem with alcohol; it seemed that's just what she enjoyed doing.

And there was Tony, the big guy behind the bar. He stood over six feet six inches tall and towered over most customers. He was a nice guy, but not very talkative. Some of the younger girls that came in late at night came looking for him. He was always happy to oblige.

Usually, Jason would come to the bar around 5:30 and would leave by 7:30, getting a bite to eat afterwards. He was normally in bed by 10:30 and up at 6 to be at work by 9. Two beers, a conversation about movies or news events, then home. Today, he looked at his cell phone. It said 4 PM. *Shit*, he thought. *It's still early.*

He raised his hand to signal Tony, who brought him a Bud Light. As he put the bottle in front of him, Jason asked, "Do you know who Willy is, from the REC Center?"

Tony responded, "Who is what?"

Jason repeated his question: "Do you know who Willy is, from the REC Center?"

Tony said, "Yeah, why? Are you looking for a hooker?"

Jason replied, "No, why would I be? Is that what he is into?"

He leaned over the bar, and spoke directly into Jason's ear. Tony said, "I don't know what he's into now, but when I see him around, there are usually prostitutes with him."

Jason knew better than to ask more questions. He said thanks to Tony and took a long drink from the beer bottle. He sat back on the stool wondering if he was over-thinking this. Anyway, it was an easy thousand bucks.

By the end of his second beer, some of the other regulars floated in. A buddy of his started telling jokes and bought him a third beer. He had several people listening. He should have been a stand-up comic, Jason thought. Some guy at the end of the bar bought everyone a shot of wild turkey. Jason wondered why he didn't do this more often.

The lights in the bar came on at last call. He looked at his phone, which told him it was 1 AM. He paid his tab and walked back to the apartment, slightly drunk. The bar made him forget his car and financial issues for a little while. It was a nice break to forget about that stuff.

A New Day Is Coming

The alarm went off at 6 AM as usual, but Jason didn't really feel like getting out of bed. He reached over and hit the snooze button at least twice. By the time he was dressed, ate his last bagel and finished his coffee, it was 9 AM. He could not locate the card Willy had given him. After searching the apartment, he finally found it in the pocket of the pants he had worn the day before – the pants he had thrown into the hamper last night.

He did not look at the card when Willy had given it to him; he had just stuck it in his pocket.

He wondered to himself where area code 212 was. It wasn't anywhere around where he lived. He noticed that the last digit was not on the card. *What is this?* He thought to himself. The card looked like it had been folded one time over the last number, which was possibly a 2 or a 7—or was that a 4? Great, he thought to himself. He tried a 2 and on the first ring, Willy answered the phone.

"Talk to me," Willy said.

"Hi, this is Jason."

"Hey, is now a good time for you?" Willy asked. "How long will it take?"

"I really don't know, sometimes it takes a while to scan for these things," Jason answered.

There was a long pause. Willy finally said, "Okay, I understand. Look, just don't interrupt anyone while they're working. The address is 1147 West 8th Street, fourth floor. You can come over now if you want."

That's not too far away, Jason thought. "I'll see you in a bit," he said, and hung up. Jason debated driving there, but remembered he did not know where his car was. He thought he could use another cup of coffee so he grabbed his laptop bag and walked down the street to the 7-11 at the end of the third block. He drank his coffee and walked the remaining thirteen and a half blocks to 1147 West 8th Street, which was a hotel. The sign that was supposed to spell out "HOTEL" flashed a measly "HO L." One of the neon lights flickered and the other was burnt out; the paint was peeling and it looked like it had been there for a very long time.

As Jason entered the lobby he thought it looked more like a flophouse. There was an older man at the front desk behind a cage, like you would see at an old bank. The desk looked more like a banker's cage than a hotel counter. It had bars that went from the counter to the ceiling, with an opening in the front to slide items without reaching between the bars. At the opposite side of the room was an old TV bolted to the wall. An old man with a white cane sat on the couch opposite the TV.

The only light in the room came from a big, grey window. Jason suspected that it was that color because of dirt, not because the window was actually tinted grey.

As soon as Jason approached the desk, the older man behind it asked, "What do you want?"

"I'm here to see Willy," Jason replied, completely unsure of his surroundings.

The man behind the desk said, "Fourth floor. Elevator is right around the corner, but it doesn't work. Stairs are through the door across from the elevator."

"Thanks," Jason said. He walked past the cage and toward the back of the hotel. The hallway was dimly lit. From where Jason stood he could not even see the end of the hallway. As soon as he turned the corner he found the old freight elevator. The sign on it read, "OUT OF ORDER." It looked like it had been a very long time since the elevator had worked. Across the hall from the elevator door was another door. He opened it and saw the stairs.

The stairwell was also dimly lit, to say the least: One bare bulb jutted out of the wall just above the door he came through, which closed with a thud on his third step. Each floor had the same light above its door. The stairwell had the scent of urine. It reminded Jason of a place where delinquents came to practice mugging people.

Finally on the fourth floor, he opened the door to a sight that didn't seem to fit with the others. Someone had knocked down all the inside walls and made a big opening. The building was narrow and long and he saw two rows of office cubes that stretched its length. The cubes made a small waiting area for whoever came up the stairs.

There were two chairs to the left of the doorway. Directly in front of the doorway and to the right of the opening in the cubes was a table with a computer and monitor sitting on it. It looked like a makeshift desk.

At the ceiling level at either end of the room were large convex mirrors. The mirrors were the kind that shopkeepers used to watch for shoplifters. Next to the mirrors were camera domes. From where he was standing, Jason could see inside all of the cubes. He then saw Willy walking down the cube row, to the entrance to meet him. Whoever had put the cubes in blocked the windows partially so you could only see the window tops above the cubes.

Willy appeared from the cubes wearing an expensive shirt, dress pants and dark shoes. He looked like he was dressed to go to an expensive Saturday-night disco. The smile he gave Jason was a grin that bordered on being devious.

"I'm glad you could come." Willy said, shaking Jason's hand. "You found us okay?"

Jason said, "No problem," and thought to himself what a stupid question that was. *I'm already standing here.*

Willy said, "Well, there is lots of work to do, come this way." He started walking into the cube row and swung a left into the hallway of cubes that were now on either side of them.

To the left and right along the way were women in each of the cubes typing on computers. In one cube, he saw web browsers and Skype open, where one woman was typing a message. In the next cube a woman was typing with multiple browsers open. He could see AOL chat in the foreground. The woman across from her also had many browsers open and was typing a message on Facebook. Jason had been in many offices, but never saw so many people all using chat clients of various forms before.

The only sound in the room was the pitter-pat of people typing on keyboards. They made an uneven clacking sound that filled the room. No one was talking. Jason had once worked in a bank where the same "silence—work only" rule was followed. It was the reason he didn't work there long.

At the end of the cube row, Willy stopped and directed Jason into the cube where there were two chairs in front of a desk. Behind the desk sat a giant Asian man. His head was shaved and he was wearing a white tee shirt. His chest and arms were covered with tattoos that showed through the fabric of his shirt. The man looked like he was between 270 and 300 pounds, and his arms were as big as Jason's thighs.

"Have a seat," Willy said to Jason. The Asian guy had a frown on his face and Willy told him, "Don't worry, man, he is here to fix this stuff and make it work right again. Aren't you Jason?" The Asian guy just looked at Jason, who suddenly noticed that his left hand was missing the ring finger. It was cut off right at the knuckle.

"You git virus bye bye," he said to Jason.

Jason replied, "Okay?" He was feeling quite intimidated by the large Asian man.

Willy looked at the Asian man when he spoke. "You help him with whatever he needs. I have a meeting." In response, the Asian guy grunted. Willy then walked out of the room. He had never introduced Jason to the Asian guy.

Jason stood upright as the Asian man did. As he rose, it was obvious that he was over six feet tall. He was actually too big to go behind the table that split the cube in two. When he went by the wall, he nudged the table to give himself some room, which made the other side buckle a little.

The Asian man led Jason to the first cube where a somewhat pretty brunette girl was typing away. She looked up at Jason, and dropped her head, almost as if to avoid eye contact. She looked as though she was in her late twenties, possibly 30. She didn't say anything, so he didn't know if she had an accent, but she had a European look. Her tee-shirt read "Yankees."

Jason watched as she closed all the programs she had opened. She came out of the cube and looked down as she passed him. She made her way to the end cube that Jason was previously in.

The Asian guy looked down at Jason and said, "Get rid of virus," pointing at the screen. Jason sat down. He found that the computer had every browser and chat installed that he had ever heard of. Also installed were tons of malware applications and two antivirus programs.

Okay, this is different. He was never threatened to clean a computer. This guy was intimidating and he sure as hell didn't want to do anything to upset him. The Asian man walked away in the direction of his own cube.

Jason immediately went into the control panel and removed one of the antivirus programs. *If they are all like this, it's going to be an easy day,* he thought. *Everybody knows you can't run two antivirus programs.*

As he did that, he looked for signs of what the computer was used for, but there were no documents or pictures. No network printers or any printer installed. The setting on the web browser said that it was proxies to an IP address that Jason didn't recognize. A proxy is a setting on computers to redirect the traffic to another computer. Many times this is used so that corporations can filter viruses and bad websites from being opened on their networks. It is also used by security teams to watch what sites are accessed or to mask the link so that the logs of the website show the proxy server rather than the computer accessing the site. Sometimes viruses will do this to steal passwords of banking sites.

Jason looked over his shoulder. No one was there. He looked up and could see the Asian guy in the mirror staring down at something. He quickly turned back. He had to open a web browser to find a Geo tool first after which he put in the IP address. It reported the IP was in the Chechen republic. This was obviously wrong so he removed it. He still had an uneasy feeling about this place, like he should get out of there. He could feel the dampness under his armpits, which always happened when he was nervous. *You need the money,* he reminded himself.

After updating the protection programs, he rebooted the computer. While he waited, he unpacked his computer and set it on the table next to the monitor. Searching through his bag, he took out the two network wires and small hub he always carried. This allowed him to add his computer to the network, but he was about to use it on the computer he was sitting at. He booted his laptop and changed its hardware identification number; he didn't want his laptop to be recorded on this network—who knows what is on it anyway.

He noticed soon that the computer did not have a login name; it just started automatically. Any user had full permission to the computer.

I bet these people, whoever they are, don't do anything they aren't supposed to on these computers, Jason thought. He also assumed that no one there was the least computer savvy. Willy no doubt had been the one to install the two antivirus applications.

Jason used a tool on his computer to probe the network and found 58 devices in all that were connected, including his laptop. Some of the devices were network equipment, some were computers and some didn't display what they were. There were no printers. Interesting and odd, he thought. All of the computers were logged in as administrator, and he could access the files on any of them from his laptop. The whole network was wide open. He didn't try probing any further—you never knew who might be watching. Besides he could only see 15 or so computers here not the 58 that he got back from his scan.

The router connection was a cheap home router; it had the default password set. The connection was a local cable provider. The list of connections going out from the network was huge. Every social site was connected more than once, and many other sites, too. Checking fast, Jason realized some of the addresses belonged to porn sites. Many of the computers were going to a variety of proxies, but the chat windows were made directly: Google, Facebook, AOL, Skype and some he would need to look up later to see what they were. The scan took over two hours to complete, and in that time, he figured out the login IDs for many of the users using the sites. Some of the sites had multiple IDs being used on the same service.

He ran a tool against the local computer and saw it had a number of weaknesses itself, so he started patching and downloading service packs that weren't on his laptop to the computer he was working on.

The clicking of keyboards typing was the only sound in the room, apart from the occasional traffic sounds from the distant street below. The silence was broken suddenly with the sound of his cell phone ringing in his pocket. It startled him; he quickly pressed the button on the side of it so the call went to voicemail. Pulling his phone from his pocket, he checked the number, which he didn't recognize. *Hopefully a job offer.*

Jason locked his laptop screen and looked at the computer that was still downloading patches. The connection must be pretty slow here with all of the people chatting on all these sites, he thought.

He turned to get up and noticed the Asian guy was standing just outside the cube. "I'll be right back," Jason said to him. The Asian guy didn't say a word in reply, but as he walked past him, Jason could feel the Asian guy staring at his back the entire time as he walked. He felt a little relieved when he got to the staircase. He noticed the absence of phones on his way out. He couldn't spot anyone with a phone on his or her desk.

Jason left his laptop on the desk so it could probe the network further. He had locked it with his fake screen saver. The program he had written made the computer look like a Windows screen saver with a twist. If anyone attempted to login twice incorrectly, the laptop would then begin the process of deleting its drive. If the machine was left alone long enough, it would turn the drive into a paper weight. There was a flaw in one laptop hard drive manufactures software that allowed the mechanism to scratch the disk, making it unreadable. He was pleasantly surprised to find that even the new drives by that same manufacturer still contained the flaw. Hopefully no one tested it again for him.

Once outside, he felt free. *What a place,* he thought to himself. *This is going to take longer than a day; it's been over three hours just to fix the first one.*

The voicemail wasn't good news; it was a representative of his bank, informing him that they had been notified of the car theft, asking if he could call their office immediately to discuss a payment arrangement. He sighed. Unbelievable, he thought. It hasn't even been 24 hours yet. He called his insurance agent, who was not in his office, so he left a voicemail to call him back.

Across the street was a McDonald's. It wasn't his favorite kind of food, but he wanted to stay nearby and get the job done. After ordering, he ate his lunch by the front window. He watched for signs of anyone leaving the door to the hotel. No one came or went. While he was eating, he called the placement rep to check on any new development or interviews. Nothing new, the rep reported. He checked again on monster.com. No change there. Perhaps there were a few things across the country he could apply for instead.

He was finishing his food when his cell phone rang. The rep he had just gotten off the phone with asked if he could go to an interview tomorrow at 9 AM. Fortunately, the interview wasn't far from where he was now. This was great news, a job possibility at least. Now in a better mood, Jason went back the makeshift office. As he crossed the hotel lobby, he noticed the blind man wasn't there and the TV had some soap opera on. The volume was loud and the guy in the cage was watching intently. Jason didn't say a word as he passed by on the way to the stairwell.

His cube was the way he left it. The computer was finished downloading and installing, and the scans came up with simple spyware junk and lots of tracking cookies, but nothing serious. He checked on the cookies to see who had made them, but he wound up finding lots of porn sites.

He logged into his laptop and checked its logs quickly to see if anything had tried to probe it off the wire. The exploit log gave him a list of things to address on other computers on the network. He saved the files and shut the machine down.

As he was shutting the laptop, Willy spoke from behind him. "How's it going?" The voice startled Jason. The place was just so absent of any conversations, and any chatter or noise seemed out of the ordinary. He jumped a little, and turned to face Willy.

"It's going," Jason stated. "You have a lot of things wrong here, you know. Everyone has too many rights and the configuration of this machine was not correct." Jason figured his wording was better than saying some idiot put two anti viruses on the computer and screwed up the box.

Willy didn't look surprised. "My cousin did all this up for me," he explained. "He is out of touch right now so, that's why he's not doing the work."

Jason said, "Maybe it would be better if I came back later, when no one was here. Then I could work on more than one at a time." He didn't add that he knew how to push many of the patches out from his computer and speed them up a bit. Some people get upset if a technician doesn't seem to spend enough time fixing a problem.

Willy talked over him: "There's always someone here. It's a 24-hour shop. Just like a 7-11, we never close."

Jason was surprised at this. "Okay," he said. "It's going to take a while doing it this way."

Willy smiled and said, "That's okay. Are you done with this one now? Time is money."

Jason looked at the computer screen; it had a pop-up that said the machine must be restarted. Jason said, "Sure, it's fine now."

"Good," said Willy. Do this one next, he pointed at a blonde woman, who got up from the cube across the row from him. She didn't look directly at Jason, just at the floor. She walked past him and went to the cube that he was just in. He sat down in front of the computer and started working. Willy watched him for a while, not saying anything. A couple hours later, he switched with the cube next to the one he was currently in.

After taking much longer on the second machine, Jason decided to connect to all of the computers in the room, using his laptop and scan them remotely. He also wrote a quick script to update and remove the useless crap on the other machines. He left his laptop connected and around 6:30, commotion started. All of the women got up and walked out of the room with the Asian guy. Jason was the only one left in the room for a short while. He could hear the door close and footsteps on the stairs. The room was almost totally quiet. A few minutes later, he heard footsteps on the stairs again.

A new set of women came in. A guy that was with them was Asian, but much younger and skinnier than the other one. Jason could see that he was covered with tattoos up to his neck. Jason got a glimpse of a few of the women as they passed by. One had red hair and looked sickly thin. The left side of her face was swollen, as if someone had beaten her badly. No one spoke.

Jason tried not to think about how weird this place was. All he had left to do was reboot them as he got to them. He checked a few settings, and by 7:30 he was on the 8th computer. He didn't feel like being there any longer. He was getting hungrier and more tired by the minute. He had checked monster and a few other employment sites on his cell while he was waiting and still nothing new. He sent a text to Willy that he wanted to leave and come back tomorrow. The problem he found with the speed of the computers was the same on every box. Easy to fix, just time consuming.

Willy appeared a few minutes later; he must have still been in the building because he heard him on the stairwell.

"How much more do you have to do?" Willy asked.

"Not much, but I'm hungry and need some fresh air." Jason replied.

"How many hours left, do you think?" he asked Jason.

"At least three, but I can't come until tomorrow afternoon because I have an interview in the morning."

Willy replied, "Well, good for you. What are you looking for anyway?"

"I'm really a programmer," Jason said. "I know how to do lots of stuff, but that's really what I enjoy."

"Really?" Willy said. "Good for you. I checked out that first computer you worked on and it is a lot faster. What kind of programming do you do?"

"I code in java and C sharp, but prefer java. It's really powerful you can do virtually anything with it. I have worked mostly in the banking industry."

"Really?" Willy sounded excited. "Anything?"

"Pretty much," Jason responded. "Many things run java… phones, computers, cars…it's a completely open architecture."

"You lost me," Willy said, shaking his head. "But it doesn't matter. Would you like me to order some food for you? So you can finish?"

Jason said, "Not tonight, I'm tired and I need to get some rest. But thanks for the offer."

Willy said, "Where did you park? You can use one of my spots behind the building tomorrow. It has a fence and cameras."

"Oh I didn't drive…my car is in the shop," Jason said, knowing it was a lie. He didn't think Willy needed to know his business.

He remembered where he was suddenly and was pretty sure something here was not okay. He felt he really needed to get out of there. "I'll be in tomorrow and finish .There are only a few more," Jason said, as he was stuffing wires into his laptop bag.

"Good luck tomorrow," Willy said.

Jason thanked Willy and, once outside, crossed the street and went back to the McDonald's. This time he just ordered a Coke and sat down at a table a few rows back from the window. He wanted to take another look at that hotel from the outside. He could see a least two cameras mounted on the exterior of the hotel pointing at the sidewalk below. He wasn't sure, but it looked like another one was mounted to the hotel sign as well.

More Things Go Amiss

J ason walked back to his apartment, stopping at a street vendor along the way for a hotdog and chips. He ate them as he walked home. He was tired and just wanted to go to bed.

As he neared the end of the block, he could see the police car blocking the road completely. All traffic was detoured so no one could drive past his apartment or any of the others on his street.

When he turned the corner, there were more police cars and an ambulance sitting directly in front of his apartment building. They could be there for the building across the street too; there was no one on the sidewalk directly in front of either of them. Jason stood there for a while waiting for some activity to tell him which building they were interested in. It had been a long day.

There were police everywhere, some in small huddles talking or drinking coffee, and others filling out forms and writing diligently in their report books. They all seemed busy doing something, and there was no real indication which building they were interested in.

No one seemed to pay any attention as Jason walked up the three steps to open the front door.

"HEY, YOU STOP!" he suddenly heard someone shout from the street. "WHERE DO YOU THINK YOU'RE GOING?" Jason turned around to see two police officers on the street walking quickly towards him.

"I live here", Jason said.

A man on the sidewalk wearing a '70s plaid jacket spoke: "Would you mind coming over here for a minute, mister?"

"Um, mister?" the cop to his right said.

"What's your name, dumbass?"

The other cop said, "Would you mind stepping on the sidewalk and talking to Detective Smith, sir?"

Jason was unsure who they were talking to and assumed it was him. They stepped apart to let Jason walk between them toward the guy in the plaid jacket, whom he could now see was wearing a police badge on his pocket. The badge was highly polished; the light coming from one of the police cars reflected off of it, making it appear that he had a flashing light on his front jacket pocket.

Detective Smith asked, "Do you have any ID on you?"

Jason said "Sure," pulling his driver's license out of his wallet and handing it to the detective. He asked, "What happened here"?

The detective pulled a small flash light out of his rear pocket and shined it on the license so he could read it. "How long have you lived here?" he asked. He didn't wait for the answer; he started walking away from Jason with his license in hand. He walked about twenty feet, and Jason followed. They stopped under a street light. Then the detective put the flashlight in his back pocket, pulled a small notebook out of his jacket with a pen and started taking notes from Jason's license. "How long have you lived here?" he repeated louder.

Jason walked to where the detective was and replied, "Um, about eight years I guess. What's going on?"

"You live upstairs in 2A?" Detective Smith asked.

Jason was starting to get annoyed that his questions were being ignored, but he tried to hold it back. "Yes," he said.

Detective Smith asked, "Where were you tonight?"

"I had to walk, I was working late," Jason said.

"I know your car was stolen."

"Yes, it was."

Detective Smith asked, "Who do you work for, Jason? Is it okay if I call you Jason?"

Jason responded, "Yes, it's okay. I work in computers I was removing a virus from someone's computer." Jason thought he might have said too much.

Detective Smith asked, "What time did you go to work this morning?"

"I left around 10, I think."

"You don't have to be there at a specific time?" the detective asked.

"No sir. Um, it's a temp job just for a few days," Jason said. His laptop bag was starting to feel heavy; it was digging into his shoulder. He took it off and set it on the ground. When he did, he heard the clank of metal hitting concrete and turned to see two guys in white taking someone on a stretcher covered in a tarp down the steps.

"What's going on here?" Jason said as he turned back to the detective.

"Do you have the phone number for the place you were at today?"

Jason started to pull out his cell phone and thought, *now what do I do? Willy's guys would probably do something to me if I gave them Willy's phone number.* He opened his phone and looked at the call history; he gave the detective the phone number of the bank off the screen, and said, "I think that is the right one."

The detective jotted down the number. As he did, the sound of two doors slamming came from the back of the ambulance. Another guy in a dark suit called out, "Hey Dave, you have a minute?"

The detective raised his head and spoke loudly to him in return, "In a moment." Detective Smith turned back to Jason. "So you were at work since 10 and you are just now getting home?"

"No, I left around 10. I had to walk there, so it took me 20 minutes..."

The detective began walking away as Jason spoke. While Jason was still talking he said, "Stay put, I'll be right back." Jason watched as the two men in suits had a short conference on the landing of the apartment building.

The building super walked up to Jason; he had seen him around before, though he'd never needed his services. Pat, Jason thought his name was, but he wasn't sure. He was a 50-something ex jock who'd played professional baseball for six months. At least that was what he overheard in the building. He was now the superintendent of several apartment buildings owned by an investment group. He was wearing a bright red t-shirt with bright gold letters reading 'CCCP' and a hammer and sickle printed on it; dark highwater sweat pants with stripes down the side; white socks; and white running shoes. Actually, Jason thought he looked like the poster boy for the word "dork." He bet he didn't still live at home, as he couldn't imagine a mother willingly dressing her child that way.

Pat turned and saw Jason. "Well that sucks, huh?" he said.

Jason thought for a second and responded, "Yeah, he was a nice guy."

"She was such a sweet lady... who could do such a thing?"

Finally, Jason had an idea of what was going on. Mrs. Green was an older woman in her 70s who had a cat; she lived downstairs. She was a nice older lady and she dated Mr. Jones across the hall. They were both divorced, and had met each other in the apartment building. They would have dinner in each other's apartments or watch TV together. Every once in a while she would make chicken soup and leave a small Tupperware container outside his door. They had been seeing each other for years, long before Jason had moved in. Once when Jason was in Mr. Jones's apartment, he was telling him some story about the Vietnam War while sipping straight whiskey. He had been through some pretty scary stuff. He told Jason he was a tunnel rat. Whatever that meant. Jason wasn't sure…but it didn't sound good.

"Both of them?" Jason asked Pat. "That is horrible. Do they know who did this?"

"I don't think they have any idea," Pat said. "Ted, your neighbor from across the hall, came home and found blood on the floor coming from under Mrs. Green's door and called the police." The man who lived across from Jason's apartment was Ted, the security guard. Ted worked all the time and was practically never home. In the eight years of living in the apartment building, Jason saw Ted maybe twice a month, when he picked up his mail. He came and left at all hours. Mrs. Green had said once that he had a wife and child somewhere and just worked to send money home. All he knew about Ted was that he lived across from him. He never really had a conversation with him, other than saying hello.

Jason looked back to the two detectives on the landing. They were in some sort of heavy discussion both with their notebooks open. The detective looked at Pat and Jason and called out, "Mr. Duffy, would you come here?"

"This is not good. I don't make enough money to clean this up…" His voice drifted as he walked away. Jason realized that Pat was talking to himself and not to Jason. *What an idiot,* he thought. He watched Pat join the detective on the landing. He saw Pat pull out his cell phone and start talking to someone in front of the two detectives.

Eventually, Detective Smith came back to where Jason was standing. "Here, you can have this back," he said, giving back Jason's driver's license. "Do you have anywhere you can go?"

Jason replied, "For how long? I live here."

The detective frowned at Jason before speaking. "This may take a few hours."

"Was it really both of them?" Jason asked.

The detective asked, "Were you close to them?"

"Not really. We talked every once in awhile," he said. He thought about it and he should have said he spoke to Mrs. Green every once in a while.

Detective Smith said, "You should go somewhere for a while. At least a couple of hours." At that moment, Jason's stomach rumbled. The hot dog he had earlier wasn't agreeing with him.

As Jason turned, he said, "Sure, there's an all-night coffee shop down the street."

The detective turned and walked back to the landing. Jason pulled out his cell to see it was now 10:46 p.m..

Jason was tired; it was a long day, and it was late. Doris's Coffee House was a city fixture. Doris had died several years ago, but the building still had her name in bright red neon letters out front. The coffeehouse was originally built in the 1950s; it was white with chrome accents everywhere. The years had slipped by and the interior had become dingy and run down until a couple of years ago. Some movie company used it to shoot a movie and had redone the entire building. The movie and its actors won awards and made lots of money for the movie business. Jason had never seen the film and had no idea what it was about.

As he entered the coffee shop, a female voice came from behind the counter: "You can sit anywhere." As he got closer, he could see the voice came from an extremely pretty girl in a 1950s style uniform. She was making a pot of coffee. There was some older man hunched over at the end of the counter, staring at her.

There was a 30-something couple in one of the booths, leaning over the table, staring into each other's eyes. Jason took a booth towards the back. He sat down and opened his laptop. As he was waiting for it to boot up, he noticed something he hadn't seen in years: A payphone booth with a payphone inside.

The waitress, who looked like she was in her 20s, came over. "Do you need to see a menu?" she asked.

"Does that thing work?" Jason asked, nodding at the payphone.

The waitress said, "I think so. You have to use dimes though."

Jason stuck his hand in his pocket pulled two singles out. "Could I have a menu," he asked, placing the bills on the table. "A decaf and two dollars in dimes."

He logged into his computer and changed his machine ID number again. He saved the old ID as he would need it for tomorrow at Willy's. That is, if he went back. He thought he would have to just finish and get the money. The restaurant had an open Wi-Fi, so he joined it and opened a web page.

He logged onto one of the local television networks and came across the story about his apartment building. He looked through his bag for his ear buds, but couldn't find them. So he turned the volume down so it was just loud enough for him to hear.

The reporter stated: "Two people were found dead in their apartments. Police say the victims were attacked around 4:30 p.m. Both victims were elderly and police say that it is possible that it was an invasion robbery gone horribly wrong. The names of the victims are being held until the next of kin can be notified. If you were in the area and saw anything around 4:30, please call the local crime stoppers."

He didn't notice the waitress standing over him with his coffee. "Oh, I heard about that when I came into work, it is not far from here," she said.

"No, it's not far from here I think," he said. As soon as she left, Jason pulled out his cell phone and looked up Willy's number. He went to the pay phone and deposited five dimes for the first two minutes. Willy picked up the phone on the first ring.

"Talk to me."

"Hey Willy, sorry to bother you but something bad has happened," Jason said.

"Jason, is that you?" Willy asked concerned.

"Yeah, it's me."

"Where are you man?"

"Doris's Coffee House. It's on…"

"I know where it is. I'll be right there," Willy said and hung up.

Jason listened to the dial tone and finally hung up the phone. He looked over at the waitress, who was talking to the guy at the end of the counter. It sounded like he was trying to ask her out, but Jason wasn't sure so he sat back down in the booth.

Jason drank the coffee black and looked at the menu. He went to another station's website to see if the story was any different there. They had featured an interview with Detective Smith, but did not really give any more information.

The waitress came back to take his order. He sipped his coffee. It wasn't long until Willy appeared at the front door along with another black man dressed in a sharp suit. He looked like a lawyer. Willy smiled when they made eye contact and walked back to the booth where Jason was sitting.

Willy sat on the bench seat and scooted over to make room for his associate. "This is Anthony Do you have any cash on you?" He asked.

Jason was not sure what was going on. He replied, "Uh, yeah, I have some cash, why?"

"Can I get five dollars, from you?" Willy asked. Jason reached in his pocket and produced a five-dollar bill and held it up so Willy could see it.

"Hand it to Anthony," Willy said.

Jason did. "I really don't understand," he said. "Look, I called you because I had something happen at home."

Willy said, "I heard about that. It's tragic how our community has become so violent."

Jason ignored him. "The police wanted to know where I was, they asked for a phone number," he said.

Willy looked shocked, and then smiled. Through his grin he said, "You didn't give them my cell number, did you?"

Jason replied, "No, I gave them my bank's number. I didn't want to give them your number. But when they find out I gave them the wrong number, I'm going to need a number to give them."

Anthony handed Jason his card. It read: Robinson, Caruso and Cowe, Attorneys at Law. Anthony H. Jones, ESQ. *You have to be joking*, Jason thought to himself, *what a loser of a name.*

Anthony said, "You were at my office all day," he said. The address on the card was the 36th floor of the City Tower Building. Jason had worked in that building once in the past at a temp position and remembered it had lots of floors. It was the tallest building in town. "Why don't you stop over tomorrow and acquaint yourself with my staff?" Jason was not sure what was going on, but this did not sound like a good idea.

Willy asked, "Did they ask you where you were?"

Jason replied, "I didn't say anything. I told them I was working and I do computers. I just gave them my bank's phone number. I can say it was a mistake if they ask."

"You did the right thing," Willy said. "I knew you were a bright guy." He smiled at Jason and pulled an envelope out of his inside jacket pocket and put it flat on the table. He slid it over to Jason. "This should cover your time at Anthony's office," he said. "Stop over and finish at my place too, tomorrow, okay?" The envelope wasn't sealed and Jason could see that there was a stack of money inside. He felt a little guilty of something he wasn't sure of. He really hadn't done anything wrong.

"Is that for me?" Jason asked.

Willy nodded yes; Jason took the envelope and put it in his laptop bag. Anthony began to get up from the table, and the waitress appeared carrying Jason's order. She was blocking him for a moment from rising to his feet. She set the plate of grilled cheese sandwich, pickle and potato chips on the table. "Can I get you anything?" the waitress asked Willy and Anthony.

"We are not staying," Willy said as he a rose from the booth.

"Enjoy your dinner," Willy said to Jason. Then he turned to the waitress and said, "I have another question." He, the waitress and Anthony went over to the counter at the far end and Willy spoke to her out of earshot.

Jason bit into the sandwich and watched as Willy pulled something out of his pocket and handed it to the waitress. Willy and Anthony walked out of the restaurant. Jason pulled his laptop back out and pulled up a news site as he ate his sandwich.

Jason always hated that they put pickles near the chips with the grilled cheese. It made the chips soggy. He didn't eat the pickle or the wet potato chips.

The waitress came over and asked if he would like a refill of coffee and Jason agreed. She filled the cup and went back to the kitchen. He looked around the restaurant, and noticed he was the only customer.

After Jason finished the sandwich, he reached into his bag and pulled out the envelope Willy had given him. The envelope contained a stack of hundred dollar bills almost an inch high. He held it on his lap and counted under the table. He could tell there was at least $5,000 in the envelope. That was a lot of money. *Willy must really be making money*, Jason thought, *and that attorney must have something to do with it.* But what was the deal and did he really want to know?

Around 1:45, his cell phone rang. It was Pat telling him that the police had left, and all the tenants could return. The building had four floors, and eight units. Jason's apartment was really two rooms and a bathroom. The living room was split with the kitchen. He had moved there from home because it was close to school. Back then, someone else owned it, and the rent was much cheaper. The building had changed hands a number of times. The most recent company to buy the building had it repainted on the outside. They hired a designer to make the building look more appealing. Now, the exterior always had a basket of flowers. The once dark common hall was transformed to a bright, cheerful place with a painting near the mailboxes, under the stairwell; the painting was changed once a month.

As he hung up the phone, four obviously drunk guys walked into the coffee house. They talked loudly to each other as they found a booth to sit in. Jason waved his hand for the waitress, to ask her for the check. From over by the counter, she shouted across the room, "Your friends paid for you already."

Jason asked her in a raised voice, "How much was it? So I can give you a tip."

She said, "They gave me a twenty and told me to keep the change. Your bill wasn't even half that. Do you want the change or something?"

Jason smiled at her. "Keep it, never mind," he said. He packed up his laptop and made his way past the unruly four guys in their booth. He walked into the warm early autumn morning. His route home was uneventful, not even one car passed him on the street.

Just inside the doorway of the apartment building was a hallway. To the left and right were the doors leading to the individual apartments. The hallway was wide and just to the right was the stairwell up. To the left of the stairwell was the hallway that led to the mailboxes. The police had created large X's made of yellow police tape and affixed them to both doors on either side of him. The door to his right looked as though it had been chopped with an ax. Someone had put plywood over part of it in an effort to hold it together.

To his left, it looked as though the door had been pushed in. The door frame was broken at its hinges. That door too had the large yellow barrier in the shape of an X. The plastic tape had POLICE CRIME SCENE DO NOT CROSS written on it in black block lettering.

Jason was tired, but he stood there for a few minutes staring at the doors. He wondered where the cat went; maybe it was a victim too. He started climbing the staircase to his floor. At the top, he turned and opened his door. Once inside, he sat his laptop bag down next to the couch and pulled the money out of its envelope and counted it. There was $6,500 in hundred-dollar bills. He put the money back in the envelope. In the far corner of the living room, the rug was loose. Once he dropped something and it bounced into the corner and under the baseboard. The wall didn't meet the floor there, and there was a gap that the carpet hid. So he picked up the rug and slid the envelope in, but it was too fat. He found another envelope and put half the money in that and slid them under the baseboard and inside the wall. He put the carpet back over them, and went to bed.

Showing Off

T he morning came too quickly; he was still tired from the night before. He wasted almost fifteen minutes trying to get a spot out of his favorite tie before giving up and grabbing a blue one. He spied his ear buds lying on the floor near the couch in the living room. He put them in his laptop case. He took a shower and had a cup of coffee. It was 8:15 when he closed his door and walked back downstairs into the crime scene.

The morning came too quickly; he was still tired from the night before. He wasted almost fifteen minutes trying to get a spot out of his favorite tie before giving up and grabbing a blue one. He spied his ear buds lying on the floor near the couch in the living room. He put them in his laptop case. He took a shower and had a cup of coffee. It was 8:15 when he closed his door and walked back downstairs into the crime scene.

The interview was with a Human Resources person who was not technical at all. The company was screening for an experienced programmer for a long-term exciting project. They were looking for people for three positions. Actually, Jason never found out what the product was. The HR person had no real details; and since he didn't have a bachelor's degree, and had only nine years of hard coding experience, he made it very clear that Jason was not qualified to work there.

By 10 AM, Jason was in the elevator of the attorney's office, which was on the top floor. The doors opened to a large lobby. A professional older woman was behind the desk answering phone calls and typing on a computer. She acknowledged Jason's presence and stuck one finger in the air. She snapped to a more official upright pose in her chair. She looked as though she was in her late 40s or early 50s. The suit and the jewelry she wore didn't look cheap. Jason couldn't place it, but she didn't look like she shopped at the average retail stores. Some people have a natural air about them and she had just that.

"May I help you?" she asked.

Jason said, "I'm here to see attorney Anthony." He wasn't sure if this guy was a partner at the firm or what. He realized that he never got his full name the night before. It was on the card, but he didn't remember what it was.

He pulled the card back out of his pocket and looked at it again. Robinson, Caruso and Cowe, Attorneys at Law. Anthony H. Jones, ESQ. He handed it to the receptionist. She looked at it, then handed it back.

"Please be seated, someone will be right with you," she said, motioning to a row of chairs.

As Jason sat down, he watched her handle another call. "Please hold," she said, pressing a button on her phone. The phone didn't make any sounds; *it must be ringing in her headset,* Jason thought. On either side of the elevator were a set of four chairs and a small table. The chairs were dining room chairs, with leather backs and bottoms. The tables were topped with marble. There was a small vase with a bouquet of flowers on each table. The border around the waiting area was a half wall of cherry panels that wrapped all the way around. Above each set of chairs on the wall were large paintings in gold frames. Jason sat down under the painting of a hunting party with men on horseback and a dog carrying a large bird in its mouth. On either side of the reception area were large, dark, wooden doors. This separated the area from the actual office space.

This place didn't look cheap at all. Jason had seen upper class things on television, and in the movies, but this was expensive. He could just tell. The receptionist was continuing to take calls. He could hear her calmly saying "please hold," or, when someone wasn't in, "would you like his or her voice mail?"

A few minutes went by and the lack of sleep was beginning to wear on Jason. Sitting in a chair and waiting was not easy on such little sleep. He pulled out his cell phone to check his email and monster.com.

The door on the right opened revealing a short white guy who looked to be in his 20s. He was wearing a white short-sleeved shirt and tie. He walked directly toward Jason and introduced himself as he walked.

"You must be Jason. My name is Harold Ramsey; it is very nice to meet you." Harold held out his hand to shake Jason's. As Jason shook it, Harold said, "This way, please." Jason stood up with his laptop bag and followed the man. Harold turned to the receptionist and told her they'd be in conference room B. He held the door open for Jason to enter.

The office was large and had a perimeter made of glass. Outside of each office were large desks, each with a computer and a printer. Behind the desk were a series of cubes made from dark wood panels. Each desk had a professional-looking female either wearing headphones and typing, or talking on telephones. Jason could see that there must be at least a hundred people in the office. He also noticed that some of the glass offices had another door on the opposite side. It was a glass door that would slide to open. There was a large balcony outside that looked like it went the length of the building.

They had passed maybe twenty of these glass offices when Harold opened the door to a glass conference room. It had a large table in its center and had fifteen or eighteen chairs around it. On one wall at the far end was a large flat screen television. At the near end was a giant white board. Coming out of the ceiling in the center of the table was a large arm, with a big silver ball attached to its end. The ball was shaped kind of like a soccer ball, with many more sides than that. It almost looked like a giant version of a fly's eye. It was folded up to the ceiling but looked like some kind of robotic control was attached to it.

Harold said, "Please sit down. May I get you anything? A coffee or water?"

Jason was puzzled (to say the least) about the object in the ceiling. He replied, "Sure, a coffee would be great."

Harold pressed a button on a small panel in the center of the table and said, "Sue, can we have a coffee and water?" He spoke in the direction of the center of the table.

"Would you like something with it?" A female voice responded from the speaker in the table.

Jason said, "Milk, if you have it."

The voice from the table replied, "Be right there."

Harold sat down at the table in the seat next to Jason. "So…you work on computers?"

Jason replied, "Yeah, I program and tinker here and there; how about you?"

Harold said, "I keep things working safely around here. I'm an administrator and do support. I don't know how to program." He said it in a way that Jason detected to be a sense of pride in his voice. Jason looked up again at the ball thing hovering in the ceiling.

Harold said, "That thing is really cool, we use it for depositions. It tracks who is talking automatically and takes video with fifty separate cameras, all at the same time. It works in a kind of panoramic. Then we edit the video in the lab downstairs and make a single video to show in court hearings. We have a staff psychologist who sits in the control room and tells the attorneys how to react to the questions of the person being deposed. She tells them through wireless ear buds. When we stitch the final video together, key questions may have the room frowning or smiling. Even though the images end up really small in the final video, our research and others suggest that the jury or the judge subconsciously react to the additional emotional input. There are many tools here like that. I have a really cool job sometimes."

Jason asked, "You guys actually have a shrink on staff?"

Harold replied, "Well she does other stuff, too…we use her on jury selection, and actually she sublets an office from us downstairs. We have three floors in this building."

Jason asked, "How big is this firm? I originally met Anthony… um… I uh, didn't catch his last name. Is he a partner here?"

Harold said, "No, he's one of the junior partners. We do all kinds of work here. We actually have hundreds of associates worldwide. I don't know how many are in other places, but there are 430-something in this building."

A female in her 20s in business attire dressed very businesslike opened the conference room door with one hand, carrying a tray with the other. It looked like she had some past waitressing experience. She placed a cup and saucer in front of Jason and a glass and water bottle in front of Harold. She put a small creamer pitcher filled with milk on the table in front of Jason as well as a napkin and a spoon. "Thank you," Jason said, looking in her direction.

" You're welcome" she said. She left the room, pulling the door shut on the way out.

The coffee cup, saucer and pitcher looked old in design, but were clearly new. They all had a matching red design. Jason poured a little milk into the coffee cup. Taking a sip, he looked directly at Harold. "Why am I here?" he asked after swallowing.

Harold said, "I got assigned to show you this office, show you around and give you a tour of anything here you want to see. I thought you knew that you're supposed to run some kind of security sweep or something on our network and get my boss into hot water. He's in New York. But instead of getting here yesterday, you got here today so... I was told that your flight was delayed or something. You were supposed to break in and stand in the computer room and call his boss. That is what I was told, so since you are here and I know who you are, breaking into the network isn't necessary."

"So," he continued, "If you show me something wrong, I can write a report and back date it to yesterday, say you were caught and tell my boss. This way everyone is happy. There are lots of politics and back stabbing in this place. I've been here four years; I just do what they tell me to do."

Jason now understood that this was an alibi for yesterday. But he didn't really do anything wrong and didn't really need an alibi. Willy needed the alibi and this law firm must have something to do with him. *This is big time, though, not the flop hotel,* he thought. He also thought this was a little fishy. How much do they really know about him? He certainly didn't give Willy a résumé. *Hmm, maybe I'm being paranoid but...*Jason asked, "What do you know about me?"

Harold replied, "I received a cover letter saying you're some kind of security consultant. It's got your résumé attached." He pulled out his phone and searched for something, then handed it to Jason to read.

Jason read the document carefully; it said he was an expert in security-related issues. *Interesting,* he thought. The attached resume was one of the versions he was using for network security—the same one that was on monster.com. He figured someone just looked for him and composed a cover letter. *All right,* he thought, *so this is making a little more sense. Now how do I get out of here, talk to Willy and find out what this guy wants?*

Jason asked, "How secure is your Wi-Fi?

Harold replied, "It's secure, you have to have a password."

Jason pulled out his laptop and booted it up. It took a while since it was an older model. His base system was a flavor of Linux. The bonus was virtual operating systems, and he had them all installed. Through the virtual application, he could make his machine appear to be any of several versions of windows or operate like a Mac notebook. He could make the machine literally into anything he needed in just a few minutes.

Hmm. He took a sip from his coffee cup and looked at Harold who was watching him.

"So if someone logs into your Wi-Fi, they have access to your entire network?"

At the prompt, he listed the Wi-Fi names his computer recognized. A long list with their names, Mac addresses and signal strengths appeared after a few seconds. The building was so high up—36 stories—that many Wi-Fi networks showed in the list.

He found one that was named "guest," which was wide open, and pointed at R&CClaw firm, which was secured with *WPS. It is a really bad form of security,* he thought. Jason tried to check his smile.

Jason asked, "Is that it here?" he pointed at the screen. By this time, Harold had wide eyes. He wasn't saying anything. He nodded yes.

Jason typed in a command to crack the Wi-Fi. Jason said, "This may take a while." He hit the "Enter" key.

The computer just blinked its cursor and Jason took a sip of his coffee. With his other hand, he flipped over the saucer so he could read the name on the bottom. Tiffany and Co. The cup he was drinking out of was worth a few hundred bucks, he realized. He lightly put the cup back in the saucer.

Harold just sat silently, watching the cursor blink.

Jason said, "Why don't you show me around your office; this may take more than a few minutes. Sometimes it takes hours."

Harold then exclaimed, "Holy shit." Jason looked at the screen. The prompt had moved down a few lines and read:

Pin number: 18111823

Password: "Letsgetworking"

SSID: R&CClaw

Jason thought Harold looked like a Windows guy, so he launched Windows XP, and it came up fairly fast—in a minute or two. After it launched, he clicked on the Wi-Fi and connected to the network using the password.

Harold sat with his mouth wide open. Eventually he murmured, "Is it really that easy?"

Jason said, "You just watched me. Many things are that easy, but you can make them harder. You have a Windows domain?"

Harold sat for a moment in silence. He didn't say anything for quite a few seconds. He just nodded.

Jason thought about it and this seemed like enough of a show for the kid. He was impressed already. No sense in showing him someone's desktop.

Jason launched a web browser and searched for Radius. "If you hook this up and get a real certificate, it will make it harder to crack," he said. He slid the computer in front of Harold and grabbed one of the legal pads on the table and a pen and scribbled a few notes.

Jason said, "I really just do this stuff for fun. I prefer to write code. Can I take a rain check on the tour? I have something I would rather do today."

Harold just said, "Thanks a lot!" in a nervous, excited way. "If you want to come back anytime, just let me know."

Jason said, "Sure, anytime you want, it was really nice to meet you." Jason put his hand out and Harold stood up to shake it. "Yes, it was nice to meet you, too."

Jason packed up his laptop and was escorted to the elevator. *I wonder*, Jason thought. *Was this some sort of test? Who knows?*

The office building was in the opposite direction from his apartment than the run-down hotel that Willy's office occupied. Going outside and looking at the bus schedule, he only had to wait five minutes for the next one to appear. It ran only a block from the apartment, so he went home to change first.

As he neared the front entrance of the apartment building, a car door opened from a car that was parked in front of the building. Detective Smith and the man he saw the night before got out of the vehicle.

Detective Smith said, "Do you have a second"?

Jason replied, "Sure."

"We have a witness who claimed that a couple of large men, one possibly white and one possibly Asian, may have something to do with the incident here yesterday," he said. "Have you seen anyone fitting that description hanging around your building?"

Jason said, "I don't know, I recently got laid off from my job and haven't been here much during the day."

Detective Smith asked, "Did Mrs. Green or Mr. Long, um, Jones have any money that you know of?"

Jason thought for a moment. "Mrs. Green used to get checks in the mail, but I don't know from who or how much," he offered. "Mr. Jones was in the military and I think he was living on a pension."

While Jason was speaking, the police detective pulled a small notebook from his inside jacket pocket. He wasn't wearing his badge on the outside pocket. Today it was clipped to his belt. He started taking notes as Jason spoke.

"The phone number you gave me last night is not where you said you were," Detective Smith said.

Jason tried his best to act surprised. "Oh, it wasn't? Sorry about that," he said. He fished in his pocket and found the business card from the law firm. He thought about it for a minute because he knew Willy's group was dangerous, but the law firm was something bigger. He handed the detective the card.

Jason said, "I was there. You didn't ask me where I was, you asked me for the phone number. Sorry, I must have given you the wrong one." The detective took the card and began scribbling notes from it. Jason added, "You can keep it, I really don't need it anymore."

Detective Smith's partner spoke up as he walked directly in front of Jason. "Would you mind showing us your hands?" he asked.

Jason put down his computer bag and held his hands out, flat arms stretched forward.

The detective's partner said, "Would you mind rolling up your sleeves?" Jason complied, he held his arms out straight again.

"Could you turn your hands over?" they asked him. Jason stood there, palms up.

The detective's partner exclaimed in a condescending tone to his partner, "This guy is a waste of time." Then he turned his head to face Jason. "Have a nice day, sir."

Detective Smith looked at his partner who was standing there with his hands on his hips. Smith looked kind of disappointed. Jason realized that the partner was the supervisor of the two.

Jason paused for a moment, waiting for a protest or another order. A few seconds went by. He rolled his sleeves down, picked up his bag, put it over his shoulder and climbed the three steps to the door. Once he closed the door, he began to sweat uncontrollably.

He went upstairs and changed his shirt. He got the money Willy had given him and pulled out $1,000. He put it in his pocket and put the rest into the one envelope and put the envelope into his laptop case. The police tape still crossed the two doors. When he opened the front door, he could see the police car was gone. When he came back outside, he went back to the bus stop and had to wait ten minutes. He could have sworn he saw his car in the distance, but they all looked alike.

He went upstairs and changed his shirt. He got the money Willy had given him and pulled out $1,000. He put it in his pocket and put the rest into the one envelope and put the envelope into his laptop case. The police tape still crossed the two doors. When he opened the front door, he could see the police car was gone. When he came back outside, he went back to the bus stop and had to wait ten minutes. He could have sworn he saw his car in the distance, but they all looked alike.

Now Finish The Project

J ason sent Willy a text message as soon as he sat down on the bus. There were some things they needed to discuss. The text said: "just got done at lawyer's office.

Can you meet me at restaurant directly across the street in 15 minutes?"

Jason received Willy's text message when he stepped off the bus. It said: "OK." The McDonald's was only a few steps from the bus stop. Willy was already inside waiting for Jason.

"Hey, I heard you put on a great show at Anthony's office," Willy said smiling. Jason was not really amused.

"You want anything to eat?" Willy continued.

"No, let's sit over here," Jason said. They took a four-person booth not far from where a mother was struggling to get her three children to eat their food.

Jason sat down first with his back to the window. The hotel across the street was behind him, thirty or forty feet away. Willy sat across from him. Then he asked Willy, "What is this all about?" Willy tried to look surprised, but Jason thought he did a really bad job at it.

Willy responded, "Wha ya mean?"

"Try again," Jason said. He really didn't like that answer.

Willy knew Jason was smart; that's why he was picked. He said, "They want something from you."

Jason sat there for a minute thinking if he really had anything that anyone would want. He really didn't have anything to speak of; he didn't even have a car. He figured his credit was okay, so he could fix that. But the burning question for Jason wasn't what he had; it was who those guys were. This guy he could understand, maybe the office was doing something. But that law office was huge, big money. He doubted that Willy got invited to the Christmas party for them. "Where did you send me today?" Jason asked.

Willy leaned over the table, so his chin was almost resting on the top of it. He spoke quietly and slowly: "They told me to run into you. It wasn't my idea."

Jason responded, "Who's 'they'?"

"They are really big fish, and I, my friend, is the guppy."

Jason sat puzzled for a moment. "That doesn't make any sense."

"They want you to write some program—that's all I know," Willy explained. "They said you should come over to my office and fix my stuff; after that they would offer you something to do."

Jason felt a chill on the back of his neck. He realized that Willy had his head down because Jason's body was blocking the cameras from seeing him from across the street. His car was missing. He was paranoid. He thought, *what have I really done? Nothing really. Gave a cop a card, big deal. Is it all tied together?* Jason asked, "What kind of program does whoever want?" He was becoming increasingly impatient.

Willy pulled out his cell phone and put it in front of his face and pointed at it. One of the kids from the table somewhere else in the restaurant screeched. He pulled the battery out and placed it on the table. He put his forefinger in front of his lips. Jason caught on and removed the battery from his phone. *Good thing I don't have an iPhone*, he thought to himself.

"What kind of program do they want?" he asked.

Willy shook his head and said, "I don't know, you're just supposed to fix my shit. And I ain't supposed to be telling you this shit." Jason understood this guy was obviously not the brightest crayon in the box. At the same time, it was obvious that he wasn't in control and that he was being truthful. He was starting to doubt how much Willy really knew.

Jason asked, "Who are the people in the hotel?"

Willy paused. He said, "Look, I can't answer that. I'll tell you that you are lookin' at ghosts, people that are not there. If you're smart—well shit, I know you're smart—you really don't want to know that. They will kill you and me."

Jason stared at Willy. He wasn't sure what he should do. Maybe he should disappear, but on second thought, the cops might notice something like that. "Okay, tell me what you do," Jason said.

Willy scrunched his face. He licked his lips and said, "Look, these people you can't fuck with. You have some work to do; they already paid you for it. If you're that bright, you can figure that out on your own." He winked at Jason and sat upright. He put his battery back in his cell phone and closed the cover. "Is it true you can listen in on these things even if they're just turned on?"

Jason was putting his battery in too. "Yup," he said. "You know dude, thanks; I know better and I would have totally forgotten." Jason was well aware that some cell phones give their location to the tower even in the user-off state. Some can be used as listening devices by turning on the microphone and broadcasting whatever it hears over the internet connection. Spy agencies don't need to place as many bugs anymore; just knowing the cell phone number is enough to listen in anytime.

Upon leaving the restaurant, they waited for a couple of cars to pass and they crossed the street in the middle of the block. They entered the lobby; an older Indian guy was behind the cage. Willy opened the door to the stairs for Jason.

As Jason walked by, Willy whispered into Jason's ear: "Look up." Jason entered the stairwell and looked up as Willy instructed. Up in the corner was a small camera dome. When he got to the second floor, he looked up, and there was another camera dome. He almost forgot to open the door on four, and continued finding cameras on each floor.

Jason held the door for Willy; he stopped for a moment and said, "I have some stuff to do. I'll see you in a bit." Willy continued up the stairwell.

Jason looked in the mirror, and a skinny guy wearing a baseball cap was in the back cube. He was leaning back in the chair with his feet on the desk. This time, there were three empty cubes. He set his laptop up and while it booted, he started working on the computer in his cube. Most people don't know that with just a couple of programs and a few keystrokes, anyone can see what is on someone else's screen. It's harder when there are real firewalls in the way because you have to get them to open an email or download a program. But it's easy when you're on the same side of a router. Wi-Fi in public places, coffee houses and airports are actually dangerous places to use computers. There is no protection there.

Before the computer he was working on could complete its virus scanning process, he had four computer screens being logged on his laptop. The computers were going to a variety of pages and were active in chat sessions—three or four chats each. It was way too much to follow in real time. He would look at it later at home.

Jason had a remote script somewhere on his laptop. It took him a few minutes to find it. The script was a set of commands written in java; he remotely installed the script to the machines, which sat busily doing their users' requests logging into websites and typing on chats. The script took pictures of the screen and had a keyboard logger. It also dumped the clipboard buffer if it changed. When a user copied or cut text, or had a program that stored passwords, the mechanism used the paste buffer. By using this approach, anything the user did was recorded. Since Jason could tell they weren't talking or doing video chat, there would be no benefit to capturing audio or camera data.

While he was busy snooping with his laptop, the computer in the cube had finished its scan and had found a virus. Jason looked up what it did, and checked the connections. It was a Trojan that gave someone on the outside remote access. Those are common on the Internet; even the so-called safe sites have their issues. He disabled the program and looked for where its logs were located. It looked like no one had used it yet. Maybe it was lucky for them they didn't.

It took Jason the rest of the afternoon to finish cleaning the computers, resolving problems and upgrading software. When he was done, he packed up his laptop. He sent Willy a text that read: "All done, getting ready to leave."

Willy sent him a text back saying: "Hang out for a minute, be right there."

Jason looked at Monster again on his phone; there wasn't anything new. As soon as he was through here he would take the bus over to where the cheap, low down-payment cars were. He didn't know what he could afford, but hoped he could find something decent. Maybe he would go over to Tony's after and get a beer. There really wasn't anything he had scheduled for tomorrow anyway.

Willy arrived with the large Asian guy and another equally large man covered with tattoos. Although he didn't say anything, Jason guessed by his looks that he was Russian. The tattoos had Russian writing in them. Willy didn't have a gun in sight, the other two did. They both had their guns pointed at Jason.

Willy smiled at Jason. He said, "Give me your cell phone. You're a really bright guy. Guess what, the cops found your car today."

He called out to the smaller Asian guy in the back in Japanese or Chinese, Jason really didn't know what was said, just that he spoke very quickly and it sounded like an order of some sort. Willy looked back at Jason still with his smile on and said, "Sit down over there."

He was directed to one of the waiting room chairs, the one furthest from the doorway leading to the staircase. The women in the room lined up in single file and left with the thin Asian guy. When the door shut, Willy continued speaking. "The police found your car today, with items that they can link to your neighbors' unfortunate robbery. When they get a search warrant and look in your apartment, they will find what looks like a very bad drug habit. They will find empty baggies, all kinds of goodies and residue. By tomorrow, they will have an arrest warrant for you." He motioned to the Russian guy and said something to him in Russian. The Russian guy grabbed Jason's computer bag.

Jason's heart was racing; he sat silently and just stared in Willy's eyes. He was afraid and there wasn't a sole that knew where he was.

Willy got the other waiting room chair and put it directly in front of Jason. He sat down, stretched his neck, and said, "I got busted a little over two years ago. I had a couple girls workin' for me. One of them named me when she got busted, so the cops arrested me. In the lockup was some rich guy drunk off his ass. We started talkin' and he wanted to know how much I knew about drugs and girls in the neighborhood. Oh, I told him all kinds of shit – that I could get whatever he wanted, bullshit like that, you know? He looked like he ate it up, impressed or something. He asked me about my drug use. I smoke pot mostly, I told him, I don't want to make it a habit. I'm a businessman after all, I told him. He asked me if I wanted to make real money like, who don't, you know? Geco, a gang banger, and a big dude who's a Crips member was in there too. I talked to him for a bit. I have no bones with the gangs, I just stay cool you know. Well, the white dude just sat and watched me. He really looked like he was just drunk. So it was a busy night and arraignment wasn't till the next morning. I was chattin' it up with everyone stuck there that felt like chattin'. I actually knew quite a few people from around that were in there that night. Anyway, the cops come and get the white dude out, and I tried to sleep a little.

"The cops take us all over to the court house for arraignment the next mornin' and there is that same dude hungover sitting with this brother named Anthony in the gallery. When they call my name, Anthony gets up and comes over to me and asks me if I want an attorney. I say hell yeah. He gets bail set and says they will pay it in cash, like on the spot. Anthony, you know, he knows shit, so I have my bail paid and he says we're going to have a meeting, but that I needed a shower first. So he says to follow him to the parking lot, and we get in his Mercedes, I figure he was a high-priced faggot or something. He says the people he works for could use someone that has business savvy. I say yeah? And he says, 'You just do your job, and you will make some money, someday you can have a car like this if you want.' I already had a few new cars. Well, they were stolen, but I still drove them around for a while. Okay, I thought, nice. 'But what kinda drugs you sellin'?' I ask. He says this division doesn't get into drugs, you believe that division bullshit? Meanwhile, he isn't askin' me where I'm stayin', but driving the right way, I figure okay, he wasn't makin' passes at me or nothin'. At the time, I was stayin' in a motel and payin' cash. My bitches were livin' in the same motel, but they were just doing outcall, you know. I didn't want the cops coming to the motel.

"So Anthony pulls his car into the spot in front of my room and tells me go take a shower and wear somethin' not flashy but businesslike. He asked me if I had a suit, and said that he will wait. I take a shower not knowin' who this fucker is. I look for my piece, it was a little 22. I have had it for a very long time, and it's gone.

I grab a small knife just in case and put my suit on and clip on a tie. I had this phone on Boost, an extra you know. I only used it to call the girls. So I hear my cell and the Boost phone chirp at the same time with a text message that says *would you hurry up?* So now I'm ready to shit, I go outside and get back in the car and he hands me a tie that already has a knot in it. All I had to do was pull it over my head. He says, 'No clip-on ties, you need to learn how to tie them.' I think, well fuck you, too.

"He drives me to this Italian restaurant, parks, and when we go inside, there is some big Italian guy standing at the door with some sort of machine gun. In the middle of the room, there is a round table and two white guys sitting at it—a Russian guy and the dude from the night before, and we are the only two brothers in the place. There is nobody else there, just us and a white waiter. I figure that it's the mafia or something. The waiter comes over and they order a bottle of some red wine I never heard of, and the white dude from the night before says to me, 'Would you like to make more money than you ever dreamed possible?' I said, 'Sure, who wouldn't? What do I have to do?' He says they will let me know and I am to do whatever they ask, any time, night or day. I will move into one of their locations. And I will keep my mouth shut.

"I am not supposed to be telling you any of this. The Russian guy says that if I fuck up just once, I will wish they burned me alive. Then he asks me, 'Do you eat fish and do you like pasta?' What kind of question is that? I looked at Anthony and he didn't say anything. So I looked back at the white guy and he says, 'You like women?' I said, 'Sure I like women.' He says, 'Fine, you can do that for a while.' And I say 'What, like, fuck them?' and he says to me, 'You need to pay us back and make money first, then you can think about screwing around.' I said, 'What do you mean, pay you back?' The white guy says, 'Anthony here is 450 bucks an hour. You just got bailed out, bail was $20,000. For this service, you owe us $30,000.' Well, I said, 'this is bullshit, fuck this,' and started to get up. The Russian guy looked at me and said, 'we really don't need this piece of shit.' The white guy all cool says, 'Sit down, or die here.' I thought about it and sat my ass down. The white dude says, 'You know people like yourself that have been in that neighborhood forever.' He says they need someone that can talk to the street people and know what they know. So that's what I do, I keep tabs on everyone in the neighborhood, who does what and who talks to whoever.

"In a couple more years, I'll be living on the Mediterranean on a boat. I've seen it—they took me there and showed it to me. You don't know just how perfect you really are. You don't have a girlfriend or anybody that you're really close to, so nobody is going to look for you. You're smart as fuck and you can write and all that stuff. It pays to know the neighborhood. Now what you're going to do for me is make me $100,000—no, $200,000—shit, I have no idea, but you're going to get it for me."

Willy was excited and grinning from ear to ear. Jason's heart felt like it was going to leap out of his chest.

"So what are you guys, the mafia or something?" Jason finally asked.

Willy answered, "That's kind of hard to say." He shook his head and shrugged his shoulders. "Yeah, from what I know, we are that too. Since the Internet came around, and the world of everything being instant communication, the news and people just thought the big companies expanded into it. Well, so did a bunch of other people. The world crime organizations did too. The Russians, Hungarians, Japanese, Koreans, Pakistanis and a whole bunch of others, the local gangs here and in other countries, the Mexican and Columbian cartels and their billions. We all work together now, not in the open, but together, and our collective net worth is more money every year. In fact, it's more money than most countries' individual gross for domestic profit. I saw some of this myself when I was in the Army. I was stationed in Japan and the Balkans. The governments of the world use some of our services to spy on other governments. They don't admit it, but they make money with the same stuff we do: guns, women and drugs. Some of them work with us; others for us and some fear us or just try to compete with us. But after 9/11, some other things changed. It forced us all to compartmentalize and become separate units. So if one thing gets busted, the others stay intact. But that's the big picture of things, way above my pay grade. They put me here to run an operation, and that's what I do. I run a low risk operation that makes a profit every single day. You wanna sandwich or something?"

Jason wasn't hungry. *This sucks,* he thought. If he left, the police would arrest him for something he didn't do, and how do you explain that? *And that law firm I bet will screw me worse,* he thought. He shook his head no.

Willy said, "You think about it for a while then; you will get hungry. You will do what we ask of you. There is one other way, but it's not really enjoyable…if you know what I mean." Jason took it as a threat, and it was meant to be one.

Willy said something in Japanese. The big guy then said to Jason, "You git up an' come wit' me." He motioned with his gun at the same time. Jason got to his feet and was led to the door. He was instructed first up a flight of steps, next down the narrow hallway to room 508. The doors all had their deadbolt locks installed backwards facing the hallway. This way, the person was locked in without having a key.

The room was not nice. The wall by the windows had a big piece of wallpaper missing. Out of the windows was a fire escape complete with a heavy chain and pad lock on the mechanism. It was doubtful that these guys cared anything about fire code.

The bed was old; it squeaked when he sat on it. The dresser was empty with a mirror that had flakes of its reflective material lost. There was a bathroom with a shower, toilet and sink and a few towels. He lay down on the bed and noticed the camera dome in the corner. It was still light out. He watched a pigeon land on the railing. Then it flew away. When the sun began its descent, he walked over to the door and knocked. A voice on the other side in broken English with an Asian accent said, "What you want?"

Jason said, "I want a burger, fries and a beer. And something to read." He waited for a bit, and said, "Anyone there?"

The voice on the other side said, "Okay, okay."

He sat down on the bed. There really was nothing here to do. He heard a distant bump that came from one of the other rooms.

It was getting dark now. He found the light switch to the small lamp on the dresser. He heard the lock click on the door. The door opened and a tray slid on the floor past the door. Then the door closed and locked again. On the tray was a plate with a cheeseburger, some French fries, a small container of ketchup, another small container of mayo, a plastic knife and fork, a paper napkin and a six-pack of Pabst Blue Ribbon beer. He could tell this wasn't takeout food. This place must have a kitchen. Under the food and beer were several back-dated issues of *Time, Newsweek, People* and *US* magazines. The area where the address was supposed to be was ripped off the covers.

Jason set the tray on the bed and began eating while flipping through the magazines. After he finished, he put the tray on the dresser. He continued reading until he got tired. When he turned off the light, he could see a red glow coming from the camera in the corner. He guessed it was an infrared unit that could see in the dark. He got into bed and finally fell asleep.

6

The First Day Of Captivity

Jason woke to the sound of the door opening. A new tray appeared. This one had scrambled eggs and toast; plastic utensils wrapped with a paper napkin; a plastic mug with coffee; and a small container of milk. The tray slid on the floor past the door opening. Then the door closed.

After eating the food, Jason took a shower with only the bar of soap that was in the bathroom. He dressed himself with yesterday's clothes and sat on the bed for a while. He thought about yesterday's events; he had dreamed of being shot and beaten several times during the night. He thought about what Willy had said about him, and it was true—no one would notice if he was gone. If the police found what he was told, he was screwed.

Innocent or not, on top of everything else, he was bored. There was no way to leave. He had noticed that the cameras couldn't see in the bathroom. *Maybe there's a hidden one in there,* he thought. They were everywhere else. He paced a little. He walked to the door and

64

back to the windows. Finally, after going back and forth 20 times, he waved to the camera making a come over here motion. While he did that, he spoke out loud: "Let's talk." It only took a few minutes to hear the lock click open and Willy to appear.

He was alone; the door lock clicked behind him. Someone must have locked it from the other side. Willy said, "Look, we don't want to hurt you. You can make more money than you ever dreamed with us."

Jason said, "Great, but I want out of here."

Willy smiled at Jason then put a serious look on his face. "There will be a time that you can leave; hell, you can come and go… maybe. Right now the police are looking for you, and you are more important to us here. We don't want you to get arrested and go to jail. It doesn't help us."

"You arranged that, so un-arrange it," Jason scolded.

"We just ain't ready to do that yet," Willy said.

Jason said, "Okay, so if I'm stuck here I want some things. I want some clothes, things like a razor, toothbrush… you know, if I'm trapped here."

Willy pulled a small notebook from his back pocket and searched his front pockets. "Hey, do you have a pen?" he asked. The door opened and a pen was handed to Willy. As soon as Willy took the pen, the hand withdrew and the door closed and locked again. Willy handed the pen and notebook to Jason.

"Make a list for me," Willy said. I'll make sure you get what you need."

Jason then asked, "Why the fuck me?" It sounded whiny to Willy.

Willy smiled again briefly and said, "You know the reasons we picked you. You're a smart guy."

"What do you want from me?" Jason asked.

"I read that it was possible to video a person using their web cam and without turning the little light on," Willy said.

"So…" Jason said.

"We want you to write a virus or something that allows the computer to record using the camera without the light, and allows us or you to read documents and emails on the infected computer. Is that something you know how to do? Be honest."

Jason thought about it. It was possible to do something like that, he mused. "That's not something I have ever done before," he said.

"Well, that wasn't the question," Willy stated.

Jason thought a little more about this situation. *If I tell them I don't know how to do this, they may hurt me.* Finally he said, "I would need to look some things up and see if it is something that can be written. I really don't know for sure."

Willy said, "Okay, that can be arranged. You think about it for a while. Think about what you would need, and make me that list of yours. I have some things to take care of. When you are ready, just slide the list under the door." Willy turned toward the door and said, "Something to think about also, is what you want for doing this. Where do you want to go, what do you want? You and I are about to make a lot of money. I know you can do this." He knocked on the door once. The door opened and Willy stepped out. The door closed and locked behind him.

Jason thought about this for a while. It sounded crazy; he had heard of people doing this sort of stuff in other places but was it possible? He began writing a list: Toothbrush, shampoo, hair dryer (so he could then fill the tub with water and electrocute himself—fleeting thought), jeans, t-shirts, etc. He thought about the alarm clock in his apartment. The only things he had left were the pictures of his parents. It would all be gone and there would be no way of getting it back. *If these guys could do what they say, hmm…*

He started on a new sheet and wrote on the paper, "I want my stuff. My desktop, my clothes, my toothbrush, everything from my apartment— small stuff anyway." He also put "clock radio" on the list. *Let's see if they have as much power as they claim,* he thought to himself. He slid the list under the door, and he waited.

He sat down on the bed and skimmed through the magazines again. He read everything he skipped the night before. The door opened, and a beautiful 20-something woman with dirty-blonde hair came in carrying a tray. Once she was inside, the door shut and locked. She looked at him; she had large green eyes that had almost an Asian slant, or perhaps Persian or possibly Greek in shape. The color was piercing. Her high cheek bones and the shape of her face were definitely European. She was stunning, in every sense of the word. She looked like a woman from the movies or television, or even the pages of magazine advertisements. Honestly, her face looked like a number of famous actresses. He had seen the pouting lips trend in the movies and stars; she naturally had them too. She was a woman that looked so rare and exotic, and so beautiful. She was wearing a t-shirt that only came to the top of her stomach, white shorts and white tube socks with no shoes.

In what sounded like an Eastern European accent, Russian possibly, she said "Here is your lunch, sit there," and motioned him to sit at the end of the bed.

He sat where he was instructed and she lightly placed the tray on his lap. The tray contained a grilled cheese sandwich and a plastic bowl of what looked like tomato soup. She watched him stare at her for a second or two and said, "Eat." Jason took a bite from his sandwich, chewed and watched as she picked up the trays from the night before. She then turned around, pulled herself on to the dresser and sat there. Jason was staring again and she said simply, "Eat your food."

Jason ate as she watched, and likewise, he watched her every move.

When he finished, she took the tray from him and stacked it with the others. She turned back around slowly and stood in front of Jason. She then got onto her knees. She reached for his belt and said, "I am here for you." He was startled as she reached for the zipper of his pants. He pushed her hands off once; when she tried again he took hold of her hands.

She looked into his eyes. "I have to, please let me…" she whispered. Jason was shocked. He thought about the camera, and the place he was in. He started to push her back again.

She said "Please…" still, staring directly into his eyes. He let go of her hands. She slid open his zipper, and pulled his pants down a little. She took him into her mouth. He was partially afraid, but it did feel good. As he stiffened, she continued. She continued, taking all of him down her throat. She continued until he couldn't take it anymore and released. She swallowed him and made direct eye contact with him and smiled.

Jason didn't know what to think, this was wrong in so many ways, she put him back into his pants and slid his zipper half way up.

Jason cleared his throat and asked, "So what is your name?" He finished zipping his zipper. She got back to her feet and as she cleared her throat, she said, "Tasha."

"Nice to meet you, Tasha, my name, is Jason."

She started restacking the items on the trays. Tasha said, "It was nice to meet you, too." She began to pick up the trays, and it looked like she would leave.

"Please don't leave," Jason said. She set the trays down. He slid himself to the head of the bed with his back to the wall. He patted the bed by his side. "Come here," he said. She complied and sat next to him, and reached with her hand back to his pants. He grabbed her hand, and looked in her eyes and said "no" softly. She put her hands back on her own lap.

"How long have you been here?" Jason asked.

Tasha lost eye contact with him and looked at the camera dome in the corner and said, "Don't ask me questions like that." Jason understood. Everything said and every move made, someone was watching.

"Your English is pretty good, how long ago did you learn it?" Jason asked.

Tasha responded, "I learned it as a little girl, I always dreamed of coming to America."

"I grew up here, where are you from?" Jason asked.

"Romania," she said.

"How many languages do you know?" Jason asked.

Tasha started listing them: "Romanian, Hungarian, Ukrainian, Polish, German and Russian. What others do you know?"

Jason said, "I know some French, but not much other than English."

It had been a while since he had been with a woman. He had in the past had a few girlfriends, but none of them lasted for long. He had gone out with Lisa the longest but she decided that she didn't like men and the last time he saw her she was dating another girl.

This wasn't a girlfriend, he thought to himself. She would have never even looked in his direction if it wasn't for this situation. She was a hostage just like him. He thought about that for a moment and realized she wasn't a hostage, she was actually a slave.

He thought about what to say next. He really didn't want her to leave. "This guy goes into a shop to buy a parrot and says he's looking for a parrot that won't scream or swear," Jason began. "The owner of the shop says this one here recites the Lord's Prayer. If you pull on his right leg, and if you pull on his left leg he cites the 23rd Psalm. The guy says that's great and asks what happens if he pulls both of his legs at the same time? And the parrot says 'I fall off my perch, you idiot.'"

They both laughed at the joke. It was one of the few he remembered from Buddy. She was really beautiful, he thought. What a tragedy that she came into his life this way. He also knew that women like her were out of his league, and he would never meet someone like this on his own.

"So tell me about your childhood," he said to her—anything to talk to her that would keep her there.

Tasha said, "I lost my mother and father in the war many years ago. My older sister took care of me." Her voice began to change. She continued, "My sister is a painter, she paints portraits, she is very talented. She won a competition once; she painted a portrait holding flowers. It hangs in a museum."

"Do you paint?" Jason asked. Tasha shook her head no. "What about music?" Jason asked.

Her eyes opened wide with interest. "I used to play the violin, I miss it very much," Tasha said.

"What songs do you play?"

"My favorite is Tchaikovsky, but I can play Mozart and Schumann," she explained.

Jason was impressed. He didn't know who all of them were, but recognized some of their names. Classical music was something he never really got into. "Did you ever perform anywhere?" he asked.

"Only a few times in school, I used to practice while my sister painted. She always told me it made her inspired."

"I don't know how to play anything," he said.

"I learned to play when I was very young. My mother made me practice every day," she replied.

"Did she play the violin too?" He asked.

"No, she played the piano. My sister used to play trombone but she stopped a long time ago…" her voice drifted as she spoke.

Jason had been stuck in this room alone with really no one to have a conversation with for a day or two. It didn't matter to him what they talked about. Just speaking and spending time with someone was what mattered. It didn't hurt, he thought, that she was beautiful also. "I would really like to hear you play sometime for me," he said. "I understand that some days you're the dog, and some days you're the hydrant," he added.

She looked at him. "What does a hydrant mean?"

"A hydrant is the thing on the street that firemen plug their hoses into."

Tasha sat for a second and nodded, then burst out laughing. "You're funny" she said. He laughed with her. It felt good for him to laugh even for a moment. Their laughter was stopped abruptly by the click of the door.

"I must go," she said and got up quickly. She collected the stack of trays and left the room. The clicking of the door lock signified her departure.

He sat on the bed, thinking about what had just happened. *That was wrong,* he told himself over and over.

Willy came through the door a few minutes later. Jason was still sitting where he sat next to Tasha just a few minutes before.

Willy smiled at Jason. "Hot ain't she?"

Jason suddenly felt dirty. *Keep your cool,* he thought.

"Wow, is she ever," he said, humoring Willy.

"About your list…" Willy said.

"Yes?" Jason said.

"Some of the items here…we can get for you in time. However, I'm not sure how soon."

"What do you mean?"

"Well, the police are camped out across the street from your apartment building. So I don't think it would be a good time to get some of the things from there. Some of the items you listed are computer things."

Jason replied, "Yes, and?"

Willy said, "Make me a new list of computer items you need."

"I don't like to sleep where I work. Can we set me up with a table or an office?"

"That shouldn't be a problem. "

Jason looked around on the bed and on top of the dresser for his notebook. He looked on the floor of the left side of the bed. There was the notebook and pen. It had fallen off. He picked it up and began writing his list.

"I will need Internet access, of course," Jason told Willy as he wrote.

Willy at first made a face. "Okay" he said.

Jason said, "I will need a couple of computers, a couple of monitors, some networking wire..." he was writing as he spoke. "My laptop and..." *Crap.* "Hmm, did anyone screw with my laptop?" he asked.

"No," Willy replied.

"If anyone does, I will need a new hard drive for it, too." He said it in an offhand kind of way. Willy looked at Jason, puzzled by what he meant by that. He didn't look at it, but the kid upstairs might have.

"It's really okay, I'll just need a new drive." Most of the stuff I can download off the net anyway. There are a couple tool kits on my drive in the apartment that really would come in handy."

Willy asked, "Why can't you just log into it from here?"

Jason said, "Well, it would be challenging since it's all turned off. Is there any chance of just getting the hard drive out of my tower?"

Willy thought about that request and said, "I'll have to let you know." Jason knew it would be hard for them. Maybe the cops would catch them in the act. He thought maybe the whole crew would get caught.

Willy's phone rang in his pocket. He pulled it out and said to the person on the other end, "Hold on." He put the phone against his body and said to Jason, "Write everything on the list you think you will need and slide it under the door. I have to take this."

Willy knocked on the door once and it opened. He exited and it closed again. Jason got off the bed and walked into the bathroom. He put the plastic cup against the wall so he could hear Willy on the other side.

"I think he might play ball, but I'm not convinced. He's going to make me a list. No, I'm sure..." Willy's voice trailed off as he walked away from the door. *Hopefully there is no camera in this bathroom,* Jason thought. He inspected the bathroom for one. The mirror looked old and was hung by clips. He looked at the air vent. He didn't find anything out of place.

Jason sat back on the edge of the bed and continued writing. He added everything he could think of including multiple monitors for the workstations. If he was going to duplicate a website exploit, he would need to copy the website locally. He would need a machine or two for development and a couple for regular workstations. He thought about it and five boxes, or full-size computers, should be able to do that. No sense in being cheap for this asshole. He was on his third small sheet of paper. He added more magazines, too. He ripped the pages from the small notebook and slid them under the door. He also slid *Time, People* and *US* under the door as well, since he had already read them cover to cover.

Jason thought about the encounter with Tasha he'd had earlier. He felt guilty, but at the same time it was the first woman he had been with in quite a while. There was no one, as Willy had so brilliantly pointed out, in his life now. He liked women, but it was difficult to start a conversation, let alone find someone to date. Jason wasn't a big guy, and didn't really care about sports—or even watching them. He always thought of himself as not really a team player. He liked to work like that, too. When he would take on a project, he preferred to work on sections of it on his own. He would meet with others that he worked with, but he was the typical programming introvert.

Throughout the night, he could hear distant bumps from somewhere else in the old hotel.

Things To Do

Jason woke up with the first glint of sunrays. He had no idea of the exact time. He could not see the entire sky from where he was, just the light coming in from above the fire escape. Down below, was an 8 or 9 foot wide alley to the red brick building next door.

Occasionally Jason could hear movement somewhere in the hotel. He heard the sound of running water in the old pipes. In the distance were sounds of trucks and cars, occasionally blowing their horns: the sounds of people going about their daily lives. He used to be one of those people. They were oblivious to him and to his fellow captives.

"This doesn't happen here, not in America," Jason thought. Slavery was over years ago. Yet there he sat. He wasn't in jail, and calling out wasn't an option. They…whoever they were…were keeping him captive, in a room with peeling wallpaper and rickety furniture.

He took a long bath. He never had the time to take baths; he usually took showers. Here he had nothing but time. He warmed the water several times. He got out when his skin started to wrinkle. He dried and dressed himself with the clothes from two days ago. He washed his socks and left them to hang dry.

Jason went back to the bed and lay down. He began reading the remaining magazines cover to cover. From the bed, he heard the lock click. Then the door opened. He sat up.

A male Russian voice spoke saying, "Stay back."

A tray scooted on the floor with scrambled eggs and a coffee. As soon as the tray cleared the doorway, the door closed and locked again.

Jason sat on the bed and ate with the tray on his lap. He was hungry. He hadn't eaten, since yesterday. The coffee was black; it tasted okay—slightly bitter. When he finished the coffee, he filled the cup with water and drank that too.

Several hours had passed. Jason had no way of knowing the time. Suddenly the click of the lock broke the monotony. The door opened and Willy came in, partially out of breath, and looking as though he had just been running. He was sweating, too, and carrying Jason's laptop case.

Willy said, "Here's your case. Nobody has screwed with it. I made sure. That's a pretty big list of things you want there."

"I need to build an environment to test in," Jason explained. "One that duplicates some of what is out on the internet. I also need to test the potential victim machines. It takes multiple machines and CPUs to do that." Either Willy didn't understand and he was just going along with it, or he did understand. Either way, it didn't matter.

Willy looked at Jason. "Grab your stuff and come with me," he said.

Jason thought about that for a second. The only thing he had were the clothes on his back. He grabbed the magazines, and got his socks from the bathroom, which were still slightly wet.

He found his shoes and put them on. Willy watched as Jason did all of these things.

Willy knocked on the door once and it opened. The big Russian guy was standing just outside with a pistol in his hand. Willy turned left and walked down four doors with Jason behind him. He stopped at a door on the opposite side of the building. He opened the door and stepped in. Jason noticed it was a little cleaner than the last one. The room had newer carpet and the wallpaper, although it was the same, wasn't missing any pieces. The adjoining room had a bed put on its side and a couple of long collapsible tables were set up. Two old, rolling office chairs were there, too. The dresser was not there and bolted to the floor was an old television and stand. Both rooms had a bathroom. Jason looked at the camera position in both rooms. They were in the far corners, so there was a great view of the entry door, but not of the bathrooms. "*Interesting,*" Jason thought. He then saw that the mirror could be used to see into the bathroom if the door was left open.

While Jason checked out the second bathroom, Willy called out from the first room, "we will see what we can do. I'll be back in a while. I have stuff to do." Jason heard the door close and lock shortly after.

Jason turned on the old television, and static came on the screen. He pushed the button marked "radio" on the top and music started coming out of the speakers. He turned the radio to a rock station. He put his laptop case on the table and ran his hand into the inside pocket. The money was still there. He put the laptop on the table, and he stood back noting the position of the camera. He moved the table and sat the laptop up so his screen was not in view of the camera. He moved a chair to the table, and looked for an outlet.

He found his power supply and plugged it in while he waited for his laptop to come to life. After the system loaded, he typed in his user name and password. The first problem was the Internet. He got a list of Wi-Fi names, but all of them were locked. He used his Wi-Fi cracking tool and as luck would have it, in less than 30 minutes, he had a connection to the network of a florist shop.

He first typed his name into Yahoo News in the web browser, but he didn't find any hits yet. He did find a few local stories about the invasion robbery. There was no mention of him by name. He searched for a few of the published viruses. He was looking for something that gave a similar look and feel. He ran a number of searches on all the search engines. He was looking for anything that had been published that did this already, but didn't find anything. That was good, he thought, since maybe no one would be looking for his new java code either. Well, not yet, anyway.

The door opened in the other room. A slender woman with short, dark brown hair came in wearing a black Nike t-shirt, white shorts and black socks. Jason locked his laptop. He went into the other room. She had just put a tray down on the dresser. The tray contained a sandwich and some potato chips. She looked down as soon as he approached.

Jason looked at her and said "thank you." When he reached for the tray, she stepped back. She did not utter a word to him. He picked up the tray and took it to the room with tables. He set the tray on the closest table and grabbed a chair. He pulled the tray in front of him and bit into the dry ham and cheese sandwich on white bread. He looked up, and the girl was standing in the doorway. She was still looking down and avoiding eye contact. Jason chewed and then took another bite. She was still just standing there.

After he finished his sandwich, he said to her, "My name is Jason." She didn't speak, just stared at the floor. He bit into a potato chip, and she just stood there. He spread out the napkin and put the remaining chips in it. He picked up the tray and handed it to her. She took it, and he turned his back to her and went back to his laptop. She was still standing there holding the tray and staring at the floor.

Jason spoke over the music, which really wasn't turned up very loud. He asked, "Is there something I can do for you?"

She just stood there. 'Okay', he thought, 'fine, stand there.' He continued looking for some example code. There was one that was similar called "Flame," which was reported by Kaperski Lab. It was blamed on the United States and Israel as a follow-up to the stuxnet virus. It was the first time a weaponized virus was used on the Internet. The virus weapon was used against the country of Iran to dismantle part of its nuclear program. The follow-up "Flame" virus, among other things, recorded Skype and made videos using the attached camera on computers and cell phones. Computer viruses are sometimes made just to be destructive. They would alter or delete information on the infected machine. The people who wrote them were just individuals. Now most well written viruses are written by groups of people or governments for surveillance, theft and destruction. There are arguments among computer people that would classify flame as the first computer germ and not a virus.

The program his handlers wanted written didn't actually need to be a virus. Many people mis-classify computer terms all the time. The difference between a virus and malware is that a virus can self copy or duplicate itself. Once it's duplicated it sends a copy of itself to someone or something else. Malware doesn't copy or clone itself; other than that, there really is no difference.

What he needed to do was get remote control of the computer at the other end. Or at least get a program he wrote to run at the other computer. Stored passwords are in files, copying them and opening them should be the easy part, which was actually, getting email passwords remotely. This could be done, but once a user stores the password using the web browser stored password function, it can be picked off.

He had been reading on the web for about a half hour or so, and when he looked up, the girl was still standing there.

Jason got up and went over to her. "Is there something I can do for you?" He asked. She whispered to him in broken English, "muzick." He thought about it for a second. He walked over to the closest office chair and rolled it over to her.

"Sit," he said. He realized that he had spoken to her as someone would do to a dog. She sat down. He went back to his computer. He thought about looking at the data he had collected yesterday, or looking at his email. He sat there simply to bore the crap out of whoever was watching.

A little while later, the door opened. The girl got up and took the trays. It locked behind her after she left. The time on the computer was 3:30 pm. For the rest of the afternoon, he looked on the web for a way to turn off the web cam light. The problem he found, was that there were literally hundreds of webcam manufacturers and several ways to turn the light off. He would need to add a few laptops to that equipment list.

Around 5:30, the door opened in the bedroom side of the suite. The big Russian guy came in first, carrying a large box marked "Dell." He put it on the floor. Then the skinny Asian guy brought in another box. Then the Russian returned. They alternated bringing in boxes for a while. When they finished, they closed the door with a slam. On top of the stack were two bags from Wal-Mart; one had clothes, the other had some toiletries. He opened a couple of the boxes, pulling the computers out. He set them on the tables. As he unpacked, he noticed that there were not enough power outlets in the room for all of the equipment. His power strip didn't have enough either.

Jason realized he was getting hungry, so in a raised voice, he asked, "someone going to bring dinner soon? "

Fortunately, he had a couple blank DVDs in his laptop bag. He would need to download one of the versions of Linux to install on a couple of the new computers. After he downloaded them he could burn onto the DVD's using his laptop. The florist network was really slow to download the files he needed including the java software development kit (SDK).

The door opened on the office side this time and Tasha came in carrying a tray. Jason smiled at her as she set it on a table. All he could think to say was, "Hi, it's nice to see you." She smiled at him as she set the tray down.

Jason asked, "Have you eaten anything?" Tasha just shook her head no. He called out to whoever was listening, "I want another tray."

"Sit please, here, have this one," he said offering her the food on the first tray. She didn't move; she had a look on her face like she had done something horribly wrong. He reassured her. "It's okay. Really, it's okay." He put his hand on the small of her back and pushed her toward the chair, and repeated, "Please sit down." She hesitated and looked around the room as if she had to ask permission. She looked confused and finally sat in the chair. The tray of food was on the table, and Jason slid it in front of her. A few minutes went by, and the door opened again. The silent girl wearing the Nike shirt came in as the door closed and locked. She carried another tray of food. This time without hesitation, she put the tray on the table and went directly back to the door, knocked once, it opened, and she walked through. Then it closed and locked.

Jason grabbed the other chair and set it on the other side of the table from Tasha. She was still looking at the two pieces of fried chicken and mashed potatoes.

"Eat," was all he said. She attacked the food as if she hadn't eaten for a while. She was thin, but not what he would say skinny to the bone. He ate his food and watched her eat.

He went to both bathrooms to get two plastic cups, which he filled with water. He put one in front of her. She gulped it so quickly that he gave her his to drink while he refilled the empty cup. Tasha broke the silence after looking around the room. "Lots of computers," she said. She spoke while chewing her food.

Jason said, "Yes I, am building something."

"You are like us," Tasha said.

"What do you mean?"

You are locked in."

"Yes that's true," Jason said.

"You were working on the computers downstairs. They seem faster now. You must be very smart," Tasha said. Jason thought for a moment and said, "Not smart enough not to be locked in, like you." He smiled and so did she.

Jason hoped that whatever the end result of this was, that all of them could leave this place. Not just himself. How, he had no idea, and if he proved to be profitable to these guys, how much would be enough? He knew no matter how much money someone had, it would never really be enough. And when people are no longer needed, they are let go. He figured that being let go of in this crowd had more permanent meaning.

They finished dinner and stacked the trays. Jason refilled Tasha's water again, before they were through eating.

"How long has it been since you've last eaten?" Jason asked.

Tasha shook her head. Okay, he thought, maybe that was out of bounds. Anything about this place must be. While he thought what to say next, he got up and changed the radio station. He dialed it to the low end of the FM band. "Tell me when you like the music," he said. He stopped at each station and looked for a reaction from her. She smiled when he found a euro beat dance music. "I like that," she said. He fine-tuned the station with the old radio dial.

"I need to do something," he said and looked up at the computer screen, which was flashing a confirmation question for updates. He pressed the button and words scrolled by the screen faster than he could read them. He had no idea how long he would work tonight.

It wasn't that he expected her to be there. Although it was in the back of his mind, this is what he felt the word surreal really meant. He was happy to have anyone for company, especially someone as pretty as she.

He pulled the chair over to his laptop and took a few things out of his bag, including a small hub and a couple pieces of network wire. In the bag of supplies, he found a few more network wires. He connected the machine to the hub first, then changed a few of its settings. He stopped what he was doing and looked over at Tasha, who was just watching him from the table in the distance.

"Could you pull the chair over here?" he asked her.

Tasha wheeled the chair to the end of the table, where he was working. The table looked about eight feet long. He had placed several of the monitors on top of it. The computer towers were all on the floor. In the center of the table was a tangled mess of keyboards, mice and other wires.

The outside window in the room was near the center of the table. It faced a concrete block windowless wall that was three or four feet away. There was no view, and very little light coming in. You could not see the sky or the ground. Looking at the grey blocked building, Jason wondered what it was. He must have walked by it when he was outside.

He worked on the computer and finally got it to ping outbound on the outside. He had known in theory how to make his laptop into a router. He knew that almost all computers can do that, but he'd never had to do it before. It wasn't a permanent solution. He wanted his laptop for some other things He noticed that the angles of the computer monitors were not in view of the camera, He didn't look up to make it obvious; he put them at a 90-degree angles to the camera. The monitors all faced out in a row, so the camera had only a view of their side, not their screens. He worked on the computer for almost an hour. He set the next computer up by his laptop. He plugged in the keyboard and mouse and connected a monitor. As expected, he noted that he had run out of places to plug the power in.

Jason turned and looked at Tasha. "Having fun?" he asked. Tasha responded, "Yes, you know a lot about these things." Jason smiled at the ego boost. He liked to hear it. Jason said, "Yes, I am good at these but I am not good at these," he said, pointing at her.

"What do you mean?" Tasha asked.

"I never know what to say to people," he said. It's hard for me or something; I don't have interest in many of the things that people talk about. It's not that I don't know how to express myself. I can do that. It's building the conversation to the meaning of it all."

Tasha just sat there, with a blank look on her face. Jason realized she had no idea what he just had said. It really didn't matter, though.

The door clicked and Jason stood. It opened and Willy came into the room. The door closed. Jason took a couple of steps towards where Tasha was sitting. When he looked at her, fear took over her facial expression, which was not something he had seen in her before. She lowered her head.

Willy asked Jason, "How are you doing up here?" while looking at the computers on the floor and the maze of tangled cords on the top of the table. Jason responded, "I found some things that look interesting."

Willy studied the computers and spied the pile of boxes. He looked directly at Tasha, and said, "Take them out of here" in a demanding tone. Jason looked at Tasha, who was standing up slowly with her head down.

Jason said, "Have someone else do it." Willy looked confused, smiled and raised an eyebrow. Tasha was already out of the chair. Willy said, "Ah, so you like this one."

Jason thought a moment about the question; "this guy is a monster and he realized that if he let on about anything, she would be used against him. "The boxes are dirty, who wants to roll around in bed with dirt?"

Willy turned to Tasha and said, "Sit your ass down." She complied.

Jason went back over to his laptop. "Here is an updated list," he told Willy. "I forgot a few things." He grabbed the pen as he spoke.

"I forgot power strips." He wrote that down.

Willy asked, "How long do you think?"

"The power strips?" Jason asked.

"No makin' it all work," Willy replied.

"I have no idea right now, I'll know better in a day or two." Jason handed the paper to Willy who looked at it, and frowned. "What do you need the Mac for?" he asked.

"There are flaws or exploits on all operating systems," Jason explained. "The Mac people think they are immune, so they don't even look for viruses. Many of them are zero days. That is, they are not publicly known or haven't been addressed by the manufacturer. Some are old and people don't upgrade their computer. In order for this to work, I am not going to know which operating system is looking at the site. And about the sites—do you know what sites?"

Willy responded, "I have a few in mind."

"Can you make a list?" Jason asked. "I am going to need some help."

"What kind of help?" Willy asked.

"Well, injecting code into a website is not something I have ever done before."

"What's that mean?"

"Well, when I have something, I'll need to get it onto the site, the site from your list. Some of that is over my head. I can learn how to do it, but it would take much longer."

"How much longer?" Willy asked.

"It could take months," Jason shrugged. "I'm really not good at that sort of thing. You said you have friends out there. You have all this high-tech equipment here...cameras, listing devices...it all costs money to install and design. There must be someone at your disposal, I'm not the only bright guy here."

Willy knew he was smart, smarter than him. He hated these guys. He forced a grin and showed his teeth. "Sure, I'll see what I can do."

Jason said, "If you want to keep it at a distance, look at the crews in Russia or China."

Willy suddenly felt uneasy. "This fucker, whoever he is, naw it had to be a guess," he thought to himself.

Jason said, "Some of it isn't a problem. I could really use that hard drive from my place and the stack of CDs on top of it."

Willy replied, "We are still working on that. The cops have been there all day."

Jason said, "Oh probably looking for me." He grinned and glanced at Tasha, who was sitting in the chair with her head down. Jason looked back at Willy. "Let me have a bottle or two of wine, and a couple glasses."

"You don't have to get them drunk," Willy said sharply.

Jason said, "I know that---it's for me. You have me trapped in a room. You're feeding me and giving me a beautiful woman. Alcohol seems to be the only ingredient missing."

"Anything else?" Willy asked.

Jason could tell he was in charge of the project even though he was under Willy's control. He can be pushed, but not yet and not too much.

Jason said, "Make it a chard, a chardonnay. You know, I think the remote connection stuff won't be that hard. I can store almost everything on the victim's own machine, but can you get me a server from the outside of the U.S. for storage?"

"What do you want that for?" Willy asked.

"Do you want the FBI running in here and swatting the place?"

Willy just stood there, looking at him. He had no idea what Jason just said, but the FBI part was concerning him.

Jason said, "You told me yourself that you ran a low-risk operation. What you are asking me for is a lot higher profile I'm sure than whatever you are doing here."

Willy nodded his head in agreement. "Can't you just plan this out a little better?"

Jason looked at him for a second and said, "Maybe. All my shit is on that desktop. My laptop is not set up for that. And besides, you hit me with something that I have never done before. There is a learning curve involved, not anything that is impossible, just stuff I never packaged up before."

"What do you have in mind?" Willy asked.

"I'm not sure, somewhere in Europe; it needs to be a server that is on the Internet. Who has it, doesn't really matter, just a Linux box that I can totally control. I just need access to it and need you to put a web server on it and a few other things. I can do the rest."

Willy nodded his head again; he really didn't know how this stuff worked. "A few grand," he thought, "as long as he comes through."

Jason said, "Can I have that list back?" He still had the pen in his hand. Willy handed him the note. One side was full so he wrote on the back: 4 network cards that are PCI express and my headphones that are hanging off my bedroom door knob. He handed the note back to Willy. "You might have to get those network cards off an online site or something. I don't know where to buy them locally."

Jason knew that this could take a while—a week or two, maybe longer. The idea that this could be done overnight is just a Hollywood delusion. Doing it for real takes time and planning.

"I have other shit to do," Willy said and turned toward the door. He knocked one time and the door opened. Willy went through the opening and the door closed behind him. When the door clicked, Tasha looked up at Jason. "What a pretty face," Jason thought. "How horrible it must be for her here and whereever she was before."

In the back of Jason's mind was a fantasy of taking advantage of others through the use of computers. Almost everyone in the industry has had the same thoughts at times, but guilt, social acceptance and the threat of losing everything keep most people in line. But if you don't have a choice and you really have nothing to lose, then what the hell?

Jason had always dreamed of screwing with systems and taking advantage. Now that he was offered the chance to do something unlawful, "well, let's do it the right way," he thought. "After all, it might actually end up being fun for a while."

Jason turned the radio up a little, and motioned for Tasha to get up. He said to her, "Let's dance." She got up and danced with him.

The hotel was manned by a rough set of "attendants" united in their dark pasts and willingness to ruthlessly do whatever they were told to get paid. For example, Steve, the overweight, balding guy at the webcam controls gazed at a monitor with Willy as Jason and Tasha dance. "I don't trust this fucker one bit, Steve," Willy said.

"Well you shouldn't, you really think he can deliver?" Steve said.

"Yeah I'm sure he can pull it off, Peter says he can do it."

"Well, if he can't, you know it's going to be your ass in the sling, not Peter's."

Steve was a wanted man. He had done time in several prisons, both in North and South America. Now hard-living and age were catching up to him. He was slightly balding and getting, as he described it, "pudgy." He stayed in the hotel most of the time, but ventured out occasionally to go to the convenience store to pick up a six pack to bring back to his room. To him the hotel was far from a prison. He was free to come and go, he was making money and when not working, he could drink and have a woman or two … even three.

He had screwed up only once inside this place. He had grown attached to one of the women. He'd slept with her every day but got drunk one night and started hitting her until she became useless to work. To make matters worse, it caused problems with Willy and the others. Willy had warned him that she was there to work and not to be his personal toy. That night, Steve returned from his rounds on the street with a large bottle of vodka and downed most of it. When he woke the next morning, the woman's lifeless corpse was crumpled up in the corner. To make matters even worse, Steve didn't get paid for several months after. They withheld his pay supposedly so they could replace her. And he was told in very brutal terms that if he did it again, they would kill him. There too, he wasn't worried about them killing him—he was worried about not getting paid after having to work all day. That really pissed him off.

"I know, but man, think of how much money this is worth if he does," Willy said.

"Who the hell put the radio in there? It is hard to hear," Steve said.

"I thought that TV was dead," Willy said. "I didn't know the radio worked, it's old junk that was just there." Willy then pointed at the screen. "Hey what's that?" He was pointing at one of the small images on the right side of the display board. Steve pressed a button on the control board. A uniformed police officer was standing in the lobby of the hotel talking to the hotel clerk behind the desk. Steve pressed another button and rolled his chair across the floor a couple feet to the computer. The facial recognition was quirky and sometimes it didn't work at all.

A picture of the police officer popped up on the computer screen. His name, badge number, start date and home address all showed. "He's just a newbie, trying to know everybody---no worries," Steve said.

They watched him for the next 20 minutes with audio, as he talked to the hotel clerk behind the cage. When he finally left, they watched him as he walked out, then changed views and followed him for the next two blocks. They had put battery-operated Wi-Fi cameras on the top of a few of the buildings around theirs. They had eyes in a solid four-block radius. Willy said, "So how did he get in here?"

"Well don't blame me, you're the one that wanted to watch your boy," Steve said. "Do you really want to know?

'No'" Willy said.

Another hotel "attendant" Abel was walking up the back

stairwell. He was carrying two bottles of wine and thinking about how this was another one of Willy's bright ideas. This one might get him killed. He smiled at that thought. He hoped he personally got to do it. "This guy is a fuckup" he thought.

When he got to the third floor, he went down a few doors. He unlocked the door and opened it. There was one single bed in the room and four girls sitting on the floor with their backs against the wall. He said, "Where is she?" They just looked down, not making eye contact. "Fuck," he said. He slammed the door shut, locked it, and opened the next. This room had a couple of mattresses on the floor and three girls sitting against the wall. He pointed at the bleach blonde and said, "Come with me." She got up and joined him in the hallway. He locked the door again and they walked up the hall to the front staircase. They went up to the fifth floor. They walked down the hall to the door leading to Jason's room. He handed the two bottles of wine to the blonde and reached over to unlock the door.

Jason and Tasha stopped dancing when they heard the door click. The lock made a loud sound when it snapped. The blonde woman came in carrying the two bottles while looking down at the floor. She saw Tasha and looked up at her. She put the bottles down on the table and walked back to the door. She knocked once and it opened and she left.

Jim was in a pissy mood. He had a lot to do today. Carrying a bunch of cardboard boxes to grocery store dumpsters was not making it any easier. Somebody had set the motion sensor off on camera 26. He still needed to check it out. Whatever it was, the switch was jammed and sending alarm signals every five minutes. He had met these guys when he was working as an alarm installer. This job was great. It paid him $60,000 a year, compared to the 22 thousand he made as an alarm installer. He didn't have to crawl through attics every day, anymore. All he had to do was trespass every once in a while for some old rich recluse that owned a dump hotel.

The cardboard boxes and garbage were another part of the paranoid old man. Whenever he had boxes, he had to cut the labels off no matter what they were. He'd take them home and burn them. The cardboard had to be taken to not one but four different grocery stores to be disposed of. Cardboard wasn't disposed often. When it was, he found it annoying, but "what the hell," he thought it was money.

The trash was another issue. The bags had to be dumped into another bag. The trash had to be put in a bunch of different dumpsters every time. By the third month, he was driving over 100 miles away to never use the same dumpster. It had been almost a year with them. He had found a guy that owned a farm that was 200 miles away. The farmer would bury the garbage. He kept the bags. Those had to be burned also.

When he first experimented with Wi-Fi cameras outside, he tried regular batteries that lasted a day. He knew that changing the batteries every day was not practical. When he used a car battery, the camera lasted almost three weeks. He found some solar battery chargers cheap and wired them into the contraption and the unit would stay running indefinitely. He added a motion sensor to the box so he would know if it was moved in any way. He added some materials to the surveillance rig including roofing tar and black paint. Once completed, the box actually looked like it was part of the roof. The weather did the rest to make the disguise complete.

On more than one occasion, he was almost caught in the act. He had been warned by the handy man, Willy, that if he ever told anyone about the camera network, they would make his life miserable. He didn't need misery. It was easy money to keep his mouth shut and to replace batteries.

The cardboard and four garbage bags were waiting for him on the dock. Over the last few months, there had been a sudden increase of garbage from the place. He had been there only two days ago and there were four bags. "They must have had a party," he thought. An old Indian guy was making his way out the back door as he made his garbage pickup. They waved to each other as he walked down the steps and got into his beat-up Datsun. They had this routine of seeing each other every couple of days. They never spoke though. They just waved.

Meanwhile, back in the computer-filled room, Jason looked at the recently delivered bottle of chardonnay. "Hmm, no corkscrew," he noted. He got a screwdriver out of his case, took off his shoe and banged the cork into the bottle. He still had the plastic cups and poured Tasha some wine, and then himself. He moved so that his back was facing the camera and clinked plastic cups and said, "To freedom," silently to her. She smiled at him, and he wondered if she would actually still like him if they did get out of there.

Jason had never been with a prostitute, but he sensed that this was not anything close to prostitution -- those people seemed to have a choice at some level. At the hotel, he sensed there was no choice for anyone stuck behind its doors, locked from the outside. Funny, it occurred to him, that as long as he made his captors money he would be useful, just like a prostitute. As long as he was useful, he felt he could get just about anything out of his pimp Willy, however, just like many prostitutes, his usefulness would also decide his health.

Jason drank, and Tasha got sloppy drunk. Near the end of the first bottle, she could barely walk. He opened the next bottle because he wanted another glass. He guided her to the bed where she fell face first and looked totally unconscious. He pulled her up into the bed under the covers, and started to undress her, but just left her clothes on. He left his clothes on too and lay next to her and eventually fell asleep.

8

Finding A Purpose

The morning came too soon. Jason woke up with Tasha by his side. She was still asleep. The sound of the door closing in the next room was what woke him. He had a slight headache from the wine, and he really needed to pee.

He got out of bed and looked in the office. On the floor sat a box containing his stack of CD-roms on a spool; his hard drive; his USB external drive; the Cisco bag; a box of pictures and some new power strips. The broken alarm clock wasn't there. He doubted that he really needed it anymore, anyway. He ran quickly to the bathroom.

When he finished in the bathroom, he went back to the bedroom and found the Wal-Mart bag. He pulled the tags off a new pair of jeans and put them on. They were a little large, so he found a paperclip and twisted two of the belt loops together so they would stay up. There were also a couple of T-shirts in the bag. He figured that it must be the official uniform of the hotel inmate population.

Through the mirror behind his reflection, off in the distance, was the peaceful sleeping beauty still lying in bed.

The radio was a little loud, he noticed. It didn't help his head at all. After he lowered the volume, and changed the station to light rock he picked up the hard drive from the box. It looked like the one from the tower at home. It was time to install and try it.

By the time the door lock turned and breakfast was served, Jason already had his old hard drive installed in a new computer. The computer booted up and ran normally. Good thing he didn't use Windows or a Mac, as neither of them would have worked after such a hardware change. Linux, on the other hand, was much more flexible, powerful and forgiving. Unlike operating systems people buy commercially, it just works.

The door lock clicked again and the skinny girl from the day before came through, struggling with two trays. As she attempted to set them on the table, she knocked over one of the plastic cups. Before being tipped over, the cup had held a small amount of wine from the night before. A little stream of wine ran down the table and dripped onto the floor. She began frantically wiping up the wine with her shirt. Her face appeared to be frozen in fear from what to Jason had been, just a harmless accident. When she was finished, the entire front of her T-shirt was soaked. She went to the door and knocked once to exit, never speaking a word in the process. The door opened, and she exited.

Jason took both trays into the bedroom and shook Tasha lightly, until she woke up. She yawned, stretched her arms wide. That was when Jason noticed scars on her wrists. They were on both wrists and were three or four inches wide. He wasn't sure, but it looked like she had worn metal shackles on her wrists. They had dug into the skin and cut it. And obviously this had happened more than once because the cuts in the skin had produced permanent scars.

"Good morning," they said to each other.

He got one of the trays and said "Sit up," as he placed it on her lap. He took the other one and sat next to her as they ate the scrambled eggs and toast. The coffee that day was bitter, but Jason drank it anyway.

"Did you sleep okay?" he asked.

Tasha responded, "Yes, I like sleeping with you, you are so warm."

They finished breakfast in silence. He really didn't know what to say to her. When he finished his coffee, he got off the bed and took the trays back to the dresser.

Jason asked, "Would you like some water?"

Tasha nodded yes, so he found both the plastic cups, rinsed them out and filled them with water. He took it to her. When she finished drinking it, he asked if she would like more. She said "no" and proceeded into the bathroom to wash up.

Jason went back to the office and took a seat at the table in front of his laptop. *Let's see what the hell they are up to here.* He heard the shower start in the bathroom. He realized that he really needed to do that, too. The thought passed as he stared at a video replay of one of the computers from downstairs. He figured out that they used a combination of all the social networks to communicate. There were interlinked Facebook profiles. Many of the pictures were of younger girls. Some looked like they were in their teens. There were a number of cam sites, too, adult websites where individuals or groups perform sex acts in front of a web cam for a fee, or sometimes even for free.

As he watched video, he saw the user change to a number of dating and hookup web sites. She would check for emails, or send emails to various men. The pictures she used were not the same. He doubted that any of them were really a picture of the woman working. Often, different pictures were used on different sites. Some of the sites he had never heard of, and others were long-established dating sites.

He opened the key logger file he had created on the computer. He was able to find the username and password used to log into some of the websites. Many of the websites had the username and password cached in the browser, so they didn't need to type in the log-in credentials.

He found the user name and password used to log into Facebook. He looked at the profile and the friends this user had. Many of the friends listed were mostly men; only a few women. The other female friends had the same pattern. Most of them had lots of male friends, and only a few other female friends. He found it interesting that many of the females' profiles were created on the same date, around a year and half ago.

He fast-forwarded the video so he could watch some of the chat sessions. Many of them were the same. The person at the computer was attempting to get someone to go to some other site and give their credit card number to watch a cam performer.

If someone did sign up for a site, they would check for an email confirmation that the credit card was charged. He could see that many times the commission was just a few dollars.

What didn't make sense was who the performers were, and for that matter, where were they? One of the performers was a very tall woman. He hadn't seen a woman that tall since he got there.

He could feel someone watching him. He locked the computer, and turned to see Tasha watching him. She looked horrified. He put his finger up to his lips with his head blocking the view of the camera. Jason said loudly in the direction of the camera, "I could use another coffee, can you bring me the pot?"

He pointed to the bathroom. Tasha just stood there and looked at him. He got up and walked over to the television and turned the music up a little. He went into the bathroom and waved Tasha over. She started to ask him a question, but he put his hand over her mouth, then put his ear next to her mouth and let go. She understood to speak in a whisper.

"How did you do that?" Tasha asked.

Jason replied, "Please don't tell anyone I have that."

"You know the passwords, I saw you," Tasha accused.

"I borrowed them, it's okay," Jason replied as he smiled at her with a reassuring smile.

"There is someone else here that does that and he is not nice," Tasha responded.

Jason thought for a moment then said, "Don't tell him I can do that. We need to get out of the bathroom. We can only talk for a few minutes each time." He stepped back into camera view, dancing a little as he walked. He turned the radio back down a little and danced back to his chair.

He launched Windows XP on his Dell laptop and told the virtual machine the camera was attached. It took a while for him to connect to it remotely with his new java code. He heard a single knock on the door. He turned and Tasha was standing there. Jason said, "You don't have to leave. Why don't you stay awhile? Have some more coffee, it will be here soon."

The door opened. She shook her head no to whoever opened it and it closed again and it locked. She stood there by the door.

"Would you like to come over and watch?" Jason asked. She sat in the seat next to him and watched him work for a while. Ironically, watching someone else give commands to a computer made him impatient. He always thought, 'hit the key already.' He hated watching someone else.

Jason was able to find the key in the computer registry to turn off the light. Windows uses a file called the registry to store various settings in its operating system. He was able to control his laptop remotely from the computer. He remotely turned on the webcam, and made it save its information to a file. The light to the webcam did not come on. He stopped the webcam from recording, copied the file to the computer and played it. The movie that played showed part of his body moving in front of the camera then moving away.

He looked up and waved to the camera and said, "I really could use that pot of coffee."

He thought maybe they didn't watch him all the time. *Perhaps when they aren't watching, they can't hear.* He really didn't know anything about camera security panels.

He was tempted to look at some of the Wi-Fi networks broadcasting their IDs. There was a couple he found that were hidden. That was interesting, but if he did something outside of what he was supposed to be doing, who knows whom Tasha might tell.

There were actually two problems with this girl being in the room with him—the other was that she couldn't be trusted. He didn't know who the hell she was supposed to report to, let alone whether she could be trusted to keep secrets amongst the other frightened, compliant inmates. He smiled briefly at her. She smiled back.

Jason put his laptop in front of her and went to yahoo.com. He clicked on a commercial for some kind of soap. As the commercial ran, he remotely connected to the laptop from the computer sitting next to it. He turned the camera on his laptop remotely. This time he waited for the commercial to end. Then he took the laptop back and clicked on the movie file he had made, her image filled the screen watching the laptop. Tasha blushed and said, "How did you do that?"

Jason replied, "Smoke and mirrors."

The door made a loud click, opened and Willy came in carrying a pot of coffee, saying with a smile, "Don't you two look cozy."

Jason asked, "What took so long? Did you need to steal that from Denny's?"

Willy frowned for a second, and chuckled a little. Jason laughed like it was really meant as a joke.

Jason said. "I only have two coffee cups."

Willy set down the carafe and said, "That's okay, I'm good."

Jason looked at Tasha and said, "Would you get the cups?" She got up from the chair. As soon as she was out of the way, Jason waited for Willy to sit down. "Would you have a seat?"

Jason put his laptop in front of Willy and said, "Okay, do you know how to create a new text document and store it in my documents?" Willy replied that he did. He moved the mouse to do so.

Jason said, "Okay, now rename it." Willy did so. Jason hit a few keys on the computer he was sitting at. He stood up and moved out of the way of the monitor as he pressed the enter key. The computer started playing the video that was just recorded. "Yes I know how to create a document and save it in my documents. Okay, rename it. Okay, done."

"Wow," Willy said.

"Smartass," Jason said.

Willy looked confused.

"You named the file smartass.txt," Jason said. They both laughed.

"That was done in java and using Windows script," Jason explained. "How's the progress on getting me a Mac and a tablet and laptop or two?"

"Shit man," Willy said. He looked up at the camera and spoke to it. "This guy will run shit rings around you, fool." Jason had no idea what that meant. Besides, he just made some sort of enemy and he didn't even know who he was.

Jason looked at Tasha, who was still standing there holding the cups. "You can pour it," Jason said to her. He turned his head and rolled his eyes upward. He worried that the situation he was in was severely screwed up.

Jason asked, "Is there any progress on finding someone to help yet?"

Willy replied, "Are you sure you can't do it?"

"No," Jason said. "I'm not sure I can't. I don't think I can, but you never gave me the list so I don't know what sites you were thinking of."

"Oh yeah, the list, yeah," Willy said, snapping his fingers.

Jason said, "I have a few kinks to work out before I'm ready." Willy nodded, stood up and looked at Tasha,, saying, "You keep my boy here happy." He walked to the door, and knocked once. It opened and he left. Tasha handed Jason a cup of coffee. He sipped it. It was black, but in the moment, he didn't care. It felt good.

"Thank you," Jason said. "Did you get a cup yourself?"

Tasha responded, "Yes, I have it in the other room."

Jason asked, "Do you mind being here with me?"

Tasha replied, "No I like this. I am learning things, and seeing things that I have never seen before."

Jason asked, "Do you like that video trick?"

Tasha responded, "Yes, but I don't understand how that works."

"Computers do anything you tell them to do," Jason explained. "There are really no rules, just programs. What I mean by that is that programs exist and limit the use of the computer to the program's purpose. In the computer world, there really isn't that limitation, just the limitation of the programmer."

"I think I understand," Tasha said. "You are saying the computer can do much more but they are just limited to the programs that people use?"

"Exactly," Jason replied.

Tasha said, "This place is kind of messy."

Jason responded, "Would you like to straighten it out? I don't care where you put anything."

Tasha said, "Sure, I could do that."

It wasn't that Jason really wanted a maid. He needed a little privacy. He didn't know if she would say anything to someone about what he was looking at and he didn't need questions now.

He needed answers for himself. He went back to his laptop and watched the next capture file he had from the other day. The actions were the same, a few more Facebook and Google+ profiles to look at. The casts of websites were nearly identical. What was interesting was that they both seemed to be saying they were the same performer on identical sites. It was as though they knew which performer to promote and when.

When Jason was in the room with the cubes, no one talked. The room felt like being in a morgue. If they were communicating, it must be through email or instant messages. As he checked the chat history for Facebook messages, he didn't see anything telling them what performer to promote. There wasn't an instant message telling them who, either. And the screen captures didn't have anything that made any sense. The key was the performer they all collect commissions from. He went online to the cam site and checked the performer profile. He didn't see anything odd. The sites that they regularly used, seemed to have steady performers.

In looking at the last capture, he noticed a few things that were different. Some of the Facebook profiles had additional friends. As he was looking at them, he saw that they had around the same start dates on Facebook and Google+. One profile had younger friends, young girls maybe 8 or 9 years old. The Facebook banner showed an 8-year-old girl doing a sexy pose. He looked through the posts on her Facebook wall. Most of the posts were from older men. One remarked that he had a great time hanging out with her.

Doing the math in his head, it wasn't that much money. In the time he did the captures, they had maybe $15 between the three. He got the bigger picture: doing the math in his head for 24 hours, as Willy had said, it was close to $5,000 for the day.

From what Jason figured out, the performers must be at another location. At this end, they just promoted the activity. *Now, if the inmates at the hotel just promote, and there are other sites like this, it makes more sense. That is the sort of money the law firm would be interested in.* He made a mental note to ask Tasha about this, later.

Seconds after he heard the click of the door lock, he locked his computer screen. His mind was on lunch. The same skinny girl came in carrying two trays. This time she had them balanced a little better and placed them on the table. She went back toward the door and returned carrying a box that was a little large for her. Jason took the box from her and set it on the floor. He could hear her knock and the door shut and lock behind her. He saw the violin case and took it from the box. He opened the case. It was a used one—maybe from a pawn shop—and it was complete with a bow. He slid the case under the dresser in the office.

"Come eat," Jason said to Tasha. He had set one bowl of tomato soup across from him, the plate with the sandwich in front of him. She sat down and they ate. This time, she didn't attack the food like she was starved. He noticed that she saved a piece of the bread from the sandwich to scrape the bowl. He had seen people do that before, but this time is was notable.

Jason looked at her. Overall, she looked pale. She didn't really have much color. "Can I ask you a question?"

Tasha responded, "Okay."

"Just out of curiosity, when was the last time you were outside?" he asked.

Tasha thought for a minute, and said, "I think it was in the winter. I was cold and didn't have a coat."

Jason asked her, "Was it last winter or the one before?"

"The one before, I think" she said.

"I see," Jason said. He felt even guiltier for touching her. She was such a fragile, damaged girl.

They ate their lunch in silence. As soon as she swallowed her last bite, Tasha asked, "Would it be…okay if I lay down for a while? I can stay here, but I don't feel well."

"Sure you can lie down, absolutely," Jason said.

Tasha got up and went to the bedroom. Jason moved his chair to the opposite end of the table. It must have been the wine from last night, because he still didn't feel that great, either.

He unlocked his computer and launched a web browser. He went to the site that appeared to be the one used most often to promote the performer. He left-clicked on the video, but it required a credit card to enter all the way. But of course, Jason found a freebie. The performer was not the most attractive woman. The right-click with his mouse gave the answer he was looking for: it was flash-based. He checked the next one, and the one after that, and they were all flash-based systems. Adobe Flash does many things; it is a great player, and some people even design games using the platform.

Jason got back up and poured himself a coffee. He thought about the last hour. He still needed Willy's list. *Actually, not really,* he thought. But Willy should give him the list, anyway. Jason realized it would freak Willy out if he knew that Jason had already figured out some of the sites he was using. The question that he could not answer at this point was: who was Willy after?

Willy stopped by the control booth; he sat down next to Steve, who was holding a cell phone to his ear. Steve said "Uh huh, ok… see you. That was Anthony. He is going to stop over later and take a look at your boy."

"What's he been doing?" Willy asked.

"He's just typing stuff. I have no idea what; I can't see," answered Steve, who turned the video feed from the camera on the large screen.

"I'll go check on him in a bit," Willy said as he was getting up.

Steve changed the big screen to the cube room. Willy walked out of the room, as he did.

Jason returned to his laptop and went to work on the two hidden Wi-Fi networks. Both of the networks had a strong signal. A hidden Wi-Fi router is one that doesn't broadcast its identity or its SSID. Their signals were strong, like they were actually in the building. He probed the router for the SSID ID, first on channel 8. His tool told him what the name was. Next, he attempted to connect to it, but it was locked down. He scanned the devices on the network that were connected to it and scanned for the signal strength of the devices that were active. The tool or program told him the machine identity address, or Mac address, of the most distant device. The Mac address is a unique string of numbers that identify the hardware address. All devices actually work via the hardware ID. He picked the one that had the weakest signal. He then changed his laptop to the same Mac address as the remote device. This caused a conflict. Jason called this "conflict city." He next tried to join the network, but it wasn't there yet. *"Hmm,"* he thought. He typed in a few more commands, and manually changed his network ID on his own computer to the default network address most commonly used "192.168.1" and gave his computer "253 gateway.1" and tried to reconnect.

Jason ran a scan and lots of devices started showing up. He stopped the scan. No sense in setting off a trap after all. A trap is a device that looks for connection or odd behavior on larger networks.

Steve was calling Jim to report that camera 13 just went off line. Camera 13 was on a roof four blocks west of the building. It was on 8th Street and looked back in the direction of the building. Many times, police will create a meeting point or establish a perimeter before storming in, to arrest or search. Having a series of cameras and watching them gave the building's occupiers an edge. The old bread truck was parked in the back of the hotel for just that purpose. With only a 5-minute lead time, the clever criminals could be in the truck and simply drive in the opposite direction.

Jason went back to his web browser and typed in the first address. An alert popped up that asked, "Security networks: Do you want to allow this to run?" He did. A few minutes later, he was looking through a camera somewhere in the city, which was pointed downward. He could tell it was up high. It was really a terrible viewpoint; all the people looked like ants. He could see cars passing by. There were controls on the webpage for zooming and moving the camera, but he didn't want to move it yet.

Jason tried a much lower address. The video on the screen showed him the live feed of the lobby of the hotel. *"Now this was a good picture,"* he thought. He tried another address, which took him to a picture of an empty stairwell. The next one he tried was a view of the room with cubicles. The camera was pointed at the convex mirror and the big Asian guy was in the back cube. He tried another one, and a hallway came into view. The big Russian guy was sitting in a chair next to a door. Jason guessed that it was his door that he was sitting beside.

He typed a couple of commands on the other computer and pretended to be looking something up on the laptop. He moved it so he could see it and it was facing the wall. Then he looked at the camera.

"Hey, can I have an Advil or something and a Coke? My head is splitting. Also more wine for, later?"

It took a little while before he saw any action. He moved the laptop, so whoever was looking through the camera could not see his laptop screen. He moved it on the table so he could see the laptop screen and the door at the same time. He watched as the skinny Asian guy escorted the blonde girl down the hallway and handed something to her. It was a can of Coke. The big Russian guy opened the door. Jason walked over to the door to meet her; he wanted to keep her away from his laptop. He thanked her and took the two Advils, a swig of Coke and walked away. She knocked once on the door and the skinny Asian guy jogged back to door; he must have walked down the hallway a bit. The Russian guy opened the door, then closed and locked it. The skinny Asian guy escorted the blonde girl to stairwell, down—nope, up one floor—about six doors back, and let her back into her room. The door closed. The laptop beeped twice and the screen went black. Jason looked at the machine. The battery had just died; it hadn't been plugged in.

Steve sent Jim a text message: *13 came back on its own. Chinese cameras!!!!*

Jason found the power cable and plugged his laptop back in to charge it. He didn't restart the machine immediately.

He looked through his CDs and found one that had some of the utilities on it. He saw what he was looking for: the Flash forced downgrade. Adobe Flash has lots of holes in it, so they, like Java, constantly upgrade their applications to patch security holes. One of the best tools to undermine this safety-minded solution is to force-downgrade the version installed. This way, the user won't see it coming and think he/she has the patched version. The upgraded application used needs to be turned off, which is also easy to do remotely.

He sat down at the next closest computer. He opened a web browser and searched for his name again. This time there were 18 hits on the first page. The stories were all pretty much the same. He clicked the first five, one by one. He was being sought for questioning, or he was the person of interest in the double slaying of an elderly couple in his apartment building. One TV station had his old driver's license picture with the caption "WANTED." He thought, *"perfect"*. He closed the web browser.

He took one of the desktop units and installed Ubuntu Linux on part of the drive. He needed to turn his laptop on to get outside access so he could put on the required patches. So he turned on his laptop and configured it to be a router to the Wi-Fi connection. He looked through the parts in the box and bags. He needed a special cable that wasn't there. Fortunately, he had enough parts to rig a connection. Installing the operating system and doing the updates took a good half hour.

Tasha had been awake for a little while—he could hear movement in the other room. He installed everything he thought he needed and set the machine up to emulate the Internet and placed the brand new Wi-Fi router between the website he'd created and the computer he was using.

He started setting up the last computer that was left on the floor. At this point, the table had his laptop and six screens sitting side by side down the length of it. The computers were sitting on the floor and there were four keyboards and four mice down the length of the table. Each of the screens had either a desktop screen for Windows XP, Windows 8, a Linux desktop, or simply Linux prompts. Jason did it this way, to give Willy a show. Nothing looks more impressive than flashing lights and moving displays. There was a real purpose as well—he could see the logs and monitor multiple things with the many screens.

Jason experimented with various solutions for bypassing the little firewall, but what he found was an old trick that was still not fixed on the brand new Wi-Fi router. It's called the DNS Rebind Bind Attack. The attack is simple—it uses a flaw in most operating systems to fool the computer into thinking communication is still open, when it's not. A quick search downloaded a program to use and detailed the instructions. The world of communication is not without its irony. Many companies and governments attempt to suppress hacking, exploiting of information and piracy. It is in this way, that people understand and share the security problems with various products. Instead of being forced to fix their problems, manufacturers just ignore them, allowing them to be passed along. The idea of killing the messenger and destroying the message is still alive and well, even in the information age.

Jason heard Tasha walk up behind him. She rubbed his shoulder and the back of his neck. It felt good, and he enjoyed it for a moment. He looked backward and glanced at the door and realized that he may have made a small error in judgment. "Hmm," he said out loud. He stood up, and walked over to the door and looked through the peephole. It was reversed. He turned his back to the peephole and didn't give a shit at this point if the camera operator saw or not.

Tasha walked toward the bedroom and said, "Come see what I did."

The bed was made. There was nothing sitting around. She had put the clean clothes away and put his dirty clothes in a bag. She had found his box of pictures. Some of the pictures had been taken when he was small. A couple, were photos of his parents. They were his memories that he kept locked in a box and in his mind. He preferred those things remain in their box and not on display. He looked at them tucked into the mirror frame. He started to feel extremely angry at this display. He felt his anger increase, but remembered that someone was watching. He could not show anything, no matter how much he wanted to. *"Count to ten, buddy,"* he told himself. He smiled. He knew what to say next. "Oh cool, thank you," he said, "I would have never thought to do that."

"You have so many things," Tasha said. He understood what she meant; she probably didn't have anything, anymore. Not even a photograph, or a ring. Long ago she had been stripped of more than her dignity. All her thoughts and possessions were the property of someone else.

Jason asked, "What do you do with dirty clothes?"

Tasha stood with a blank look on her face, confused.

Jason asked, "How do they get clean?"

Tasha said, "There is a big washer and a dryer in the basement."

"Oh," Jason said. It was a simple enough question, but it disclosed that the building had a basement, and big meant big power. *"220 Volts or higher, that may come in handy",* he noted. Big power can be made deadly; it can start fires and a way to get out. He also realized that the staircase he came up on must not be the only one. He thought there must be another, but he didn't see it on the floor with the cubes. Maybe it was there and he just hadn't noticed it.

Jason was starting to feel hungry. He had been making progress, just as he had said he would. Willy still hadn't given him key pieces of information to put this all together. He also knew he needed to keep many parts of this looking complicated, even more complicated than was needed. He needed them to need him, because he had an uneasy feeling about what would happen to him when he wasn't needed anymore.

"Do you, know what time…" Jason started. Then he realized she had no way of knowing, so went over to the XP machine and moved the mouse back and forth. The screen saver went away and the clock said 5:58 p.m. No wonder he felt hungry. The food here was all right, but the portions were very small.

Jason moved the tables to form an L shape. This gave more room for the computer monitors and keyboards. He left space behind the table so a chair would fit in between the dresser and table.

He moved a Linux computer nearest the intersection of the L and the Windows XP one. He pulled his chair in front of that computer and asked Tasha, "Would you like to play a game?" Tasha pulled the other chair next to Jason's and sat down. She said, "I don't know how to play any games."

Jason opened up Yahoo Games, which showed a list. "Do you know how to play checkers?" he asked. Tasha said, "No, but I know how to play Go." Go is an ancient game originated in China during the Zhou Dynasty (1046–256 BC). The physical game uses a board or lines in the dirt to create a grid. Stones are the game pieces and even called that in the computer game. It took a few clicks but he opened Go on the Yahoo site. Playing the ancient game with her wasn't pretty. She creamed him.

Jason thought he understood her strategy, so they played another round, but she beat him even worse. Partway through the third game, the door unlocked. The skinny, blonde girl walked in, carrying one tray. She put it down on the table, and knocked once on the door. She walked out and the door locked.

Jason was partially happy the game had gotten interrupted, because he was losing again. But he couldn't help but wonder, *"Why would they do that? Did they want to piss me off? Or are they sending me a message?"* All of these thoughts came quickly to him. He was tense; he knew he was in a dangerous situation. He didn't create it, but he allowed it to exist. So now, he had to get out of it.

The door clicked open again and the blonde returned carrying the second tray. This one had two bottles of wine on it. She seemed to have trouble with them because they rolled back and forth on the tray as she walked. She put this tray down, next to the first. She never made eye contact; in fact, he never saw her eyes. She knocked once to exit. The door swung inward and she stepped out of the room. The door was pulled closed and locked with a loud click.

"Would you like wine with your dinner?" Jason asked.

"Yes thank you," Tasha said.

Jason found the open bottle of wine and poured some into one of the cups, but had difficulty finding the other one. He put the cup of wine in front of where Tasha sat last.

"Do you know where the other cup is?" he asked her.

Tasha looked around. "Oh, here it is." It had fallen off the table and rolled next to the bed; it was lying on its side against the wall. Jason took it and poured wine for himself.

They ate their dinner of lumpy mashed potatoes, green beans and two deep-fried pieces of chicken. While they ate, Jason asked, "Earlier today, one of the girls stared at you. What was that about?"

Tasha said, "She is my friend. She is worried that she will never see me again. Usually when we leave, it's forever."

"Does that happen often?" Jason asked.

"I really shouldn't talk about it," Tasha said, her voice kind of traveled off.

"I see," Jason said, not wanting to press the topic. "Can we play another game after dinner? A different game?"

Tasha said, "That game was no fun for you. Do you want something easier?"

Jason responded, "That's not it. Well, yes it is. You were beating the crap out of me. How long has it been since you played that game?"

"Oh it's been years," Tasha said. "I used to play with some boys I knew from school. It was a big thing for them. It was not so much fun for them too, but it's always easier for me."

"It's easy how?" Jason asked.

Tasha said, "Well, I think of the possible moves ahead of time. You know, when you make a move, I think of the move you will make three turns from then. If you change what I think of, I see three moves from that."

"But how?" Jason asked.

Tasha said, "I don't know. I see shapes in my head. They come to me as I play. I just close my eyes and see what it will look like as we play."

Jason asked, "Have you ever tried chess?"

Tasha said, "I have, but I think chess is more predictable. Go and chess require different ways of thinking."

"What do you mean different?" Jason asked.

"I think chess is like playing in a box," Tasha explained. "It has patterns that are very predictable. Go also has patterns, but they are large. You know, giant. There are too many to guess."

Jason teased her, "Do you always beat boys at Go?"

Tasha said, "I used to beat almost everyone at Go! I haven't played in so long." He poured a little more wine in her cup. "Let's play some more Go, but you teach me, okay?"

Jason started a new game and made the first move.

Tasha said, "Making the first move should be an advantage, but look. If I place here, then you go here or there, that means I go here or here next." She was pointing at the game on the computer screen. "Are you following?"

Jason said, "Next you will take it further, unless I don't go there or there at all."

Tasha said, "But if you move there, I will win much sooner."

Jason asked, "Did you ever have a dog or cat?"

Tasha said, "When I was a little girl, I begged my parents for a puppy. Finally one day we got one. We named him Aurel. He was so cute. I put bows on him and pretended he was really a girl puppy. He used to follow me everywhere."

"Did you really want a girl puppy?" Jason asked.

"No, not really," Tasha said. "I just wanted him to be a girl because I'm a girl."

Jason asked, "Did you take any high math classes in school?"

Tasha said, "After the war, girls weren't allowed to go to school where I was. I was very young then."

"Are you a Moslem then?" he asked.

"No, my parents were Christian," Tasha explained. "But after the orphanage and what has happened to me, I'm not so sure."

Jason asked, "So do you believe that there is a higher purpose to everything or just chaos?"

"I really don't know."

"Do you ever study the stars?"

"Do you mean astrology?" Tasha asked.

"Yes, or look at the heavens?"

"I haven't in a long time," she said.

"How can you tell when the moon has eaten enough?" Jason asked.

"I don't know," Tasha said.

"When it's full," Jason said.

Tasha giggled and he laughed. It was nice to hear her laugh. The giggling was interrupted by the sound of the snap of the lock on the door.

Willy walked in. He stopped after a step or two and put his hands on his sides, in a very male peacock position. When people stand with their arms at their sides and elbows pointing out, like Superman or Wonder Woman, they do it to show power over others; they are making themselves large like a peacock showing all of its feathers. Many times it is for the same reasons, to show power, dominance or control.

Willy said, "Whoa now, that's what I'm talking about!" He saw the multiple displays sitting across the table. Jason and Tasha were sitting in front of a monitor that was close to the center.

Jason leaned over to Tasha and whispered in her ear, "Go to the other room because this could take a while." She got up, but kept her head down and walked to the other room. At that moment, Jason felt horrible. He really didn't mean to say it in a mean tone. He just didn't want her to be picked on by Willy. He also didn't want her to be a distraction when having this discussion with Willy.

Willy waved his hands at him and said, "So what is all of this?"

"Well this represents a number of things," Jason said. "Wait!" He stuck up his index finger and went to the box. He found the Cisco bag still packed from his former desk. Inside was a small pad of sticky notes. He moved back in front of the monitors, found the pen and wrote on the first few. "Okay," he said. "This is the victim." He put a sticky note on the monitor with the Go game on its screen. "This is the connection to the Internet," he said, pointing at the small router, "In real life, they are bigger and there are lots more of these." He held his palms up and rotated his hips confidently as he talked. "We are here." He stuck a sticky note with "Internet" written on it, on the router. "This is our web server out there looking all innocent," he said, sticking a note on the monitor on the far left. "This is our magic box—it handles Internet and manages DNS. You may have heard of it? Stands for domain name service?" He looked at Willy who had a blank stare on his face.

"It doesn't matter really," Jason said. "What does matter is that the Internet knows that this," he pointed to the web server, "belongs to this." He stuck a DNS sticky on the monitor. "This is my box," he said pointing to the far monitor on the right. He said, "This too, is on the Internet." He put a sticky that said, "My controller" on it. "If the victim," he pointed, "goes to this," he pointed to the web server, "I do this," he clicked the power button off to the web server monitor. "Then he got redirected to here," and he pointed to the box with his controller on it. "Now I own the victim's machine."

"Own?" Willy asked.

Jason replied, "Yes, I can do anything I want to, as long as he keeps the Internet connection alive. Meaning, I can install the camera recorder, but what I found is cool: What I do is put a file on his computer where any time it is on for more than two hours, it looks for this," Jason turned back on the monitor to the web server sticky. "Now all the victim's machine does is say, 'do you want me to do anything?'" On his machine, he pointed at the web server. "And this can tell that to do anything I want."

Willy said, "But you said the machine was off."

Jason said, "It is off only at the beginning and just for a little while. After that, it can stay on. If it happens to be off. The program waits another six hours and tries again."

"I don't know…" Willy said, rubbing his chin.

"It works, but I have a question for you," Jason said.

"What's that?" Willy asked.

"How are you planning to get paid?" Willy looked surprised at the question. Jason said, "Really, how are you planning to get paid?" Jason knew that whoever was watching this on the camera couldn't see the screens, but could hear all of this, so his audience was larger than the room. "Are you planning to have them send you a check or something here? That will invite the police."

Willy was shocked at the question, but couldn't answer.

"Many people dream of stealing money," Jason said. "They think it's easy to beat the systems. Master card and Visa have holds on their money, so if they detect fraud, they don't pay. How about a direct bank transfer?"

Willy sat down. He was listening. Jason continued, "The movies always make this part look easy. Well, it's not. There are ways to set up accounts and transfer money around, and not send up flairs for the FBI or other governments to follow. They are all on the lookout for drug money and possible funding for terrorism. They can be avoided at least until someone complains. Just keep in mind though that if someone complains and there is any trail left over, the government agents will be relentless.

You have to remember that there are really only two ways that government agencies make their money or get funded. They do it either by taxing people or seizing assets from criminals. In the United States, the individual agencies, federal, state and local, compete for criminal activity, not always because they want to solve crime, as much as that they always want additional funding. This type of capitalist policing exists from the smallest police department to the federal systems."

"I can set you up accounts in the U.S. but there is a catch," Jason continued. "That is, in the United States, accounts actually have to belong to someone. Now if you steal a few people's ID's and add money to their accounts, you can shift it around, but you have a limit of $7,000-something at a time without setting off alarm bells. In the big scheme of things this is small change. But you have to get to the account in order to control it. Who is the victim, Willy? Is it one person or many people? I need to know this to help you do what you want done."

Willy just sat there thinking about what Jason had said. He crossed his arms on his chest, which told Jason he was being defensive. He either didn't know or he didn't think it through.

They both turned their head when the click of the door lock sound was heard. Anthony had heard enough and came into the room.

A Meeting With Anthony

This was the moment for which Jason had been waiting. He deserved to finally meet the person behind this secretive operation and, of course, his current "situation." Anthony wore a custom-made tan suit, white shirt and black tie. His shoes looked Italian. All in all, he appeared sophisticated and in charge, certainly different than the other men controlling events at the hotel. Anthony walked to the center of the room and looked at the monitors with the sticky notes attached. When he was through looking, he crossed his arms, looked at Jason as if he were just another desperate crook on his payroll and said, "Continue please."

Jason turned his chair to face Anthony and said, "I was just explaining that there are many methods of getting money that don't attract attention. There are things people do every day that involve big money, houses, cars, jets, or boats, to name a few. Big electronic money has a shorter shelf life than that of small change. If you have it in paper however, nobody can track what you're doing. " Willy didn't understand what he meant by all of that. He crossed his arms more tightly and looked genuinely confused. Anthony however, nodded in agreement.

Suddenly, Jason turned on his keepers, "So you guys fucked up my life and stuck me in this dump." He had actually paid to stay in some worse places in the past, while traveling, but he wasn't about to mention that. "So you want a system created to do something dealing with the web, and you want to steal money from someone remotely. If you want a thing built, I can do it for you, but I need the information, man. You put my nuts in a vise, so I'm on board and I really don't feel like making a stupid play here that lands me in jail, too."

Anthony followed Jason's every word. His facial expression changed revealing a degree of surprise and surrender to Jason's gutsy push back. Jason continued, "Everyone on the Internet wants to make the big score; they did it in the 90s during the tech bubble. That was all just dreams of getting rich quickly on the web. The Russians, Pakistanis, Nigerians…they play little games with credit companies, or just scam with direct deposit. The thing is the little scammers are the ones that steal identity and fuck with people's lives. They aren't rich, living it up. There are exceptions like that guy in the Ukraine who had more card numbers than he knew what to do with. When he got sent up for 30 years in jail, he had 400 thousand credit card account numbers. He didn't buy boats or mansions; he bought hookers drinks in discos. The little guys, for the most part, use the money to buy drugs. When they get caught, the cops solve the case. The cops are all about closure. So who are you going to be stealing from? You have to plan how to cash out. It can't stay in banks, it has to move—and quickly—to cash or somewhere else."

Anthony recovered somewhat, looked directly at Jason, and uttered, "Impressive." Then he nodded his head and added, "You really thought this through, didn't you?"

"Yes, I did," Jason said.

Anthony looked at Willy and said, "Don't you have something

else that needs to be done? And take that girl with you." He looked up at the camera in the ceiling and pointed to the other room and said, "Off." Then he pointed to the camera he was looking at and repeated, "Off."

Willy got up and walked over toward the bedroom. "Bitch, get up and come here."

"Keep her nearby and bring her back when we are done here," Jason said. He realized that he might have been overstepping his boundaries. He wasn't sure that he wanted it that way but he didn't want any more harm to come to her either -- not if he could stop it.

Willy and Tasha left the room. Anthony took off his jacket, neatly folded it and set it on top of one of the keyboards, which made the computer start chirping, so he moved it and placed it on a chair back.

"Okay, this may not be the time, but this has been bugging the crap out of me. How did you find me?" Jason asked.

"One of my associates knew of you," Anthony stated. "Then one of our more legitimate operations got a copy of your resume, and, uh, Willy had this idea, um, which truthfully isn't bad, so we let him approach you."

"He screwed up my life," Jason said. "Approaching me, is saying hello."

"Well some things were a bit dramatic, but here we are," Anthony shrugged. "You asked."

"Okay, who is it you want to scam?" Jason asked point blank. "That would be a start."

"We have lots of what you would call associates all over the world," Anthony explained. "Some of them found that, if you, say, own a girl, you can make a lot of money, but it's risky because there are too many people involved. The Internet is a better, smaller return, and it only requires a web cam, a room and an, actress, let's say. There are people all over the world who pay to see the actress, and they can pay with a credit card. It's clean, and we just promote the show. We don't know where in the world the actress is, so they are insulated from us. And if the actress gets busted, and that operation fails, well, they are insulated from us. This just requires a simple investment. And it returns a constant percentage. Some of the things we promote are not what I agree with, personally, but as the shows get more exotic, they pay better. Some of the people, especially in, say, more civilized regions are breaking the law by even viewing the shows. So, Willy thought we could squeeze funds from some of those people. Apparently, he didn't think it through, we are not set up to receive money like that though our operation and I wasn't convinced that this was really possible," he pointed his finger at the table and monitors.

In response, Jason probed, "So, what you want to do is what, collect an extra $100 fine for watching a show that they would never watch again?"

To which Anthony admitted, "Well, you created something a little more powerful than what we had ever dreamed … Most of it is way over my head. Can you explain it to me simply? What can you do with all this?" he asked, waving his finger at the monitors and other equipment.

As the conversation continued Jason felt more comfortable and in control. He continued, "Okay, let me do a couple of things," He got one keyboard and typed a couple of things, and went to another keyboard and typed a bit. "Look at this," he said. On the computer was a desktop that didn't look like Windows or his Mac, or anything that Anthony had seen before. In the center was a back window with a "c:\"

"This is that computer's hard drive," Jason said, pointing at the machine that had Windows 8 running. There were a couple of icons on it but nothing was running.

He typed "Dir," then hit "Enter." A list of things scrolled down the window. He typed a long sequence of commands and waited. A few seconds passed. "Oops, I left the antivirus on," Jason said. He hit Ctrl C, and typed another long command. "Okay, the antivirus is now off. Let's try that again," Jason said as he pressed the up arrow twice and hit enter. The Windows 8 machine opened an Internet Explorer page. The keyboard and mouse were untouched and were in front of the monitor.

A new window came up on the machine he was using: the screen of the Windows 8 desktop. Jason moved the mouse on the Windows 8 machine to display the search. Anything he did was mirrored on both machines.

He went to Yahoo in the browser. Yahoo's homepage came up, and the other computer showed the same desktop displayed in a window. He clicked on email on the Windows 8 machine. He typed an email address and password.

He pressed the login button. The screen on the Windows 8 machine showed the list of emails. The other machine showed a mirror of the same display in one window. But there was another window opened that showed the email address and the password clearly readable on the next line.

"Okay," Jason remarked triumphantly, "I own this machine." He pointing at the Windows 8 machine. "From here," he said, pointing at the monitor displaying a mirror of the Yahoo page and the user name and password. "If this," (pointing to the Windows 8 machine) "is connected to a network like an office PC, I have the entire network at my disposal. I can do literally anything. I can be the owner of the computer from their own machine, liquidate their savings and retirement, I could even sell their house. Your cohort wanted to steal a measly $100 from each dupe" he said shaking his head. "That just shows a total lack of imagination."

Jason had just scared his captor. Anthony sat with large eyes looking at the display in silence. Jason broke the silence and said, "Let's go have a drink outside of here; I don't really trust these walls." He was taking a gamble pushing back on this guy, a smart guy at that. But maneuvering this fellow wasn't really that big a feat. Jason simply had to appeal to whatever Anthony's imagination could muster -- his greed made him easy to manipulate.

"Okay," Anthony said, still in a trance of sorts. He was staring at the password in view.

Jason said, "I have a problem, can you get it fixed?"

"What is that?" Anthony asked as he shook off the remaining fixation of the yahoo page.

Jason said, "Look at what I am wearing." He stood up displaying his t-shirt and jeans held up by a paper clip. He wasn't wearing any shoes or socks.

Anthony looked at Jason and smiled a little, "Sorry about that."

Jason grabbed a pen and the notebook and wrote down his sizes of shirts, slacks, socks and shoes. "Wal-Mart, even Marshall's is okay." He handed the sheet of paper to Anthony. "Can someone get me something to wear?"

"I think a shower might come in handy, too."

Jason chuckled and said, "I bet you're right."

Anthony looked at his watch and said, "I'll come get you in, say, two hours?"

"That would be fine," Jason said. "I can be ready in that time. Besides, I'm not going anywhere."

Anthony got up and took hold of his jacket. He knocked once on the door and it opened "I'll see you in a little while," he said, closing the door behind him. A few seconds later, it opened again, and Tasha came through. The door closed again and locked.

Jason threw her a quick smile. She had no idea what just took place. He said, "I need to take a shower. I stink." He grabbed his cup that still had a little wine in it and took a drink. He picked up her cup, which was empty, and poured a little wine into it. He held the cup out toward her, and she took it from him and took a sip. He was so tempted to invite her to shower with him, but held back. "I know you haven't been in a place that you had any choice in such a long time," he said to her. He sat back down and changed the Yahoo page to games and typed "Go" in the game search.

The Go game was ready to play. He rose and said, "Here's the game."

He went into the bathroom and started the shower. He was in the middle of washing his hair with soap running in his eyes when the curtain opened and the naked beauty stepped into the tub and started washing his body.

Near the end of their extended shower, they heard the door shut from the other room. They dried each other, and he looked in the mirror. He really needed a shave. He put soap on his face. He forgot to ask for shaving cream. He pulled out the disposable razor, but Tasha took it from him.

She whispered into his ear, "Let me do it." He had never been shaved by anyone else before. He put the toilet lid down and sat. She shaved his face, being much more careful than he would have been. She shaved it backwards and forward. When she was finished, his face actually felt smoother than he could ever remember.

When he went to the office side, he saw two Marshall's bags. He found a green silk shirt, (which probably wouldn't have been his first choice), brown dress slacks, brown socks, a brown belt and brown dress shoes, which all together, really wasn't a bad mix. He put the clothes on, and turned around to see the pretty girl standing in the doorway, watching him. She had a towel around her waist, but her breasts were still visible for all to admire. He walked over to her, and kissed her on the cheek. He whispered, "Get dressed, someone will be here soon." He had no idea if the cameras were back on or not. And at this point he didn't really care.

Tasha went to find her clothes, and Jason went to check the time on the computer. He realized he had no idea what time Anthony had left. He typed a couple of commands and saw the log of the password had occurred at 7:03. When he looked at the time it was 8:51.

The door clicked open and Anthony walked in as Jason was getting up from the chair.

Anthony said, "Well, you certainly look much better."

"Well, thanks for the makeover," Jason said.

"Let's go," Anthony said.

Jason followed Anthony out the door past the big Russian. He led Jason to the back stairwell and could hear the lock click and thought, *"Man, that thing is loud."* They went down the rear staircase and to a small hallway at the end, where there was a door. Anthony opened the door, which led to a small loading dock. They went down the steps and across the sidewalk. Anthony's Mercedes was parked on the street.

Once outside, Jason felt very much relieved. He paused ever so briefly in the driveway and took a long breath. The air outside felt so fresh; it inspired in him a completely unfamiliar sense of freedom. But even with the stress of that room seemingly behind him, way behind him, he was uncomfortably aware of Tasha's absence. He hadn't spent every waking moment with anyone since he lived with his parent's years ago, and the bond lingered.

Once inside the car, Jason turned the radio way up and leaned into Anthony's ear. "If you have your cell on you, can you take the battery out?"

Anthony shook his head no and pulled out an iPhone. Jason wasn't sure if Anthony was still being "company man" Anthony or "the guy who sees bigger potential." Jason took a gamble and grabbed the phone from him. He whispered to Anthony, "I don't trust this device, would it be okay if we left it here?" Anthony understood and nodded yes. Jason opened the car door and found a discarded paper cup on the ground; he turned the phone off and put the cell phone inside the paper cup. He placed the cup on its side next to a bush on the side of the road. He didn't get any objection from Anthony as he got back in the car and closed the door. Soon after, the car started moving. Anthony turned the music down.

"We shouldn't talk in the car, and we can't go to a place anywhere near here," Jason said. "I'm a wanted man, you know. Do you know any place in another area that has underground parking?" Anthony took a left at the next intersection.

Back in the building, Willy was with Steve in the control booth. He looked at Steve and said, "What the fuck was that?" They had watched as Anthony left and returned with Marshall's bags. They also watched as Anthony purposefully drove the freshly dressed Jason outside of their video perimeter.

Steve looked at Willy and shrugged his shoulders.

Jason and Anthony got onto the freeway and drove to a bordering city, which took around 45 minutes. They pulled in front of what looked like a steak house. The sign outside simply said, "Villa." Together they found a parking space in an underground garage. Jason watched to see if any cars followed them, but there didn't appear to be any. Once in the parking spot, Jason and Anthony got out of the car. As they walked toward the exit, Jason said, "I saw an Irish pub across the street with big windows. We can sit there and watch for anyone coming to look for us."

"I don't think anyone would be interested," Anthony said.

"Well, you know more about who I am dealing with than I do. Maybe I'm being paranoid. I really don't know," Jason said.

They went up two flights of stairs and opened the door at the top, which led to the street. Once outside, they crossed the street and entered the restaurant. The place had a few patrons, but the seats at the window were available. They sat there so Jason could watch the street. It didn't look like anyone had followed them, but tracking devices don't need people behind them. And GPS units have difficulty in underground parking garages. Also, the drones were out there to worry about as well.

As soon as they sat down, a waitress came over to take their order. When she was gone, Anthony said, "That is some pretty amazing stuff you do with computers."

"It's not really that amazing," Jason said. "What's amazing is the cover up."

"What do you mean?"

"Well, all over the Internet there are all these conspiracy people right? The people that think everything is a cover up, even the moon landing, 9/11, and the eventual economic collapse of money; the net is just filled with these characters."

Anthony nodded and said, "Agreed."

Jason said, "What is ironic is that everyone in charge of securing the systems everyone uses, knows nothing is really secure. The people at the top of major corporations and the talking heads don't discuss it. Most of the stuff on the internet is insecure as hell; none of them are solid. No one talks about that. Instead, they act like every security is fine. The only way you make something that someone can't get into is to unplug it and bury it. And hope no one finds where it is buried."

Anthony said, "That's a pretty funny outlook for someone in your line of business."

"I think if there's a conspiracy on the Internet, then it's a greedy agreement among powerful companies to overlook how risky it is. Those that do web-based business ignore lots of obvious risks online. They spend money on encouraging us all to use the net and they invest like crazy in the growth of the net, yet they know the system is totally without security; there's always a way in. Users are all potential dupes, there for the taking in spite of layers and layers of antivirus, antimalware, all the security. Ask any tech that does this stuff. Ask them, 'Is the site you're in charge of totally secure?' and you know what, if they respect you at all they'll look you straight in the eye and ask if you've gone nuts."

Anthony listened patiently but then remarked, "Well it sounds to me like a lucrative opportunity to make loads of money. ... Do you think governments and businesses really understand how vulnerable they really are?"

Jason smirked, "No, they don't have even a flippin' clue ... the

Internet was never intended for commerce. It was designed to send messages back and forth in the science community so groups of people around the Earth could collaborate and work together. Security wasn't a consideration because the intention was that they wanted the information they offered to be shared and spread among people and as quickly as possible."

The waitress came back with a glass of wine for Anthony and a bourbon and coke for Jason. "Would you like to keep a tab open?" The waitress asked the pair. Anthony pulled out a credit card and gave it to her. "Keep it open," he said to her. She went to the table behind them after taking the card.

Jason continued, "If there is a single group I'd pick out for pushing the conspiracy to scam people using the risks of online business, it would be the banks. They are the ones that really made the Internet into this commerce thing, ignoring security all together. The decision for this came from the top layers of ignorance and I can prove it. You know why I say this?"

"No why?" Anthony said.

"Most people understand the idea of 'atoms.' It's been put out there globally, since the 1950s. Do you know what an atom is?"

"Sure, I think so," Anthony said.

"Okay, the Internet also has its atom too; the 'packet.' It's small bits of communication that combined make up any message. Commerce is communication so it's just a collection of packets."

Anthony nodded his head and Jason continued, hoping he understood.

"The packet—this single entity that we base all of our commerce on—can be copied, changed and manipulated, which is how it was actually designed to be. This logic is the same as saying, 'I have atoms and I can change them to whatever I want them to be.' It is the same on the Internet, although the alchemist of old was a dismal failure at turning lead to gold. Today the hacker is the alchemist, manipulating the electronic system of payment into whatever 'gold' you want: precious metal, paper currency, anything. It even touches the futures market where people bet on the price of gold before it's dug up or re-melted. Anyone who bothers to learn the details of the internet understands all of this, the true weak point; it is insecure and is totally glossed over. That is why 'ipv6' is the next thing. Do you know what that is?"

Anthony shook his head. "No I don't."

"Never mind, it's really not that important," Jason said. "But do you understand what I am getting at?"

"I think so. So what can you do for me?" Anthony asked impatiently. He made direct eye contact with Jason as though he was carefully listening, but in his peripheral vision he was looking for any body movement that indicated the hacker before him was somehow full of shit. Was Jason really as smart as he sounded; was he that alchemist he described? That last question burned in his brain.

"What is it you want done?" Jason asked

"I want a new life."

Jason really didn't know how to respond. "Seriously?" he asked with a blank question on his face.

"Well, you claim to have all this power over the computers."

"I don't claim anything; this idea was not mine," Jason responded.

"Well you talk like someone who has more than an idea of how this has been done. I have had clients who were bright, even brilliant, but I never had someone say to me, 'There is someone's life. All of it,'" he motioned with his arms like he was holding an invisible tray and made a motion toward Jason with it. "I have represented hitmen, and murderers of all types. Eventually a body is found. You see, that's why I get involved; the evidence of their past comes back to haunt them. I need something so complete that no one will ever know and every record is erased."

"What are you looking for?" Jason asked.

"I want a new life, one where I don't have all this shit following me around. It isn't me, I am not really like them."

"Like who?" Jason asked.

"Some of the people that I work for…the firm, it's complicated, of course; there are people within the firm who if you were to look up 'evil' in the dictionary, their families are listed. The firm, at least part of it, is really old; one of the partner's great, great, grandfather or something like that."

Anthony took a large gulp of his wine; he looked around the room for the waitress and once he made eye contact, lifted his glass up over his head, signaling for a refill.

"I got sucked into this crap and I really am done, but I'm in a job you can't exactly quit. Getting 'fired' is not an option; I like life a little too much for that. These people would look for me; hell I call out the dogs to look for runaways myself, so I know how it works."

Jason asked, "What do you mean by dogs?"

"Private investigators and bounty hunters, sometimes bail bonds people or street trash, it depends who is reaching out for whom. People always screw up, there is no perfect crime. No one escapes forever. I still ask myself why I brought you out; maybe I need my head examined. But then that's how I ended up here. What I noticed is that everyone they go looking for, they find because they contacted someone they know. So what I need from you is a way to make them not look for me. I need you to kill me in the system."

"I don't know how that even works," Jason said.

Anthony observed, "Well you seem to have a pretty good idea how lots of things work. You put on a pretty good show for me back at that hotel."

But Jason began to shrink in confidence, sputtering, "I didn't say I can't figure it out, but you seem smart -- how the hell did you end up with…"

The waitress came back and put their drinks down on the table in front of them.

Jason asked her "Could we have a couple of shots? Do you do 'Wild Turkey'?" He looked at Anthony who nodded in agreement. Jason held two fingers up and said "Two shots of Turkey," to the waitress. As soon as she left, he continued. "How did you end up running the firm's operation? I look at you and you don't really look like you fit in with Willy and the people at the hotel. I mean I visited your office as you wanted me to and saw that it was a big firm with real money. Why would your firm even mess with this small time crap? It really doesn't make any sense to me."

Anthony sighed and slowly began to explain, "It is a lot larger than what you see. The hotel operation for example generates a lot of money. It may look like small change but each computer workstation makes 30 grand a week. This is only one operation; I know of others which are even larger than this. The law firm I work for is a really old one. They've existed, from what I have been told, since before the United States existed. One of the named partners of the firm was a trader in the 1600s. The connections for the firm go back to the early European aristocrats and traders of spice and sugar. The firm's main client base still deal in whatever are the biggest of money issues, globally. So our clients sell guns, drugs, people or labor---some call it the Big Three. We have attorneys who work on every type of law. The biggest are corporate clients, of course. Some parts of our firm deal with international issues. In the United States we follow whatever are the biggest money markets at the time. Currently that market is immigration and class action.

"Once you understand the history of the firm then you can see how impossible it's gonna be to hide from its reaches ... just like the law ... it has very long arms."

Jason said, "Well it depends, I guess, on how you want to live. Can you afford to retire?"

"I haven't really given it that much thought, I have some money and investments socked away for retirement. Right this minute I can get my hands on some cash, most of it is tied up in investments though."

"You can't use any of that. It has to be left alone. I mean other money," Jason said.

"Hmm I hadn't thought of that," said Anthony, "but you're right though. If I take or touch any of current investments, then it would set off alarm bells for anyone looking."

Jason continued, "The thing almost everyone who is on the run, forgets about when dealing with money, is that you have to have cash in order to avoid leaving a trail, and also to live on. Do you have that kind of cash lying around?"

Anthony thought for a moment, "I have some cash around and a few things I could sell that no one would miss, but not enough to live on long term or anything."

Jason offered, "We can work on that if you're really interested. I would need to keep some of the money, be paid for my time. Do you think that would be possible?"

Anthony appeared to warm to Jason and said, "Well, we're here talking, so give me an idea of what to do,"

Jason was already ahead of this question, "So, this is just a thought, but in the United States, I've heard there's a problem with the county coroners' offices, like, the people who do autopsies and process bodies are not certified by any national board or anything. There's no accreditation and some of them work part time. You know, like that scandal in New Orleans after Hurricane Katrina; same sort of situation in Kansas and Arkansas… The officials just can't keep up with all cases and even when they do there aren't enough experts to verify the identity of every corpse."

"Ok, so go on," Anthony said.

"Getting a new identity isn't the problem; getting a past identity is really the problem. This is just an idea, but if we were in an area where there is lots of violence, someplace where it's common for black men to die and not be identified. If someone had access to that system, it would be possible, from the inside, to swap the identity of a living person with some deceased guy. Then, if some random junkie suddenly starts paying taxes, holding assets and stuff, he'd probably fly under the radar, just as he did during his miserable life. By the way, it would be even better if you could find a body that was really unrecognizable; do you have any relatives? "

"Why do you ask?" Anthony asked. As he did, the waitress came back with the two shots of Wild Turkey. She put the shots on the table in front of them. As she left, Jason reached over and took one of the shot glasses.

"To commerce," Jason said. He held it in the air, until Anthony took the other glass and held it up. They downed the shots forcefully and clapped the glasses on the bar.

Jason continued, "Well, I was wondering if anyone would search if suddenly disappeared; it's a fair question. Is there someone that would be upset, contact the police, ask a lot of questions?"

Anthony though for a moment and replied, "Not really, I don't have any family that I'm close to. I have a few cousins in Chicago but no one around here, not living any way."

Jason quickly remarked, "Well you can scratch Chicago then, if you die somewhere you don't want the police contacting anybody in the same city, even if it is a distant relative. That includes … Jason paused for a moment and became more cautious. "I gotta ask".

Anthony noted the change, "Ask what?"

Jason continued, "You said that only part of your company knows the stuff that is going on; so, does that mean everybody or just a few people know what is going on?"

Anthony thought for a moment and replied, "In my office there are six others that I know of, who have things going on that are outside the legal practice. I mean the hotel that you are at and another place not far away. Peter and I do the hotel; actually I got stuck with watching over this hotel, since Peter's wife got tired of Peter hanging out at the hotel. Her father is one of the senior partners of the firm and Peter married into money, if you know what I mean."

Jason finally got the chance to ask, "Maybe I'm dense but why do you bother with the hotel and that business anyway? Does it actually turn a profit?"

"Sure," Anthony replied, "The hotel investment cost us almost nothing, the building is owned by an offshore firm that deals in arms through a shell corporation. The hotel is used as a tax deduction and loses money by design. Off the books however, the hotel generates between 25k and 30k per month. It also boosts some of our offshore operations by 30 to 40 percent. Peter would know more about that end of the business; I'm not really in that loop and honestly, there are things, I don't want to know. "

Jason took the opportunity to ask, "Who at your firm knows about me and do they have any idea that you want out of their organization?"

Anthony started to answer, "Hell no, there isn't any one that…" the waitress came back to take the shot glasses and Jason held out two fingers and made a circular motion above them. Anthony said to her, "Two more of those and could I have a vodka tonic? Jason, do you want another round?"

Jason answered "Yes thanks." The waitress went back to the bar taking the empties.

"Where was I?" Anthony continued, "No one really knows anything at all. A couple of people know of you exist but just as a temp to fix our slow machines. It was actually Peter who first brought you up; your resume was given to him, but he had other resumes too. So it came down to who Willy could set up. Willy thinks a lot but specializes in screwing things up or at least making things more complicated. Actually, I really don't know much about you, except you became Willy's latest crazy plan … and now then little demonstration today"

"So," asked Jason thoughtfully, "if I were to disappear now, would your people go looking for me?"

Anthony began to see where the conversation was going, "Well at this point, that decision would belong to me and that depends on what you can do for me while appearing to take care of Willy. Do you think you can provide what Willy needs?"

Jason replied confidently, "I am pretty sure I can pull off what he wants. It doesn't look that hard, but to do your stuff is going to require keeping tabs on your firm. I think it would be a good idea to monitor them for a while."

Anthony's eyebrow indicated surprise, "How would I go about doing that?"

Jason continued, "Well I don't think that you should really do anything personally and if you're going to leave, it should be suddenly. It should be in the middle of some sort of big project, completely unexpectedly. And you should really plan confusion and real work for someone if they decide to track you."

"You lost me, kid," Anthony said.

Jason probed, "Do you use any of the social networks?

Anthony chuckled, "No, who has time for that?"

Jason's became very intense as he revealed a plan, "I think you should make time, you should make an effort every night to reach out to people on the social network. Connect to Twitter, Facebook, Google---all of them. I also think you should look for strangers to communicate with. You should play games and meet people from all over the world."

Anthony was puzzled, "Why would I want to bother doing that?"

Jason continued, "Because in a couple of months, when you have that tragic accident and your firm starts looking into what Anthony was interested in, there is busy work for some P.I. to do. The more information you can put on the Internet, the better. Use you work email address, too. Make it easy for whoever is going to look you up; let them find all kinds of strange and interesting gems of information. Hopefully it will be such a distraction from what has really happened that eventually, you'll just be forgotten."

Anthony continued to look uncertain, "So why bother even

doing any of that?

Jason tried to explain, "Because people who hire people to look into other people's lives, expect some kind of report. It's just a guess, but if your information is harder to find, then someone will make the effort to find out the truth, somewhere. But if you can fill them with shit, they will use that and create an easy report. People are, for the most part, lazy; so if you give them something to report about, they won't dig very deep and will go on to the next issue. Do you see what I'm driving at?"

"That's really not a bad idea; what do you think it would cost to set up the mont…." The waitress appeared with their shots and their drinks. She picked up their empties and Anthony waited for her to leave before speaking again. "Salud," he said finally to Jason as they drank the whiskey shooter. Jason was starting to feel the effect of the alcohol; he hoped that Anthony who weighed slightly more than he did, would start to feel its effects, too. He saw Anthony take a large swallow from the mixed drink; he knew now, that this guy might be just a little tipsy.

Jason kept the conversation going, "I'm going to need some money to buy some gear to get some things setup."

Anthony seemed entirely on board, "How much are you going to need?"

Jason had to think about it for a second or two, especially as the drinks were messing with his head. Finally he spoke, "Around thirteen grand I think, but I need it deposited in foreign banks under new accounts; the accounts should have no ties to the US system."

Anthony struggled to keep up with the request, "Why foreign banks?"

Jason explained, "Because American banks have FDIC records. Every night, the balance of every individual account in every bank, is given by law to the FDIC. If anyone wants to know transactions in American banks, it is easy to do. It's harder with foreign banks;

you have to have the government involved. Again, people need to be interested enough to go to the effort and since you're American, do you travel outside the county a lot?"

"No, been there on vacation a few times," Anthony responded and then added, "So why would I have a foreign bank account?"

Jason quickly replied, "You wouldn't, but I need a way to buy some gear that I don't have, preferably through the Internet using wire services or through checking accounts."

Anthony started to seem overwhelmed, "I don't know how to do that, set up some sort of account; can't I just give you cash or something?"

Jason reassured him, "Thanks, but we don't need your cash. Maybe you're worried about being tracked down; do you think I want that to happen? No way. I don't want anything to do with any records or purchases. Besides, the police probably already have a trap on my bank account in case I try to use an ATM. Can you get someone to set up a blind mail drop and bring it to me over at the hotel? There are these mailbox services; go to one and set up 2 mailboxes, tell them one is for a new company you're starting. The clerk will have some forms to fill out, fill the one out for your personal one, correctly. Fill out the one for the company with whatever you want. If the clerk looks really young, or really stupid, that is even better. The company one will be the one that you will give me. The personal one will be the address you give the banks you set up. Prepay both of them for 6-8 months. Do you have someone you can trust to pick up what I have shipped there, and then bring to me?"

"I think that can be arranged." Anthony nodded his head as he spoke in agreement.

"Would you rather go to New York or LA for an impromptu weekend?"

Anthony raised an eyebrow at the question then took a large sip of his drink before answering, "I have never been to LA."

"Well, maybe LA would be a good place to go later then, so could you go to New York and set up three new bank accounts? I am thinking Bank of China, Bank of Saudi Arabia and Bank of Africa," Jason said.

"I can't just disappear; people at the office would ask questions."

"It would just be for a weekend. I'll send you an email; you won a contest, all expenses paid. You, of course pay cash only, for the entire trip. Have you ever been to a Broadway show?"

"No I haven't," Anthony said with a slight slur.

"There is a ticket booth in Times Square. It's where they sell tickets for the shows. Go there, buy one for cash and go to the show. Secretaries at your office will want to know all about it; tell them about the show and make a big deal over going. Buy a statue or plate or something and leave it in your office. People where you work will ask you about it and you can tell them about winning a contest, and going to a Broadway show. You seem smart; how in the hell did you get mixed up with these guys anyway? What did they use over you?"

Anthony sighed. "I had a part-time intern thing at the firm, and had just taken the bar exams. I had a girlfriend, Lisa, who I had been seeing for a couple of years. The studying for the exam was intense. Alan, the attorney whom I was assigned to, had some big case going on at the same time. He was on trial; well, his client was on trial anyways. I found some box of files that were mislabeled to another case in the archive room. I told him about the box and put it in his office. The next day I had my exam and afterwards, we went to a party to celebrate. Some people there had cocaine and I tried some, I only did a little and so did Lisa.

"I didn't drink a lot that night, from what I can remember. I have played that night over and over in my mind. We were talking to these other people we had just met, and one of them went to the bar and got us drinks. That was all I can remember from that night. I blacked out. I really don't know what happened until I woke up in a hospital and was told that I was in a terrible accident. My Lisa had died at the scene. The police told me I was driving and drove into a tree and she had gone through the windshield." Anthony's eyes were getting red as he spoke.

"The police had found a half a pound of coke in the car. I really don't know where that came from either. Neither of us ever had that kind of money and I had never even tried it before that night; neither did she. Someone from the firm was waiting at the police station when they brought me in. The police took me directly to an interrogation room where the guy from the firm was waiting. He told me that I had a choice to make in the next hour—that I could join the law firm full time, erase everything forever that has happened, or I could face my destiny. I was so upset. Lisa was my life and I wanted to marry her. I remember he told me one more time, 'one hour.' Then he left the room." Anthony was sobbing at this point. "Who wouldn't want to erase everything?"

"I want to smoke; do you smoke cigarettes?" Anthony asked.

"No, I d…one second," Jason got up and went to the table directly behind where they were sitting. They both had watched the guy behind them smoke a cigarette outside. He had just come back into the restaurant. Jason went up to him and said, "I got a deal for you." He pulled out two $20 bills from his pocket and put them on the table in front of the guy and said, "Here is $40 for your cigarette pack and your lighter."

The stranger looked confused. "Well, the pack is not full."

"It doesn't matter," Jason said. "Take the 40, and give me what you have."

The stranger put the items on the table. "Okay," he said.

"Thanks." Jason picked up the items and held them up so Anthony could see and flashed him a smile. They went outside to smoke the cigarettes.

Once outside, Jason and Antony both lit cigarettes. The street was not very busy; only a few cars went by. The air was slightly cool;

it was autumn, so the trees still had their color and had not changed yet.

"I need some more information in order to figure out this firm and keep tabs on whoever could be interested in me once you're out of the picture." Jason stated

"What kind of information?"

"Names of people would be a good start. Could you write down a few names on a napkin or something so I know who to keep tabs on."

"I think I could do that for you. You know I have thought about this for a long time. I always knew that I made the wrong choice back then. To say I really understand why I brought you here with me would be a lie. But I am glad that I did, you gave me a ray of hope."

"Well I'm not convinced that your firm is really as powerful as you believe it to be. We are standing within a real hornets' nest."

Anthony looked at Jason with a rather blank expression. Jason continued "What I mean is that the US government and all of its resources pitted against your law firm, the firm would be no match for them," Jason said.

"So…?" Anthony said.

"I am just saying that if some new terrorist group was started in some far away region of the world, all because some US-based company pulled some shit and your law firm represented the terrorist group and had information on its computer network, then the power of the government would crush this firm and any of its associates."

"I think you give the government too much trust to do anything; the firm is very old and has been doing politics long before there even was a country here," Anthony stated.

"Perhaps, but don't you think it is worth a try? Besides, do you really want them putting effort into looking for you at the same time or spending their resources fighting ghosts? Can I have another one of your cards? I need your email address, I lost the other one."

Anthony pulled out his wallet and handed Jason one of his business cards. Jason slid it into his back pocket after examining the card to make sure nothing was bent or missing.

"The sooner you go to the city to set up the account, the sooner I can get started. Just make sure to spread the money between the banks. Small amounts don't attract very much attention. I need to buy some items from China for doing some of this. Some of the parts are illegal to own in the United States. One thing I forgot, make sure you don't order any credit cards for the accounts, the credit system would tie the bank accounts to you. Just get basic checking accounts," Jason instructed Anthony.

After the second cigarette, they went back inside and drank one more shot of whiskey together, paid the bill, went back to the car and drove back to the hotel. Fortunately, the cell phone was still where Jason had hidden it. When he handed the cell to Anthony, he said, "Walk me up to the room and make sure it looks as it did. You know I'm under guard. Can you do one more thing?"

"What's that?" Anthony asked.

"Around here is some florist," Jason said. "Please have someone buy a bouquet of flowers for my room every week. I'm borrowing their internet."

Anthony said, "That can come out of Willy's budget."

Jason said, "You do realize Willy is watching our every move."

Anthony said, "Not every move. I park here because it's a blind spot."

They both laughed.

By the time Jason got back in his hotel room, Tasha was sound asleep. A thought occurred to Jason: *"Doesn't that Russian guy ever sleep?"* He looked around the room and gathered the towel and his bag of dirty clothes and put them all in whatever bags he could find. He knocked once on the door. He waited and knocked again. The door opened and the Russian guy looked very confused and pissed off. Jason put the bags on the floor at his feet.

"Dirty," Jason said.

He had no idea if this guy even spoke English, but it didn't matter. He went back in the room; the door locked behind him. He went closer to the camera and waved his hand in front of it and said, "I need some towels for taking a shower in the morning."

The day's events were a bit much. He wasn't really that tired, although it really was getting quite late. He took off his clothes and got into bed with Tasha. He thought about the day. He could have just bolted as soon as he was out of the city. With what though? *A few thousand that he didn't take with him?*" Then, of course, there was the warrant for his arrest, which left flying, out of the question. "*I want Willy's boat,*" he thought to himself. That was his last conscious thought before slipping into unconsciousness.

10
Making A Plan

Jason awoke to gentle nudges from Tasha. She was wearing only a T-shirt. "Wake up, it's morning, sleepy head," she said affectionately.

He slowly became aware morning was well underway as the breakfast trays had already arrived. She got him to sit up and put a tray of food on his lap. She got a second tray and they sat side by side, enjoying breakfast in bed together.

"I must have been sound asleep," Tasha said. "I did not hear you come back last night. The way you got dressed up and everything, I thought maybe you left forever." She talked very fast and he could tell she still seemed nervous.

"There are many things in life that aren't meant to be forever," Jason said thoughtfully. "But my time with you is something I want to keep for as long as I can."

Tasha smiled. "You are such a nice person."

Jason grinned back. "Well, I think you're pretty nice, too."

Tasha slowly shook her head. "I'm not really that nice a person. I have done some bad things."

"We all do bad things now and then," Jason replied. "Sometimes people force us to do bad things. Like what I need to do here. But it's what is inside of you that counts."

Tasha looked doubtful, "I don't think so," she remarked.

Jason was saddened by her doubts and asked, "What do you believe about yourself, inside?"

"I think I have been a bad person," Tasha confided.

Jason shrugged. "So change," he said. "Be a good person from now on." He thought for a moment. "Well maybe not yet."

They both chuckled at the irony of his comment as they hungrily finished off breakfast. The coffee was better today.

Jason could tell Tasha was curious about last night, "Did you have a nice time wherever you went?" she asked.

Jason nodded, sipping his coffee. "Yes, it was more of a business meeting. Anthony really wants me to get things going here and wanted me to figure out how to do this, alone. He really wants me to succeed and make Willy happy." Jason was mindful they were still being monitored and used it as an opportunity to misinform whoever was listening.

Jason watched Tasha get up and remove the trays from the bed. As he sat there, his gaze wandering to the ceiling and he thought about the things he needed to get working on, especially the email he needed to create and send to Anthony that morning. He would also meet with Willy and try to smooth over last night's meeting with Anthony.

Tasha had other things on her mind and pulled the cover back slightly. Jason was thinking about how to receive payment when he felt Tasha's lips around his genitals. As soon as he was hard, she got on top and slowly slid him inside of her.

He started to move away and she leaned in and kissed him lightly and said, "Shush, let me." Tasha leaned close to his face and whispered, "I want you inside of me, let me feel you."

She created a rhythm, each time arching her back then sitting upright again. She repeated this sensual motion over and over for what seemed a blissful eternity. When Jason felt he could not contain himself he whispered, "I can't hold it much longer."

Her response was to pick up the pace and intensity.

"Let me feel you cum," she rasped. "Come on, you want me; let me feel you."

He could not hold back any longer. He released with an ecstatic growl and by her raspy sigh it appeared that she came too. She rolled off of him, and lay on the bed next to him. They laid there for quite a while in each other's arms, kissing lightly.

"We have new towels," Tasha finally observed.

"Are you telling me I need a shower now?" Jason joked. He got up and walked into the bathroom. Tasha joined him and they washed each other's bodies. Each of them took extra care to wash and massage each other as they went. They took the same care in drying each other, too. Tasha took a towel and wrapped her hair in it.

Jason made a lather to shave. Tasha took the razor and seated him on the toilet lid and shaved him again, a caring touch to which he was becoming accustomed.

When they were through, Jason walked out of the bathroom, naked. He went to the dresser and found two pairs of jeans that were clean, two T-shirts and several paper clips to hold them up on Tasha's thin waist.

Once they were dressed, they looked in the mirror and laughed at their wholesomely clean but offbeat fashion statement.

Then it was time to get down to business. They moved the two chairs in front of one of the computers. He would need Photoshop, which wasn't installed. ("Great," he sighed impatiently.) Then there's Adobe, the leader of the digital editing world who regularly changes their software so every new version is different from and barely compatible with the last! So unlike their earlier versions, it now takes hours to learn each new and "improved" version.

While downloading the trial of Adobe Suite, he turned to Tasha and asked, "Do you know how to use Photoshop?"

"No, what is that?" she asked.

"It's a great image program," Jason said. "I'll show you how to use it."

He opened Notepad and created a new file called "Order list." He added a color printer, photo paper, an old laser printer, an iron, gold and silver laser foil, a spool of 21 gauge wire ground, 3g router with rj45, a battery backup power strip with network, set of tools, pliers, soldering station, Chinese femtocells and a Cubieboard.

He looked up at the camera and spoke to it. "I need to speak to Willy, can you send him in?"

Tasha had no way of knowing what was going to happen, and even Jason wasn't sure he could pull it all off. Nonetheless, while he waited for Willy, he patiently browsed the Internet.

The door unlocked and Willy appeared. He didn't look extremely happy.

"Anthony and I had a long talk about your idea last night," Jason said.

"Oh you did, did you?" Willy snapped, barely concealing his anger.

"Here's what I think," Jason said calmly. "You use your victim's bank account and also find a lifer's identity."

"What?" Willy asked.

"Find someone who is spending their life at a state run institution, not a federal one," Jason said matter-of-factly.

"What for?" Willy asked, somewhat annoyed and yet curious.

Jason explained, "Many inmates have very bad credit …. They also don't do the things like you and I do; like buy things, have bank accounts, that kind of stuff. No one will notice if you steal the identity of an inmate."

"Go on," said Willy, still annoyed but quickly catching on.

Jason continued confidently, "One of the problems of just stealing money is how to get it, how to put cash in your hand,"

Jason said. "Most of the people doing drugs buy stuff online and sell it for pennies on the dollar so they can get high. But what we need to do is take money and move it to someone's account, you know, someone's account besides yours or mine -- someone who's not likely to be checking when we put in extra funds or make withdrawals. And when the feds investigate, and they eventually will, they'll find the account holder *already in jail*. The trail will stop their leaving the Feds scratching their heads. All they can do then is try to follow the paper trail out – but there won't be one because we'll use a debit card to tap that bank account and just withdraw the money from an ATM. If it works right, at best they'll only have ATM pictures of someone wearing a hat."

Jason got up from the chair and sat on the table and continued, "This is what we do. You show me who were supposed to shake down for watching the 'performers.' But instead of that scam, let's use my plan get things going. O.K.?" Jason waited for Willy to show agreement and then continued, "So let's first jump on the websites. Can you show me?"

Willy sat down and typed a URL in the browser for one of the cam sites Jason had been at earlier. The screen filled with pictures of performers. There was a "log in here" button and a banner running across the top.

"Do you have a login you can use?" Jason asked.

"I don't trust you using that," Willy said.

"Dude, I'm on your side," Jason protested. "I need to understand this site if it's one that you want to mess with."

Willy sat there for a second, then typed in an ID and entered a password.

Jason said, "Okay, now click on a model. I bet they are all the same."

Willy clicked on a model in the middle. The page changed to a live video feed of a woman lying on her stomach. The camera angle only showed her face and part of her shoulders. She was typing on a keyboard and the text scrolling across the bottom. It showed many people all talking to her at the same time. The list on the right gave a total of 65 people chatting with her. Down the left side of the screen was a large advertisement for enlarging your penis.

Jason pointed at the penis ad. "That's how we get to your victim."

Willy looked on, confused.

"Sometimes you have to think outside the box," Jason explained. "You see that ad? Click on it."

"I don't need—" Willy started.

"Just click on it," Jason interrupted.

A new webpage launched with string at the top. "Can I see the mouse for a second?" Jason asked. He took the mouse and clicked on the web page address and copied the entire webpage URL. He opened Notepad and pasted the long string into it. He minimized Notepad and closed the website brought up by the advertisement. He closed the performer and was at the homepage to the site. He clicked on another performer. Once the performer page was loaded, he clicked on the penis ad and copied the URL. Then he opened Notepad and pasted the long string of information on the next line.

The strings of information were almost identical. Both of them started with "https://" and the "/" was used several times. There was an "ID=" and a short string of letters and numbers that were the same on both lines until he got to the end. The last 12 or 16 letters and numbers were different.

"That's it!" Jason pointed at the URLs.

Willy was startled and desperately scanned the screen, "I don't understand," he said perplexed.

Jason, with a triumphant look, explained further, "The ad is the answer. If everyone that looks at this page runs a javascript, I can tell who is looking at a particular page. If I own this advertisement, then I know the IP address of everyone that views this ad. If the ad had a refresh built into it, I can log into the computer looking at this ad. I can't tell you which of these I am logged into, but then again does it really matter?" He pointed at the people logged in chatting with the model. "So my script in theory would be able to connect to the people who you want to connect to. If I know their IP address, I can log into their computer."

Willy shook his head cautiously and smiled. "I get it," he said. "Why an inmate again?"

"You need an account to dump money into, someone who's not YOU. Someone who the police will look at instead of YOU," Jason described, then he asked. "Do you have a victim in mind, someone already who isn't 100 miles away, whose ID you can use to open an account?"

"Maybe," Willy stated.

Jason said enthusiastically, "Okay, we'll use that person. I'll just need a checking account number, and a routing code, a canceled or voided check. I need to have control of it so I can get the change sequence."

"What is that?" Willy asked.

Jason thought for a moment and came up with a simple example, "When you set up a PayEasy account, they want to be sure you own the account. So they'll put small change in the account, like 16 cents and 12 cents, or something. The amounts are random. To complete the security of linkage to the account, you have to put the amount into their system. If you use someone else's account, I'll have to get the information secondhand. Are you sure you want to deposit thousands into the account? It's really up to you. You might run into problems either way."

"Whoa, what do you mean problems?" Willy asked.

"Well, our clueless inmate may have screwed themselves out of a bank account," Jason noted. "It's common for people with a bad banking history to be reported to the Chex system. It's a credit agency for banks and checking accounts."

Willy asked, "What do you do to free the account?"

Jason said, "You'll have to clear it. That is, you'll have to pay off whatever they owe."

"How much will that be?" Willy asked.

Jason shook his head and shrugged, "I really have no way of knowing, sometimes it's hundreds, sometimes thousands,"

Jason pressed on, "You know people that couldn't get an account?"

"I did that to myself, I know what to do," Willy said.

Jason typed in the search "African web hosting," and found a page for Linux pro hosting. "Get an account here for web hosting," he said.

Willy looked at the page. "Why this one?"

"Africa has many scammers from some very small nations and they get daily requests from the U.S. Government for disclosure," Jason explained. "They are overwhelmed with requests. Africa takes its sweet time doing everything. It could take them months to find out somebody bought this and for what? A penis ad. Nobody will be interested."

"Is there anything else?" Willy asked.

"Yeah, I need a mail drop set up, not at a post office," Jason recalled. "Those mailbox places are fine, just don't get anywhere near it, and have whoever gets the mail from there bring it to me.

Willy gave Jason a skeptical look. "Why do you need that?"

Jason said, "I'll need to purchase a few things, including special equipment to make a new identification. Someone seems to have done a job on the ones I have now."

"You can do that?" Willy asked.

Jason nodded. "Yup, I've done it before. I'll even make you a new one if you like, too."

Willy was feeling a little uneasy about Jason knowing how to create IDs, not to mention telling him how to do everything. He was still questioning why Anthony just took off with Jason, but now Jason was offering him a golden goose on the platter. Nonetheless, Willy decided to play along. "Okay, I got a name for you," he said with a sneer.

Jason interrupted and warned, "If I were you, I'd use someone that isn't connected with this place at all. That way, we can just burn it. … I mean that figuratively. I don't mean burn the building down. You should pay for it for a year up front in cash. There is no telling how long we will need it."

Willy got up and went to the door. "I'll think about what you said and see what I can do." He knocked once on the door. It opened and he left.

Jason had just set into motion two opposing wheels. [EXPLAIN by briefly describing each wheel] Hopefully one of them would come through. The other he would need to push through. He checked on his download. It was complete.

Jason and Tasha worked through lunch, creating an impressive voucher for two free tickets to any Broadway show to be presented at the booth at Times Square. At the bottom, it disclosed, "No cash value. Offer expires in 15 days." Tasha had quite the flair for creating the voucher; she had more talent for graphic design than Jason did. The final mockup looked pretty good. They also put a website on the voucher, to go to; www.entertainment-link. com was the ticket agent and it really existed. They were just spoofing the email to look like it came from them. Hopefully Anthony got it.

Jason set up a new email address for communicating with the cam website. He asked them about pricing for advertising. Judging from the ad used, it seemed that they made referral money based on clicks, which was just a few cents per click.

The answer back was surprisingly low; it took six emails to strike a deal for what was needed, which was $300 USD for six months. That could be paid by wiring the money or PayEasy, plus 5%. "Dirty deeds done cheap," Jason chuckled as he ploughed through the work.

Eventually, Jason decided that there was much remaining for the others to do today. More importantly, he really needed to work alone for a while. So he asked Tasha, "Do you like movies?"

Tasha said, "I like them very much, but I haven't seen anything for many, many years."

Jason got up and looked through the boxes for his headphones. He plugged them into a machine at the other end of the table from where he was working. He opened a web browser, went to Netflix and signed up for a trial account. He also got the pad and made a new sheet for usernames and passwords, since he didn't want any of his identifiers on that site. Just logging into something could produce alarm bells, now or later and he certainly didn't want whatever happened on the site to come back to him personally.

Jason gave her the headphones to put on, and helped her navigate the movie site. Her first pick was an old Audrey Hepburn movie, *Breakfast At Tiffany's*. It charmed him that she picked one of his favorite movies.

Jason went back to the computer at the opposite end of the table. His first thought was where to start. He opened Excel and a web browser. After he opened the website of the law firm, he discovered that the firm had well over 500 attorneys. It also had well over 800 support staff in 14 countries. He took the next hour to copy the names and sort them on Excel worksheets. When he was through, he sighed at the list of names and thought, "*Well, it's a start.*". Next he focused on the principal partners and filings within the United States. The record for the Secretary of State yielded more names in corporate filing, and Uniform Commercial Code records gave even more information on prior land purchases. One of the databases linked officers in corporations. He had made progress just scrounging. Looking up more information in the paid databases would have to wait.

Now the hard part, he thought. He downloaded a database program and spent the rest of the day creating a program that would allow him to link and display the information more easily. It was a daunting task, confusing enough with just the principals—all 18 of them.

11

The Daily Grind

Someone once said "an army runs on its stomach", and that definitely applied to the imprisoned slaves at the hotel. Unlike kitchens in an actual army or a genuine hotel, the inmates relied on the good graces of a surprisingly devoted cook. Gladys cooked three industrial-sized meals a day. For her sizable effort she was only paid minimum wage, but she was happy to have work. Now in her late 60s she was becoming very grey-haired, yet her work-ethic never faltered. She worked nearly every day, often seven days a week. Her day started at 5 a.m. and usually involved 12-hour "shifts." Each morning, just after 5:45 a.m., she also would make coffee for herself and the staff. She also felt free to take frequent breaks and spent time watching games and talk shows on the small television that sat on the table off to the side of the room. It was out of her sense of duty, specifically to the blind and disabled, that she gave herself to the hotel's kitchen. It was a shame that there weren't other 'foundations' that committed themselves so entirely to the

150

blind and disabled like hard-working people at her workplace. She was a regular at St. John's Bingo and loved to talk about the nice Mr. Willy and the work of his charity foundation; she gained such as sense of pride working for him.

Gladys had mistook the hotel's "cook wanted ad" as an appeal for volunteers in their front as a charitable foundation. She had no formal restaurant experience or résumé, which meant there was scant record of her employment -- the perfect profile for employees of the hotel. She had taught herself how to cook on a group scale. The work wasn't difficult, and the long days were filled with endless cooking, dishwashing and cleaning up the kitchen. She was quite content with that routine. The only problem she ever experienced was with the kid doing the grocery shopping; many times he would bring back spoiled vegetables. That boy just didn't know how to shop. One time she found a receipt down in the bottom of a bag that had a name on it that she never heard before. She had grown up in the area and knew every grocer. He must live far away, she realized, and shop near his home. *"Too bad,"* she thought and wondered what it would take for her to take over that task too – the hard working charity workers deserved better. *"Even more so because they work so hard; work themselves to skin and bone!"*

Gladys was witness to a lot of strange procedures at the foundation. She had to stay in the kitchen for the entire shift. Moreover they went to odd lengths to save money. For instance, all of the garbage had to go into huge plastic bags. The bags were bigger and heavier than any normal woman could lift.

Over the last year, though, she sensed they must have gotten a lot more clients. She was now struggling to cook for over 20 workers. The last time she saw that nice man Mr. Willy, she told him that she might need some help soon.

It was getting hard for her to cook for that many people all by herself, every day. He told her he would "look into it."

Today the grocery boy was late again. This caused Gladys to get a late start on dinner. She deep fried close to 40 chicken legs every day. The chicken came in big boxes from some wholesaler who gave the foundation a special price. But the quantities were simply huge; she could not pick the delivery box up from the freezer until it was almost empty. So, she resorted to carrying the fry basket into the freezer to fill it up. Under such conditions she really needed more help.

Willy was on his cell phone, checking back with Anthony about Mexican illegals who might fill in as cooks. He decided that if they showed they could keep their mouths shut, maybe he would throw in the laundry as a task for them too. That would make it less risky than having the inmates do it. But Willy also worried that each additional worker risked more witnesses to the inmates and their activities, more people to cow into submission. He shrugged. He would just have to limit the new workers to the first floor. Besides, he could pay two illegals the same amount he had to spring for just the one dizzy old bag. No one would notice if she suddenly disappeared, he coolly plotted. But all this was just daily grief. He recalled that Anthony said he might stop over later and unwind with the girls. That always dug into their work, but it wasn't his problem; Anthony was, after all, the boss.

About a half hour later, the redhead entered Jason and Tasha's room with food trays. She put them on the table and left without uttering a word. Jason was getting sick of the menu – it arrived like clockwork and properly cooked but there was no variety. Maybe being shut in made food a particularly big deal. *"At least they're feeding us in this dump,"* he thought, and considered whether it was wise to demand takeout just as he had the wine. Tasha and Jason finished off the leftover wine with their meal.

Willy was with Steve in the control booth. They watched a medical emergency underway two blocks away. There were two fire trucks, an ambulance and two police cars. The control panel before them consisted of a large board with various dials, a keyboard and the video display unit, which was made of a series of LCD flat screen monitors for computers. They were lined up, six across and six down, to make a large video display square. The computer system made it so the display could show one large screen and a number of smaller screens around it. Each screen involved a different camera. The operator could make any camera's image become full screen view or run any combination of images in smaller view. This arrangement gave them eyes and ears inside the entire building.

Willy asked Steve, "So what do you think?"

"What about?" Steve asked, puzzled.

"My boy," Willy insisted.

"I think your guy is capable of just about anything," Steve said. "Just one question though."

"What's that?" Willy asked.

"What Internet is he on?" Steve asked. "I can tell he is using something." He pulled out his phone and retrieved the list of Wi-Fi names available. "I don't see anything open."

"I guess he is using something else," Willy said. "Did you hear what he did over at Peter's office?"

Steve shook his head.

"He broke into the lawyers' Wi-Fi with their security tech guy sitting right there. Then Jason told him that he could get into their files and shit. It scared the crap out of him," Willy admitted.

"So what makes you think he's not in our shit?" Steve asked.

"Like that's my department?" Willy scoffed. "Anyway, the computer for this building isn't on the Internet or anything else, so I really don't care." Then he thought for a moment, "Is this secure?" he asked pointing at the video display.

"I think so," Steve said. "I'll leave a note for Randy to look at the stuff overnight. I'd just screw it up."

"Well we wouldn't want that again," Willy said in a familiar condescending tone.

"Well fuck you," Steve said. "You know that wasn't my fault. Did you hear the bullshit from last night?"

"Yeah I heard," Willy said.

"That twisted kid Ivan is gonna rip his head off," Steve said.

"He knows if he does they will end him, whether they need him or not," Willy observed.

Steve asked, "When are you gonna get some backup anyway? We're all doing double shifts as it is. Having Ivan standing by the door isn't helping anyone. And running shit for this little pecker ain't right," Steve said sarcastically as they both looked on at Jason and Tasha.

"I know, we need somebody else; Anthony is working on it," Willy said. "There's somebody they are looking at now, I heard."

Steve said, "Well, I hope it's soon, it's boring as fuck up here."

"Just do your job … and don't get stupid about your 'recreation'," Willy said with a hint of anger. "We can't have another problem coming from you."

"That wasn't my fault …" Steve declared in a quiet, subordinate tone.

Willy got up, with a sigh and said, "Yeah, keep tellin' yourself that." Then he left the room.

Steve watched him leave the room. He truly hated Willy and couldn't resist mumbling under his breath, "Time will tell, little fucker…"

After dinner, Jason and Tasha played another game of Go. He was getting better, but she always beat him. It was rather humiliating, losing to her over and over. But in the back of his mind, he felt she actually needed the victory, no matter how small it was, more than he did. Besides, it somehow made her even more attractive. She wasn't just a sex object; there was something more.

Jason watched *Pretty Woman* with Tasha. After the movie ended, Jason asked if she wanted to watch another and she declined.

"That is my favorite movie," Tasha said.

"What makes it your favorite?" Jason asked.

"The clothes they wear," she said.

Jason didn't really understand. He attempted to play along. "What about them?" he asked.

"They all wear such fascinating clothes," Tasha explained. "They are so colorful, and they are so different. They seem to match wherever they are."

"They have a person who does that," Jason explained.

"They are all so beautiful, the clothes and things. Is that really how it is for Americans?"

"Well, it can be I guess," he pondered. "But not for most people. Most people have other things to think about so all that fashion isn't so important. But then there people who just like to dress up, who express themselves with what they wear. You know, it's self-expression, not required."

Jason could see it in her eyes that Tasha didn't quite understand. He continued, "It's a choice. Americans tell you who they are by what they wear … I think."

"You have a choice?" Tasha asked.

Jason realized that somehow something as seemingly basic as choosing one's fashions was stripped from Tasha long ago. Choice wasn't something that she understood—that he was free to change his clothes and more to the point, go where he pleased, have sex with only partners he found attractive. He took so many things for granted which somehow made him as guilty as his captors. No matter how he tried to be kind to her, he was taking advantage of someone who had no sense of choice. He had violated her and needed to put that right. So much needed to be put right in this crazy "situation" … and it all hinged on the plan that was coming clear in his head. He just hoped he could pull it off.

"Some people think that they don't care what they wear, but they do," Jason said. "They use fashion to identify who they are or how far they've come in life. But I don't believe fashion is something that most people actually value. Would you like to watch another movie? There's one that I think you'll like ... Have you ever seen *The Devil Wears Prada?*"

"No, I don't think so," Tasha remarked with a look of eager curiosity.

"Let me see," Jason said, walking back to the computer. For him, accessing movies was as simple as logging on. The Internet and its open policy of free information is something that news, television and the movie industry neither comprehend nor accept. They play along, but like angry children, kicking and screaming all the way. He quickly searched several sites until he finally found the movie. He had to sign up and used his junk email address, which he had to click on to confirm only to find the email box had 1,500 new messages, all spam. When he logged in, he had to choose whether or not to infect the computer with a virus, which would steal whatever information it contained (it was a new install, so there was nothing to steal) or a bot so it could be used for attacking others. He chose to go for the infection. He turned off the other machines first though; no sense in infecting everything.

Finally, he was able to start the movie. He then paused it, so they could get the mattress off the wall and the pillows from the other room and watched it together on the floor. It was more comfortable than the office chairs.

Somewhere in the middle of the movie, which he had seen several times, he fell asleep.

Willy went to see one his former workers, one of his "bitches." She was addicted to crack cocaine which she obtained by streetwalking for Big Maurice, a dealer and user himself. They lived in a low-rent apartment building that was filled with people who lived by any means possible. The more upright residents weren't much better off and had no choice but to allow the pimps and dealers in their lives. They feared harm to themselves or, more importantly, to their children. What could they do? They were trapped together in poverty and neglect from society. The apartment building was nothing more than an enormous older house that had been chopped up into a series of small apartments. The entire neighborhood used to be affluent housing with plush green manicured lawns, but was now reduced to cracking sidewalks and raw dirt patches where grass now refused to grow.

Big Maurice was well-known on the streets, so it wasn't hard for him to find them. He sitting on a stump in plain view on the street, waiting for a crack customer to come wandering by when Willy approached.

"Hey, what up brotha," Willy said.

"Whoa, it's mista money bags, whatcha been doin'? You looking for rock?" Big Maurice said using his best sales pitch voice.

"No, I was looking for your old lady. You still banging that crack ho Wanda?"

Big Maurice stood up. "What you want with her?"

"It's cool, its cool," Willy said. "I got money for you to do something for me. I just need to talk to her. Is she around? You can listen, it's cool."

"Wanda, git your ass out here," Big Maurice yelled.

"How's "business goin'?" Willy asked.

"Good, man," Big Maurice said. "I can't ever have enough rocks, you wanna sample on the house?"

"No man, it's okay," Willy said. "Really, no, I don't want any. You know I don't participate."

"Come on, bitch!" Big Maurice yelled to Wanda.

An extremely emaciated and wobbly woman, came into view. She had a face that you could tell had been pretty at some point, but now her skin sagged and was creased into a mask formed by years of toxic drug use. Willy hadn't seen her for almost a year. In that time, he thought she had lost maybe 20 pounds and aged at least 15 years. When she smiled at Willy, he could see she had lost her front teeth.

"What you doin' around here, fool?" she said.

"Lookin' for your ass," Willy said.

Wanda exclaimed, "What you want with me?"

Willy said, "I need your photo ID and your name for some things. I'll give you money to use 'em."

"Why?" Wanda questioned. "Whatta you up to?"

"It's nothing hard," Willy said. "No worries. I need your credit to buy a new car."

Wanda, Big Maurice and Willy all laughed at the thought of credit. In their world there were seldom bank accounts, let alone any sort of credit.

"Tomorrow around noon time I'll be back," Willy said. "If you go with me and sign some papers I'll straight up give you five hundred. We just hafta stop at a few places."

Big Maurice looked at Willy. "Five hundred? You have that much? Let me see it."

Willy stepped back. "I don't have it on me now," he said. "Don't do something stupid, I'll bring on some heat." He pulled back his jacket to reveal to Big Maurice a Glock tucked into his waistband.

"I'll be back at noon," Willy repeated. "Big Maurice, you come too. I just need some shit signed, that's all. Aw right?"

Willy backed up a few steps on the sidewalk so he could watch Big Maurice.

"No, I ain't signing shit," Wanda said, shaking her head.

"Yeah we'll be ready," Big Maurice said.

Willy backed up a few more steps, "Okay, tomorrow around noon."

Wanda said, "I'm not doin' it."

"Shut your mouth bitch, I'll fuck you up," Big Maurice told her with a sure but menacing look.

Willy stepped back a little further, turned and walked away briskly. He knew he could count on Big Maurice to focus on the dollars.

He'd make damn sure he and Wanda were front and center come game time. Willy walked down the street and up the next checking over his shoulder for Big Maurice. Willy knew it was stupid to trust crack dealers – Big Maurice and Wanda would appear tomorrow all right; ready steal every cent. But as usual, Willy's extensive history as a vicious character himself would help him keep the upper hand and put his plan in play.

Setting Up A Way To Transfer

Jason awoke with Tasha still sound asleep, her head on his chest. He could hear her slow, steady breathing. The sky wasn't visible from the room, yet he could just make out the dim beginning of sunrise. It occurred to him that he must have fallen asleep early the previous night and for a moment he was disappointed in losing the opportunity to share the movie with Tasha. He lay there a while, not wanting to disturb his cozy bedmate. But while he was coming to savor this nurturing yet reality-defying routine, he was wide awake and itching to get the day going.

He was able, with a little affectionate effort, to move Tasha's head onto a pillow. After he went to the bathroom, he shut off the computer they had used to view the movie, now undoubtedly infected. *"I'll just rebuild it,"* he thought. After all, he had plenty of time to do that and other procedures he'd usually find more tiresome. Then he paused and thought, *"Maybe I'll look at the code and see what it did first."* He might be able to use it in his private library. He kept his library on Google Drive now. The files were changed in a way that if anyone ever accessed the ones in his private stash, no one would care or want the ones on Google. This is how encryption embedding typically works. First he would encrypt a file, scramble his code, stick it into a picture file, then upload. All that the casual observer would find was a picture file that was huge but nonetheless a picture of other people's pets. One of the best backdoor Trojans he ever found was stored in a picture of a bulldog. In the early days of the internet this was a common practice of spy networks. They would send messages to each other with the message inside of graphic pictures like Viagra ads in email. The spies would simply send the same ad to everyone.

He booted up his laptop and thought that he should really take a look at the camera network again. He kept a text file containing the notes he took on his computer. It was much easier to log in this time. "Whaddya know," he murmured. He was looking at the video of the hallway outside of his door. The Russian guy wasn't there. They were at work on the computer floor with the cubes. It dawned on him why he couldn't see the back stairs on that floor: something else was behind that room. He could tell approximately how long the building was by the camera view on his floor. There must be more rooms that are only accessible by the back stairwell. That would explain how Willy and Anthony could get there so quickly. The camera room must be just half way down the hallway and down a floor. He was beginning to get his bearings in the hotel.

He was keeping notes on which cameras were in known places as well as those in unfamiliar places. He could see that some of them were moved or rotated from the center, and he didn't want to upset that, especially if someone else was watching. He saw a number of girls asleep in one room. He could see a black man sleeping with two girls in another room.

He couldn't tell who—it wasn't light enough, and he didn't want to move the camera. He found the Russian guy and the big Asian guy. Their IP addresses were lined up one after another. There was an older lady in a kitchen. Then he saw the control room. The operator, whoever he was, was tall and thin and wearing a baseball cap. He was sound asleep.

The camera feed in the control room was much better than some of the others. Jason could see some of the other views from the display on the wall. He also could see himself—at least it could be himself, in the lower right corner of the display console in the lobby of the hotel. It was large in the center.

He counted the screens and saw that there were six across the top and six across the bottom. The big video playing in the center was made from several smaller monitors. It looked like four high and six across. That meant he had found more cameras than they had monitors, so they must not be able to see all the cameras at once. That was, unless they could make the pictures smaller and put multiple cameras on one computer monitor.

He traced the network again and found the name of the control board they used. He would have to research it later since this Wi-Fi network seemed to have no internet access. For good measure, he logged into the router. It had the default username and password and was one of the cheap ones sold in many retail stores. He added the Mac address he assigned to his computer for this task so it could log in "securely" next time. Looking through the event logs, he ran into a dilemma. The list was huge. The router had no way of modifying the log. He could see the log entries he had caused by trying to get into the router.

He deleted the logs from the device and reset the logging events to maximum logging. This action would fill the log with useless data, so the next person to look at the logs had something to see. It is obvious when people attack systems because they remove the logs. If someone is looking, it's a good way to tell that someone else has been there if the logs are missing. Most people though, don't even bother looking at the logs.

He left the picture of the control guy up. If he moved, he would need to stop what he was doing. Now that he could see the control room, Jason could take the cameras out for a test drive.

He was able to tell which side of the building the cameras were in by pointing the camera at the windows. On his side, there was no view, just a concrete block building next door. He spent the next hour or so looking at the camera system. He thought maybe he found them all and could figure out which side of the building they were on. There was no way of telling which floor they were on though.

Through the hallway camera, he could tell there were 12 rooms per floor, except on the fourth floor. The problem was, he had 22 rooms with cameras that meant that there must be at least three floors of rooms, but all of them must not have cameras. He finally disconnected from the camera network so he could look up the user manual for the control panel. He was still looking at the instruction manual when Tasha woke up.

The two spent the rest of the morning storing the mattress and taking showers. He gave her a set of jeans that he hadn't worn yet. They continued to use paperclips to them keep them up over her hips. She also wore his last clean t-shirt.

The door opened and a thin brunette girl carrying the meal trays walked in with her head down. That was until she saw Tasha. When she did, she lifted her head and made eye contact with her. Without saying a word, she moved her head left, then right then again. It looked as though she was saying 'no' with her head motions, to an unspoken question. She placed the trays on the table and went back to the door. She knocked once, the door opened and she left the room; the door closed and locked.

Before Jason could sit down, Tasha launched herself on him. She whispered in his ear, *"Bathroom."* Once inside the bathroom, Tasha whispered, "Something bad has happened. That was their signal when someone dies or gets very hurt." Whatever it was, it was bad; that was obvious. She looked very worried, but while he wanted to console her, he felt powerless to do anything. All they could do was go back to the table and eat their breakfast; they ate in silence.

Willy had breakfast with Ivan and Akio. They were the two largest men in the building. They also were the two with the most experience in security. Both men were no strangers to murder. Either of them would do it for money or simple entertainment.

"I need to run an errand today and need backup," Willy said.

Akio looked at Ivan. "I go, you stay, or I stay, you go. Not both. Someone needs to watch here."

Ivan looked at Akio and at Willy. "I go, sit behind you, if anybody fuck up, I'll kill them, no problem," he said.

"How's about you drive?" Willy asked. It would be nice to have a chauffeur for the day.

"No, you drive, I sit behind so I can see and take care of business," Ivan said.

So it was set. Akio would stay. He never liked to leave the hotel anyway. Willy had offered many times to take Akio with him and he always declined. On his off hours, Akio usually stayed in his room lifting weights or meditating.

The recently departed Spider, a former outlaw biker who also used to work in the hotel, was a very big man. He would often suggest that Akio was gay because Akio never wanted to get with any of the girls. One day, Spider was passing Akio in the hallway and whispered "faggot" into his ear. Akio turned and hit him in the chest with such force it broke Spider's ribcage. A rib punctured his heart and he died instantly. This was why the work crew was essentially short by a man. In spite of their intense homophobia Steve and Willy respected Akio's need to respond to even the slightest hint of disrespect. These were hard men and accepting insults usually led to more fatal treatment, so they would have reacted to Spider in the same way; or at least they would have tried. Akio seemed to spend all his spare time preparing to do combat, so both Willy and Steve were apprehensive of mentioning the incident with Spider to Akio, let alone risking any new comments he might find insulting.

After breakfast, Jason showed Tasha the program he had written yesterday. He opened the spreadsheets and had her work on data entry and importing. She was a fast learner and immediately found a bug. While Jason worked on the bug she played Go against the computer. Once the bug was fixed, other information needed to be added. They both worked on the data input. The list of names was now over 900 people. Jason had no way to really begin on names as Anthony hadn't told him who to look at yet. Meanwhile, there wasn't much he could do on the Willy project.

Willy drove and Ivan sat directly behind him. They stopped the car not in front of the building, but across the street and back about 500 feet. They got out and Ivan stood by the trunk on the opposite side of the house for safety. Willy honked the horn twice and walked down the sidewalk to the front of the house and waited.

Big Maurice and Wanda slowly came out and squinted in the light of day. They saw Willy standing on the sidewalk. Big Maurice gave his usual welcome, "Hey, what up?"

"I'm cool, you cool?" Willy asked.

"We be cool, you have the cash?" Big Maurice said. "Who that?" he asked, pointing at the large white man standing by the car.

"That's my boy, Ivan, he's going along for the ride," Willy said. "No problem."

"What is this?" Big Maurice demanded.

"It's nothin'," Willy said. "He's my helper; we're cool. Look, if you just want Wanda to go, we will bring her back, I got no problem with either of you. I just need a favor, that's all and I'll pay five hundred when we're done."

"I'll go, just checkin' you know, it's cool," Big Maurice said cheerfully, though his eyes still suggested angry suspicion.

They walked over to the car and Ivan opened the front passenger door for Big Maurice, who got in. He opened the rear door for Wanda, to get in behind Big Maurice. He waited for Willy to get in the car before getting in behind him on the driver's side.

The 4–year-old Lincoln Town Car had not lost its flair; it still was a low-key but 'righteous' ride. Leather interior and a new air freshener gave the interior that 'new car' aroma. Nonetheless, soon after they began to travel, Big Maurice felt it necessary to ask, "Can I smoke in here?"

"Don't be smoking nothing in my car now," Willy said.

"Just askin'. Where we goin' anyway?" Big Maurice asked.

"We're going to a mailbox up the road," Willy said. He turned the radio to a rap station to appease Big Maurice though he personally hated it. He was more of a 'soul' fan. He made the turn to get on the interstate.

"Which mailboxes you going to?" Big Maurice asked.

"Up the road," Willy said, pointing ahead. "Just sit back and be cool. We'll be there shortly."

The same girl as earlier [girl from that morning] brought Jason and Tasha their lunch; she came in and kept her head down. She was too intimidated to even whisper to them. She put the trays on the table quickly. Each tray had a baloney sandwich and a bowl of soup. She left quickly, without lingering at all. When Tasha and Jason sat down to eat, they found the soup was cold. It was clear the soup had never been heated. Moreover, the sandwich was dry, just two slices of baloney on white bread.

"Would you like some water?" Jason asked Tasha.

Tasha nodded. Jason found the cups, washed them out and returned with them filled with water. They ate their lunch, and then returned to the work with the computers.

Tasha logged onto one of her Facebook accounts, and opened a chat with someone named April May. Jason looked on at their chat session:

T: Hi

AM: Hey, good to know you are okay

T: What happened?

AM: Tracy died from that pill they gave her

T: Oh. Well tell everyone I'm okay

AM: Gotta go someone's coming

"What happened?" Jason asked.

Tasha turned and stared at him. She got up and they both went to the bathroom to whisper.

"One of the other girls got pregnant and they gave her something to make the baby go away," Tasha said. "But the girl died."

"Was it someone you knew well?" Jason asked.

"We all know each other okay," Tasha said. "It's not my turn yet, that's all. Some day it will be, or I'll go to another place first. Then it will be my turn."

Jason heard her deep despair and offered, "I care about you, and I won't leave you," He hoped nobody else ever realized his affection for Tasha was genuine, but he needed to let her know at least.

Willy pulled into the parking lot of the mailbox site. Willy had arranged a mailbox that was near the interstate and in a very upscale section of the city. A white college kid stood behind the cash register in a pompous, richer-than-thou uniform. He seemed stunned and cautious as they approached. It was obvious to Willy that he had never done business with many black people before. The clerk acted very uncomfortable at first. Wanda was able to fill out the form and showed him her state issued ID. The kid took it to photocopy, then returned it to Willy who paid $721.50 dollars for a medium-sized box for one year in advance.

The next stop was a small bank in the same plaza. The bank manager, an older white-haired woman, met them at the door, and the black security guard gave the pair a dirty look and stared in their direction the entire time they were in the building.

The older white woman wearing a blue skirt and matching blazer over a white blouse and way too much lipstick approached the two and said, "May I help you?"

"We need to open an account," Willy said.

"Come with me," she said, leading the pair to an office near the entrance. The desk had a computer and a single chair behind it and two facing it. She motioned Willy and Wanda to sit in the two chairs. Once everyone was seated, she asked again, "What can I do for you?" She smiled at them with lipstick stuck to her tooth.

"We need to open," Willy repeated with emphasis, "a checking account."

"May I see some sort of identification?" the woman asked.

Willy said to Wanda, "Give her your ID."

Wanda pulled the ID from her pocket and put it onto the desk. The woman picked it up and typed a few things on the keyboard. "I will need your social security number," she said to Wanda.

Wanda sat silent after a moment.

"What's your social number?" Willy asked.

Wanda spoke slowly, working very hard to recall each digit.

She gave the woman too many numbers. The woman looked confused as she was typing the numbers. "That's too many numbers," she said. "Do you have a social security card?"

Wanda pulled out the tattered paper card from her pocket and put it on the desk.

The older woman pressed keys on her keyboard, then frowned and said, "You have a flag on your account. I'm sorry, I can't help you."

Willy was expecting this. "How much and where?" he said.

"The flag was set by Global Commerce Bank," the woman said. "It doesn't say the amount. You will have to settle it with them."

"Can you find out for us?" Willy asked. "She really needs money. Just look at her."

The older woman stared at Wanda's emaciated face. She frowned and picked up her phone and dialed a number. "Hi, this is Susan at the Federal Hills Branch," she said. "Could you look up something for me? My account seems to have an issue; it won't pull up full information." Willy and Wanda sat as she spoke. The woman gave the person on the phone all of Wanda's information and then paused. "Yes, I got that far. What's the amount?" She listened and wrote something on a blank sheet of paper. "Thank you," she said, and hung up the phone.

She turned to face Willy and Wanda and said, "The amount you owe is $836.27. You are going to have to settle this with Global Commerce Bank, there is really nothing I can do." She slid the ID card and the piece of paper toward Willy and Wanda. Willy picked them up and thanked the woman. He stood up and he tried to shake her hand. She was a bit hesitant, but then shook it. Wanda was still sitting there gazing into space.

"Let's go, come on," Willy said softly while helping her out of the chair.

Wanda rose and walked with Willy back to the car. Once inside the car Willy said, "One more stop." He started the car and backed out of the space. Against Jason's advice, Willy drove straight to the city that the hotel was in to set up an account at a local bank.

Adding to his growing respect for her, Jason found that Tasha was very good working on the computer. She adapted very well and helped him make the design of the data entry screen flow a little faster. Once all the information Jason had collected was imported into his program, he set her up on Facebook, collecting more information, names of relatives, vacation spots, phone numbers and email addresses. If they came up with possible matches, he used the pictures from the law firm's website to confirm. He didn't know what he would need, so he collected anything and everything that might help. At this point there was no way to eliminate people from the list, so more was better.

Jason's intent was to collect as much personal information as he could about the employees of the law firm. This would give him an advantage, since with the boom of social networks, people share everything about themselves. From all this sharing it is easy to build simple profiles about likes, attitudes and even politics. He signed up for trial accounts with a number of investigative and genealogical sites to gather additional information on the employees, including their relatives. There were now at 1,052 people in the database. Some of the information lists offered an avalanche of details so he added a general interest page for activities like beaches, skiing and boating so Tasha could add personal details on the fly.

He showed her how to copy and paste the information, which made the input much easier. She suggested at one point that it might be useful to add children's ages to the database. So while she did input and kept notes, he modified the program to accept their expanding collection.

Willy and his companions pulled into a Global Commerce Bank parking lot. They were only a few blocks from the hotel.

Willy and Wanda entered the bank and sought out a black clerk to wait on them hoping to minimize both hassles and suspicion. "Hello I'm Kasha Smith," she said. "What can I help you with?"

"We'd like to open an account," Willy told her.

"Come this way," she said, directing them to her desk halfway towards the back of the building. She offered them chairs. "Can I get you anything, a cup of coffee or a bottle of water?"

"Could I have a water?" Wanda asked.

"Nothin' for me," Willy said.

"Sure, I'll be right back," Kasha said.

Willy and Wanda sat and waited for Kasha who quickly reappeared. She offered a small bottle of water to Wanda, and then took a seat behind the desk. "What can I do for you today?"

"We need to open her a checking account," Willy said, pointing to Wanda.

Kasha explained that they offered many types of checking with many options. All of them came with internet access so that they could withdraw and deposit funds. They even had applications for cell phones for depositing checks. With very little effort, they were able to establish an account and Willy paid the prior balance due of $325, as Kasha was able to reduce almost all of the late fines. She opened the account using the mailbox address and didn't order any checks. They set up a new temporary debit card and set up a pin number. Willy reminded Wanda to write the number down, so she would not forget it. She wrote it on the paper sleeve for the debit card. When it came to the email address, Willy used his own for the account.

Once outside the bank, Willy and Wanda walked up to the car where Big Maurice and Ivan sat. Big Maurice had his window down. Willy said to Wanda, "Okay, there's the money, let me have the card." He held the envelope in his left hand and held out his right hand.

Wanda handed him the card, and Willy gave Wanda the envelope with the cash. "See you Willy," Wanda said, walking away. In spite of his bulk, Big Maurice leapt out of the car and followed after Wanda, or was he chasing her? Whatever the case, it was no longer Willy's concern.

Willy got back in the driver seat and held the card up for Ivan to see. "It's a start," he remarked triumphantly as he started the car and drove back to the hotel.

When Willy and Ivan got back, it was close to 5 p.m. In the back of the hotel was a station wagon, and inside was an object that looked the size of a body wrapped in large plastic bags and tape, the same bags used for their secretive garbage removal. Willy's anger was quick and obvious upon coming upon the scene: it was in plain view … anyone passing by could see it. Moreover, no one was with the car. He snapped a curse-strewn command to Ivan in Russian street slang: "Get on this shit, now!". At the same time Willy bolted toward the control room.

Steve spoke as soon as he entered, "Well, she bought it."

Willy asked, "Who?"

Steve said, "That skinny blonde that wouldn't eat."

Willy asked, "Well who the fuck's car is out there? And why was she left in it?"

"The car belongs to Jim," Steven said.

"So why the fuck is it out there and not gone?" Willy's eyes were bright with anger.

"I don't know," Steve said suddenly sensing things were out of control. "Someone needs to watch over things. I can't leave here for long, you know that."

"Find him," Willy barked and shoved him toward the control panel.

Steve was too alarmed to stand up for himself. He started searching through the cameras trying to find Jim. He found him in the room by himself, sitting on a bed. He appeared to be alone. "He's in 502," he told Steve.

Willy quickly exited the room and made his way quickly to 502. When he opened the door, he found Jim sitting on the edge of the bed rocking back and forth, staring into space. He did not react to Willy entering the room. At this point, Willy was standing right in front of him.

Jim had worked for the firm for quite a while. He was the only one who worked there longer than Willy. Spider and Jim had been there from the start. Jim worked the late-night shift and helped himself to the girls, a little too often. He was a friend of Peter's and had a house some place far away from the city. Willy had the impression that Jim originally had dealings with Peter, bought a girl from him, or some other trade.

"What the fuck is wrong with you?" Willy demanded. Jim rocked back and forth two more times. On the forward motion of the third rock forward, Willy hit Jim on the side of the head so hard Jim keeled over onto his side.

Jim lay on the bed totally motionless. Willy thought maybe for a second he had killed him. He leaned over his body and could hear him breathing. "FUCK!" Willy screamed and stomped out of the room. "Totally fuckin' useless," he uttered as he slammed the door and marched back down the stairs.

Pissed off and fuming, Willy went down to the kitchen. He was now seriously shorthanded. Gladys had the table full of trays. She had made trays and covered every possible surface. As soon as he entered the room, she spoke. "No one has taken them; I don't understand where your helpers are today."

"We had a problem upstairs and I was away," Willy said. "It's okay, I'll get things going shortly. Are you done?"

"Not really," Gladys said. "I need some room to make more trays and I need to do the dishes."

"It's okay, we will take care of the rest of it," Willy said. "Why don't you just go home? You had a busy day."

"But I'm not finished," Gladys said, confused.

"I know and it's fine. We are short-staffed today," Willy explained. "It's not your fault, just go home, it's late. We will take care of this." He went and got her purse off the arm of a chair. There were trays on both of the chairs and across the top of the table. He handed her the purse. "It's really okay, we will take care of this." He escorted her up the steps, to the back door and to the dock. "It's been a long day for you. I know we just had a really long day, too. Just go home."

"But there is so much to do," Gladys insisted.

"It's okay, don't worry," Willy repeated.

Willy watched her walk across the small parking lot behind the hotel and get into her car. He noted that Ivan and the station wagon were not in the parking lot anymore.

"Where the fuck is Ivan?" Willy mumbled to himself.

He locked the back door and went back to the kitchen. This mess was nothing, he thought. When they first started this operation before he hired Gladys, it was like this every night. He walked back down to the kitchen and talked directly to the camera. "Get your fuckin' ass down here and help."

Ivan was having a problem. It wasn't often they lost inventory. When they did, Willy took care of it with his drug buddies. It was easy to leave a body at a crack house. Nobody wanted to see you or what you were doing. The cops would get the body, make the assumption that it was drug-related, and bury it with no ID. A detective would come by every so often. The advantage was that no one really did know anything about the girls. Since none of these girls were from the United States anyway, they weren't on any missing record system. The cops had more local characters to deal with and would simply let the mystery corpses lapse into cold cases, most of which were never pursued, let alone solved. But now he had to do this himself – and not where anyone would see him. He was a big man, covered with tattoos he had accumulated during years in prison, each one broadcasting his association to groups feared both in lockup and on the street. Back home in Russia, tattoos meant respect. But here in the United States, he might as well be wearing a clown uniform. Add to that he was 1.9 meters, almost six and a half feet tall which caught people's eye no matter how hard he tried to blend in.

As he drove on the interstate, he felt very conspicuous and dreaded every moment. Eventually, he got beyond the city, even the suburbs and arrived in the county. He got off at an exit onto a state road; he was in the middle of farmland and seemingly abandoned houses. He would have preferred to arrive later in the day. In the dusk you didn't need a flashlight, yet people couldn't make out details like his face or the make of the car. He drove down the road for several miles took a left at an intersection to head north. He found what he was looking for.

He focused on the abandoned houses that dotted the farmlands; many of them had fallen into disrepair. These were perhaps the homes of the farmers who had once owned the land, but one by one, they were bought up by the big food corporations. For them, the land was theirs to exploit on a massive scale. The houses were in the way, but it would cost too much to knock them down. They might use the barns, but most of the houses had no remaining value and were allowed to rot.

Ivan pulled in the dirt driveway of an older abandoned house; it had no barns and corn was growing up to its foundation on the far side. When he got to the back, the corn was growing right next to the dirt driveway. This offered a blind spot to hide the car and Ivan from the view of the road.

Ivan pulled the plastic mass out of the back of the car and carried it to the open back door of the house. He put the body down on the ground and pushed open the door. The floor had rotted to create a trap for anything that entered. Looking down in the hole, he could see what looked like scattered bones of various animals. There was also fur on the floor in the dark hole, which was the basement of the house.

He attempted to remove the plastic, but the body was still stiff due to rigormortis. He looked through the car in vain. There were no gloves in sight. He had to tug and pull on the plastic to get it off the body. He was concerned about leaving evidence. He made sure to avoid touching the body directly with his hands. Moreover, some of the tape used to wrap her might have fingerprints, so he carefully pulled it off of the skin of the girl's corpse.

At one point, he pulled on the tape and plastic so hard it flipped the body over, revealing a pain-stricken, contorted face. As hardened as he was, Ivan looked away as he struggled to remove the material off remaining plastic. After that, he pulled out a pocket knife to cut off her clothes. Finally, he picked the body up using some of the larger pieces of plastic and dropped it into the hole in the floor of the house. As soon as the body hit the floor below, he could hear something moving in the space below—probably some hungry animal he thought, which only helped his cause.

Ivan took with him the plastic and the rags that were once

clothes. He got back in the car and drove to the hotel. The body, if found, would produce no clues. That is, if the scavenging animals left anything at all behind.

He backed out of the driveway and got back onto the road. He didn't see a soul or even a car again until he got onto the interstate.

Once Ivan got back to the hotel, he found the back door was locked. No one responded to his wave at the camera, so he was forced to go in the front entrance. He preferred staying out of sight because people stared at his tattoos.

Jason was hungry, and the dinner was usually there by now. He stood under the camera and asked for a couple bottles of wine. He was actually tired, and so was Tasha. They had been entering data all day.

As Ivan arrived, Willy and Steve were supervising the girls to deliver dinner, provide additional plates and do the clean-up.

"Any problems?" Willy asked in English.

Ivan responded in Russian, "No, taken care of."

Willy responded in kind. "I sent Peter a text to get over here."

Ivan, annoyed, remarked, "That idiot again?"

"Yes, now help him, I'll go watch the cameras."

Willy took a tray and went back to the control room. To Willy, the control room was the first line of defense and offense. It needed to be manned all the time or it was useless. He considered it the most important room in the building.

From this single spot they could watch and listen in real time on not only what happened inside the building, but blocks away. The state of the art computer and facial recognition system contained the images of all known law enforcement. The newest feature was the lockdown button, which had only been tested but never used all the doors, and could be locked magnetically by pressing a single button. He checked on Jason and saw he and Tasha were eating their dinners.

Peter arrived about 30 minutes later. Willy saw him walking

down the street. He never parked his car anywhere near the hotel anymore—not since the police in the city started installing license plate scanners, which record the location of cars when the camera mounted on the police car can see them. They are also at many intersections. Many police departments store away this information forever so they can track the history of a car's movements.

Peter came into the control room and sat down next to Willy, who was intensively watching a drunk on the sidewalk who was staggering toward the hotel entrance.

"Hey Willy, what's going on?" Peter greeted him.

"Hi Peter," Willy said. "We had a little problem today and your boy flipped a lid or something. He's up in 502."

"What happened? Peter asked.

"That skinny blonde bitch who wouldn't eat bit the dust," Willy said.

"So what's that have to do with me?" Peter asked.

"Like I said, your boy is a basket case upstairs," Willy said. "I'm really short on manpower as it is. Are you guys coming up with somebody for me soon?"

Peter replied, "Well, the guy we had lined up got pinched trying to enter the country, so right now I don't have anyone for you. What happened to Jim?"

"I really don't know," Willy said. "I had an errand to run. When I got back, his car was out back with a body in it and he was upstairs sitting on a bed rockin' like a fuckin' baby. I really don't know. Could you see if you can do something with him or have someone take care of him?"

Peter raised an eyebrow. "Sure, I'll go take a look."

"Thanks man," Willy said casually. To him, Peter was responsible for providing more reliable help, which included replacing basket cases like Jim.

Peter walked up to room 502 to check on Jim. He was laying flat on the bed. When Peter came in, he sat on the bed and faced Peter;

He noticed Jim had a good-sized welt on the left side of his face.

"I'm sorry," Jim said.

"So you're better now?" Peter asked.

"Yeah, I'm okay now," Jim insisted. "Really, I'm good."

"Okay," Peter said. "Did Willy do that?" He pointed to the welt.

"I think so," Jim said. "I was sort of out of it earlier. I never had to do that ….body stuff before."

"As long as you think you're okay, we need you," Peter said.

"I'm cool," Jim said. "I'm just going to stay here tonight – you know, party a little."

Peter nodded. "Okay, well get some sleep today. We need you tonight." Peter left the room and went back to the control room where Willy was still watching the drunk hanging out in front of the hotel.

"Don't pop him again, you little asshole," Peter said to Willy. "By the way, your numbers are a bit weak."

"Well, we're doing the same, and we haven't had any specials lately," Willy said. "You know how it goes."

"You need 1,200 per machine, per day, every day," Peter said. "The last couple of weeks you have been light a couple of hundred. You can't do that. You have to hit that or even higher."

"You know what specials do for us," Willy said. "We will make it up and then some—you'll see."

"Show me the room," Peter said.

Willy brought up the room with the cubicles on the full-screen on all the monitors. Every cubicle was occupied. They watched for a little while. Peter put his hand on Willy's shoulder while he got up from the chair. "I'm going to take off."

"See you," Willy said.

Peter left the control room. Willy watched as he left the building and went down the street. "That punk has no clue how things really work around here," he fumed.

Jason and Tasha were watching a movie together. She hadn't seen *Sleepless in Seattle* so they pulled the mattress onto the floor to watch. They used all of the pillows and blankets they had to make themselves comfortable.

Willy let himself into Jason's room. He shut the door behind him. He looked at Jason and Tasha. "Don't you two look cozy?"

Jason got up from the mattress. "I'll need a minute," he said to Willy as he walked over to the computer. He got his headphones and plugged them in for Tasha, and handed them to her. He whispered in a low voice, "Put these on, it's okay."

After she did, Jason asked, "So what's the occasion?"

"I have an account set up and a mailbox rented," Willy said.

"Sounds cool," Jason said.

Willy handed Jason the temporary checks and a slip of paper with the address to the mailbox. "You should have everything you need right here."

"I found a deal for getting an ad to run on that website you showed me," Jason said and went to the computer at the other end of the table from Tasha. He typed the name into the browser and brought up the page.

"Inside ads, which play when a user clicks, are cheap—$600 for six months."

"Why do we want an ad?" Willy asked.

"It's not the ad we want, it's something to run inside of the ad," Jason explained. "I can insert my code into it and do my thing. It is the easiest way to do this without outside help."

"Oh, I see," Willy said.

"I'm going to need to set up that server first. Did you order it?" Jason asked.

"No, I was busy all day," Willy said.

"I can do it," Jason said. "Is there money in the account?"

"Nah, maybe $100," Willy said.

"It's going to be more than that," Jason said. "I will need money for the ID stuff too, and a wire to run down to your computers so I can see what's going on. Or you can add a Wi-Fi router and I can pick it up here."

"How much do you think you will need?" Willy asked.

Jason rattled of a list, "A die cutter is $50, a laminator is $100, a color printer is $200, the website is $600. I think something like $1,500 or $1,600." Then he added, "We can get started as soon as I have the server built and the ad in place."

Willy had had a rough day and this sounded like a lot of work, "How much is just the stuff you need for now?"

"What do you mean? I need the printers for what I'm working on. It's hard to just work off the screen. It takes longer. Besides, I thought you wanted to get things going quickly?"

"Fine," Willy said. "I will put $1,500 into the account. You need to start makin' money before you get the rest."

"What is the email for access?" Jason asked. "I don't see it here."

"Oh, I forgot." Willy walked over to the table and wrote on the pad "wclarke8640@aol.com, password: tulip123."

"That password needs to be changed," Jason said. "I'll let you know what I change it to."

"How long do you think it will be?" Willy asked.

"Well, I have a good start," Jason said. "I just need to do a few things and wait for some stuff to come in. Maybe next week, maybe sooner."

"I'll get the Wi-Fi router and have it installed," Willy said.

"That would help," Jason said. "Well, we are getting there. We just need a few more things."

"Yeah," Willy nodded.

"I asked for some wine earlier," Jason said. "I guess you didn't get the message."

"No, they forgot to tell me," Willy replied. "How about I get you several bottles and give you a refrigerator? There is one around here someplace."

Steve was watching all of this in the control room and knew the only refrigerator was in his room with beer in it.

Jason got excited. "That would be great!" Changing the subject, he said, "So when will you tell me who we're going after?"

"I'll let you know," Willy said vaguely.

Jason tested Willy's boundaries, "Look, if you don't mind, I can go get some wine," Jason said. "I've got too much invested in all of this to skip and you, after all, do have the cops looking for me."

"No way," Willy said. "If you get caught, I'm back to square one. I'll get it."

Willy opened the door and walked out into the hall, and locked the door. He walked toward the front staircase and stopped under the camera and looked up.

"I'll be right back, I have an errand to run," he said to the camera.

Jason lay back down on the mattress and pushed the pillows from the bed around a bit. Tasha unplugged the headphones and laid her head on his chest. He ran his fingers through her hair. Jason had heard that lock thing. Willy must have been alone with no one else at the door. He thought he should add a lock pick gun to his list too.

Willy returned 20 or 30 minutes later. He opened the door just far enough to put the three bottles inside, and then closed and locked it.

Jason heard the door and saw the maneuver upside down. "Would you like some wine?" he asked Tasha.

"In a little while," she said. They were close to the end of the movie anyway.

When the movie was finished, Tasha's head was still on his chest. As the credits started scrolled down the screen, she rubbed her hand across his balls and started playing with him. She finally moved her head so he could kiss her. They kissed while she played with him and pulled off her jeans and his. "Time for you inside me," she said.

He got on top of her and after a half hour of intense kissing, he entered her slowly. They continued for a while, in a slow, steady but increasingly powerful rhythm, lightly kissing each other. She was so beautiful and willing, so wet; he could feel himself getting closer; he tried to pull out and she pulled him back closer and they came together. At least that's what he hoped had happened.

They rolled off of each other. The situation had its perverse aspect, as they were well aware they were providing a show for whoever was watching on the camera system.

Jason asked, "Would you like some wine now?"

"Sure," Tasha said.

Jason got off of the mattress naked and found the two cups and pushed another cork in with the screwdriver. He filled the cups with wine and handed one to Tasha.

"So what do you want to be when you grow up?" Jason asked.

"I want to be rich and famous," Tasha answered.

"Not me," Jason said. "Too much heartache."

"I want big houses and cars," Tasha said.

"You want people following you around and not being able to have any secrets?" Jason asked.

Tasha pointed at the camera. "It isn't that different than being here, except you get to dress better."

Jason thought that was funny. He laughed out loud. "Well, style is not exactly a requirement here."

"That is so true," Tasha said. "You know it's not as bad here with you."

"Not as bad?" Jason said.

"Yeah," she said.

"Do you want some more wine?" Jason asked.

"Sure," she answered.

Jason refilled the cups. They talked well past the point of the bottle being empty. Eventually they turned off the lights and held each other until they fell asleep.

13

Some New Discoveries

Jason awoke with the dawn. He and Tasha were still lying together on the mattress. He stood up on wobbly legs, stretched to fully regain his senses and then headed straight to his laptop.

He logged onto the camera Wi-Fi network. He first needed to know if he was under surveillance, so the first camera he checked was the control room. There was the guy with the hat, sound asleep again. Accessing the control board, he found that it had a web server built into it that allowed control of every camera. The web server gave him the name of each camera: 201, 202, etc. This made it easy to click through them. The interface also revealed which camera was in operation. He noticed his room was not listed, so no one in the control room, including the sleeping attendant, was watching him now.

He found he could instruct the console to play back any file. He looked to see if there was evidence of stored videos. Instead, it the system appeared to overwrite videos on a daily basis leaving no

183

extended record. He watched a little of the video of himself and Tasha from the night before. The camera wasn't focused on them; it was left on the two chairs from when he had been talking with Willy. *"Good,"* he thought, *"...not really comfortable with Tasha and me becoming porn stars for these losers."* Then again, it would hardly register for the camera attendant when the women at the hotel were used as sex slaves on a daily basis.

Jason was surprised that even that early in the morning, the cubicles were occupied and supervised by the skinny Asian guy, who instead of monitoring the girls was, just as before, completely distracted with a game on his iPad. Having accessed each camera, he closed the interface. After reflecting for a moment he concluded, *"At this vulnerable point in the daily routine, it wouldn't be that hard to unlock the door and simply walk out of the hotel"*

Jason moved on to the bank website. He logged on and saw Wanda Williams was the account holder. The balance was $100. He decided to get familiar with the site. Personally, he would have never used Global Commerce Bank. They offered an option to transfer money to any account on their system so he could create a check and send it anywhere. He opened a new email address which he named "wanda123408" on Google. He also opened a PayEasy account under that email address using the address of the mailbox as the registered email address. He started the linking process on PayEasy, so they were directly connected to the bank account. He expected the connection to set up instantly, but it was made to wait ... he would have to come back later to follow up the process.

He looked around the web for any activity related to Wanda. She was either inactive on social media or somehow hidden from all of the social networks. He found almost nothing about her. He tried her name in the state criminal database. It was hard for him to imagine anyone so outside the cyber world. Then again, he found an avalanche of online information that others had collected on her. There were numerous arrest records for prostitution, drugs, criminal impersonation, and more petty crimes. More important, under known associates, he found records for one "Wilson Lattimer," A.K.A. "Willy Lattimer."

There were no criminal records for Wilson Lattimer, which was surprising, unless his records were somehow erased. Not only did he not use someone not known to him, he used someone he was associated with. *"What an idiot,"* Jason thought.

The door lock clicked and it opened. Without panic Jason quickly locked the screen on the computer. A short, redheaded girl in the now familiar T-shirt, shorts and socks delivered breakfast. Her entry awoke Tasha. The girl looked confused and uncertain about what to do with the trays, so she cautiously put them on the floor. She didn't look up or at Jason or Tasha. Once she left, Tasha went to the bathroom and freshened up while Jason moved the mattress and set the room back into its day mode.

While they were eating, Tasha pointed out, "She is new."

"How do you know?" Jason asked.

"I have been here for over a year," she observed. "I know all the girls, but I have never seen her before."

Jason asked, "How many girls are there?"

"There were 32…um, 31 of us here," she said, thinking. "But I'm not sure since I have been here with you."

"Are things always bad for you and the others?" he asked.

"No … sometimes," she thought aloud. "There used to be a really bad man here that used to hit me, but he is gone now."

"I'm sorry," Jason said.

"Why are you sorry?" Tasha asked. "You didn't hit me, you're nice."

"I'm sorry that anyone would hit you," Jason said, looking at her.

"I have seen many things, worse things," she said, her eyes starting to well up.

"You don't have to tell me anything you don't want to," Jason said.

"You are so sweet," Tasha said. "One day you will leave, too."

"I can't promise, but I will try very hard not to leave you," Jason said. "That is, if I ever get out of here."

"You will leave and forget me," Tasha said.

"I doubt very much I could ever forget you," Jason said.

"You are sweet," Tasha smiled.

Jason and Tasha finished their coffee in silence. There was nothing he could do for either of them at that point but keep them working on the plan. He had Tasha look up information on Facebook. The net they had cast on the lawyers and their families was now completely out of hand; they had 1,400 people of interest and another 2,350 supporting characters. The list included spouses, children and parents. Jason noted three men named "Peter" at the law firm, and focused closer attention on them. Eventually he was able to rule one out because he had no children or a wife. He did have an attractive girlfriend who liked exotic vacations. That left two Peters, one of which had to be his drinking partner from the night before.

Jason had made up several new profiles on Facebook. He took advantage of a generation of kids addicted to "liking" each other and collecting as many 'friends' as possible. He found pictures of especially attractive little girls and little boys, some of them from professional modeling sites. He used the made up profiles to 'friend' some of the children of the people at the firm. This way he could get more information from their kids' accounts.

The door lock clicked. Jason looked at the time. It was a little early for lunch. When it opened, the redheaded girl came in carrying a vase, which contained a very nice bouquet of assorted flowers. She put them on the table, and then she exited the room.

"Oh, how pretty," Tasha said.

"I thought you might like them," Jason said.

"It's been so long," she exclaimed and looked at Jason with genuine glee and affection. She shot up and immediately walked over to rearrange them.

"I'm glad you like them," Jason said.

"My parents used to have a garden," she said excitedly. "In the spring, so many flowers would grow there. I remember running around and playing with the puppy in the garden. It was so full of color and…they are very nice." She returned to the monitor and hugged him around the neck. Then, in a very robotic fashion she sat and resumed looking up information on Facebook.

Jason was pleased but had no idea of what to add or say. It was as if she only existed as a real person in the past and now only understood serving as a slave. Then again, in their time together there were flashes of a very affectionate, promising person he yearned to recover. There were lots of things he wanted to say to her—that is, without the camera.

Tasha broke his train of thought, "I have a question," she asked, "This one has a Twitter account, but you didn't add a place for that?" He had put her to a task and she demonstrated another aspect of her special quality: a determined intellectual quality compatible to his own.

After looking at her thoughtfully for a moment, Jason replied, "Okay, I'll add that," He set upon writing a module that tracked Twitter, then showed Tasha how to set up new email accounts on Yahoo, Google, AOL and Outlook. That way, each Twitter feed also had a unique email address. This required him to add the email address and password used into the program. The social networks all try to find things in common so they can suggest new people you might know. But the way Jason set things up, no site would recognize from the Twitter posts that the new IDs had any relationship with each other.

If you want to probe the life of a stranger, social networks are a wealth of information. He needed to collect what he could especially because security questions he might need in the future were posted in the social networks. Cracking a person's security codes can unlock details about every aspect of their business and private life.

Lunch came and Tasha and Jason took a break, though he was eager to be done with the program modifications.

Tasha asked, "Would it be possible for the computer to get all the information from the screen automatically?"

"Well, I could set up a scraping tool," Jason said.

"What is that?"

"The information on a computer screen has two basic types," Jason said. "They may look very similar to each other, but they are very different. I don't mean information that you get *out of* it, I mean information *to* the computer—it means something. A picture on a computer just displays a picture, and you can't really do much with a picture. Well, you can convert the picture if it has words or letters or even numbers on it. That process is optical character recognition or OCR. The process tries to read the picture and convert the data back to computer information. But pictures are mostly of things like people or their pets so it's not always very useful. Do you follow what I'm saying?"

"I think so," Tasha answered with an expression indicating her attention to every word.

Jason continued, "So what web pages are good at is displaying information in basically the same place on the screen, over and over. So what a scraper does is read the information on the page and allow users to use it somewhere else. A screen scraper is something that opens a web page, then, based on the site, automatically gets the information requested, like this page. See, the name is always here."

"There are so many to do," Tasha said. "It is going so slowly."

"I know, but there is another source of information we don't have access to yet. We'll have access soon. Some of this stuff we won't even need. That's why I included a button to eliminate people and information that is not important; irrelevant to us."

"I was wondering what that was for," she said.

"Pressing that button on a specific person makes the information tree we're building stop, and they stop appearing in the work queue list," Jason explained. "All of the branches around that person also drop out of the queue. About how many items do you have in the queue now?"

"It's about 10,000," she said with concern.

"That will go down significantly once we have more data," Jason said. "Your suggestion on scraping was great." Tasha was proving to be so capable that Jason asked, "Do you know how to write computer programs?"

"No, I never did anything like that," she replied matter-of-factly.

"I can download something that can teach you, a visual toolkit, and show you how to use it if you'd like. Maybe you can learn to help write programs."

"I don't know about that," Tasha shook her head warily. "I'm not that smart."

Jason chuckled. "You don't have to be that smart to use this tool. It helps, but it really isn't required. Do you want to try?"

"Sure," Tasha said.

While Jason was chewing the last bite of his lunch, he started downloading the Microsoft visual trail software onto the machine Tasha was using. He set her up on another computer to run the program he had written. It was web-based, so it could be run by any computer in the room. He then reconsidered what he was doing and turned to Tasha. "I have something for you, close your eyes," he said.

He got up from the table, reached under the dresser and pulled out the violin case. He opened it and set it in front of her. "Okay, open."

Tasha opened her eyes and looked down. Her hands fell to her lap, and she stared at the instrument for quite a while. She tipped her head to examine it without touching it. She looked at him with tears filling her eyes.

"Pick it up," Jason said.

She ran her hand down the string board. She picked it up and pulled out the bow. She took time with each string, making sure it was properly tuned. Her tear-filled eyes concentrated on the instrument. The struggle that she had in seeing was not affecting her hands. Her hands moved a lingering, loving memory of their own. They caressed the violin and moved gracefully into position.

She rose to her feet and stroked the instrument. Jason did not know much about classical music, but whatever she was playing must have been classical. He did know a few people who played but made regular squeaking mistakes. Tasha's touch showed none of that. From the first stroke, she created flawless notes. Whatever it was she was playing was deep and filled the room. She played from a distant longing heart. She was a prisoner in a place that steeped her in the depths of hell. Yet as she played, there was a freedom in her expression and movement, if only an instant.

Steve called Willy on his cell. "What the fuck is that noise?"

"Don't worry about it," Willy said. "You should have seen what I did."

"I heard already," Steve said.

"He knows his shit, and soon, money will come," Willy promised. Don't worry about it, man."

Through the vents and walls the women enslaved in the cubicles could also hear the music; they spontaneously all paused their endless instant messaging while it played. As soon as it was over, the tippity-tap sound of the keys nervously resumed.

When Tasha finished playing, Jason clapped. He was touched. It was true, unbridled passion, he thought. "That was beautiful," he said.

Tasha held the violin close to her face as if to hug it. She slowly slipped it back in its case and tenderly put the bow back. She slowly closed the lid.

"Thank you so much," she said, sliding the case away from her body on the table.

"It's yours, you keep it," Jason said.

"Thank you, but it is not allowed,"

"It will stay here, anytime you want to play it."

Tasha looked at him; her eyes were full of tears. "I forgot how to cry," she said just before bursting into tears. He walked over to her and held her for a moment. He let her cry on his chest. Eventually, she rose and held his hand. She pulled him toward the bedroom. He was unsure. She was so damaged and he wasn't going to take advantage. She didn't understand since all the men she knew for the last few years expected sex. Instead, he lay down with her. She started to touch him and he held her and whispered, "No," A few moments later, she was sound asleep. He thought about a nap too, but a different idea came to mind. He got out of bed and went back to the program and worked on it until Tasha woke up.

An hour later, Jason showed Tasha the basics of visual dot net. He had to refresh his understanding of it too, since the basic version didn't use the same syntax as "C" or "C sharp." She actually looked happy when she made her first program. It was a form with a button. When she pressed the button, the top of the form flashed "Hi Tasha."

Jason taught Tasha all through dinner. They opened a bottle of wine and finished it, then opened another. By 10 o'clock, he showed her how to connect to the database and get records from it.

Around 2 a.m., They were both drunk and tired.

"But if I do it this way, why doesn't it work?" Tasha slurred.

"Let's go to bed, it's late," Jason said. "We can pick it up tomorrow."

"But why?" she asked, too drunk to accept that she was exhausted.

"Come on, let's sleep, I'm beat," he said. He reached over and shut the screen off. He shut the screens off on all of them, then grabbed her hand and paused so she would get up. They went into the bedroom. He shut off the light as they passed the switch.

14

Tasha Pitches In

An unexpected exchange was growing between Tasha and Jason. Today, it was Tasha who awoke at sunrise. Ordinarily she would meekly allow Jason to sleep, waking him only to make sure he enjoyed breakfast while it was still warm. However, she had become sensitive to the urgency around his work, so she didn't wait for breakfast before nudging to wake him. She got him to sit up in bed and become more alert. He had a headache from the wine the night before and felt crappy but was grateful to get a start on the day. The food arrived soon after and she quickly sat his tray on his lap. She was in a great mood and eager to get on the computer again. Their partnership was in full swing.

"I had a great time learning about the computer yesterday," Tasha said.

"I'm glad you liked it," Jason responded, smiling weakly and trying to catch up with her enthusiasm.

"I never understood how they worked before," Tasha explained.

"It's really not that big a deal," Jason reassured her.

"I see that now," she offered, "but what can you do with it?"

"Really anything," Jason explained, "you can work almost anything using a program."

"What do you mean?" Tasha asked.

"Okay, for example, take cars" Jason said.

Tasha nodded cynically. "OK."

"Well, these days little computers run programs that run the cars: the engine, accessories, and, of course, GPS, and so on," he listed. "… Programs operate other things too including sensors which are like little switches. They can turn a device on or off, depending on what is needed, based on a number. If the number is three, then the device does one thing. If the number is five, then it does something else."

"So everything runs programs like that?" Tasha asked.

"Today, just about everything has a computer chip running a program or lots of programs," Jason explained. "Everything—TVs, DVD players, even some refrigerators. All you need to understand is that programs like the one you wrote can be used in other devices."

"Will the program I wrote work on something else?" Tasha asked.

"No, what I mean is, programs in general work other things," he said. "You're working in what's called "visual studio." You know how we switched from 'basic' to 'C' programming? The same thing you did looked the same but the instruction was different?"

"Yes, I saw how the two did the same thing," she said.

"Well, there are other languages that have the same rules," Jason told her. "Remember when we used the brackets?"

"Yes, I messed that up several times," Tasha admitted.

"Well, that's just a particular language," Jason explained. "Other languages can do the same thing, but have their own rules about how you write them, called 'syntax,' which is just the way to put the statement together."

"Which one do you use?" Tasha asked.

"Well, the program that we use to put information in the database is called PHP," Jason described. "I use Java, which has similar rules, but they all have their own strengths and weaknesses. It depends on the language and what you want to do with it."

Tasha finished her coffee and got up from the bed. "I'm going to go work. You can go back to sleep. You look tired."

He lay there a bit longer, flirting with falling back to sleep, but her enthusiasm inspired him. In spite of his hangover he willed himself out of bed and into to the bathroom. When he walked into the office, he found Tasha picking up from yesterday. She had found a couple of websites containing programming lessons. She skipped over many of the lessons since she had so quickly absorbed the material.

Jason sat at the computer he had been using the day before and checked on the bank deposit. He was surprised to find it had not yet arrived. He logged out of the bank site and opened the email account he used to send Anthony an email. He had a new message: "I booked a flight for Friday, thanks buddy." It was sent yesterday at 10:45 AM. He had to look at the date to see that today was Thursday. He realized he had lost track of days. Friday was tomorrow, but in this place, there would be no weekend.

He looked at the camera and waved. "Need more coffee and Advil!"

"Why won't this work?" Tasha asked, glued to the screen.

Jason moved his chair next to Tasha's and sat down. "Let me see what you have," he offered.

Tasha clicked on the code screen, and Jason looked it over. "May I have the mouse?" She let go and he took it. "See this right here," he pointed with the mouse. "You have to have a '{' there and '}' there. They are important; it's one of those differences between the languages."

"I see," Tasha said.

Jason pressed "compile" from the menu. He watched for errors to appear on the screen as it changed the code into a program able to run. After seeing that there were no errors, he launched the program and watched it do its process.

Jason got up and pushed his chair back to the other computer. Tasha was doing amazingly well at learning to program. While Tasha went back to the lessons on the webpage, Jason decided that he would install the visual platform on that computer, too. He thought that since she was getting ahead, he might as well write the screen scraper in something she would be able to follow.

While he waited for the install of the visual studio to complete, he returned to investigating Peter, or for the moment, the mystery of the two Peters. He uncovered a difference between them: One had younger children, two girls, 13 and 14 years old which meant he had found his man. Jason found as much information as he could about *Jonathan Peter Long.* By the time lunch arrived, he collected the names of his wife and kids, his mother's maiden name as well as his date of birth, wedding date, telephone numbers, prior addresses and even the name of his mortgage company and his wife's, as well. The building plans to their house were online, too. He couldn't locate a Facebook account for him, but his wife posted pictures of the kids like crazy for her mother, Gail Cowe, who resided in Minnesota. In response, the mother seemed to post on her wall after every picture she received.

Jason pulled up Google maps and used the geo tags on the wife's phone to find the park where she had taken many of the pictures of the kids. He also planned to add a field to the program for vehicle information along with a couple of the images from their driveway which provided clear images of the cars. One had a good shot of a license plate on a black Mercedes.

When the brunette came in carrying a lunch tray, Jason realized that his headache was still there, and no one had brought coffee. She set the two trays on the table. She didn't look like she had showered in a while. Her hair was oily. She kept her head down and Jason couldn't really see her face. She was wearing the official uniform, he realized. She exited quickly.

"She's new, too," Tasha said when the door closed.

"Really?" Jason asked.

Tasha nodded. "She will get in trouble for not being clean."

"What kind of trouble?" he asked with a look of concern.

"Maybe they will beat her," Tasha said matter-of-factly.

"Huh, is that so" Jason murmured. Hers sounded like the voice of experience and he did not need to know any more than that. He wondered for a moment where all the girls were coming from, but before he could finish the thought a large thump was heard that shook the building.

Jason looked at Tasha. "What was that?"

"I don't know," she replied.

They waited for any other sound. They could hear the rush of cars on the street, but it was mostly silent. Jason really wanted to look at the cameras, but thought better of it. It wasn't that he didn't trust Tasha; he did, but this sent his mind into some questions he wasn't sure he wanted to answer. She did pick up programming quite easily. But it was strange that she had no questions or anything to say about her captors. He shook his head. He was being silly.

They finished their lunch, which included soup and sandwiches. The chicken soup was warm today.

"I am doing much better now," Tasha said.

"I see that," Jason said. "Do you want to try some harder stuff?"

"I don't know," Tasha said.

"When we finish, I'll show you how to use libraries," Jason said.

"A library?" Tasha asked.

"That is a program that gets its information from another program," Jason explained. "Many times, people don't understand that the main program doesn't have to do all of the work. These little programs are also what open many of the problems with computers."

"What do you mean? Tasha asked.

"Well, libraries can have security holes or viruses that may tinker with the libraries to create problems in the main program," Jason said. "Windows uses names for them—'dot sys' and 'dot dll', but they can be named anything."

"Okay, I think I got it," Tasha said.

Jason finished his soup and looked at Tasha. "I think you should beat me," he said.

"What do you mean?" she asked.

"I think I need a shower myself," Jason said.

"Oh, I get it," she stood up. "Should I punish you?"

"Yes, please do," he stood up and took her hand and led her into the bathroom. They took a long shower together.

Willy was having his own difficulties after his errand to the bank to add funds to the account. He did it so Jason could buy what he needed. He stopped in an office supply store to purchase a Wi-Fi router. When he got back, Steve was still pissed at him over giving the refrigerator over for Jason's use. He refused to listen at first and so did not realize that there was another fridge not being used. It was in Spider's old room. Willy had to actually show the unit to Steve just to get him to calm down. Steve picked up the refrigerator to carry it, but tripped on the rug and fell with it. The result was a large thump, which seemed to shake the entire building. This revealed the level of readiness at the time of day because everyone available came running to the sound. Instead of a crisis or escaping girl they found Willy and Steve carrying the refrigerator.

Willy went back to the control room and made Steve deliver the refrigerator. When he looked at the video from the room, it appeared empty. A chill went up his back. There was no one there. He saw Steve in the hallway opening the door, so he ran down to the room. Steve had just put the refrigerator down inside the door of Jason's room on the side with all of the computers. The screens had gibberish on them—some sort of computer codes. As the pounding in his ears subsided, he could hear Jason and Tasha taking a shower. Shaking his head in relief and disgust Willy pushed Steve through the door which they locked behind them.

Once in the hallway, Steve, perplexed by Willy's erratic actions asked, "What? I can't put a refrigerator in by myself?"

"No, forget it," Willy said. "I don't think he is going to be a problem at all, but you are right … She's keeping him occupied. That'll be very useful if he gets out of hand."

"I wonder if we should push him," Steve said.

"There is no need, man, he is right on top of what we want him to do," Willy said. "Look, you want to stay with this shit, you know what's keeping us here."

"What?" Steve asked.

"*Identification and money,*" Willy said knowingly.

"Huh?" Steve said and looked at Willy with more than a little annoyance.

"Look, let's talk in the room," Willy pointed down.

They went back to the control room. Steve sat down in the chair and changed the big monitor to focus on the lobby. Willy sat in the other chair. "What keeps us here is who we are and lack of funds, right?"

"So?" Steve said.

"If we had another ID and money and we went somewhere else, there would be no problem with us."

"I don't get it," Steve said.

"If he can make us ID cards and we had a couple of hundred grand, then we don't need to be here anymore, and all we'd have to do is stay low and keep out of sight of the others," Willy said. "You know?"

"But if they find you, they will kill you," Steve pointed out. "I'm not getting into that kind of shit."

"Look," Willy pointed out, "If we can come up with new identities then we wouldn't need to stay in this rat hole? You're wanted as 'Steve.' But if you had another ID that said you're 'Tom' or 'Dick', and if had you some serious cash, then you could think about comin' outta here and livin' large."

"I could go to Bolivia and open a pool hall," Steve said, dreaming aloud

Willy nodded. "Yes you could, and live very well, and these fuckers would never find us."

"You better stop talking that way, there is no 'us' shit," Steve said.

Willy got out of the chair and walked to the doorway. He turned back to face Steve. "You're right. But just think about it, dude. Our little boy here can be the golden goose."

After another shower, drying and shaving session, Jason and Tasha went back to work. They saw the small refrigerator sitting by the door. Jason moved it closer to an electrical outlet and plugged it in. He then put the half bottle of wine into it.

Tasha went back to her studies, learning C for beginners, and Jason turned on his monitor, which still had his database up and the page with Peter's picture and information on top. He closed it and checked the bank account, which now contained a balance of $2,500. *"All right Willy!"* he thought.

"Hey, I want to change up on you," Jason said, turning to Tasha.

"What?" Tasha asked.

"I want to change what you're doing," Jason explained. "It will be easier and you will catch on fast."

"Okay," Tasha said.

Jason took control of the keyboard and brought up PHP for beginners. "This is similar," he said, moving to the machine next to the one he was on and installed it. "You can leave this up and run the tutorial here. It's going to be a little different, but you will understand it soon enough."

Jason showed her how to edit files on the other computer and how to see them on the first one using a web browser. He started with the famous "hello world" example, with him sitting there. He left her to work through the problems. He went back to his machine and sent an email to the website for advertising on their website. He checked PayEasy and the bank account, which were now linked. So he signed up for an account on the African Linux web host using the PayEasy account to pay for the service.

He was still configuring the website when dinner came. The same brunette came in with two trays containing meatloaf, mashed potatoes and string beans. She put the trays down on the table and left quickly. It seemed she still hadn't bathed; she had new black bruises on her inner thighs that ran down both legs and showed though her thin white shorts.

Tasha and Jason sat across from each other and ate their meal. Tasha looked at him with exhaustion and fear, "Do we have to work anymore after we eat?" she asked timidly, "…Maybe we can we watch another movie?"

"Are you having problems?" Jason asked.

"No, I understand, but I'm getting tired," Tasha said. "I just want to relax."

"You're right, we should stop," Jason agreed. "I'm getting a little tired, too."

After dinner, they pulled out the mattress and looked for a movie to watch. She preferred a comedy that made Jason wonder if her taste was perhaps very different than his own. Nonetheless, they pulled the mattress down and set up the computer to watch the piece. Jason fell asleep halfway through.

Making The Advertisement

Jason startled awake. His first awareness was a terrible taste in his mouth, then he became conscious that he had been awakened by Tasha's loud snoring. He blinked hard and studied her closely; she appeared too frail to create such a racket. It seemed at odds with her beauty, but somehow, it reminded him that she was a full person. He scoffed fondly and mused that at this moment she was a "full volume" person. The slivers of light in the window told him it was daybreak. The overhead light had not been turned off from the night before. He slid off the mattress and went to the bathroom to brush his teeth. When he finished, he went back to the room and stood over Tasha for a few minutes. She had stopped snoring and looked peaceful, like an angel, he thought. *"Why couldn't I have met her outside all of this?"* he wondered. In a more normal life, would such a beauty ever have looked his way? For a moment he was filled with doubt and guilt. Who knew how her life would have worked out had she not been kidnapped and trafficked? She was certainly damaged from her experiences. Hopefully he had not added to the

201

tragedy. Hopefully, he could help her find a path out of this life.

Jason went to his computer and logged into the email that he used with the website advertisement. He found they had sent him a contract PDF. He downloaded and read it, then downloaded an application that allowed him to sign the PDF using the mouse. He signed Wanda's name to the application, paid using the Wanda PayEasy account and, finally, submitted it to the website advertisement.

Next, he went to his laptop and logged into the camera Wi-Fi system. Today, surprisingly, the guy in the booth was wide awake and watching Tasha on the big screen as she slept. Jason was caught off guard and immediately logged out. He noted where he was sitting and the position of the surveillance camera. If the camera was focused down a little bit more, the man in the booth would have had a full view of what he was able to do on the computer. *"I have to be more careful,"* Jason thought to himself. He set the Wi-Fi router to connect to the florist shop so he didn't have to use his laptop for that anymore.

Jason scanned for Wi-Fi names and found a new one listed under the name "Netgear." That name was listed as having a full signal, which meant it must be the one that Willy had obtained. He didn't bother cracking it; he would just wait to be given access.

Jason turned his attention to the *penis* enlargement scam page for a bit. It occurred to him that Tasha would be better at designing the page, so he worked on testing the Java code to download to the victim side. It seemed to work fine, so he just needed the small slideshow, which would make the computer reconnect often, giving him the control he needed.

Jason knew there was a chance that his code might be caught by an antivirus, so he copied the virtual XP machine 10 times. This process gave him 10 different Microsoft XP computers to test with. He downloaded every antivirus he could think of and installed one of each on the virtual machines.

He was halfway through testing when Tasha woke up. She still looked sleepy.

"Good morning," Jason said.

"Morning," she replied dreamily, not yet returned to the situation at hand.

Tasha left the room and went to the bathroom. Jason tried testing the antivirus against this program once again. However, this time the antivirus caught and identified malware. This meant that what he had was discoverable, which was not good. He was looking up the virus definition on the web when Tasha came back into the room. She put her hands on his shoulders and kissed him on his neck, and now fully awake, whispered in his ear, "Good morning."

He got up from this chair to sweep her up in a long embrace. As they kissed, they heard the door unlock. They separated only to face the same girl from yesterday, still unwashed and bruised, bearing two trays. She walked around the mattress more quietly than any mouse. She placed the trays on the table and removed the ones from last night. As usual, her head remained bowed with her eyes to the floor the entire time, even as she exited the room.

By now the girl's broken and cautious ways had become just a familiar part of life in the hotel. After a momentary glance acknowledging her plight, Jason and Tasha sat down to eat breakfast. Tasha worked to change the mood, "I really enjoyed learning yesterday," she said. "But I'm having a problem with the PHP."

"What is it?" Jason asked.

She responded thoughtfully, "I don't understand why you would need the PHP if you have the web code anyway."

"They work together," Jason replied. "Some languages, or in this case scripts, use the best features of each other so they can do what is needed."

"I really don't understand all the way," Tasha admitted.

"You will today," Jason reassured her. "I need help with my penis advertisement."

"You are going to advertise your penis on the Internet?" Tasha asked, confused.

Jason laughed at the question, but realized that much of what he had said was lost in translation. "No, I'm not selling my dick," he explained. "I'm using the penis ad to help with a page I'm creating. It uses PHP, HTML and Java all together. It's a small ad that we're going to use on a website."

Tasha thought for a moment then laughed at her question, quickly getting in on the joke.

Jason finished his coffee, held his cup up and looked directly at the camera. "Coffee!" he demanded.

Tasha stacked the trays and sat on Jason's lap. He held her there enjoying the moment, all the while wondering what hell was on the other side of that door, not just for him, but for her and the others. *"How many girls are there in all?"* Ultimately, he was playing with fire. If he no longer appeared to offer something valuable, the threats and violence to the girls would also apply to him. The sound of the door unlocking broke his train of thought. Tasha jumped to her feet ending her comforting embrace.

Willy came in holding an old automatic Mr. Coffee machine under his arm, and a zip-lock baggie containing a brown dry substance. He placed the items on the refrigerator. He had finally answered Jason's request for decent coffee.

"Where we at?" he asked sharply as he pulled a stack of filters out of his pocket. In spite of bearing gifts, Willy's tone made clear he had an agenda.

"Well, there's some glitches, but I have a good part of it working now," Jason said.

"What sort of glitches?" Willy asked. "Or is it something I won't understand?"

Jason decided it wasn't worth the effort to explain or to argue with Willy so he bit his lip and said, "Nothing major. I have to do a little research on it."

"Okay then," Willy snapped, "Any idea when we will be up and running?"

"Maybe a day or two," Jason stated flatly.

Willy handed Jason a torn slip of paper and pointed out, "This is the password for that Wi-Fi box."

Jason took the paper. "That will help," he said. "Did you name it anything special?"

"Nope, just plugged it in," Willy said.

"That won't work," Jason said with obvious concern. "You have to set them up like I described to you."

Willy had trouble taking in the news, "What won't work?" he asked impatiently.

Jason kept his cool and focused on simply fixing Willy's clueless effort. He unplugged the wires from the Wi-Fi router box and calmly noted, "You have to set up new routers." He used a paperclip to reset the box. While he waited for it to reboot, he got his laptop and plugged the router into it. "This will only take a minute," he said. He opened a file on his laptop that had the result of his scan of the machines downstairs. He found an unused IP address and gave it to the router.

A few minutes later, he unplugged it and handed it to Willy. "Here, plug it into any of these ports, just not that one," he directed, pointing to a series of four plugholes on the back of the unit. "Don't use the yellow one."

"So you got the server and everything? Willy asked, as he put the router on the table.

"Wanda has a PayEasy account now, too," Jason said. "Do you want access to it?"

"Sure," Willy said.

Jason grabbed the pad and wrote down the email address and the password to the PayEasy account. He had to look those up in his log sheet, which, at this point, had nearly 50 email addresses and passwords.

"What's all that?" Willy asked.

"It's the email address I am using for a number of things," Jason explained. "I don't use the same server or password anywhere. The only linkage right now is that florist shop somewhere nearby."

"Is that why you have the flowers?" Willy asked. "I thought you got them to impress her."

Jason thought about that for a second, since she was sitting there. "Well, I'm using their Wi-Fi to mask where I'm at, so I thought it was fitting."

Willy turned his gaze to Tasha, who lowered her head and fixed her eyes on the floor. "You don't have to get 'em flowers or get 'em drunk... she knows what she's good for."

"The flowers are for me," Jason said feeling his temper rise.

Willy looked at Jason for a moment and decided he must really be gay and just playing straight for some suspicious reason.

Jason changed the subject, "Anyway, later today or tomorrow I need a couple of bed sheets ironed—one blue, one black." Jason said. "I also need a box of thumb tacks."

"What for?" Willy asked.

"I need to take pictures for making IDs. Make sure after they are ironed, use lots of starch and don't fold them; it will create lines in the material."

"Okay," said Willy, giving into yet another of Jason's strange but certain demands.

Jason picked up the router and handed it to Willy. "I really need the new one back. I can't do anything until I have it."

Willy pointed at the back of the router. "One of these?"

"Yes," Jason said. "Not the yellow one."

Willy nodded and left the room. Surprisingly, he didn't lock the door. Tasha looked at Jason. Jason shook his head and mouthed "no" to Tasha.

He walked toward Tasha and whispered into her ear, "We'll get out of here together soon. But not today, it's too risky."

While Jason waited for Willy's return, he went over a few questions that Tasha had on PHP. She had learned a lot so her questions were becoming more complex. She asked about how the program flowed, and he showed her how to use libraries.

"If you put program code that does a process in a separate file, this is called a library. You still use the separate file within your program. The process is called 'a call' or calling your library. Let's say I want to use the code again in some other program. Libraries make this easy." Jason said.

Tasha pointed to the visual studio and asked, "So you can do that in this?"

Jason nodded. "Yes, but there are several ways to handle it. But they end up being just like that. I'll show you one I'm using in the code I'm working on now in Java. It really is the same thing."

Jason went back to the computer and realized that he couldn't show her how to do it. He needed the router back from Willy. He decided it was time for a coffee break. "Do you know how to make coffee?" Jason asked Tasha.

"Yes, I make it strong," she said and headed to the bathroom to fill the coffee pot with water.

Willy returned to the room with the router Jason requested in his hand.

"Okay, good, let me see." Jason got on the laptop and successfully connected to the Wi-Fi router he had just given to Willy. He pulled up a web page just to check.

"So, you have everything you need for now?" Willy asked sarcastically.

"Maybe some more wine?" Jason said, unable to resist pushing the boundaries. "We kind of drank it all. You know, it's stressful being locked up like this."

"Well, it's all about business," Willy remarked as he walked out the door, this time locking it behind him.

In that moment Jason unknowingly reached the same conclusion as all the other slaves (and monsters) occupying the hotel. Willy was indeed the head "asshole."

In their confinement, something as basic as brewing coffee became a major event. Jason had to guess how much coffee to use for the four cups. He took the water from Tasha and filled the water reservoir. He turned the machine on and was halfway across the room when he heard Tasha ask, "Don't you have to plug it in?" Jason looked back and realized he had been caught spacing out. Tasha smiled affectionately as she plugged the unit into the wall outlet. They were beginning to function this way in many of their tasks. The room soon filled with the aroma of their combined effort.

Jason sat down to reconfigure the wireless router. He made it hook to the florist shop so it acted as a repeater for the shop's Wi-Fi network. Down there they thought their Internet was safe. They had no idea that nearby their Internet was being used to perpetuate a number of state, federal and international crimes. Jason was, for once, glad that few people think about the security of their Wi-Fi.

Tasha went back to working on learning the basics of PHP. After Jason got the Internet back up, he ran the test on the rest of the antivirus programs. It was the only one that detected it. But it was one of the big vendors, so it needed to be handled. It turned out that the fix was actually easy. Most antivirus and malware applications just look for a string inside the code to detect a virus or malware. Many times, just changing the string a little is enough to bypass them. By just adding a few useless characters into his file, he made it undetectable.

Next, he returned to his pet project. He called Tasha to join him. "See this advertisement?" He showed her a penis enlargement advertisement. "I need to duplicate this and make several slides that look similar," he explained. They pulled the file into Photoshop and within a few minutes had several variations that looked correct.

Jason moved the files back and put them on his web server in Africa. He also set up a new domain name and DNS Server for his trick to work.

Lunch finally arrived around noon. This time, a blonde with extremely long hair came in. She smelled like perfume. Like the rest, she looked down until she made out Tasha in her peripheral vision. Jason saw Tasha smile at this new girl just for a second before she put the trays down on the table and left.

Jason and Tasha ate their sandwiches and chicken noodle soup. "Did you eat like this every day before I came here?" Jason asked.

"Sometimes we are punished and so no food … Sometimes just they forget to feed us," Tasha said wearily.

"You've been punished?" Jason asked.

"You learn what you must do, but some girls don't learn fast and so nobody gets food, or if you are too close, then …" She made a harsh snapping noise. "… you get hurt."

Jason was disturbed by her matter-of-fact acceptance of the violence and abuse; it was obviously a regular and long-term feature of her life. She grew quiet and he suddenly felt bad for making her self-conscious. He attempted to change the subject, "So tell me about the first time you kissed a boy," he asked a bit awkwardly.

Tasha worked with him and answered, "My sister dared me to kiss the boy next door so I did," Tasha said. "Afterwards, he ran to his mother crying, saying that I hurt him." She smiled and giggled recalling the innocent incident.

Jason chuckled along. "Where did you kiss him?"

"On the cheek," Tasha said. "I got in so much trouble!"

"How old were you?" Jason continued.

"Four or five," she replied and returned with her own flirtatious question, "How about you Jason. When did you kiss?"

"I don't kiss boys," Jason joked, then turned more serious. "It was a girl on the playground when I was in grade school. Her name was Jean Shroder, and she told everybody I kissed her. It was really embarrassing to me then. Yeah…" he sighed, "she ruined me, that's why I'm so shy around women now."

"You don't seem shy to me," Tasha said.

"Well, you're beautiful and I like your style," he fondly recalled. "It was hard to feel shy after what you did when we first met!"

They both laughed and finished their lunch. Then it was back to their computers.

However, a little while later Jason couldn't resist asking, "Do you know that girl that came in?"

"Yes," said Tasha, "We were put together when we came here"

"She wears perfume," Jason noted.

"That's for the Japanese man," Tasha said. "He likes perfume. Bad perfume," she added dryly, pinching her nose to further make her point.

"I see," Jason said and realized that they were becoming distracted. He shook himself and decided, "Let's get back at it … I'm making some progress. How about you?"

They moved the chairs back in front of the computer Tasha was using. She seemed to sigh and offered, "I'm coming along. I mean, I'm getting part of it but the syntax isn't right. It doesn't tell me when there is an error, there's no error message."

"There's another program you can use," Jason said. "Let's start building the scraper together on your computer." He went back to the visual tool. He opened a web page to find Ajax for visual studio. "Ajax is just another one of those programs or scripts that provides features," Jason explained.

The two worked on the scraping script for Facebook until dinnertime. They were making some headway and could pull needed information off the Facebook page.

"That will really save some time," Tasha observed proudly.

"I know," Jason agreed. "You know, if it works, we can get all of the information directly from Facebook. I wish I had the tool they give the police, so you don't have to do all of this page by page."

"The police look at Facebook?" Tasha asked.

"Sure, it's the first thing the cops and private investigators do," Jason said. "It's becoming a huge source of profit to cellular and other companies – nowadays they all have department specializing in selling their information to law enforcement."

"How soon will you have the Twitter thing working?" Tasha asked.

"It's still a work in progress, but maybe we could adapt what we are doing here to that. Or maybe something someone already wrote." They worked for a little bit longer.

Tasha asked, "Tell me about your parents."

"My father was a very kind man," Jason said. "They had me when they were quite old, so my father died before I graduated from college. My mother got dementia or Alzheimer's—no one seemed to know for sure, but she ended up in a nursing home and she died almost seven years ago. When I was young, my father was interested in everything. He wanted to understand how everything worked. If you couldn't figure it out, he would either buy the item or get it out of a trash can. It didn't matter if was electrical or mechanical. He would take hours explaining things to me. He bought books to tutor me. He brought home a payphone telephone once and showed me how to make a box so you didn't need to pay. But the catch was I had to understand how it worked, or I couldn't have it."

"How about your mother?" Tasha asked.

"My mother was kind, too. She liked to bake when I was younger. I remember the wonderful pies she would make. She used to make me try different food. 'You just have to take one bite,' she would say. She loved the garden and grew a number of kinds of flowers. She knew all of their names, but I never caught on. She would repeat them over and over, but they just never stuck in my head. I really don't know why." Jason paused and turned the attention back to Tasha, "How about your father?"

"Poppa was a very nice man," Tasha began. "He had really big hands, and they were as rough as sandpaper, but he was so gentle with my sister and me. He worked so hard so we had a house. He would work night and day for weeks. We wouldn't see him and then he would come home and have money to take us somewhere or buy my mother a new dress. When I was really little, he would read me stories. He would always ask if I heard them before and I would say, 'No, Poppa, never in my life,' even if I had heard the stories many times before. He would swing me around which made me so happy but it made my sister angry because he stopped swinging her when she got big, at least that is what he would say. My mother made everything good. She washed the floor twice a day and we were never to make a mess. She planted a wonderful garden, a garden just for cooking, so when she cooked, everything was fresh. She grew oregano, basil and lots more. When I was little, she would put mint leaves on me to smell nice. Now, when I smell mint, I think of her. Even now, she tells me that I will get out of this place and have my life back."

Tasha paused for a long moment, then continued, her voice quavering with sadness, "One day a bomb blew up the house while we slept. My ears rang for a very long time after that, and sometimes I can still hear them … everyone dying. My sister and I ended up in an orphanage for a while. In that place she was my mom, my second mom, you know? When she was old enough, she got a sewing job and a small apartment and sent for me. I was still very young; I wasn't in high school yet. She wanted to meet a very special man but she had her little sister at home. It was so long ago… I hope she met someone."

Tasha looked at Jason, her eyes filled with tears and genuine grief and her English failing more and more with each word. "I think you are the first nice person I have to talk to for many years," she lamented. "So many people leave me in my life. Maybe it is meant, you find me."

"I'm not sure I was meant to find you," Jason said. "But I know for certain I'm happy that we met -- even in this crazy place you make me feel lucky." They sat quietly holding hands and falling deeper into their growing affection. Finally, Jason realized they had done all they could for the day and it was time to simply surrender the day. Nonetheless, he asked Tasha, "Do you feel like working on this anymore tonight?

"No, not really," she sighed weakly.

"OK, I think we're both really tired; let's go to bed," Jason said. He grasped her hand and led her to the bedroom, flipping off the light on the way. Once in bed, they laid in each other's arms in a silent, warm embrace until sleep finally overtook them.

16

Buying The Needed Tools

J ason woke up with Tasha still asleep in his arms. He lay in bed
for a while wondering why he tended to wake up so early at the
Hotel, while at home he never got up early and would
instead hit the snooze button for an hour or more. But here he
was, suddenly alert at the crack of dawn most every day. He carefully
slid out from underneath Tasha, who was taking her turn at being
the sleepy one. After time in the bathroom, he brewed more coffee.
It was nice to have coffee when he needed it. Then again, Willy's 'gift'
reminded Jason that the clock was ticking. "Guess I just answered
my question," he grumbled to himself, realizing that Willy wasn't
trying to be nice but instead offering caffeine to push things along.
Finally, somberly considering his situation, Jason mused, "Better
the carrot than the stick."

It was time to get to work. Being very careful about where he sat
in the room, Jason reconnected to the Wi-Fi on the camera network.
The guy with the baseball hat was back to his usual early-morning

siesta. After poking around for a while Jason was able to observe 25 women -- though he knew there must be at least 30, since there were two shifts of 15 women working at the computers. He came to the conclusion that there must be additional rooms with no video surveillance containing the missing women. Jason disconnected from the Wi-Fi and moved on to another machine, the one he worked on most. He checked the connection log for the web server he had built in Africa and was surprised to see that the script was installed on hundreds, if not thousands, of computers throughout the world. So, curious, he tried one of the computers with the script.

Jason shut down the web connection for a single IP address, waited, ran his program and made a connection. It was that easy. Many home and corporate routers are vulnerable to this trick, called the "double bind attack." He typed "Dir /s" and the entire contents of the hard drive appeared as a list. He pushed over his little script and installed it as service so it would request or "ask" the server what to do every six hours, but only if the CPU was less than 60 percent busy. It only runs if the computer is not busy doing something else which might raise attention to the attack.

Suddenly he found something unexpected. "So what do we have here?" he murmured. He ran a few commands to get the name of the person logged in. He opened a web page and located the IP address to an area in Philadelphia. He looked into the documents folder. There were millions of them! He found one called "invoice920.pdf" and copied that to his computer. He opened the file, which was an invoice from a law firm to a client for services. He checked and the computer was on a network with drives mapped, so he simply listed the container of a folder called "Accounting," and found a "QuickBooks" file. He copied the file which took quite a while, since it was so large. He went back to the documents folder and found a folder called "Personal." Inside was a resume. He downloaded the file but didn't have a program to open it. It was in "WordPerfect" format, and he needed QuickBooks to open the accounting file.

Jason disconnected from the computer and downloaded "Open Office." In an effort to open the WordPerfect file. It took awhile to find QuickBooks and install its trial version. When he tried to open the QuickBooks file, it turned out to be the wrong version, so he had to wait for it to convert to the version he had installed. Once upgraded, it wanted a user name. He tried "admin" and for the password he tried "password," which, as clueless as it seems, sometimes worked. But today, there was no such luck. He tried to search the Internet for a "password crack" for Quickbooks and got back 400,000 hits. Most of them claimed they could do it for a fee, but there were a couple, that were free. The first one he downloaded didn't work. The second one, however, popped up a little window that listed all of the usernames and their passwords. The instruction at the top of the program screen was to leave the file up and copy and paste the credentials into QuickBooks.

Jason opened QuickBooks again, entering the user name and password. The program loaded and displayed a bank balance of $453,702.74 – a very nice war chest for his secret plans. *"So, let's see,"* Jason thought. *"I could write a check, but have no way to print it. Let's just store that file for a bit, he thought to himself."*

Jason closed the program. He opened the résumé of an attorney that listed the office address and phone number. He was a named partner in a small firm of four partners. Jason was increasingly excited by his success in this new arena. He had dabbled in petty hacking schemes before but he had never been particularly serious about stealing money, let alone a lot of money. His program worked a little better than he expected. He downloaded the log file from the web server and found the connection log had well over 10,000 distinct computer addresses in it. He had access on each computer just for going to the wrong website.

With his success it was time to do some shopping. Jason went to an internet auction site and checked it against a few of the online stores for a color laser printer, an inkjet high-quality photo printer, an all-in-one printer with fax and a box of thin foil in four colors – in particular, gold and silver. He also needed toner and ink for the printers; an ID lamination machine; a die cutter for ID-sized cuts; a standard iron soldering iron; a multimeter; hot glue and a hot-glue gun; Dremel tool and lots of bits; and a set of screwdrivers. To avoid the wait for deliveries from China, he focused on sellers near his location. Jason smiled with satisfaction but decided that was enough for now until he could verify that his efforts were successful. Besides, he could hear Tasha beginning to wake up.

Jason got her a coffee and crouched on the bed, grinning ear to ear.

She saw his delight and asked sleepily. "What?"

"You're absolutely beautiful," Jason said.

Tasha blushed. "You are crazy man" she mumbled with a thick accent.

"You really are beautiful," he insisted.

"If you think so, okay, but I don't know that. I think you are in a very good mood," she observed.

"Good morning, then?" Jason offered.

"Good morning," Tasha said politely, then headed straight to the bathroom.

"Okay, I have your coffee," Jason said holding her cup as she whisked by him.

Tasha spoke from the bathroom. "Oh yeah, we have coffee now," she said a bit preoccupied. "But I think we need tampons today."

"Yes, isn't it great?" Jason said.

Tasha replied a little confused, "What is great, coffee machine or tampons?"

"Yes," Jason replied, still celebrating his newfound appreciation for coffee when he really needed it. "This machine is a good one," he added. Then taking in what she had said he spoke into the camera in the bedroom. "We need some tampons, O.K.?" After he said it, he wondered how all the muscle-bound men around him managed the realities of holding so many women hostage. It must involve lots of up-close encounters with feminine hygiene products.

Tasha finally came out of the bathroom and took her coffee. As he handed it to her, he kissed her on the cheek. While holding the coffee, she put her arms on his shoulders in an embrace. "So what makes you so happy this morning?" she said.

"I'm making great progress---things I only dreamed of doing before," Jason said.

"What do you mean 'things'?" Tasha asked.

"There are things that most people just don't do..." Jason started. Then he paused, stuck for a moment recalling where they were standing, and the life that she led; the 'things" she had to endure, including the horrors. Compared to her experiences, the 'things' he was doing suddenly seemed like nothing, unimportant, unworthy of his excitement.

Tasha was waiting.

"It's just really cool stuff," Jason said. "I'm mostly lucky you're here with me."

"I am many things," Tasha said. "But I am not lucky, my dear."

Instead of trying to talk her out of it, Jason and Tasha laughed at the strangeness, so hard in fact they managed to spill some of their precious coffee.

"So you want to get back to the code?" Jason finally asked.

"Sure," Tasha replied, feeling heard and accepted.

They went to the computer and reran the code for scraping the user list and immediately encountered a snag. "When you don't have permission, there is no data," Jason noted. They worked had to find a clever route around that problem.

"You know, we may have overlooked something important here," Jason remarked.

"What's that?" Tasha asked.

"Their lists of 'friends'," Jason continued. "We should track that too." He slid over to the other machine and brought up the configuration screen he had created for fields in his database, and made a few changes. He went back over to Tasha, "For each friend, look and see if they--- uh, never mind," he muttered as he worked the problem.

"Okay," Tasha said.

Jason ran the program on the other monitor. They watched the work queue jump from 10,585 to 30,492. Jason stopped the program. "Well, that shouldn't have happened."

"Well, you added people," Tasha said.

"What do you mean?" Jason asked.

"Well, you added friends, they have friends and so on," Tasha explained. "They are not what you call the primary group. They are six or seven. You called them branches or something, anyway."

"Oh," Jason uttered in surprise at Tasha's growing skill, then made sure to add, "I get it now, thanks!". He went back to the other computer and typed and clicked furiously. He slid his chair next to Tasha. The work queue number changed back to 10,585. Jason ran the program and he and Tasha watched the work queue: 10,585, 10,586, 10,587, 10,586, 10,584…

They admired the beauty of their joint effort and barely noticed as it became fully daylight. It was a surprise when the door unlocked and the brunette appeared. Her hair looked clean and the bruises on her inner thighs had healed to a sickly yellow. She put the breakfast trays on the table and cleared all the old items. She had been quickly brought in line with the others, moving quietly, head down and without a pause. As soon as the door closed behind her, Tasha and Jason sat down for their breakfast.

"See?" Tasha said.

"See what?" Jason asked.

"She is controlled now so they cleaned her up," Tasha observed. "She has no value here until she is washed up … Other places I have worked don't care about that, just that you are 'working,' but here, you have to be washed."

"I see," Jason said. He could tell that she had become an authority on being trafficked. Moreover, Tasha's comfort level in talking about such matters was growing, so much so it began to simply merge with their working chatter. "So what is reading now ... I can't see it from this angle?" he asked her.

Tasha leaned back to read the number. "9,482."

"Very cool, we'll let that run," Jason said.

"I want to learn more about C today," Tasha announced.

"Okay, but after we eat," Jason replied. "Things are really picking up so you can only use one monitor, not two."

"I don't care," she replied. "How many more things are you going to add?" Tasha asked.

"I really don't know," Jason pondered. "There is some more information like home addresses, list of cars and bank stuff that has to be done by hand, but for a very few."

"Some of these information is from other countries," Tasha said. "I saw someone from Romania ... there are a lot of people there and other places."

Jason was sitting with his back to the camera and put his index finger up to his lips and looked at Tasha. "When are you going to play for me again?"

Tasha understood that they were changing the subject for the camera. "I don't feel like playing now," she said. "I want to be a coder."

"Really? You don't look like a coder," he said.

"What do you mean?" she asked.

"Most coders are overweight boys," he mused.

"Really?" she said, surprised.

"Yes, it's not usually a 'girl thing,'" he quipped.

"Well, I like it," Tasha said, revealing an unexpected side-effect of existing outside of mainstream society.

"That's great," said Jason supportively, "then let's get you set up," With that he set her up on the other computer with C sharp and found her place with the tutorial.

"I don't see my stuff," Tasha said, distressed. Then she shook her heard. "Never mind, I don't need it."

"Okay," Jason said. He was already hard at work and not fully conscious of what she was talking about.

Jason glanced at the work queue. It had gone above 10k again, but then back down again while he stood there. It was perhaps a bulky collection of information, but worth it. The program was taking the information from Facebook names of relatives and friends and figuring out who was part of the primary list of 1,500. Even if someone doesn't have a Facebook account, his or her wife or kid may have one. Jason didn't have facial recognition nor had he ever worked with it, so he had no idea of whom or what he was dealing with. They were a group of very powerful people. This little information-gathering exercise would buy him a huge edge in this situation. These people were his primary interest and would be the key to his plan.

Jason remembered he needed to rebuild the computer that was infected by watching the online movie. So he got started. Luckily, just by pressing the F11 key at startup, a factory restore started, erasing all changes to the drive since it had left the factory.

Tasha got up and went to the bathroom. Jason looked on then recalled her request. He looked up at the camera, annoyed, and said, "Hey, tampons, did you forget?"

He returned to the penis enlargement website to check the logs. There had been over 20,000 visitors to the advertisement. He was in the middle of connecting to another computer located in Montreal, when the door opened and a tall brunette entered. Jason had never seen her before but she seemed like she knew the drill. Her head was down and she avoided eye contact. Her hair was long and Jason could not see much of her face. She brought in a small cardboard box that contained two bottles of wine and a box of tampons. She left quickly, the door locking behind her.

Jason put the wine away and called out to Tasha that the tampons had finally arrived.

She called out from the bathroom matter-of-factly, "Could you bring me one?"

In another moment of strange but growing domestic life, Jason took her the whole box and put it at her feet as she sat on the toilet.

"Thank you," Tasha said gratefully, as someone who had long become unaccustomed to being accommodated.

Jason went back to the computer to check on connections that were active. The first few he tried didn't work. He knew that the process was not foolproof. The third one, however, made a connection. There really weren't any files on the computer in documents, only a few pictures. Unfortunately, there was no way of opening files remotely. He had to download them instead. The pictures all looked like family photos. One showed small children playing in leaves. Another showed the same children playing in the snow.

Jason checked to see if that computer was connected to any others. There was nothing.

Tasha was back at the computer and remarked, "I don't understand why this won't work … Can you help me with this?"

" "Let me take a look," Jason offered, disconnecting from the remote computer. She had generated a lot of code and it took a while for him to find that she had missed a closing statement. "You need this semi-colon here," he noted and pointed at the screen to a typical mistake made by starting programmers.

"Oh, how did I miss that?" Tasha moaned, frustrated by how such a small and easily made mistake could be so crucial.

"It happens all the time," Jason pointed. "The good news is that there's a website that can check the code for you," he said enthusiastically. "Let me in there and I'll find it for you." He sat down and looked in a web browser for a site that he had used before. After a few minutes and plying through several false leads, he found it. "Just copy your code into this box and press 'validate'," he instructed enthusiastically. Tasha, encouraged by the new tool, returned to coding without a word.

Jason connected his laptop to the Wi-Fi network connected to the cubicles on the floor below. He opened the screen of one of the computers and watched for a while. That particular woman was on Facebook as well as several chat sessions at the same time with multiple clients.

Jason asked Tasha to come over to him. "What is she doing?" he asked. "I don't get it."

"Oh, that's what we all do here," Tasha said. "We get people to sign up to watch web shows, and let them know when there will be a 'special,' you know, when there is some girl who is with a lot of men. It doesn't matter if she wants that, she must have sex with all of them so the customers can watch."

Jason struggled with the now familiar atmosphere of enslavement and rape, but tried to stay on task. "How do you contact them for a special?" he asked.

"I have many Facebook accounts, each for every type of special," Tasha said. "I also have one that I use for joining, so I can tell someone online that my friend is interested in that."

Jason thought for a moment, then asked with additional alarm, "Are some of the other specials with children?"

"Yes, we all have Facebook profiles for those, too. We let our friends know when something is going to happen."

"Are all of your customers your friends on Facebook?" Jason asked.

Tasha shook her head. "No, most of them we email, some we text—it depends on how they contact us. She pointed to the screen. "See that? That is a program that has a cell phone number. The person they are chatting with is on a cell phone."

"So what is this person selling?" Jason asked. They both looked at the screen, reading the chat messages on AOL.

"She is telling him that she has a 'performance' on one of the websites," Tasha said. "This guy is new, so we make money from the new member when they sign up, and if the performer is one that is with us, we make some from what the performer makes while other people watch."

Jason paused for a moment in amazement of the efficiency of the scam as it economically benefitted from both the 'johns' and 'performers' essentially as new-age pimps. "So who is the performer now?" Jason he continued.

"It doesn't matter," Tasha explained. "It doesn't look like she is working with a special or anything, so the performer doesn't matter. She is maybe telling him that it is her who performs."

"I see, but how do you know when someone wants something else?" Jason inquired.

"They will tell us," Tasha said. "Sometimes they say weird things or ask for something they want. Sometimes I have three or four people on at the same time so I have to send the customer to someone else, maybe someone sitting next to me."

"So how did you get picked to do this?" Jason asked.

"I understand computers, so they sold me here," she replied matter-of-factly.

"Did you ever do the web performance thing," he asked then thought better of it. "Maybe I shouldn't ask?"

"No, I never did that, and no, you should not ask," Tasha said offered.

Jason kissed Tasha on the cheek, and whispered, "Thank you."

Jason got up and went back to his experiments when the door unlocked. Each time he heard the lock. He glanced at Tasha. He never looked at her when the door had opened before and noticed she paused and put her head down and waited to find out who entered. He wondered if she always had that reaction. The girl that entered was the same one with the bruising on her legs. The bruises were almost gone. She brought in lunch and picked up the older trays. Then she robotically turned around, knocked on the door was gone with barely a sound.

"I am so hungry today," Tasha said as she devoured grilled cheese sandwiches and warm chicken soup, which surprisingly appeared homemade.

Jason looked on and commented "Yeah, you must be hungry…" Then he decided it was as good a time as any to follow up on what he had observed moments before. "Why do you put your head down when the door opens? And why do the girls always have their head down when they come in?" he asked cautiously.

"We are not supposed to look at their faces," Tasha said. "You get in trouble if they can see your eyes."

"I was just wondering," Jason said, still puzzled but beginning to get a deeper idea of what it meant to be a slave and how vicious the men must be to generate such fear and obedience.

The door unlocked and Willy came in looking wild-eyed. "How close are you?" he asked sharply.

Jason had to swallow before speaking but tried to behave with confidence, "I'm pretty close, I guess. I tested a few things. Not the video part, though."

"In 15 minutes there'll be a show that you can test it on," Willy said. "What I want is for you to record the screen and the email address. You also need to record the webpage at the same time. Can you combine the picture … like put their image at the bottom or top or something and put it together?"

"I haven't tested that far," Jason said. "It may not work all the way."

"You can do all of them though, right?" Willy demanded.

"It doesn't work that way," Jason explained. "I can only do one at a time,"

Willy only partly took in his response then said "It's time to do your stuff."

"I understand," Jason offered, "but I told you I'd need a couple of days."

"So can you do any of it?" Willy asked with increasing impatience.

"You didn't tell me the method of payment or what it is I am actually doing," Jason said.

"I just did," Willy said shifting his posture to stand with his hands on his hips.

"I can try," Jason said trying to keep control of the situation. "I can't tell you if everything will work, and a lot of it has to be done by hand. I don't know if I can get the email address just now. That might take a while. I never wrote the scripts for that either."

Willy pulled out his phone and looked at the time." You have 12 minutes to figure it out."

"I can try, but I can't guarantee anything."

"Well, get to it."

"What's the page?" Jason asked, noting that he was quickly losing control of events.

"Look for the video called 'Mable'," Willy said. "Do you have a log-in for the site? … I can log you in as me," Willy said as he tried to figure out which computer he could use. "Which of these should I use?" he asked.

Jason looked at the one he was rebuilding. It was still busy. He went to the one that Tasha was using and pulled up a webpage. Willy walked over and logged in.

Jason looked over at Tasha who was sitting with her head down and her hands by her sides. A part of her sandwich was still on the plate.

"Tasha, could you take your food to the other room?" Jason asked.

Tasha still had her head down but he saw her as she flashed him a smile.

"Take my soup away, too," Jason said, so she could eat that too. Tasha walked into the bedroom.

"Okay, she isn't on yet," Willy said. He looked at his phone again.

Jason went over to the other machine and looked at the web log.

"I need it to start first so I know which log entry to look for."

"Any time now," Willy said annoyed.

Jason checked his script to detected webcams on his laptop and it failed to find his. "This is wrong," he said.

"What's wrong?" Willy asked.

"The way I check for web cameras doesn't work right."

"So you can't record a video?"

"I told you I wasn't ready," Jason said. "I asked you for a couple of laptops and you never got them for me."

"Fuck man, now you're bullshittin' … you know good and well you can do it!" Willy said angrily.

"I can do it, just not now" Jason said dryly. "I still need to test it. I told you yesterday I needed a couple of days."

"Shit," Willy said. "Okay, look, if you can't do it…"

Jason sensed in the ultimatum and tried to get things back under his control. "I said I need more time," he said. "I need the laptops. Right now, I can only detect some models of webcam and turn them off; it's not foolproof."

"So this is a waste of time then," Willy said glaring at Jason.

"We're well on our way to making this happen," Jason said firmly. "But I need the laptops to test with and the webcam. All the stuff on that list I gave you. You need to do your job and get me that equipment."

Willy glared at Jason then shook his head and seemed to back down. "Okay, okay, I get it," he said, but then shook his finger at Jason and threatened, "I'll get you the stuff, but you better be ready next time."

Willy walked towards the door.

"I'll do what I can, but I need time to test this stuff," Jason repeated.

Willy slammed the door behind him. The lock clicked a second later.

That was the worst exchange yet between them. Willy was a loose cannon and threatened to jump the gun on Jason's plans.

Jason regained his composure enough to realize that Willy had made a serious mistake. Jason return to the computer Willy had logged onto. It had a search page up. Mable was in the "search for" field and the result said: NO RECORD EXISTS, PLEASE TRY AGAIN.

Jason looked at the clock and waited for a minute to pass. Tasha came back in and was standing behind him.

Jason hit the search button and a screen popped up. The penis enlargement advertisement was on the side of the screen. Jason reached over and unplugged the wireless router. He was still connected on the florist network and he didn't want whatever was going to appear to be there, but instead be on the network downstairs.

It took a few minutes to reconfigure the network so that the connection was downstairs. When he was reconnected and logged into the web server, he reached over and pressed the refresh button on the web page. It popped up with the message: PLEASE LOG IN AGAIN, YOUR SESSION HAS EXPIRED.

Jason sat for a minute, thinking. He looked at the monitor and saw the "youpostit" note that said "victim." Then he smiled. He looked for his hidden directory that the keylogger that he was experimenting with had created. He pulled up the log, which was enormous. It had captured every keystroke made on the machine including the code examples Tasha was working on. He had to download a program since Windows doesn't have the basic tools for viewing files from the end.

A few minutes later, he had Willy's log-in and password, 'longbanana.' Jason went to the website, logged in and searched for Mable. What came on the screen was a web camera video feed of a man that looked like he was possibly Filipino receiving oral sex from a young boy that looked like he was 10 or 12. What went through Jason's mind was total disgust. He reached over and hit the print screen button on the keyboard.

Jason looked at the log and found a computer that was watching the video. He tried his web cam as he found that "script it" failed, so he manually looked at the remote computers' installed hardware list. There was no camera installed, at least not one that he could find. He connected to another computer. The log file had about 875 computers looking at the live video feed, at that point.

It took eight computers until he could find one that had a camera installed. It was not one that he could use however, as it was a brand that he had never heard of. He opened another web page and looked up the manufacturer and how to turn off the light, but he couldn't find anything. So he disconnected from that one. The process was slow. Tasha silently watched his efforts. She could tell just by looking at him, that he was getting frustrated, but didn't yet have the skills to help him on the computer. She began to rub his shoulders while he worked.

Jason tried a few more machines, but none of them had a known camera. The entire experiment failed. He had some work to do.

Jason logged onto the web server and set a command for his remote to dump the registry of all the infected machines and store it as a file, and copy it to the web server. The file would be named the IP address of the infected computer. This would give him the last known public address of the infected computer. Jason worked on that script for the next several hours.

Tasha came back and rubbed his neck a bit more. She whispered into his ear that dinner was there. He hadn't heard the door open or seen who brought it. He needed this to work. He wasn't ready to put his plan into action and didn't want Willy to conclude he had literally outlived his 'usefulness.'

Jason took a break to eat dinner. He and Tasha sat down to chicken and mashed potatoes. Tasha looked at him sympathetically and asked cautiously, "Jason what happened?"

"The part of the recording remote video didn't work right," Jason explained. "Some of the computers didn't have cameras. Others had cameras, but I couldn't them."

"Is there anything I can help you with?" Tasha asked.

"I don't think so," he said thoughtfully, then smiled to note her generosity.

"Can I sit with you while you work and watch or does it bother you?"

"Oh, no, you don't bother me," said Jason suddenly.

"Do you know how to fix it?" she asked.

"I'm not sure yet, maybe," Jason said rubbing the side of his head thoughtfully.

"Maybe you need some wine?" Tasha offered responding to his obvious stress.

"Yeah, good idea," Jason agreed gratefully.

"I'll get it." Tasha offered Tasha as she rose and went to the refrigerator. She took out a bottle out. "We still don't have an opener," she said looking at him.

"Sure we do," Jason reminded her as he reached for the bottle, took his screwdriver and pushed the cork inside the bottle. He poured each of the a generous amount and they resumed their meal.

Tasha continued to try to distract him from his worries. "What are you like out there?" Tasha asked.

"What do you mean?" Jason replied surprised by the question. "We've been spending all this time together."

"I know, but only here, in this place. You spent time out there, you know, in 'America.' What are you like there?" Tasha asked.

Jason chuckled at the unusual question. "Well, it's hard to say," Jason thought a bit. "I work, sleep, look for love. Every once in a while, I go to a bar or pub and have a drink or two, then go home or to the movies. I really wish there was someone like you to spend time with..."

Tasha smiled in response to the compliment, "What kind of love were you looking for?" Tasha asked with a hint of flirtation.

"I'm not sure how to answer that," Jason said. "You know, I looked for a girlfriend. Someone who was smart, nice, kind—someone one I could marry and have a family with, I guess."

"Do you like children?" Tasha asked.

"That's hard to answer. I haven't spent much time around children, but I would like that," Jason said, suddenly turning the tables on her. "How's about you … do you want a family?"

"I used to dream of a life that had a big house and things, but when I first came here, I cleaned a big house, and took care of an old woman," Tasha said. "The people made me stay in the house and clean and polish everything every day. I worked so hard… I never want a big house. There are more important things."

"I see," Jason said, noting that she hadn't fully answered the question. "Well I never lived in a big house. I grew up in a small house and then I moved to a small apartment.. Then I came here." They chatted a bit more and Jason did in fact feel better, more relaxed and able to focus. When they had finished eating, he took his cup of wine and went back to work.

Throughout the wee hours of the night and beyond he worked on his script on both of the computers and on his virtual XP computers. It looked like it might work, so he copied it to the web server and had to wait for the six hours to elapse so that his automatic script would run on the infected machines. He forced the connection and checked it. It looked like it worked, but he was too tired to appreciate it.

He turned around and saw that Tasha had already gone to bed. The time on the computer was 3:31 a.m. Jason shut off the light and joined her.

17

More Data Collection

Tasha shook Jason awake. "Good morning, sleepy one. Wakie, wakie," she whispered into his ear affectionately.

"What time is it?" Jason asked, rubbing his eyes in confusion.

"I don't know, but breakfast is here," Tasha said.

"I was at it until late," Jason muttered, still half-asleep.

"Yes, I went to bed first," she replied. "Do you want to eat here?"

Jason staggered to his feet and put on the pants he had been wearing for the last two days. He headed straight for the bathroom. When he came out, he found Tasha waiting for him at the table in the office. He could smell coffee in the air. He sat down and took a sip of the coffee, it was very strong. He smiled at Tasha. Waking to her presence was about the only perk for him in this crappy adventure.

"How did it go last night, did you make progress?" Tasha asked.

"I think so," Jason said. "I'll see today if everything works right.

I will need your help looking through a bunch of files I made to do different kinds of things. In your tutorial, did you cover opening a file and comparing strings yet?"

"I did some of that," Tasha answered. "But I don't know about opening files."

"That's okay, it's easy," Jason said. "Man, I miss bacon."

"What?" Tasha asked struggling to interpret.

"Life is just better with bacon," he quipped, momentarily homesick for normal life.

"I don't understand," Tasha said, looking entirely too serious.

"It's okay," Jason chuckled. "You're better than bacon!"

She continued to stare at him, perplexed, but his smile reassured her. Jason found himself once again marveling at Tasha's natural beauty. He could grow old happily looking into those eyes... Suddenly he snapped back into reality – regardless of his attractive company, they were expendable meat in an increasingly dangerous trap. And he really could no longer remember how many days he had been locked away, or for that matter the date or day of the week. The days in the hotel just seemed to run together and it took all his willpower and energy to keep working -- he needed to get the hell out of there

Jason finished his cup of coffee and held it up so the last drop would run into his mouth.

"Would you like some more?" Tasha asked.

"Sure, but can you fill it halfway and put water in it?" He handed her his cup.

"Did I make it too strong?"

"Never!," Jason said, "but I need to keep my cool."

"Cool, huh?" she responded, charmed by his seeming confidence and self-control. He was so unlike the men at the hotel, most of whom were impulsive animals and slaves themselves – to drugs, sex and most of all, a fearfulness that made them need to brutalize others to prove their strength.

Tasha got up to make more coffee. As Jason chewed the last scrap of toast, he stacked up the trays and cleaned. He realized he was procrastinating and finally moved his chair over to the computer. He had left the monitor on and the connection to the web server. He found thousands of files that were the copies of Windows registry files from the remote computers. He deleted the script so no new machines would run the command and copy more. He had plenty of data to work with.

Tasha sat a coffee down next to Jason then rolled a chair beside him so she could watch and learn. Jason started the process of downloading the files. Tasha could see that the Windows registry was the main setting file for the Windows operating system. It lists not only every device installed, but it also includes the settings of every program installed. Most of the time, no one pays attention to this file, but Jason needed to examine it to understand what he was dealing with. He made sure that he grabbed the log file also so he could limit the machines that were looking at the video later.

Jason worked with Tasha to build a program to look for just the files that were associated with the video. The files had yet to be downloaded and there were 36,000 computers now running his code. Jason was worried that sooner or later someone would discover the software he had written. Then, one by one, the antivirus companies or the spyware companies would start blocking his program. It would take another two hours for all of the files to be copied to his local computer.

They tested the program they had built and it seemed to do just the first part, sorting them correctly. They ran the program and found that there were 3,801 computers that had given their computer registries that had also watched the video. All the rest were computers that had watched other videos on the website.

Now they had to write something to look for the presence of a known web cam. Jason first wrote something to break them up by computer manufacturer. The program took awhile to process them all. The files by this time had finally downloaded, so they ran the sorting process again. Only one additional computer was added to the watched video group.

Lunch came, and Jason was still working. Tasha was increasingly contributing but decided it was better that Jason kept working, so she collected the food from the trays and brought it to the table for them to eat as they watched the programs run. Her support helped him get over the hump. After he sorted the data, Jason finally had the information he was after.

He looked up at the camera and raised his arm to wave, then abruptly stopped. He waited a moment to make sure Tasha was finished eating. As she finished he suddenly waved to the camera and demanded, "Tell Willy I need to see him!"

Jason was still making pie and bar charts when he heard the click of the door. As if on cue, Tasha walked into the bedroom as the door opened.

Willy walked in. "Well what do you have?" he said flatly, not attempting to seem friendly.

"I was able to find out some things about your group." Jason began. "Of the 3801 machines that I collected information on, only 421 had web cams installed or at least ones that that I could find."

Jason handed Willy a pie chart showing what he was explaining. "This small sliver represents the 52 webcams that will work with the code that I have written. If you get me the laptops to test with, I can probably guarantee that I can make them work. However, without having the laptops I asked for, I have no way of knowing if the camera is even on. There's also lots of old machines. This chart is a breakdown of the same 421, by computer manufacturer."

Jason showed Willy another chart that had lots of slices. "This is a breakdown of the machines by manufacturer. Not all of these have cameras installed, but it gives a clearer picture of what they are using."

"That's a lot of computers," Willy sighed, slowly shaking his head.

"Yes," Jason said. "What I need to do is alter the script a bit so it checks and notifies me if a connected machine has the supported hardware … recording video that is."

"I think I get it," Willy said. "Do you still need the laptops?"

"Well, it would help add to the collection, but you still didn't tell me how you wanted to get paid."

"That's what I set the bank account up for," Willy said.

"If you want to use the PayEasy that's already set up; do you have an email set to go out?"

"No, I don't have that yet," Willy said.

Jason was annoyed by Willy's inability to keep up with the scheme, but he continued in a matter-of-fact tone, "Another issue is the email account." Jason brought up another pie chart showing a breakdown of different web browsers. "These were the browsers used to connect to the video," he elaborated. "Now I can tell which of these has installed a version of local clients like 'Outlook,' but I have no way of knowing if they use webmail. I can get into their history and look at what they have gone to, but it would take a while. I think what would be best is to just record them and save the file, and figure out later what they use and go back and find what they use for email."

"That sounds okay," Willy said, perking up a bit. "How long will it take?"

"I honestly don't know," Jason replied. "I can get more information from the ones in the small 52-person group and see what more I can find. Do you have a way to get the email address they used to log-in to that web page?"

"I think so," Willy said. "I'm not sure there are many reports on how much we make. It might be listed … I'm not sure."

"Can we look?" Jason asked.

"Which computer do you want to use?" Willy asked.

"This one," he said pointing at the one Tasha typically used and, more importantly, the one Willy had logged onto before.

Willy pulled up a chair and logged onto the website. He clicked on "manage account." and used some sort of access. The site listed the shows that his group had promoted and the IP addresses of the client with their usernames, but it didn't say which username looked at which show and the usernames were not necessarily email addresses. After clicking on a number of tabs in the management section of the site, even working together, they couldn't find anything useful.

"That really doesn't help," Jason concluded.

Willy, always focused on immediate gratification, failed to see the obvious and clicked desperately on a few more ways of looking at the same report. He stared at the computer, frustrated. "I guess not," he finally conceded. A useful exercise in that it justified Jason's claims.

"It'll take a little longer to figure this out, "Jason said. "Why don't you come up with an email to send them? In the meantime, I'll look at getting email addresses from the ones I have already captured and see what I can get."

"Sounds like a plan," Willy conceded. He got up to leave. "I can see you're gettin' closer," he said, almost respectfully.

"Yeah, well, it takes time," Jason repeated, unable to resist rubbing in what he had told Willy from the start.

Willy opened the door and Jason heard the telltale click. With the coast now clear, Tasha immediately came back into the room. "Can you really get back into those computers?" she asked.

"Yeah, they have a program running," Jason said. "That's how I got all of this information."

"Oh, I didn't understand that before," Tasha said. "I see now."

"It's going to take awhile to get all the information, but you can help," Jason said. "First, we need to find out what kind of programs they have. I wish I had written this before. He didn't tell me exactly what he wanted."

"It's going to be okay, isn't it?" Tasha asked.

"I think we can get there," Jason said. "It's going to take a little more work, that's all."

With that, Jason and Tasha worked right through dinner and into the night. Tasha performed more routine matters, then watched with great concentration as Jason experimented with several programming approaches she had never seen before. He set his automatic program to pull down the stored usernames and passwords from the browsers and also set the program to look for programs, and stored that information.

Finally, after hours and hours of working continuously, Tasha wearily kissed him on the cheek goodnight and collapsed on the bed. Jason worked on without stopping. At some point his thinking became chaotic. He looked at the clock; it was 4:04 AM.. *"Getting there,"* he thought enthusiastically, then fearing he was about to make mistakes that would set back all his work, he decided he had put in all he could that day.

He turned off the light and slipped into bed with Tasha. Although asleep, she now responded automatically to his touch. She turned over and ever-so-gently embraced him. Jason also responded automatically to her and felt a rush of calm before quickly drifting out of consciousness.

Starting To Make Progress

Jason woke up late and alone in the bedroom. For a moment he was confused and alarmed by Tasha's absence. Then he became aware of the smell of coffee, strongly brewed coffee, which could only mean Tasha was up and already at work. With that reassuring thought he was tempted to sleep a few more minutes, but instead he shook himself more fully awake. He really needed a shower, but the smell of food overcame him, so he pulled on the same jeans as yesterday and headed for the workroom. A tray of food was sitting on top of the coffee maker waiting for him. However, as he looked for Tasha at the computers he noted another food tray with used dishes, but she was nowhere in sight. For a moment the feeling of alarm returned. Suddenly he heard the flush of the toilet and the now familiar sound of Tasha pursuing her morning routines. He chuckled nervously at his growing reliance on her companionship.

His thoughts returning to his stabbing hunger, he sat down

with the tray of cold scrambled eggs and soggy toast. He poured himself a cup of coffee, the first sip of which hit him like smelling salts. He poured half the cup back into the pot, then added water from the bathroom.

"I tried to wake you, but you were sound asleep," Tasha said, entering the room.

"I made some headway," Jason said.

"Headway?" she said, cocking her head in that way that said 'translation please'.

"Oh, it's progress. I made some progress last night, er…early this morning," Jason said.

"I'm glad," Tasha said. "You looked so full of stress yesterday."

"Well, I'll find out what I have when I look at that box," Jason said thoughtfully.

"Things will work out, you will see," Tasha said looking at his tray of food. "I put it on the coffee pot… you know … I heated it. Did it work?"

"A little," he said.

"The flowers are not doing so well," Tasha said glumly.

Jason looked at the flower bouquet. It was starting to wilt. "That was fast," he said.

"Maybe if there was sunlight coming in," Tasha suggested.

"Perhaps," he replied.

"You know what I miss the most?" She asked.

"What's that?" he responded

"The sun," she said. "When I was younger, I used to lie in the sun for hours."

"You don't see the sun?" he asked with concern.

"No, I haven't seen the sun outside in a long time, not since I came to this place."

Jason, blinking in surprise, considered exactly how long she had been captive at the hotel and could only offer, "I hope I will be in it soon."

"I just miss it, that's all." Tasha continued with little show of concern. And with equal composure asked, "Do you like to swim?"

"Sometimes," Jason said. "I'm not a big fan of cold water."

"I used to swim in a lake," she said. "I always dreamed of swimming in the ocean."

"I did that a few times," he told her.

"I saw the ocean twice," Tasha said. "Once from a plane and then from a car."

Jason had finished eating and moved his chair over to the computer.

"Was the ocean warm?" Tasha asked.

Jason felt self-conscious describing what must be almost magical privileges to Tasha. Instead of answering right away, he logged onto the web server and found the files he was looking for. He had them compressed so that many files could fit in one file. He downloaded one at random.

"The Atlantic was warm, I mean, when I was in Florida it was warm," Jason said. Then he added, "The Pacific Ocean was cold when I went to Washington state."

Jason opened the file and found the settings for all but one of the web browsers installed on the computer. It looked like the mail address and password were there, so he opened a web browser and logged in as the remote person. The account belonged to a Dr. Henry Hawks. It had an email from a bank that was marked as read. Jason didn't want to open anything new. There weren't very many. He had many emails from various dating sites. One said he had a message so Jason opened that one. The dating site didn't ask for a password. He clicked on a profile of Dr. Hawks and there was a picture and bio. He was 62 years old, divorced with adult children, several grandchildren—and was a complete pedophile. Jason checked the connection to this computer. It wasn't currently active.

"I never went in a swimming pool," Tasha said.

"Really, never?" Jason said, trying to seem as casual and accepting as possible "Swimming pools make my eyes burn. It's the chlorine," Jason offered.

"I like to swim, but it has been a quite a few years since I have been able to do that," Tasha said.

Jason went back to the web server and downloaded all of the captured files. Out of the 52, 38 had uploaded their data. He had to wait for the data to download to his local machine.

"Someday, let's go for a swim," Jason suggested trying to sound enthusiastic. He sat back in his chair gazing curiously at Tasha as he waited for the data to download.

She turned to him, smiled and asked, "Did you get the web cam thing to work last night?"

"One part of it did," Jason said. "I have to rewrite the software that detects the web cam and lets me know, somehow. That way, I will know which connection is the one to work with. That isn't done yet."

"Is that what you're doing now?" she asked.

"No," he replied. "I'm checking the settings on the computers from yesterday."

Jason continued, "Some of the files had email login info, so I was poking around with that."

"Can I see?" Tasha asked.

"Sure, let's open one of the files," Jason said.

Jason picked another compressed file and opened it. Looking though the information, he found one file that had stored login information. He went to AOL's website and entered the email address and the password. He clicked on email. The email program showed hundreds of emails.

"Wow, that was easy for you," Tasha said, astonished at the sheer amount of information revealed.

"Yeah, lotsa stuff…," Jason said absentmindedly as he scrolled down the email account. There were several credit card billing statements. "Y'know what, I forgot something," he said. He ran the IP address of that computer indicating where the email address came from. It was in Minneapolis, Minnesota. Jason thought for a bit and concluded, "We need to wait to do this one."

"Why?" Tasha asked.

"Most people are asleep from 2 a.m. to 5:30 a.m.. We should only look at emails in that time frame. That way, people are most likely asleep and won't notice changes in their email."

"I think I get it," Tasha said shaking her head in agreement.

"Let me see if I can find someone," Jason said, skimming. "Oh, look at that, it's Monday. You know it's hard to keep track of what day it is here."

"I really don't care anymore. I haven't for a very long time," Tasha said. "I used to keep track of the days. I scratched a box lid to a pair of shoes. But they took them away and the box so now I don't care what day it is anymore." She paused and seemed to change the subject to something more pleasant. "Do you like to fish?"

Jason opened another browser and realized he forgot the password and email address he used with the emails to Anthony. He looked them up on his computer as he continued the conversation, "Not into fishing," Jason said. " I have done it a few times, though. You?"

Jason read his notes and recalled the password and email that he was using. He logged in and a new message from Anthony was waiting. The message contained all the information needed to log into three bank accounts and included scanned images of the temporary checks. Anthony also included a mail drop address. The address was from the next state over, in the name of Jim Smith. Jason logged off and connected to the email. Suddenly he realized he was using the wrong network. "Can't let that happen again," he muttered to himself. He simply could not allow himself to become distracted; there was too much at stake. After a brief pause to regain focus Jason continued. From now on he would use only his laptop for this stuff. Meanwhile, Tasha was still carrying on the conversation.

"I went with my father a few times," Tasha said. "I just don't like touching the worms."

Jason chuckled, "I'm not crazy about doing that either," he said, but his need for focus was evident as he changed the subject. "Let me show you how to find the email address in these files. "You start by uncompressing the files this way." Jason showed Tasha how to find what he was looking for on two of them. He ran into a snag when he didn't find anything on the next one, so he showed her what to do when nothing was found and got her set to work on the files.

Jason opened his laptop and connected to the florist network and started his TOR client. The TOR network allowed him to hide the location of the computer he used from being tracked on the Internet. The problem was that the web client must be clean. There must be no "flash" or other application that gives the ads and other things that make websites look complete. Once connected, he returned to webmail and opened the Bank of China's client login page. The page was messy, the Tor browser messed up many web pages, but Jason was able to find the English button. At least he could find the account page; it contained a balance of 305,426.57 Yuan.

Jason opened a translate engine so he could read Chinese. He had no idea what the page was saying. With that, he joined PayEasy in China to set up a PayEasy account. He also added the Chinese bank account to it. As he encountered the usual wait, he disconnected the connections and made plans to check back.

"I have a question," Tasha said.

"What is that?" He got up and stood behind her.

"This one has many email accounts, see?" said Jason. "Okay, well, we'll put it in a special place to look at later. Do you think you can create a program to do this?"

"Maybe, I'm not sure," she replied

"Well, you know what to look for, so let's do one together and maybe we can set it up to work remotely so we can focus on other stuff," Jason said.

Jason and Tasha sat together and started on a program when they heard the door unlock. The tall girl came in carrying trays. Her hair was very long and hid her face completely. After she set the trays down, she picked up the old ones and left. Jason and Tasha barely took notice and fell into their usual evening routine.

"Do you want water or wine?" Jason asked.

"Water," replied Tasha, still glued to her screen.

Jason got up to fill the cups with water. Tasha tore herself away from coding and set the chairs at the table and moved the trays of food in front of them.

"After we eat, we should take a nap," Jason suggested. "We have a lot of work we can do between 2 and 5 a.m.."

"You don't want to make the program?" Tasha asked.

"Well, I really want to do both, but I guess the program is more important," Jason said.

"You don't want them to be angry with you," Tasha said. "They will hurt you and I don't want that."

"That is possible, but I think for now, we're good to have the program almost done for remotely checking for cameras," Jason said. "I was able to add one manufacturer, but I don't trust turning the light off unless I can see it work. After lunch, we should check for it and see how many there are in our collection of data."

"Did you always do computers?" Tasha asked.

"Really, ever since I can remember," he replied, "It was a way to understand things. Computers and programming are just natural for me. It looks like they are for you, too."

"I don't know," she said. "I mean, I have been doing what you tell me, and I get it, sort of."

"I have been in professional programming shops where everyone codes and not many of them could get it as fast as you seem to," Jason said.

"Thank you; I try to understand. Don't you have a girlfriend or wife somewhere?"

"No, I don't have anyone but you," Jason told her.

Tasha smiled at him. "That is sweet, but you don't really want me. I am a bad person. I have done some very bad things."

"I don't think that you did them willingly," Jason said. "Whatever they are, they are in the past."

Tasha thought about that for a few minutes, and looked straight into his eyes, and a single tear started to develop. "You are so kind, but I have done so many things. Once you find out any of them, you will not want me, not like that. So don't think about me like that. You have no idea really who I am or what I have done."

"I think by now, we know each other very well, even if it is not by our choice," said Jason. "We are together here for some reason. I don't know why, but I know that you are who you appear to be. Nothing more or nothing less, as I am to you."

"You are such a kind man," she said. "I have never...since this began...I know now what..." She was fighting tears. Jason understood that she was conflicted about a lot of things and her hormones were also in play. How much of what he was seeing now were parts of her that she would not normally show, he had no way of knowing. It really didn't matter as long as they were honest with each other. He had shown her things with computers that most people don't ever see. He knew that and she had seen a side of him that he normally didn't show either.

They both finished their lunch. Jason stood up and took her hand. He pulled her to the bedroom. They laid together, her head on his chest, him stroking her hair and her back. She fell asleep.

Willy had heard their exchanges and he was pissed, mostly at himself for creating this by putting her in there. But she seemed to be learning from him. He went down to the kitchen and asked Gladys who was starting to work on dinner to set two plates aside and keep them warm. They would be picked up much later.

When Jason woke, it was dark outside, and Tasha was not there. He got off the bed and found her at the computer working on the program in C language. He walked up behind her and kissed her neck as she continued to type.

"What does that do?" He pointed at the screen.

"It keeps the item in memory so it can look at everything faster."

"Okay, well, we can't do that remotely or the CPU will get too busy. Someone will notice; do it the slow way." He kissed her neck again. He could not believe what she just said; he thought it was simply incredible.

Jason went over to his laptop and looked at the time. It was 8:30—well past dinner and no trays were on the tables. *They must have skipped us,* he thought.

It felt good for Jason to sleep; he was overdue since the last few days. He was wide awake now. He went back to the TOR network and logged into the Chinese bank and looked for the PayEasy confirmation. It was not there yet. He disconnected from the site and the network. He needed that PayEasy account to work so he could get started with the law firm.

"Tasha, how is it going?" he asked.

"I have it working okay, but could you look?" She motioned him over.

"Sure." He got up to look at the screen. "Can you scroll up a little?"

Tasha moved the screen up. It looked okay to him.

"This is really good work," Jason said. "Let's convert it over to Java and add it to the install file. It just needs a little adjustment."

"Okay, I saved it," Tasha said.

"Why don't I get in there? The java development kit is on here. I'll show you the differences." Jason rolled the other chair over as Tasha got up. Then the door unlocked. A red-headed girl came in carrying the trays. Her hair was short and Jason could see that she had bright blue eyes even though her head was bowed. Not saying a word, she set the trays down and went back to the door and knocked to leave. The door opened for her and she left.

"So the camera gods were paying attention," Jason said.

"I don't understand, what god?" she asked.

"It was a joke... they heard us say...never mind, let's eat."

"Would you like some wine or water?"

"Water for now for me," Jason replied.

Tasha went to fill the cup with water. Jason rolled her chair to where she always sat to eat. He decided to roll his chair next to hers so that they could sit side by side for a change.

She came back and stopped. He had moved the slightly wilting flowers to the table, also. She sat down and they had their dinner side by side.

"So what is your most un-favorite color and why?" Jason asked.

"Hmm...black, because it reminds me of dark and scary things that I cannot see," she answered.

"What if I were next to you in the dark, scary place?" he asked.

"I would feel better," Tasha smiled. "But I have been locked in a box for hours and hours. I don't want to think about it."

"Okay, how about your favorite color then?"

"It is the color of the sky when the sun is just on the horizon on a warm summer night. Purple or orange or a combination of the two. How about you?"

"Favorite or un-favorite?"

"Both and why?"

"Let's see...the color hot pink, because it was the color of my lunch box when I was a kid and the other kids made fun of me," Jason said.

"So you don't like to get made fun of?"

"I'm not crazy about it, no."

"You sound as though you are a little insecure about yourself," Tasha noted.

"I use my insecurity as a shield to accomplish more," Jason said.

"I just think you're the little boy afraid of hot pink," Tasha laughed.

"That's not fair," Jason said.

"So, what is your favorite color?" Tasha asked.

"I think it's green," Jason said. "The color of the grass and the color of everything when it grows out of the ground. And of course, the color of your eyes."

"That was cheap," Tasha said.

"What was cheap? I was trying to be sweet."

"You don't need to try to be sweet, you are sweet," Tasha said. "Try sincere."

Jason was confused. "Let's get back at it, shall we? Would you like some wine?"

"Sure," she said as they got up. "I'll get it."

Jason pushed the chair back over to the computer and started converting Tasha's code to Java. He could tell that it was very good—not necessarily the way he would have done it, but still very good. Tasha put her cup down next to him and filled it with wine. She sat down next to him and he converted the file line by line.

"You see how similar it is? Jason said.

"Yes, I don't understand that." She pointed at the screen.

"It is the same thing," Jason said. "The statement means the same. It's just another word."

"I see," Tasha said. "Maybe I should try Java next."

"There is more to C sharp to learn first," Jason said. "Then Java." He continued to translate the code. After a while, he finished. To test it, he tried the modified Java package on one of the XP test boxes just to see if it gave any output, and there was none. Of course, he never used a web browser there or stored a password in it or in the computer registry. There was nothing to find. "*Stupid idea,*" he decided. He copied it down to one of the machines in the cubes room downstairs and forced it to run, he checked the web server for the resulting file. He copied the file local so he could work with it. He opened it in a text editor.

"Hey that's some of my stuff," Tasha said.

"What do you mean?" Jason asked.

"Well, some of the stuff I use downstairs."

The list had at least 50 entries. Jason didn't count them all—some were duplicates for the same sites, but different log-ins for different browsers.

"Well, that's exactly why you don't store passwords in browsers," he said. "Because someone like yourself will come along and use it against you."

"Well, I wouldn't," Tasha said.

"Oh yes, we will," Jason said. He looked at the computer clock. It was only 10 p.m..

"The UK is six hours ahead," Jason said. "Let's see what time zones we have."

"How do you tell?" Tasha asked.

"I never had to do this before, so let's see if there is a tool," he answered.

Jason tried a search on the web for a Linux script and found one. The machine he was on wasn't Linux, he was on Windows 8 and was lazy so he searched the web for an IP address location tool and searched the IP addresses one by one. He soon came across one from Frankfurt, Germany. "Cool, let's try this one," he said.

The person had a Gmail, Facebook, LinkedIn, VK and Yahoo account. "Pick one," Jason said to Tasha.

"I don't know, you pick," she said.

"Okay, let's see Gmail." Jason typed in the address and waited for the page to load. Then he put in the username and password.

Gmail loaded, but there weren't many messages. "Bad guess, let's try Yahoo." He clicked "sign out" and put Yahoo in the address bar. Once it loaded, he entered the username and password. Yahoo changed to the German version.

"Do you know German?" Jason said.

Tasha replied, "Yes."

He scooted over so she could have the keyboard and mouse. "You drive."

"What am I looking for?" she asked.

"Anything that looks like a bank," he said.

"Here is something from Bankhaus Lampe." Tasha clicked on it.

"Let's look at their site," Jason said.

Tasha clicked on a few links and found a maze of back and forth. She finally found the customer login. The website was looking for a subscriber number and pin numbers.

"Let's look elsewhere," Jason said. "It's a little bank with real security; how about PayEasy?"

"Here is a PayEasy email," Tasha said. "He bought something. Looks like speakers."

"Cool, okay, let's try PayEasy with this email address and forgotten password." Jason pointed and said, "Click that reset password. Now refresh the email."

"Nothing new," Tasha said.

"Try it again," Jason suggested.

"New email from PayEasy," Tasha said. "It says: 'Click on this link to change your password.'"

"Go ahead," Jason said.

"Okay, what should I make it?"

Jason said each letter and number: "P 3 d o p h I l e."

"Okay, now we are in the account," Tasha said.

"Do they pay extra to join the special shows?"

"Who?" Tasha asked.

"The people that watch the special shows," Jason said. "Do they pay extra?"

"You mean to view a private show? Yes."

"Press send money," Jason said. "Pick product. Pick other. Under description, put four-pack DVD box set. Brutal sex with little boys. Make it a z at the end of 'boys,' not an s."

The screen read: Amount 335 Euros

"Use the email to wanda123408@gmail.com and click send," Jason said. "I seriously doubt he will report to PayEasy that he didn't order that. Click back on the email and let's copy and save it. We will delete the payment and password change emails. Now empty the trash. Click on contacts. Now click actions, export all."

As Jason rattled off directions, Tasha followed. Once she was done, Jason said, "Ready to do another one?"

"Sure," Tasha said.

"Let's do someone in the states now, they are easier," Jason suggested.

Jason and Tasha continued the process on email accounts and banks or PayEasy until 4 in the morning.

"I'm tired…I can't do this anymore," Tasha said.

"They can wait," Jason said, yawning. "We can do them later. There really is no rush."

"How many did we get?" Tasha asked.

"I'm not sure, let's look at the PayEasy," Jason said.

"I know," Tasha said. "Log off, clean out cookies, close the browser, clean the temp files. Can't we just write a program for this part?"

"What, the cleaning part?"

"No, the entire thing."

"Well, yeah, I guess it's possible," Jason said. He typed the password on PayEasy. The balance on the webpage was $9,578.31.

"Let's go to bed; I'm exhausted," Jason said.

Tasha got up and turned the monitor off. Jason turned the rest off, and they went to the bedroom and collapsed on the bed.

Working All Night

The call of nature finally stirred Jason from an exhausted and deep sleep. His hurried effort to rise stirred Tasha awake. She looked on wearily as Jason quickly shuffled towards the bathroom. They both labored to fully wake up and pull on their clothes. Upon entering the office area, it took a moment for them to process the fact that there were food trays containing lunch well as breakfast. They had slept past noon – not too surprising as the girls bringing the food were always so quiet. It also meant that their late-night escapades on the computers had gone undetected or they would have been awakened by an angry visit from Willy. Their gamble had paid off. The guy minding the surveillance cameras had taken his usual evening sleep as they plundered the system and generated funds for their own use – which were still small potatoes, Jason knew, compared to the money generated by the firm at the hotel.

He made coffee and used the last of the grounds Willy had provided. "*They could afford more and better coffee now*", he thought, amused by his accomplishment. They had stolen almost 10 grand in about 4 hours. *"But how to make purchases without raising Willy's suspicion?"* Jason wondered.

He pushed the breakfast and lunch trays around so they each had two. "There's some food here," he called out to Tasha. A few moments later, she was seated across from him eating a virtual bounty, albeit cold: cold eggs, cold grilled cheese sandwiches and cold soup, additional signs of how late they had slept.

"Well, we made some progress," Jason stated triumphantly.

"I was thinking about a program," Tasha replied more lost in thought. "Maybe it is easier to read the emails with a program," she said, pausing to look at Jason, "Or is there too much information?"

"Yeah, that'd be a lot for one program to manage," Jason said noting her seriousness. "The problem is that we'd need the computer to understand what a *bank* is, and that'd take too long … There're also too many different types of email websites for just one program to read."

"Are we going to do more of them?" Tasha asked.

"Maybe tonight," Jason said. "I want to tweak a few things in that program. I really need more cameras so I can widen the net just a little. Do you remember how many computers we found that had cameras, but weren't supported?"

"I think it was around a thousand or something," said Tasha trying to recall.

"Having a thousand cameras would be nice, huh?" Jason said tapping the side of his jaw thoughtfully.

"That would take forever," Tasha said.

"What do you, mean?" he asked.

"Well, it took us four and a half hours to get into 15 or 16 people's accounts," she explained, "…not counting the ones that did not provide enough information. So, at that rate it would take us about three or four months to finish."

Jason considered her concern and offered another way to look at the problem, "Look at it this way: how much did you make per day when you were doing chat sales?"

Tasha wrinkled her nose as she did the numbers, "Uhm … we worked twelve hours each day and had to earn at least $600 each. If you got $800 or more, you could have a day off, as long as it wasn't a 'specials' day. On a 'specials' day, you could make $1200, no problem, so nobody took a day off."

"I see," Jason said. "So, last night we made in four hours what you might make in 10 'specials' shifts?"

Tasha seemed to scowl as she replied, "No, I mean…I don't know," she stuttered.

Jason suddenly realized that he was being insensitive to what Tasha, as a slave, considered her work and her accomplishment. He struggled to change the subject, "The soup sucks, huh?" he offered.

Tasha nodded. "Yes, pretty bad … too much salt." In spite of her good-natured response, they exchanged a glance that confirmed he had struck a nerve. Jason was only just beginning to understand what being enslaved meant to her view of life.

Jason finished eating and moved the chair back to his workstation to check on the website logs and email. Tasha also finished and attempted to toss their leftovers into the garbage, which was starting to overflow.

"Wow, there're over 10,000 worldwide running my code," Jason said.

"Why are there so many?" She asked.

"Well, the ad runs inside the page of every performer," Jason explained. "So anyone who goes to this site picks up my little utility … Not that it really does anything."

"That's a lot; can we do this to all of them?" Tasha asked.

"That wouldn't be practical," Jason said. "We have to find a better way."

"You stink," Tasha said looking at him with all seriousness.

Jason worried that he again said something to her out of line,

"What do you mean?" He replied and struggling to understand where the statement came from.

"I'm going to take a shower," she stated flatly, then continued, "you need one too," She laughed flirting. "Would you like to join me?"

While he was relieved to realize she was trying to reassure him and keep their close bond Jason couldn't overlook the business at hand. "Sure, in a minute," he said, smiling warmly at her. "I just want to take care of something."

Jason checked the Chinese bank again from his laptop. Finally the PayEasy connection was there. He opened the list he had created for the law office project and ordered everything by FedEx, next-day or two-day. He only ordered two-day if the next day was a crazy price. Not having credit card numbers to use made things a little challenging, but the checks and PayEasy made it possible.

His effort took almost an hour. By the time he got to the bathroom, Tasha was drying off.

"Could you ask them for clean clothes and sheets?" she asked. "And if they can take the garbage out."

"Sure, I'll take care of it," Jason said stripping off his clothes.

"You want me to scrub your back?"

"No, you're dry already, that's okay," he answered.

Jason got in the shower and stayed in there a while. The water felt good. They were almost out of soap, shampoo, etc. After he left the shower, Tasha was waiting for him.

"Do you not like me anymore?" she asked.

"Why would you say that?" Jason asked, surprised.

"You have not touched me in days," she replied, looking down all the while.

"We've been real busy," Jason stammered. "We're together all the time. I feel like I'm always touching you ... we live on top of each other ... what do you mean that I don't touch you?"

"I don't know," Tasha shrugged. "You look at all the girls who come. Maybe I am not good for you anymore, just trouble."

Jason struggled to convey the mixture of affection and concern he had for Tasha. "You are very good for me. I care for you. I hate this place," he began. "But I know that you've gone through total hell, so I don't know sometimes what is right when we are together." Having finally put his concern out there he quickly continued, "I feel so lucky that you're with me. I would have lost it by now if you weren't here and helping me."

Jason cupped his hands behind Tasha's neck and drew her close to him. He whispered to her warmly, "I'm so turned on by you and I care about you. I can't tell you how or when we're getting out of here, but when the time's right, we leave together. We'll get out of here, and when we do, I want you with me without cameras watching and listening." Then he looked at her more sternly and made clear, "but none of that can happen unless we do what needs to be done to get out of here."

He moved his face right in front of hers so their noses were touching. "Got that? … Do you believe in me?"

"Yes, I do," Tasha looking more calm and reassured.

They kissed for a very long time, then became aware of the office around them again.

"So, you ready to get busy?" Tasha said teasingly as their lips parted.

"Yes ma'am," Jason retorted. "What time is it?"

Tasha shook her head. They were beginning to lose all sense of normal time.

Jason tried to get dressed. Wearing the same clothes seemed to defeat the purpose of taking a shower but fresh clothing was apparently not a regular part of the arrangement. He didn't have time to bother the guy watching them and went straight back to work.

Tasha was already sitting in front of a computer looking through the files for possible targets. Jason looked at the time. It was early. He didn't want to open up someone's email account at the same time they were in it, nor did he want them seeing an email stating there was a change of password for a bank account or an online payment system.

He went back to his laptop, checked on his list and found he had missed a few items. So he went back to looking for more items, like a Drumel tool, and bits among them. A couple of items were only available in China, but one seller actually carried both. He also sent an email to Anthony to let him know he got the information and was working on it. They were able to send it via DHL and said maybe it would be at the mail drop in three days from Hong Kong. Jason thought that was a slim maybe, but they seemed to be the only ones selling the items he was looking for.

After working for a few hours Jason finally took a break. He stood before the surveillance camera, waved and asked for Willy to come to see him. He went back to the machine he used to connect to the web server. He checked the connection count; he had over 52,753 unique computers or devices logged in as connecting to the server. This was a concern because of the way virus and spyware applications worked to detect the code. *"It may take a couple of weeks before some wiseass will notice all the infections and start flagging them,"* he thought.

The door unlocked and Willy came in. Jason looked in Tasha's direction. She stopped what she was doing and put her head down as soon as she heard to door.

"Any news?" Willy asked demandingly.

"Yeah, things seem to be working a little better," Jason said. "We found some stuff off of some computers last night. Thanks for holding up food for us."

"What'd ya find?" Willy asked ignoring Jason's effort to be pleasant.

"Well, we pulled some money from the computers without cameras," Jason offered.

"How much?" Willy said his eyes revealing his greed.

"Not a lot, we are working on some more," Jason said trying to lower Willy's expectations. "It's all in a PayEasy account under Wanda's name."

"Great," Willy said. "Are you ready to get busy with this thing now?"

"Yeah, but I really need you to get me those laptops and that webcam," Jason said trying not to cause and argument. "We've found from the data we collected that only a small number of computers have a camera—about a quarter of the ones that viewed that video feed. Of those computers, only about 500 had a camera I could control."

"I see," Willy said. "Well, you still think all this is worth it?"

"Yeah, it'll work," Jason said trying to keep him onboard. "And, we're getting money even from the ones without a camera."

"Okay, well, I'll let you know when things happen again," Willy said.

"And …" Jason continued feeling a bit more in control. "We're working day and night so there's some other stuff we need."

"Uh-huh?" Willy questioned with a look of annoyance.

"It reeks in here … we, Tasha and I, need stuff for the shower and some clean clothes," Jason began. "We also need some decent coffee …?" he added hopefully.

"Make a list," Willy smirked, though Jason got the impression Willy would do anything to keep the money flowing, so he continued.

"We gotta get the laptops and cameras – that has to happen now," Jason demanded. "I need them to add to the camera list."

"Yeah, I guess," Willy said. "How much did you get last night?" he asked as if to confirm the demand was worth his effort.

"I'm not totally sure, around 10 grand."

"What?! Holy fuck!" Willy exclaimed in disbelief.

"I know … We'll try to do better with the cam." Jason said trying to sound apologetic and modest.

"Fuck dude, I thought you got like a couple hundred or something!"

"It should be more."

Willy pointed at Tasha. "I watched a little last night," he said. "Is she helping you or should I pull her boney ass outta here?"

Jason was suddenly alarmed and realized that he must not let on to Willy about Tasha's growing importance to him, both personally and in his work. "Oh her? That one's helpful," he said casually, then added, "I work better when there's a nice piece of ass when I need it." With that comment he glanced at Tasha, and could tell she was working to hide a smile, thinking about his earlier comments about her contribution and not having time for sex.

Willy stared at her for a moment as if he might be catching on, then shrugged without a clue and said, glaring at Tasha, "You better be a good little bitch."

He opened the door and slammed it behind him. Jason looked back at Tasha who still had her head down so the camera could not see her face but was visibly looking at him with slyness and smiles at his performance. He had spoken like he was one of them, but he had prevented Willy from removing and possibly punishing her. She had a growing admiration for Jason's ability to size up their situation and control the people who thought they were controlling him. She offered her approval by saying nothing and starting to type again.

Jason worked to put them back in a good mood. He grabbed a pad and began their shopping list. "Shampoo, conditioner, coffee, wine ... anything else, Tasha?"

"Clean sheets, pillow cases, a toothbrush, toothpaste...oh yes, a real wine opener and new cups ..."

Jason walked over to the door and slid the list under it. As he stood up, the door suddenly unlocked and opened. He could not get out of the way fast enough and the door struck him knocking him backwards and on his butt. The girl coming through the door didn't know what to do. She was balancing two trays. She had long red hair that came down past her shoulders and the standard t-shirt & shorts.

Jason said, "It's okay, my fault, no problem." From the angle Jason was in on the floor, he made out the faintest grin on her lightly-freckled face as she walked by. He couldn't tell if she was amused by his fall or being flirtatious. She picked up all of the empty trays and bowls and was still struggling to hide her grin as she knocked once and left.

Jason got off the floor. Tasha was watching him too, grinning as well, and trying not to laugh.

"Would you like wine or water?" Jason asked.

Tasha, giggling, said, "If you are done flirting with her I would like water, thanks."

Jason smiled at her teasing, grabbed the cups and went to the bathroom to fill them. When he came out, Tasha had put the chairs side by side and was seated already waiting for him.

"I am sorry for today," she said. "I don't know why I say such things sometimes."

"You didn't say anything wrong, it's okay," Jason said to reassure her.

"I am almost done sorting," Tasha said, "Many of them have no username or password."

"Well, keep putting them in the same place," Jason said. "We can take another run at them using a "key logger. That's a program that just records your keystrokes," Jason explained. "I can have it send me the log every time they connect."

"What happens if you write a letter or something while a key logger is running?" Tasha asked catching on quickly.

"We'll get the letter or blog," Jason said. "So we just search the file for the '@' symbol and see what is around it. …I know! We'll make a few and you can write the program to find the username and password."

"I don't know," Tasha said, still uncertain of her skills.

"Come on, it will be fun," Jason said.

"Maybe, we will see," she said and tried to change the topic to cover her doubts. "Why do you like me?" she said flirting.

"Where to start?" Jason said, picking up her vibe. "I look into your eyes, your beautiful green eyes, and I see total trust and caring looking back at me. I can feel it, not only with your words or actions. I can just tell that you believe in me and you believe in what I can do. You make me feel some things I've never experienced before. I have dreams about you. We work together like one person, which I've never experienced with anyone. Neither of us chose to be here, but … I feel a freedom when I'm with you, like it doesn't matter where we are. It's like you're part of me now. If I were to lose you now, I'd be in trouble, like a getting a wound that would never heal." He gave her a kiss on her cheek and held her hand.

"…Eat your food," said Tasha, embarrassed by his confession, then asked as she had before, "So what's your favorite color?"

"This isn't fair," Jason said, realizing she was testing him. "If I say something different from before, you'll accuse me of lying. If I say the same color, you will accuse me of patronizing."

"What is patronizing?" she asked.

"It's like saying what you want to hear, so you'll like me or do what I want," Jason said.

"I don't think you can do that patronizing me," Tasha said.

"I don't think so either," Jason said smiling. They had reached a very important level of trust between them. They were becoming a force larger than Willy or the firm ever anticipated.

"Do you still want to wait a while before we begin?" Tasha asked.

"Yeah, it's way too early," Jason said.

"How much wine is there?" Tasha asked.

"About a bottle and a half, why?" Jason noted.

"We need a break" she explained with enthusiasm. "So, while we wait for time to pass let's be drinking and playing Go, and you will have a reason for losing to me!"

Jason laughed. He walked under the camera and waved his hands. "Can we get a bottle of whiskey and a 12-pack of beer?"

He sat back down in the chair behind his food. "I think getting tanked and hacking is a great idea, but if you're going to get high, do it with beer chasers," he stated flatly.

"I don't know if I like whiskey," Tasha said.

"No worries," Jason said. "It goes down very smooth … I think you'll like it," Jason said.

Tasha sat and watched Jason finish his meal. He was eating slowly. When he was chewing his last bite, she tried to get him up and over to the computer. She launched Yahoo games and started Go.

Jason had lost maybe three games before the door unlocked. The redhead was back with a stack of sheets and folded clothes. She put them on the table and took the trays. She knocked on the door once, but instead of leaving, she was handed a plastic bag with a bottle in it and a 12-pack of Old Milwaukee beer. She put those on the table, and then knocked, picked up the trays and left.

"Ah, at last," Jason said. "Let's see your cup.

"Now, the rules are simple," he continued. "Every time you move on the board, you drink a shot, then a sip of beer. Then you wash the beer down with the rest of the shot. Got it?" Jason explained.

Tasha got out of the chair. "Can I smell it?"

"No, no," Jason said. "Here," he put a shot in her cup and opened a can of beer. He handed her the cup.

Tasha smelled the cup and made a face. "Ugh, what is this?"

"Just drink it all at once don't stop or it will taste awful." He poured himself one, too.

Tasha downed the cup with the brown liquid then gasped for air. Jason held out a beer and was pouring whiskey in her cup. Tasha took a drink from the beer. "No, no more," she said.

"You didn't go to college in the U.S., did you?" Jason asked.

"No," she said, still trying to find air.

"This is required for college," he explained as he sipped the beer. "It's also a really good way of getting lucky with girls."

"What kind of girls is drinking that stuff?" she said still coughing.

"I'll get you some water," Jason finally said accepting that it wasn't her style and moving to bring her some water. "Sorry," he offered. "I guess it's not for you."

Tasha drank the water, and held the cup out. "More."

But Tasha wasn't about to give up, they had three more shots which eventually had the desired effect. Jason was finally able to win a round of 'Go'. They played a few more rounds and time flew by.

Around midnight, they stopped and returned to opening emails and searching for banks and online payment accounts. She went through the files and separated the ones without email accounts. Her work made their effort much easier and faster. Together, they did almost 30 more. Finally, in the wee hours of morning, they were both exhausted and had to stop. They fell into bed with their clothes still on. As Jason reached to click off the light, he could see the sunrise starting to peek through the window.

Monsters Near and Far

The noise of the door opening and closing was not enough to wake Jason, but it became a feature in a fitful dream. In it, he watched as Tasha, standing on the other side of the door, slammed it repeatedly in his face. He struggled in the dream to find out the reason for her brutality. However, as happens in many dreams, the answer never came and it instead moved on to other strange scenes. The next thing Jason knew he awoke to full daylight pouring through the window. This could only mean they had slept late again. He slid out from Tasha's embrace and she squirmed quietly in sleepy protest. Then he consciously heard the door open again, followed by a long pause and then the familiar click of the lock as it closed again.

Jason put his pants on and went to the adjoining room. Along with trays containing the usual breakfast and lunch there were several boxes stacked in the middle of the floor including a couple of larger boxes with smaller ones on top. Some of them appeared to contain computers. By contrast, on the very top of the stack was a can of pre-ground coffee.

Revealing his priorities, he opened the can and made some coffee. While he waited for it to brew, he opened one of the computer boxes. He took a laptop out of the box, set it up and turned it on. After pouring himself a cup of coffee, he unpacked a second laptop and placed it on the table next to the other one. Both were models with internal webcams that were unfamiliar to him. There was also an external webcam by a major manufacturer. He quickly mastered how to control the internal webcam and found it was already in his code. He had to have the camera in front of himself when he tested it; there was no remotely way to tell if the activity light was on or off. He needed the camera to operate with the activity light off so no one would know they were being recorded.

Some of the ones that Anthony had ordered were mixed into the stack. Jason put those under the table for now. None of the tools were part of this shipment.

He checked the PayEasy account for Wanda. It contained $34,072.25, an additional $18,427.48 EU and $250,000.12 Yen. There was a "charge back" listed from someone named Eugene Hill in the amount of $399. Really, they want their money back? The nerve, Jason thought.

Jason pulled out the printers and set them up. He realized he had no cables to make them function, and for that matter, no paper. The scanner printer combination had a brand-new ink cartridge kit that came with the unit. He was only after it for the scanner portion. He would need to be able to make copies. The high-grade printer was not there yet. He would need cables, ink and paper for that one, too.

He opened a web browser and went to a local office supply store website and ordered the supplies he had overlooked. The printer cables, however, were expensive. So expensive that it was actually cheaper to order them online from another vendor and having them shipped by FedEx the next day. All of the items he ordered went to Wanda's mail drop.

As he finished making online orders he realized that he had no idea what was happening in the world, locally or anywhere else, so he opened a local news website. He sipped his coffee as he read. He tried his name in the search bar and came up with three stories. Two of them he had seen before, and one of them was new. It said that the police were looking for him for additional questioning in the multiple homicides of his neighbors. He read on and learned that the two elderly people died in an apparent home invasion and the police needed more information. A local crime stoppers phone number was listed for anonymous tips.

He opened another page to see that some movie star had an accident while driving drunk. The studio was concerned since they had just completed a movie with him that was not released yet.

As he read on, Jason continued setting up the two laptops. As soon as he could, he went to the webcam site and logged in as Willy so he could see a performance and infect the computer. He checked his log and found that one of the machines was not infected. This was a problem he had not anticipated. For some reason the browser did not operate on this model as it did on all the other computers. He quickly realized that Java did not come installed on the computer. After he installed Java and went to the site and the machine became infected like all the others. Having solved the mystery and reassured himself that his virus program was effective, he shut down the machine and poured himself another cup of coffee.

He looked at the time; it was 1:48 p.m. and in spite of the trays of food, he had become too preoccupied to eat. Meanwhile, Tasha was still asleep. He didn't want to wake her. He was almost enjoying working alone for a while.

He tried to turn the camera on both of the laptops, which caused the light to come on, indicating that they were videoing. However, when he plugged in the external webcam, his code worked perfectly. There was no light, which meant that he could video undetected and it created an HD-stored file; that was huge progress. Now he needed to figure out how to make the camera only shoot in standard format. He started looking that up on the web when he felt Tasha touch. She kissed him and ran her fingers through his hair.

"I'm going to take a shower, you will come join me," Tasha asked invitingly.

"Well sure," Jason said.

Jason stopped his work and followed Tasha to the bathroom. She was out of her clothes before they entered the room and turned to help Jason shed his pants. They entered the warm spray, embraced and kissed passionately as the water flowed down their eager bodies. Jason suddenly opened his eyes. "Did you hear that?" he said in alarm.

"Hey, you ready?" he heard Willy say. "A show is going to be on tonight."

Jason stepped out of the shower and put a towel around his waist. Then realized he had to wait a moment until his raging hard on had subsided a bit. He walked out of the bathroom still soaking wet to see Willy standing there.

"There's a show on tonight at 8 p.m. …Will you be ready?" he repeated impatiently.

"Yeah, I think so," Jason said. "I just got the laptops set up."

"Can you do it with what you have now?" Willy asked.

"Yeah, probably," Jason said. "The live remote thing is not always working, but the later thing works okay."

"Okay," Willy said with a determined look in his eye. "Don't forget: 8 p.m., I'll be out on the floor for this one. It's gonna be big."

"There is a lot of money there so you might want to start thinking about cashing some of it out," Jason said.

"When can I do that?" Willy asked.

"I don't know," Jason shrugged. "Maybe later today or tomorrow. It depends on how long they wait for the transfer of funds."

"Cool," Willy said. "How much can I get?"

"It depends on the ATM."

"Huh?"

"ATMs in poor neighborhoods have limits on how much you can withdraw at a time," Jason explained. "If you go to a rich neighborhood, you can withdraw more."

"Ya don't say," Willy muttered, not willing to fully admit his ignorance of such things.

"Is there any chance of getting some real food in here?" Jason asked, pushing the importance of his work as a reason that he deserved better than the cafeteria meals served at the hotel.

"I'll get whatever you want, just tell the camera or leave a note under the door," Willy said as he headed for the door. He paused for a moment to add with a vulgar wink, "Better get back to that little bitch before she drowns."

Jason looked down. The carpet was wet all around him. He returned to the shower determined to ignore Willy's need to see Tasha as only a slave. What mattered, he thought, was that the deal was on. Let's just see what he's gonna do … Jason thought.

As he returned to the shower Tasha had shampoo running down her body. He was eager to get back to where they had left off, so he helped massage the lather into her hair. She quietly moaned in appreciation and they gently covered each other in soap.

Sex in a shower always seems like a romantic idea. However, in reality it turned out to be a bit awkward. Moreover, he could not help but notice a swirl of blood going down the drain revealing Tasha was still on her period as they wrestled in the confined space. But they were on fire and unstoppable. She bent over and he entered her from behind. In spite of their usual effort to be private, the sound of their lovemaking was thunderous against the walls of the small shower. The attendant did not need a camera to realize what they were doing and in spite of his access to the other enslaved women, he envied their passion. When they were finished, they continued kissing as they dried each other with the new, clean towels.

Sleeping late and having sex worked up Jason's appetite. ""Okay. Looks like we can have whatever we want today," Jason said. "Do you know what you want?"

"You," Tasha said playfully.

"No, I mean to eat," Jason said.

"We can get something new to eat?" she asked, then continued, "Is there a menu?"

"There's always something online," Jason noted with enthusiasm and asked, "Do you eat sushi?"

"Not for a long time," she mused, "but I love it!"

Jason continued this theme, so far from work or other pressing matters. "Do you like sashimi too, or just sushi?" he asked.

"Sashimi?" she asked.

Jason took her question as just another sign of how long she had been in captivity from the real world. "It's just the fish ... without any rice," he explained

"Oh yes ...," Tasha offered, as if she understood.

Jason began to pull on the same clothes but Tasha stopped him. "Don't put those dirty things on, there are clean ones on the dresser," she said like a scolding parent but with a smile.

Jason went to the dresser and got fresh clothes for them both. They dressed and went straight to the computers. He looked up the address for the hotel, and searched nearby for a sushi restaurant that delivered. He pulled up their menu.

"What do you want?" Jason asked her.

Tasha looked at the menu without a clue, then said playfully, "I cannot make up my mind, you order for me."

Jason plugged in his headphones on the computer and opened a new Gmail account. After going through a number of questions and upgrading the account, he added "Google voice" after finding an open "sms text" number to verify with. He put on the headphones and dialed the restaurant's number.

Jason ordered several rolls and told them to deliver to the hotel lobby. He was informed the total would be $47.50 and that it would take 45 minutes. After he hung up, he went to the camera and waved. "I ordered some food; it'll be in the lobby in 45 minutes. It's $55 with tip." He followed that up by writing a note that said the same thing and slid it under the door.

With food on the way, Jason went to one of the laptops and typed a few things. Then he went to the computer he used to control other's cameras and tried his remote script. "Tasha, could you sit here and tell me if the light is on?"

Tasha rolled the chair in front of the laptop and waited. Jason tried his remote script on her computer but it didn't work at all. He searched through a number of possible explanations. Finally, he changed his script to more specifically support the laptop's camera. Almost instantly Tasha exclaimed, "The light just came on." Just to verify the matter Jason closed the script and waited only briefly for Tasha to note, "Light is off."

Next Jason looked remotely at the registry on that computer. He found the settings for the device and a value called "lightalwayson." The value was 1. He changed that to a zero and ran his script. He waited for a second, canceled it, downloaded the recording and played it. It was a video of Tasha sitting in the chair.

"OK, I figured out how to control that on that one," Jason said.

"What about this one?" Tasha asked.

"I didn't try that one yet," Jason pointed out.

"It's asleep, does it matter?" Tasha asked.

"Yes, press the space bar or move your finger on the pad to wake it up." Jason noted.

"Okay, it's starting up," she described.

"I can't identify your unit from the others. What's the IP address?"

"I don't know that," Tasha said.

"Hit search and type in 'CMD'" he instructed her.

Tasha did as told and clicked on it.

Jason, looking on continued to instruct her, "In the black box, type 'ipconfig,' then hit enter," he said

"So many things are coming," Tasha observed.

"Read me the 'ipv4' address, it's shorter," Jason said.

Tasha read it out, "192.168.1.131."

Jason adjusted his script to the specific computer, "One sec," he said as he tried the script.

"The light is on," Tasha said, catching on to the procedure.

Jason looked through the registry and then online for additional answers. He was still looking when the door unlocked and the girl with the bruises came in carrying a folded shopping bag. Her bruises were virtually gone. She put the bag on the table, and walked out.

"Dinner," Jason announced.

Tasha walked over and admired the special delivery. "I'm now very hungry," she declared and wrung her hands in a gesture of eagerness.

Jason, enjoying this small triumph, also wrung his hands, "Me too" he declared.

They excitedly shoved the chairs back to the table and tore at the delivery bag containing at least 10 pieces of sashimi and easily twice as many sushi in aluminum tins. There were also two large containers of soup. They were so accustomed to eating from the trays that it took a moment to sort out the food. There were also chopsticks and Jason attempted to show Tasha how to use them with little success. Finally, hunger won out and they used their fingers and large spoons to devour everything.

An hour later, they leaned back in their chairs rubbing their full bellies. "I'm stuffed," Jason observed.

"Me too, that was good," Tasha agreed. "I have not seen sushi in many year."

It took a long time for them to recover. Finally, they began to store their leftovers and return to working.

"I don't even know where to begin with the webcam built into that laptop … Can you look up how many machines on the list have this manufacturer?"

Tasha nodded and set about the task.

Jason went back to the computer and searched page after page trying to understand why it did not respond to his script. Online sources had little to offer.

Finally, Tasha broke his concentration. "There were 256 of that group, I think," she announced.

"That sounds about right," Jason said.

Tasha offered a guess, "Is the manufacturer of the chip the same?"

"What do you mean; the same as what?" Jason asked, breaking off his web surfing.

"Is the maker of the chip the same as one of the others?" she explained more fully.

"Well, it's a different brand," Jason said. "I don't know."

He looked up the chip being used and saw that it was the same as the one he originally had written the program for. He looked at the registry entry for the camera he knew he could control and recreated the entire set of keys to the laptop. Then he ran the script. "Any light?" he asked.

"No," Tasha said.

Jason stopped the script and copied the video file. He videoed the door in the distance.

"It worked," Jason declared.

"All right!" Tasha congratulated him.

Jason approached Tasha still seated and hugged her. "That was a smart call, I didn't think of that," he said beaming at her.

"Glad I could help," Tasha said modestly.

Jason smiled. "You really are a super chick."

"Thank you, sir," Tasha said looking not fully taking him serious. "I think!" she added.

"Could you start up that program and get through those names again?" Jason asked. "We haven't done that for a while."

"Sure," Tasha agreed, feeling more and more effective in their efforts.

Jason upgraded his program so he could incorporate all he had learned today. He set up the program to regularly update itself. This way, anyone that had the old code would automatically get the newer version thus saving him the effort to checking every targeted computer to see if his script had installed.

"Hey, Tasha, could you write a program to take screen shots of the desktop every few seconds?"

"Sure, just show me how to do that," she offered enthusiastically.

"Look on 'sourceforge.com' for a screen capture program and just modify it," Jason explained.

Tasha struggled with the endless list of strange names, "What was the name again?" she asked.

Jason repeated it and asked, "What kind of number are we on?"

"It's on 7,563 and going down," Tasha said.

"We need to add a few sites to it later, 'LinkedIn' for one," Jason said.

"You never finished the Twitter program either," She added.

"I know, I'll do it in a bit." Jason replied. He looked at the clock. It was 4:15. They only had a few hours to go, and they needed everything to work this time.

"I'm having a problem," Tasha confessed. "I don't understand some of the code."

Jason got up and walked over to see what was on Tasha's screen. He looked at the code. "Can you scroll down a little?" Jason read and looked up. "What's the issue?"

"What is that? I don't understand," Tasha said pointing at part of the screen.

Jason look on briefly then said confidently, "Oh, I see, you need to set the output type to a file … It's not a problem … Let me in there."

"For this, we'll just store the files as images in 'PNG' format. It's a graphic file format, you don't need a lot of this code," he said highlighting the unnecessary code with the mouse. Then he stood up. "You need to skip all of that garbage about calling the form to save the file. Just put in a 5-second wait. The machine will be busy, but who cares."

He sat back down and continued on his program changes. He was almost finished when Tasha announced. "I have it, I think."

Jason was a little surprised and got up and look over her coding.

Tasha typed something on a prompt; she clicked on an Internet Explorer window. It had a single file that was called 190408.png. She double-clicked on it and the paint program opened with a screen shot of the entire screen.

Jason was impressed, "That looks great," he said. It was now 7:06 p.m. They only had 50 minutes left. "Just make it wait a few seconds and loop."

Jason went back to his work. There was no time to test it again, so he uploaded it to the web server and copied it to the laptops. They seemed to work, too. They had 15 minutes to spare.

Jason went back over to where Tasha was working. She looked frustrated. "What's wrong?"

"I can't get it to stop," she said.

"Let me see." Jason tried the keyboard. The mouse only moved a little and stopped and started again. He reached over and pressed the reset button on the computer. The screen went black. "You didn't put enough time in the sleep value," he explained.

"Oh, I thought it was enough," Tasha said. "It said 500."

"When it comes back up, try 50,000," Jason said.

Jason and Tasha waited for the windows machine to launch. It seemed to take forever. Finally, it came to life and Jason logged in and got up. "Could you find your project? I don't know where to look."

He got out of Tasha's way and she opened the development studio and found her code. She went to the sleep statement and started to change it.

"How many files are there?" Jason asked.

"Uhm, how many files of what?" Tasha asked, beginning to show signs of lack of sleep.

Jason didn't want to spoil her growing confidence or enthusiasm so he simply offered some instructions. "Open the place where the files go," Jason requested.

Tasha clicked on Explorer and went to the folder where the files were being written. There were hundreds for every 1/10th of a second.

"Just make it 5,000, and delete all of those," Jason said.

Tasha deleted all of the files, and changed the value to 5,000 and compiled the program. She went to a prompt and typed a command. Every four seconds a new file was created.

"I think you're ready," Jason said. "Let's log in to that site. Did he tell me the name to search for?" He checked the clock. It was 7:56 p.m.

"I don't know … no, I don't think so," Tasha recalled.

Jason went over to the camera and waved to it. "Tell Willy I need the name to search for. He never gave it to me." Jason went back to the computer that Tasha was sitting at. "Can you log in to that site and make the screen big?"

Tasha opened a browser. The computer paused for a second every time the program ran. It was okay though; it was doing its job.

"Do you want me to log in?" she asked.

"Sure," Jason answered, "do you have a user name?"

"We all do." She replied as she logged in.

Since no one responded to his last request, Jason went back to the camera and waved more vigorously. "I need to see Willy," he stated with impatience.

In a few moments there was a knock on the door and a slip of paper appeared beneath it. Jason picked it up and unfolded it. It had one word: "Sammy123."

"Look for Sammy123," he told Tasha.

She took only a moment and replied, "Okay, I found it."

The video was of a little girl, maybe eight or nine years old. She was sitting on a bed. The room looked like a cheap hotel or motel room with a bedspread that only such places would use, never in someone's home. The camera angle changed a little showing part of a nightstand with a lamp and a white telephone in the background. The girl just sat there on the edge of the bed with her legs dangling over the edge. It was obvious that someone was holding the camera. The bait had been set.

Jason went to the machine that he used to connect to the web server. The server log showed that there were only 10 computers logged in at this point. He refreshed the count and it changed to 35. He attempted to make a connection to the first computer on the list. He could not connect. The next one, however, he was able to turn on the web camera and record. He disconnected and tried the next one.

Tasha had pulled a chair over by him and was watching him work. This process went on for the next twenty or so minutes. Jason glanced over at the video of the little girl. She was being held down by two men. One was removing her panties. They did not have the audio on and Jason was glad. He really didn't want to have the sound of the little girl being raped in his head. Jason tried not to look. It was disgusting and made him start to feel ill. Even more revolting, he checked the log of connections. It was now well over 300 active connections. One by one he connected with the viewer's computer, checked for video connection and started their camera recording. He was keeping a list of the real IP addresses that worked in a file so he could go back and retrieve the video files. After about 30 minutes, he stopped the video and uploaded the files to the web server.

Jason glanced at Tasha who was watching him. She was unmoved by the "performance", no doubt because it was a familiar image in her life. The video now showed a man on top of the girl. Jason's task was slow and tedious: connecting, stopping and starting the upload disconnecting. Each time, he had to reconnect their connection to the server. When he finally ran down his initial list, he started connecting to new ones. He connected to about 15 more but started the stop video upload process at number 12. He couldn't connect to any of them anymore. He looked at the screen. The video was over.

To complete the process, Jason downloaded all of the video files that were created on webcams by the viewers. He had cast his net and it was full. He would use this victory to justify the next phase in his plan.

21

A Business Lesson

Jason had surfed his share of online porn. But the website at the hotel included images and videos that shocked even his experienced eye. The 'models' were so young, just girls … which made the images more disturbing than sexual. "Are the specials always like this?" he asked Tasha.

"What do you mean?" Tasha asked.

"Really young girls … all the violence?" he asked.

"Oh" she said casually, "they can be anything … once, they took a man and his wife from the street. They were just tourists, German people. The husband, he tried to fight them, but they held him down. They had sex with his wife and forced him to watch, then they had sex with him, then they had sex with both of them at the same time. The Germans did not want it and tried to fight, so they beat them until they were both screaming that they liked it and wanted it. Even when it was all over the Germans were still screaming that, 'please fuck me', 'fuck my dear wife,' 'fuck my dear husband,' all those things."

Jason looked on as she spoke and felt a whole new level of awe at what Tasha seemed to treat as daily life. He struggled to keep his feelings contained. "Is that so…?" he said to her calmly. "Is it always the same group of men?"

"No, but the men on this video, I have seen them before," Tasha said matter-of-factly. "They like young boys and girls, you see, much younger than this." For just a moment Tasha seemed to pause, perhaps with the memory of what she had witnessed … or perhaps had experienced herself.

"There are others you see with children?" Jason continued.

"Not always," Tasha said. "Sometimes it's a group of men and a girl, you know, kidnapped from the street. Sometimes it is little boys and men. Once in a while, it is very violent. When we work, we don't have to watch what is done to the models, we just have to check and see if our customer is there or not. Most times, I don't look at the screen … I just try to look at the customer. They are usually staring or they pleasure themselves. But it is still better than watching the screen."

"Are they always from the same place?" Jason asked. The little girl and the men look Asian, or maybe Polynesian?"

"No, I never saw her before," Tasha said pointing at the young model grimacing and struggling to escape her obvious rape. "But there is a man that I have seen lots of times. He is fat and has white hair. When he speaks, it is Dutch."

"So, it's usually the same groups of people?" Jason asked.

"No, they are from all over the world," Tasha said. "Biechas is here now but she was in London. She said she was in a club with some friends and then she passed out. When she woke up she was on a bed naked. The men showed her a video of all of them having sex with her and then they put it on the Internet. They told her that she must work very hard for them or they would send the video to her family." Then Tasha recalled something even more to the point. "They made a video here too, of one of the girls … a long time ago I think, before I got here. Another girl told me about it, but she is gone too.

"There are lots of the women that I remember because I must tell customers about them. You know, to make business. They use some of them for longer than I have been here."

Jason started to feel overwhelmed, "I think I want a drink; would you like something?" he asked Tasha.

"Just beer, I didn't like the whiskey," she said giving him a hard look.

But Jason wasn't listening. Instead, he was trying to act like everything was okay. "I'll get it," he said. "Did you see how I added the computers to the list to get their computer files for email addresses?"

Tasha noticed he was acting strange, but quietly shook her head yes.

What Jason had just witnessed was one of the most disturbing and depraved acts he had ever seen in his life. In spite of Tasha's comment, he grabbed the bottle of whiskey and the cups. He took the lid off the bottle and took a swig straight from the bottle. He poured a cup for Tasha and one for himself.

"Here," he handed the cup to Tasha.

"No beer?" she asked. "I'll get it."

Tasha got up and took two beers from the refrigerator. She handed one to Jason and opened her own.

Jason downed the cup of whiskey and opened the beer.

The door lock clicked and Willy stepped in excited. "Did you get it?" he asked.

Unable to control his feelings Jason uttered, "That video was one of the sickest things I've ever seen," However, it was immediately obvious that it was business-as-usual for Willy too; he was completely unmoved. So Jason gave into the moment and explained, "Yes. I captured 30, maybe 40 viewers."

Willy's expression changed from hostile to happy. "That's great!" he said. "So you got 'em. Now do your stuff and take piece out of their ass."

"I can't believe this," Jason said revealing much more than he had intended.

"Believe what?" Willy asked, suddenly sidetracked from his victory.

"That is one of the most horrible, depraved videos I have ever seen," Jason repeated in a disturbed voice as if his concern would somehow force Willy to care.

"Ah shit, that ain't nuthin'. Man, what you just need to do is make it rain, make me rich," Willy said, cutting him off and returning to his usual threatening glare.

"This is what you brought me here for?!!" Jason exclaimed.

"Whatta you think, punk-ass kid?" Willy said flatly. Then, realizing that his golden goose was starting to crack he added, "You just need a drink. Hey bitch, get me a cup," he said over his shoulder to Tasha.

Tasha instantly got up and headed off to get a cup, her head bowed towards the floor.

"You can get angry all you want…" Willy continued "They are some truly sick bastards, every one of them. And you know what? There ain't one person out there that can stop 'em doin' what they want. There ain't a soul that can make anything right about this business. But there's only one motha-fucker who can make 'em pay … and here ya' are -- my personal goldmine."

Tasha poured whiskey into the cup for Willy and handed it to him. Willy snatched the cup from her. With head down she stepped back.

"So you want me to do what, take their money?" Jason said, checking his disgust for a moment.

"Take whatever," Willy said. "Boats, planes, cars, houses…you do whatever you want. But make me rich. We have a deal."

Jason poured a little more whiskey into his cup. He looked around the room to find Tasha in the corner under the camera, standing with her head down, completely still. He took a sip of whisky and reminded himself to stay calm and stick to the plan.

"So show me what you got," Willy said with a hint of annoyance.

"Tasha, stop the screen capture and pull up a frame near the middle," Jason said. He sat down in a chair and played the video he recorded of a camera. The video was of an older man with glasses smiling at the camera. He scrolled up the frame and could tell the guy was masturbating. It wasn't visible in the video, but you could tell by his face. He closed that one and opened another. This one was of a man in his 30's that looked Indian or maybe Pakistani, who had a smile on his face as he watched. Jason closed that file and the next video was the top of a bald man's head. He fast-forwarded the file, but it didn't change.

"That's no use," Willy said.

"No use?" Jason said becoming frustrated.

Tasha tried to come to his rescue, "Here is a picture," she said. The image showed the little girl struggling under the large, sweating man on top of her.

But Jason wasn't trying to cooperate. "Thanks, now shut that monitor off Tasha," he said firmly. Then he returned Willy's glare. "I don't know what you expect from me" he point out. This stuff is sick; it's not my world, it's yours. You have all the images you asked for."

Willy got up. "Look, kid, you do your thing. You have time. But bottom line, I want 30 grand from these motha-fuckers." He walked to the door and opened, it still glaring into Jason's eyes. "You get me that 30 now. You go ahead and drink on it, sleep on it, cry like a baby or whatever you need to do 'cuz I really don't give a fuck, but get me my 30." He opened the door and left, pulling it sharply behind him with a loud click.

Jason sat in angry silence for a while. Tasha sensed his feelings but could not understand why he would be so upset about what seemed typical to her. She wanted to comfort him but her experience with men left her fearful that even he would become violent. So she gave him space.

After stewing for an hour, Jason did what he always did when facing a bad situation; he got back to work. He copied the Photoshop trial to the two laptops and set up a network share which gave them a place to work as well as to open the videos. The process was relatively simple since the video captures were named by their computer's media access control or MAC address, the hardware ID of the network chip. Jason and Tasha had no idea who the owners of the individual files were, but the second process that ran on the computer would make it so they could figure out who was who.

The program that Jason and Tasha created did a few things. For one, it read settings from various locations of the computer, then saved them into a single text file and uploaded on the web server. The infected computer checked the total CPU usage. If it was higher than 59%, the program quit and waited six hours. If the total CPU usage was lower than 59%, it attempted to open a page on the web server. If the page was not there, the program quit and waited six hours.

Jason and Tasha had to wait for the infected computers to upload their own setting files. They would then edit the videos, convert them to a series of still images, combine the still from the web page and save it as a single-image file. The process was simple for Jason with the right software installed.

"Did you set the computers to send us their setting yet?" Tasha asked.

"No, I kind of got sidetracked," Jason said.

Jason created the necessary files on the web server. When he was finished, he checked the output directory, which is the place where the computers uploaded their information. There sat 278 files. He moved them to a new directory and started downloading them. This was starting to get confusing to Jason even though it was his own process.

Tasha was beginning to tune into his every mood. She was amazed at the number of tasks he seemed to manage at one time but could also see his mounting stress. "Can I do something to help?"

Jason looked at her and smiled, "Sure, can you start by copying all of the old work files to the share I created?" he said. "Make sure you keep the same structure. We'll just follow that."

Tasha pulled the chair over to the computer at the end of the table and got straight to work.

Jason was occupied with both laptops, working with the installation of a Photoshop trial. They both started to download updates, which would need a few minutes.

After a few minutes Tasha admitted, "I'm not sure what you want me to do."

Jason looked up at Tasha, who was sitting in a chair in front of the computer, her hands by her sides. He went to her and kissed her on the cheek, then started clicking on icons. "Copy all the work folders over to this," he pointed at a new network drive 'Z:', He went back to the laptops and finished the install. "You know, we need a program with a database."

"What for?" she asked.

"So far, we have looked at so many machines…email accounts and password files—I'm starting to get confused. This file I have right here—I don't know if it's new or what. And now we're getting all this new stuff and …" he confessed with a look of affection and trust, "I'm not sure what I want us to do…" They both laughed and went back to work realizing that they were together solving the challenge.

After a few minutes Tasha stated as if it were a grand victory, "Okay, the files are done; What's next?"

Jason went over to her machine and logged her into the server. He typed so fast it was hard for Tasha to follow.

"You see these files?" he asked. "Each of them is what makes the machine at the other end send up data. Go through all of the ones we have done." He opened an Explorer window and pulled up the structure that she had just copied. "Now, if we worked on it already, delete the file from this window using this command RM filename."

"So I delete this one?" she asked, pointing.

"Yes; do it for all of the ones we have done," Jason said. He went back to the laptops, which were still updating. Then, he returned to the computer that he had copied the video files to and put those in the shared folder. He checked the web server; it had two new files. He checked their names against the video files and one matched. This was what he was waiting for. He made a new directory, which he named after the current date, and moved the files into it. He downloaded the matching one.

The refinements to the program made it much easier to find stored information. The list included banks, two obvious email accounts, several dating sites, a stock trading account and several other sites that Jason didn't recognize. It was progress.

He opened Photoshop and picked a number of images taken from the web video and made them small so he had 12 images that made up one image. He thought the images were disgusting. Just possessing them was a violation of many laws throughout the world, especially the United States.

He took another swig from the whiskey bottle; he didn't bother with a beer chaser.

He felt compelled to locate the pervert featured in the clip they located earlier in the day. The IP address came back to New York City. He opened a browser and logged into his email. By reading the emails, he could tell this guy was some sort of stockbroker or investment advisor. He had tons of emails about investments and his sent items included a number of emails to clients. There were a few personal emails too. One of them he found interesting. It was to his wife about a dinner invitation.

Now that Jason had the guy's name and where he worked, he attempted to find him on the Internet. His email account was all over the place and he gave advice on a number of stock boards. There was also a YouTube link. Jason turned on the speakers and watched an interview he did on CNBC.

Jason closed the browser and he moved all of the notes to a separate place. This guy was different—someone of wealth, like a doctor, not the sort Willy and his crew were accustomed to dealing with. Rather, a really privileged type that could cause real trouble … or be extorted big time.

Jason checked the web server for another file. He didn't understand why the file was made so quickly. The people watching the video should all have a six-hour wait before they start sending their information. There should have been a longer wait. Why had it been generated so quickly? He suddenly worried that the program was misbehaving. There should have been a wait, he thought. He downloaded the access logs and went through them to find out the answer. This one actually had been infected much earlier because he and Tasha had covered a bunch of shows on the website. So that's why it was generated so quickly, it was just dumb luck.

"How's the deletion job going?" Jason asked Tasha.

"I am still working on it," she said. "Can we write a program to do this part, too?"

"You can later if you want," Jason said. "Now, we have too many other things to do. Do you want some help?"

"Sure,"Tasha said.

Jason starting working the list that Tasha had, from the end backwards. After deleting 10, he was starting to agree that it might be a good idea to write something to automatically delete the work files from the web server. He opened up his development tool and started writing the application.

"I think I got them all," Tasha said.

Jason didn't get very far. He closed the development platform because he didn't want to save the file.

Jason's stomach churned. The liquor wasn't agreeing with him. He stood up and felt dizzy. Jason could feel the blood suddenly rush to his head. He sat back down and looked at Tasha, who was typing at the keyboard.

"I don't feel well," Jason said.

Tasha stopped what she was doing and looked at him. She stared at him for a second, then got up and walked over to him. "Stand up," she said.

Jason stood and instantly felt dizzy. Tasha guided him to the bathroom doorway. He moved quickly to the toilet and knelt. After fumbling with the lid, he emptied his stomach into the toilet bowl. He could feel Tasha's hand on his back.

He lifted his head from the toilet while he was on his knees.

"Do you feel better?" Tasha asked.

"I think so…" he said. He started to stand and immediately leaned back to the toilet and threw up the remainder of his stomach's contents.

When he had finally stopped retching, Tasha got a cool washcloth. She then helped him to the bedroom. They lay down on the bed together. As she cradled his head in her lap gently dabbing his sweaty forehead with the cloth, Jason watched as the room spun, then fell into an exhausted sleep.

More Than Greed

Jason sat hunched over a computer, his attention entirely focused on a new problem. The program he'd just run generated only a blank screen – not what he would expect from the program. When he opened the program to look at its instruction, only gibberish appeared and he didn't recognize any of it. He hadn't written the code and he couldn't make out any clear logic in it, so he tried to run the program again. Suddenly, he heard the door unlock and swing open. No one came in though; it just swung open. Jason could see the door across the hall from where he sat. He thought Tasha was working next to him, but when he turned to her, there was no one there. He got up from the chair and went to the bedroom. She was nowhere to be found. He cautiously looked down the hallway. The left side was longer than he remembered—much longer than the right. He stepped into the hallway and went left, which should have led him to the rear stairwell. The hall was eerily silent. Finally, he reached the stairwell, which led downward from the lighted hall into complete darkness. He cautiously took a step down the stairwell, but it seemed to fall out from under his foot and he fell headfirst into the pitch black. Overwhelmed with panic, he opened his mouth to shout then suddenly … he woke up.

It was still dark outside. He could feel his heart racing and he was covered in sweat. Tasha's head was on his chest and she was sound asleep. He lay there for a while, staring at the dark ceiling, intending to get up. However, he found himself awaking again and this time he could make out that it was sunrise. It looked early from the amount of light coming through the window. He tried to slide himself from under Tasha, but she stirred and moaned a little.

"Are you feeling better?" she said groggily, still not fully awake.

"Yeah, I feel better," Jason replied. "Good morning."

Tasha sat up in bed and stretched. "We were sleeping forever."

Jason headed to the bathroom. "I think maybe we can get breakfast today. It seems early enough."

Tasha hurried around him playfully. "I need to pee!" she laughed.

Jason brushed his teeth and looked at himself in the mirror. He saw a strange change in his reflection. The guy looking back at him was no longer the straight-laced, virtuous, law-abiding citizen he'd always believed himself to be. The person looking back was becoming something new. He was engaging in acts that he had only thought about in the past, but dismissed as inappropriate, illegal or perhaps immoral. He was becoming a hacker, like the ones that go to Defcon. But the forces imprisoning him were monsters, and the monsters they served were no doubt much worse. "But," he wondered, "Are they really worse?" They are easily different than their victims, left violated around the world. "How could these monsters exist?" They abused so many people, day and night, and in the broad daylight of publically available internet. Why didn't he read about their abuse in online media or the newspapers or see it on TV? This wasn't some backwards developing country. America possessed all the technology needed to detect the abuse and many levels of authorities to act on it.

He had grown up in this city and was aware of all its many police and human services agencies. How was it possible that monsters could be so free to force people to do unspeakable acts? He then considered that he had become one of the people being forced into acts he had never before committed. He would never have done any of this on his own. Jason felt anger swell up inside. "There has to be a way out of this," he thought. The police seemed like an obvious option. He could call them anytime with the Internet connection; maybe they would call in a SWAT team. However, the police are paid to find crime. The entire system is geared to just arrest, convict and incarcerate. They would be short-sighted and wouldn't be able to attack the long reach of the firm and its powerful clients. They were unsophisticated and essentially powerless to deal with the power of the Internet. In the face of such technology and power, local forces would choose to not believe him without the help of a high-powered attorney, one he could never afford.

Jason looked up and saw Tasha near the coffee maker – here was his ally, his partner in taking on the monsters. He walked toward Tasha as she was coming out of the bathroom with a coffee pot full of water. He grabbed her by the waist and kissed her deeply, taking the pot from her. He pushed her back towards their sleeping area and they fell on the bed. In spite of his mixed feelings about adding to her abuse, in this moment he felt deep passion for her both as the one spark of beauty and promise in his life in that moment, and as the closest thing to a lifeline, he was not alone in all this. They made love lustfully yet tenderly.

Afterwards they lay catching their breath and covered in sweat. Tasha considered asking why Jason was suddenly so passionate. But something was changing. She was beginning to understand, or perhaps remember, that sex could be lovemaking. So instead she sat up suddenly and announced, "I'm going to brush my teeth now"

After Tasha left the room Jason realized that he needed to get the day underway which required coffee at just the right dose. He poured Tasha's version of coffee grounds back into the can and re-measured carefully into the filter. With that priority in hand he walked back to the computer and sat down. He didn't need to look at the computer clock to realize that it was still early. The door swung open slowly and the red-haired girl brought in two trays of breakfast. She put them quietly on the table. Without a word she turned and looked around the room for the old trays. Seeing there were none to collect, she turned and knocked on the door which immediately open and then closed behind her, the lock clicking loudly. Jason looked on with full awareness that whoever was watching the cameras had witnessed his passion with Tasha in the bedroom and had waited until they had reappeared before ordering in breakfast delivery. He and Tasha were no better than "models" for the watchers but Jason didn't care anymore. He would set all this right.

"Food's here," Jason called out as he got up to get the coffee pot. He had to clean out the two cups before he could use them. By the time he came out of the bathroom, Tasha was sitting at the table and had moved the chairs into position. Jason put the cup in front of her.

"Thank you," Tasha said.

Jason went to get the pot to fill both cups. He sat in the chair opposite Tasha. "We have a lot to do today," he said.

"Well, just tell me what we need to do," she said. Then, switching gears she asked, "How are you now?"

"I feel fine ... now," Jason said.

"You looked green yesterday, like a zombie," Tasha said. "I have never seen a zombie."

"I guess a lot of things just didn't agree with me last night," Jason said.

"Yes, you were very sick," Tasha said.

"How did you sleep?" Jason asked.

"Good," she said. "After we eat, can we take a shower?"

"Are you trying to tell me something?" Jason teased.

"If you want me to say you smell, I will," Tasha smiled. "You smell like whiskey."

"Okay, I'll go first," Jason said.

After they finished eating, Jason got up and went to the bathroom. He turned the water on and waited for it to get warm; he then turned on the shower. He didn't have clean clothes to put on, so he went back to the bedroom and found pants and a shirt. He went to the office to get Tasha to join him. He peeked in and saw that Tasha was in a chat with someone on the computer. He went back to the bathroom, thinking that was odd. He would look at it later, since she was on the machine that he tested the key logger on.

Tasha came in the bathroom while he was drying off. "My turn," she said smiling.

Jason shaved and got dressed and went back to the computer at the far end to start the download process. There were hundreds of files to choose from. Each of the files had the possibility of having passwords in them, but he wasn't interested in all of them, only those with videos.

Jason connected to the computer that Tasha was using earlier and looked at the web history. She had been on Facebook. He downloaded the key logger log file and read just the last few lines:

"www.facebook.com"

"ann333tayor8782@aol.com"

"Bluebird1"

"Hi"

"Yes"

"He is so nice"

"I never felt like this before"

"No"

"I don't know"

"Ok"

"Bye"

Jason closed the file and went back to work. The files were still downloading so he started deleting other files off the server so the computers wouldn't run that script again. He was in the middle of that process when Tasha came back into the room. She had a towel on her head with nothing covering her body. She sat down in a chair.

"I feel fat … do I look fat to you?" she said.

"You look very chunky to me," Jason joked.

"Really?" she said worriedly.

Jason got out of his chair and walked over to her. He climbed on top of the chair by straddling her chair, with his legs hanging over the arms of the chair. "You are perfect in so many ways to me. You have no idea."

"But you said…" she said.

"I wouldn't care if you were an elephant - although you must work must harder if that's your goal." Jason put his arms around the back of her head and pulled her close to him. "You're so good for me…," he said looking at her fondly, then added, "I really was kidding; you're a very beautiful woman."

"You think I'm…?"

Jason kissed her for a while. When he broke the embrace, he leaned back a little too far. The chair gave way and it fell over. They landed on the floor tangled up in the chair, and her towel had fallen off in the process. They both started laughing.

"Are you okay?" Jason asked.

"Nothing hurts," Tasha said.

"Good," he said. "I come in peace," he joked, then whispered, "You've been hurt enough."

"I … I hope you will rescue me from these people," she replied in a hush, breaking from her usual acceptance of a tragic life.

"Maybe *you're* rescuing me…!" he whispered back and their eyes locked for a moment in a glance that suggested a new level of trust. They kissed for a little longer before getting back to their feet.

Then Tasha brought them back to reality. "We have some work to do," she said.

"Yes ma'am," Jason replied. "Maybe you could cover up some of that beauty?" he noted smiling slyly as he took one more glance of her striking lines and gentle curves. He set the chair back upright as Tasha, smiling over her shoulder as she moved gracefully towards the bedroom where her clothes and memories of lovemaking lay waiting.

Jason opened a window so Tasha would be able to see all the files. He also made a connection to the server so she could delete the ones they didn't need any more. He went back to the computer he used and logged into the PayEasy account to set up a transfer of $7,000 to the bank account. He noticed that now there were four charge backs in their resolution center. He started working on a note and sent the note to each of them. It read:

"We note that you request return payment for four sets of DVDs featuring exotic performances featuring our most novice models. We would be happy to return your money. However, please be informed that with all such returns we email everyone in your contact list identifying you as a major consumer of this material as well as other products we provide. This policy is to insure that others in your networks might appreciate our inventory and the interest of influential patrons like yourself by name, position and location. If you decide to move forward with your request, please let us know your decision in the next 48 hours…"

Jason looked over his note with satisfaction then signed it more ominously,

"The grave robber"

Jason signed off the system. He went back to matching and moving files so that he had the data with the video. He called out to Tasha, "When you get done with that, can you check the data files again and see if it got any email addresses? We need to weed out the bad ones so we have a working list…" From the looks of it, there were 41 matching file sets. Hopefully all of them had email addresses.

The door unlocked and the redhead and a tall blonde that Jason had never seen before came in carrying boxes. Jason took the box from the tall girl, since it looked heavy. "Thank you," he said. She said nothing, but looked down, turned and opened the door. She picked up another box to bring in. There wound up being several boxes. One of them was from Hong Kong, according to the postage.

The redhead came in last with a vase filled with flowers. She put it on the table and left the room, the door locking behind her.

Tasha stood up and inspected the flowers. She took the old ones that were still alive and moved them into the new vase. She tossed the dead ones in the garbage stack and emptied the water in the bathroom.

There were 14 boxes in varying shapes and weights sitting in front of Jason. He opened the first small box and found a small tool set, soldering setup and a spool of black 16-gage wire. He took out the shipping material and put the items back in the box. He put it with the other boxes for the Anthony project. He grabbed the box from Hong Kong and put it there, too.

Tasha opened the box that the blonde had struggled to carry in. It contained paper reams. "Where do you want this?" she asked.

"It doesn't matter," Jason said. Tasha put it under the table near her.

Jason and Tasha continued opening boxes containing printer toner, the connecting cable for the printer and a cable for the all-in-one printer and ink. They stacked the empty cartons near the door. When the boxes were put away, Jason sat back down and downloaded the drivers for the printer.

"What's all that for?" Tasha asked.

"Something I need to do for Willy's boss," he said, "you know, the guy I left with."

"Oh yes," Tasha said, then noted, "I'm done with the server."

"Could you look for email addresses?" he asked her.

She nodded a silent 'yes,' staying focused on her work.

Jason got a ream of paper and put it in the printer. When he flipped the switch, it made noises and came to life. He printed a test page and put a few sheets of paper into the all-in-one photocopier and printer fax machine, and tested them, too. Now he could print, and soon there would be a lot to print out.

After a while, Tasha exclaimed, "I'm done!"

"Let's use these," Jason said and pointed at the new laptops that were sitting between them. Jason took one and Tasha took the other.

"Open Photoshop," Jason instructed.

"Ok…" she said, waiting. "It's taking a while."

"Yeah, 'shop's like that, my copy too," Jason explained.

"Ok, now what?" Tasha asked when it opened.

"Mine is still loading," Jason said. "I think your machine is faster. Can I use it instead?" he said with a serious look on his face.

"Sure," she said and started to move it.

"I'm kidding!" he joked, still amazed at her trained quickness to comply. I don't need it," Jason confirmed. "Now pick a video and play it. You need five shots of them. Here, watch me."

Jason started a video and an older, rather ugly man was sitting back from the screen. The speaker started playing the sound of the webpage. Jason turned the volume off. Then he hit the "Prt Scr" button. He paused the video and switched back to Photoshop. He opened a new document and pasted the screen into it. He went back to the video and scrolled it forward, making it fast forward. He paused on a single frame, which was the image of the man beating off. He hit "Prt Scr" again capturing the image. He switched to Photoshop and created a new image. He did this process five times.

"Now we need to create a template file," Jason announced. He found a number of images of the men and the little girl. As he looked, he tried not to comprehend what was being done to her. It was like trying to look into the sun without noticing that your eyes were blazing in their sockets. He opened all the images in Photoshop and resized it to an 800x600-sized file. He made the image look as though it was a series of images taken from the video. He saved it as template ".psd". He cut and resized the images of the man and put those images across the bottom then saved the file as "pedofile.jpg".

He turned to face Tasha. "Did you follow what I just did?"

"Do I have to make the … 'template'?" Tasha asked.

"Just open it and you can use the same one," he said. "That's why I named it 'template'" Jason made the file "read only" to help her avoid making the same mistake that he would also likely make were he just learning this process.

Jason had done two more, when they heard the door unlock. The brunette with the now fading bruises brought in lunch. She set the trays down on the table then looked up in surprise at all of the computers and equipment around the room. She quickly recovered, lowering her head and silently scampering from the room.

Jason offered Tasha water.

"What, no wine for you?" she teased.

Jason shook his head smiling, "Not today."

"OK, bartender," she continued.

While Jason went to clean out the cups and fill them with water, Tasha pulled the chairs to the table and moved the flowers closer to where they eating.

Jason sat Tasha's cup in front of her, and sat down.

"They are so pretty," Tasha said pointing to the flowers.

"He was wrong, you know," Jason said.

"Who was what?" Tasha said.

"You need flowers," Jason said. "They are almost as pretty as you." Tasha looked at him affectionately. Jason tasted his soup and made a face. "Wow, this is salty," he exclaimed with raised eyebrows.

Tasha took a sip and grimaced as well. "Oh no, that is too much salt."

They both sat for a moment, their lunch interrupted by the vile-tasting soup.

Tasha tried to recover, "We haven't had the radio on for a while," she said enthusiastically.

"I could put on an Internet radio station," Jason noted and went to a computer. He carried his sandwich with him and took bites from it while he used the mouse to navigate to an Internet station.

"Is the Grateful Dead okay?" he asked.

"I don't this person who has dead," Tasha replied looking uncertain.

As soon as he turned the volume up the classic rock tune "Truckin'" blasted across the room. Jason, bouncing his head to the music, sat back down and finished his sandwich. Tasha listened to the unfamiliar sound and fell for its upbeat tempo. Soon though the music became just part of the background and they were back to work. "How many do you have left?" Jason asked Tasha.

"I don't know, maybe five," she said.

"No way!" Jason said, shocked. "I only got a couple done. Are you doing them right?"

"I think so," she said. "Maybe you are slow, like old man."

"May…be," Jason agreed in good humor.

"What do we have to do next?" Tasha asked.

"Next I have to call Willy down here," Jason said. "We are almost ready to go, and I have no idea how he wants to collect the money. "

"Why don't you mail it?" Tasha asked.

"That would be risky," Jason said. "The police will be interested, and I really don't want them busting into this room. There is too much here that no one would understand."

"I don't want that either," Tasha said. "I am not legal citizen, I would go to prison."

"What do you mean?" Jason asked.

"Illegal people go to solitary prison in America," Tasha said. "I do not want to be locked alone."

Jason thought about what she was saying and knew that it really wasn't true, but it didn't seem the right time to inform her. They needed a way out of that room, and a way out of that hotel. They also needed a legit way to live after their getaway.

When they finished eating, Jason went to the laptop and checked the images that Tasha was creating. He was impressed to find that they were all done correctly and that she had indeed done more than he had.

"I'm going to get Willy in here," Jason said, then, trying to spare her the usual humiliation he added, "Why don't you tidy up the bedroom?" He gave her a kiss on the cheek.

She took the hint instantly replying "Okay," as she quickly headed to the other room. Jason waved at the camera and ordered, "Get Willy."

Jason went to every computer and pulled up an image that he or Tasha had created. Each of them was different. Jason sat down and continued to work with the other images while he waited.

A few minutes later, the door unlocked and Willy appeared. As soon as he heard the lock, Jason changed the window he was working on and opened one of the finished images. He displayed the image at full screen on the monitor so Willy could see it.

As he entered Willy immediately noted the graphic images on every screen: A red background and what looked like a series of still frames from the rape of the little girl. Across the bottom of each of them was what looked like screen shots of a video made of the men, watching. The image was on all eight of the screens, including the two laptops.

"These are the images of the monsters you asked for," Jason said.

"Wow, it's…" Willy exclaimed excitedly as he moved in closer to inspect each of them.

"All that's left is for you to decide how you want to get paid," Jason said dryly.

"You really did it … !" Willy said in disbelief, still fixed on the images.

"It was a lot of work, but yeah," Jason replied. He pointed at an image and changed programs on the closest laptop. He opened the text file that Tasha had created, which had a number of websites and passwords listed. He chose the Facebook one. He opened Facebook and entered the user name and password. A Facebook wall of Eric Akins displayed.

Jason opened another page and opened Yahoo. He logged into it and clicked on "email" and the page filled with emails. Then Jason stood up.

Willy looked on in shock. "Wow, man, I had no idea for sure," he said slowly. He then looked up at the camera and shouted to the watcher. "You won't believe this shit."

"Okay, you have good old Eric," Jason said. "I have him doin' the nasty. If he is not a complete uncaring sociopath, he'll be freaked out that someone has caught him at his shit. So I can make good old Eric play any tune we want."

"What is the 'social path'?" Willy asked.

Jason was stunned by Willy's ignorance but replied, "It doesn't matter," "Look I…you…we have good old Eric by the balls. But there is a problem and you need to fix it."

"What problem?" Willy asked.

"I can get in touch with Eric here and make his life fucking miserable," Jason clicked with the touch pad on the laptop and pulled up the "about" page for Eric on Facebook. "It looks like Eric is married. Want to send her a copy of the image there?"

"Okay," Willy said unconcerned, "I get it, but what's the problem?"

"Eric is in Miami, Florida," Jason said. "Last time I checked, that's 2,500 miles from here … and that guy…" Jason said pointing to another monitor "is in London, England … How do you want to get paid?"

"We have the mail thing set up?" Willy asked.

"Yes, we do, and we're using it to mail items to pick up," Jason said. "If one of them tells the police, they will find their way here. Is that what you want?"

"No," Willy said. "So gimme another option."

Jason worked to remain patient, "You can have them send it through the wire service, but someone will have to provide ID to pick the money up," he explained. "The advantage is you can pick the money up anywhere in the world. The downside is they can flag the transaction to call the police. Also, some locations don't have a lot of cash, so you can't make the amounts too huge."

"Is that the only option?" Willy asked.

"Well, there is a hole in wire service," Jason observed. "That's why they are set up with governments—to track transfers of large transactions. They assume the sender and the receiver are real people. So they don't watch the sender but they're all over the receiver. That is, the receiver can have a flag at a terminal. The system is not designed to track the sender, so what we do is make this guy send money to a password recipient. Those are blind to the system and anyone can pick up the money anywhere in the world. But not just one—we break it up so they send two payments of $500 each to two different password recipients. This makes the payment blind to the system. Following so far?"

Willy nodded. "Yeah, but how do we know they sent the money?"

"We tell them to send us proof, like the username, password and security questions, to get into the wire system account via email," Jason said.

"Then you can check and see if they sent the money?" Willy asked.

"From anywhere in the world … you just don't want it sent here," Jason pointed out.

"But you said you have 30," Willy said. "That's only 30 grand. I need more than that. I want 100 grand."

"You'll have close to that," Jason said. "Right now you have $7 grand waiting for you to pull from ATMs and close to $60 more in PayEasy. There are 41 at $1k each. That makes 100 and change."

"But how many people watched that video?" Willy said sarcastically, "Hundreds! But, you only nailed down about a quarter of 'em. Nah man, you need to get me more, I want all of them. I want $400 grand, you give me 400 and I'll let you out of here." Willy got up and walked to the door and knocked. It opened. With just a glance over his shoulder he said, "You have a good start, but I need all of it. You get me 400, we'll talk about this." He slid through the doorway and made it lock tight behind him.

Jason knew that this was an endless, no-win situation. This guy was never going to let him go. He knew that from the start. It seemed funny that Willy only now decided to say so up front. His greed was bottomless and it would only get worse with each boatload of money Jason served up.

Jason became calm as his plan came more into view. "Tasha," he called out, "coast is clear,"

"I heard him," she started. "Such a pig, always like a pig."

"I have an idea," Jason thought aloud, "Let's finish those images."

Tasha and Jason got the rest of them completed in a few minutes. Jason opened his laptop and encrypted the entire directory. He copied the key and saved it on the laptop. He deleted the originals. "How many watched that video?" Jason asked.

"I don't know," Tasha said.

Jason went over to the computer Tasha used most of the time. The tune "Fire on the Mountain" was playing. He closed the picture on the screen. He made a connection to the web server and downloaded the log file. He opened the file and scrolled down almost to the end. Then he went back up. Anyone who watched any performance on the video site downloaded his program. There were hundreds of thousands now. "Count how many unique IP addresses had this," he pointed at a long string of numbers.

"How do I do that?" Tasha asked.

"Write a program or you could do it on the server," Jason said, then added, "But you know how to write the program … save time, okay?"

Tasha smiled at his confidence in her and went straight to work.

Jason got to work too. He pulled boxes out from under the table, and started taking the uninterruptable power supply apart. He had two large batteries that weighed close to 20 pounds. The unit was intended to be a battery backup that had several outlets, two LAN ports, two cable connectors, and a single cable for plugging into a wall. He took off the back and took out his wire cutters. He removed all of the electronics from the unit first. He got the box out that had his spool of wire and soldered the switch to control the unit directly to the input line. Then he soldered the outlets to the input line; this made the box nothing more than a large power strip.

There were several items he had to take out of their own plastic cases to fit into this new plastic box home disguised as an everyday battery backup unit. The first was the cellular VPN router, which provided access via the mobile network's Internet connection to it from anywhere in the world. The next item was a femtocell box, which made a local hotspot for cell phones to connect to and acted as a gateway for the cell networks. Femtocell boxes are sold by cellular companies to supplement their cell towers. This particular one had a way of using it as a spy device. It allowed the user to connect it to a network and copy any text message or any other data sent through it to the network access.

Next he installed a miniature computer with Ethernet. It required 12 volts and had no cooling fans. Jason plugged the very large solid state hard drive to it. It made no noise and none of it had moving parts. He had to make the cables so the Ethernet ports on the outside of the box would plug into the router. He plugged a monitor into it and plugged a keyboard in and turned off one of the laptops. He took it apart enough so that he could remove the DVD player. He wired that to the tiny computer. He needed the drive to install an operating system since he didn't have any thumb drives.

The door unlocked and an unfamiliar brunette walked in. She was short and rather 'big-boned' with a huge chest. She was wearing glasses and had trouble with the trays she was carrying. Not saying a word, she put them on the table, and then, while trying to keep her head down, knocked on the door and was let out.

Tasha looked up, suddenly aware of the smell of food. "I'm so hungry; we must eat" she said.

"I'll be right there," Jason said. He pressed a random key as the installation instructed him to do. When he was done, he had built a 'Pwned' box. In the hacker world, Pwned means 'owned', or defeated. He had never needed one of those before, but he would need to test on it a bit before deploying it. This all-in-one model allowed monitoring of the local network and all cellular traffic, and it cost slightly less than $800.

Tasha looked on with fascination. "You work with taking things apart, too?" she asked unsure of what to call the parts or what he was doing.

"Yeah, and every once in a while I can put them back together" Jason joked. "Do you want water or something to go with supper?" he grinned at her as he spoke.

"Water," she said. "So many wires there, sticking everywhere."

Jason went to the bathroom to clean out the cups and get water. "They keep the smoke in."

"What smoke?" Tasha asked.

Jason came back with the cups and handed one to Tasha. "Why, the magic smoke, of course."

She looked at him doubtful. "You're making it up," she said.

"Nope," he replied as he sat down before her, "I'm not, it's the way things work,".

"You're making fun of me … don't do that," Tasha said.

"No, really," Jason insisted. "If you let the magic smoke out of the thing, it won't work anymore."

"Hmm, I don't believe you" Tasha said.

"How's the program coming?" Jason asked, changing the subject.

"I'm having a little trouble," Tasha said.

"I thought you might," Jason said. "A log like that gets created every day."

"There are so many," she sighed.

"I know," Jason said. "I bet there are well over 100,000 computers running that code now."

"So many?" Tasha exclaimed in disbelief.

"Yep, and we can get them all to do whatever we want," Jason said. "That is the power of a 'bot'—even a small one like we have."

"Anything we want?" Tasha asked.

"Well, we have been getting them to fork over information about single users info, like the stored passwords on them," Jason said. "You noticed some of them don't give us the file we want, right?"

"Yes," Tasha said. "Your code doesn't work with some of them."

"That's expected," Jason said. "Some people don't store their information that way. Some use a program to store passwords. We can get into those, too. It will just take writing a little more code."

"But we have so many now … more than we can take care of in a year," Tasha said, "you know … doing it this way."

"I know," Jason said. "I've been thinking about that. Maybe we should try another tactic."

"What do you have in mind?" Tasha asked.

"Nothing at the moment, I'll come up with something," Jason said. "You know what I miss?"

"Like what?" Tasha asked curious to find out his next move.

"Chocolate cake," Jason smiled. "The first thing I'll do when I get out of this place is get some chocolate cake."

"I like lemon," Tasha joined in, quickly realizing the game. "I had it once, it was yummy."

"Starbucks has that," Jason said.

"Starbucks?" Tasha asked, trying not to reveal yet another American thing she did not know.

"Come on, you don't know what that is?"

"No, what is it?"

"Overpriced coffee," Jason explained. "But it's good."

"Overpriced is good?" Tasha asked.

"In this case, yes," Jason said.

Jason had finished eating and was waiting for Tasha to finish. "So what's the issue?" he asked.

"I tried to do that trick you showed me with a database, but it won't connect," she said.

"Okay, let's see," he got up and looked at the screen. "You're missing a semicolon again, and…" he started typing. "I fixed it for you. What are you doing, just duping the entire thing?"

"Yes, I'll sort it after," Tasha said.

"Okay, that's the smart way of doing it," Jason said.

Jason went back to his project. He hoped Willy didn't appear with more questions and that their conversation would keep him out of the room for now. Jason looked at the board and wires; it was going to be a tight squeeze back into that box. He turned the power off and fitted the parts into the box. The antenna needed better isolation from the AC wires, so he cut and made the wires longer so he could pin them to the side. He would need to cut the plastic to get the back of the unit on. The AC adapters were giving him the biggest problem. He read them and decided to try to just use one instead of three. The one that came with the computer was five watts, which should have been overkill for powering USB devices, but he wasn't using any.

He tried powering everything back up and it all seemed to work. The router came up on its own. The computer still needed to have the power button pressed that was just a setting in the chip. He made that correction.

After making noise cutting with the dremel and making the air smell foul with the hot glue gun, he was able to get the back onto the unit. He plugged a computer in and checked out the cellular monitor. The 'Femtocell' came from China; it was a copy of a Verizon or AT&T unit that had three modes of operation: only one or the other or both. It took him a while to understand how to control it. The software development kit was not documented at all. When he made the program from the source code, the resulting test program was in Chinese. There were two cell phones that were listed as attached. When he turned it into diagnostic mode, he could capture the voice output to a file. He had to wait for the call to be completed. There was no way out of it. So he waited. The file closed on its own at the end of the call.

He copied the file over to the local computer he was on and got the headphones. There was no telling what this was. He put the headphones on and played the file back:

"Bored as hell"

"Where are you?"

"I told you. I am working."

"Oh, sorry."

"I have to sit here until 11, and then Jerry takes over. Kiss the kids for me."

"I will, I'll wait up for you."

"Okay, I love you."

"I love you, too."

"Goodbye."

The record on the web page of the femtocell box gave all kinds of information, from the number to the start time, which looked like it did when he turned the unit on.

Jason opened another web page and tried to look up the two numbers. One was a cell and he knew that the other belonged to a residential unlisted number.

Jason looked at the current connection page and found three cell phones attached. He refreshed it and only one attached. It was the same one who had the call he listened to. He put it back in diagnostic mode and was able to get data from the phone and what type it was. He clicked on messages and there was a new outgoing text message, which read,

"Hey baby, wanna hook up? Off in 10."

Jason closed the message and waited. He was about to hit refresh on the page again when the page changed itself to a new incoming text message, which read:

"ICW"

Jason wasn't that into text messaging so he had to look up the meaning of the initials. The first website he went to, his antivirus gave an alert. It blocked downloading a Trojan that stole banking information. Too ironic he thought. Finally, he found a site that offered that "ICW" meant "I can't wait."

Jason sat there for a bit longer and refreshed the connections a few times. At one point, there were eight cell phones, then six, then two, then one. It stayed, and it disappeared.

Jason tried the VPN box. He had to register it for service with one of the month-to-month carriers. He paid for an unlimited monthly data plan service using Willy's money. After an hour, he was able to get it on the cellular network. He used his laptop to connect to it and had the building's network plugged in to test. The unit worked, however he noticed that it got a new IP address every time it connected. He would need to write something that told him what the IP address was. The box did allow him on the network and he knew he had a few things to do.

"I think I have it," Tasha suddenly said.

Jason looked up from his project, "Have what?" he asked.

"There were 636 connections to that video, they were watching."

""I don't remember how many were there last time"

"Me neither," Jason said.

A while later Jason had worked so furiously that he hit the wall, "Wow, I'm losing it. Do you feel like watching a movie?"

Tasha looked up from her computer, willing to continue but seeing Jason's tired eyes. "Sure," she offered, "would you like some wine or is it too early for that?"

"Nah, not yet," Jason said, still regretting the night before. "Maybe some sushi?"

Tasha slowly walked the refrigerator. "Yes, there is some of that," she reported.

Jason pulled the mattress it to the middle of the floor and went to the bedroom to get pillows. "What will we watch?"

"Something funny. We need to laugh" Tasha insisted.

"Okay, let's see…" Jason found something on Netflix—a Martin Short comedy. It really wasn't his thing, but he thought Tasha would enjoy it, so he put it on.

They lay on the mattress together but before the movie was half-over, Jason was asleep with his head resting on Tasha's thigh. She looked on wondering at what he was really planning and doing with all the wires, puffs of smoke and the smell of burning.

23

Betrayal

It was still dark out when Jason awoke. He lay there for a few minutes staring at the black ceiling. The computer screen was still on and lit the room with an eerie glow. Tasha was sound asleep, her head slowly rising and falling on his chest.

He slid out from underneath her and went to the computer. He jogged it awake with the mouse and noted the time—3:45 a.m.. He grabbed his laptop and logged into the camera network to see if the coast was clear. First, he checked the control room. The guy in the hat was sound asleep. Jason grabbed a screwdriver and stood on the chair behind where the camera was mounted. He poked two holes into the ceiling tile. He took the black wire and clippers and mounted the webcam near the ceiling. He ran the cable to one of the new laptops. Then, with his laptop, he adjusted the webcam to match the angle of the camera in the ceiling. It wasn't the same, but it was close.

He set one of the test laptops up with a program to record video from the webcam mounted on the ceiling. He moved the unit, so it

311

was sitting on the table. At the edge, someone would need to turn the camera backwards to see the wire or the camera.

Jason went back to the mattress on the floor. He gently slid Tasha's head back onto his chest. Eventually, he fell asleep again. After a while, Tasha moved a little, which woke Jason up. They gazed at each other for a moment with a now familiar combination of wonder and desire. "Good morning," he greeted her.

She did not reply, but her gaze turned even more sensual and wanting.

Jason pulled her close to him and kissed her deeply and slowly, taking time to stroke her back and lightly kiss along her neck on both sides. He rolled her backwards and kissed the back of her neck. He took his hands and slowly rubbed his palms across her nipples. He kissed and rubbed once more. She slowly reached back and stroked him a little. He slowly moved a hand down her front and across her stomach to the top of her pubic hair and stopped. He rubbed her nipples again and stroked her ever so slowly. Each touch further ignited her eyes, her breathing and body heat. She turned slightly to fully face him, a final savoring before giving over completely to the moment. She then reached out and firmly pushed him onto his back. As she slid on top of him they joined effortlessly in a smoldering moment of intense pleasure. They continued that way with no sense of time, perhaps an hour. Eventually, Jason was on top and kept their dreamy pace. However, Tasha could no longer bear the building tension and she pled with him in her native language, but he needed no translation. He pounded their bodies together in a determined frenzy which continued long after they had each groaned in orgasm. Eventually, they collapsed in a sweating, gasping mass of arms and legs. They lay stroking each other quietly until sleep overcame them once more.

An hour or so later, the door unlocked. The door opened and hit the edge of the mattress.

The redhead came in with the trays. She looked down and saw Jason and Tasha on the mattress and seemed as if she was confused as to what to do with the trays. Jason looked up at her and said, "Just leave them here on the floor."

She did as she was told, turned and immediately left the room.

Jason got up and made some coffee. He headed to the bathroom to relieve himself, brush his teeth and admire the devastated look that comes with good sex. On the way out, he found the cups and put the trays on the table.

While they had probably treated their watcher to a sunrise porno, Jason still felt the need to put some pants on. Tasha slipped into the bathroom so he put the mattress back on its side against the wall. As he waited for Tasha to get out of the bathroom he sat sipping his coffee, enjoying a moment of peace before breaking into work.

Tasha walked into the room and sat down across from him. She sipped at her coffee and shared the moment with Jason, until a strange look came to her face. Her eyes glazed over in sudden anger as she caught site over Jason's shoulder the web cam wired to the ceiling behind the camera. "Where did that camera come from?" she thought and feared their handlers had managed to enter the room as they slept.

Jason, seeing her alarm, leaned forward and put his index finger to his lips. He smiled and winked at her. "Well good morning again."

She suddenly understood and replied happily, "Yes, good morning."

"Do you think you want to look for emails or write something to automate some of this?"

"I don't know," Tasha said. "I see everything fit nicely."

"Huh?" Jason said. "Well, yes, your body is amazing."

Tasha tilted her head back and laughed loudly. She pointed at the table. "Your wires, they all fit," she poured out. "I see you fit everything into the plastic box."

"Oh yeah," Jason replied with a slightly embarrassed look, "I got them all in there. I've got a thing for glue guns … hot glue saves the day."

Tasha was charmed by his odd admission. "It's a rainbow of pasta spilling from a black bowl," Tasha said embracing his achievement.

Jason, realizing how strange his zeal with the glue gun must sound, replied more soberly, "I guess it looks like that, I suppose."

"Why do you put movies on you don't like?" Tasha asked.

"What, which movie; you mean last night? I liked it," Jason lied.

"No, you slept," Tasha pointed out. "When, you put something on that you like, you stay awake."

"I never thought about it," Jason replied wondering where she was going with the conversation.

"I have seen it happen," Tasha said. "You put things on that you think I will like but you sleep, so I know you have no interest. Next time, put something on you think I won't like and you will."

Jason went along with her proposal, "I guess I can do that," he offered, "But why would I put on something I don't like?"

"No silly, put something on you like and don't worry so much if I will like it," Tasha explained. " That is how you will learn that I like many things."

"If we have time left in this life, it will be my mission to understand that," Jason said, pleased but somewhat puzzled by Tasha's growing openness.

"You're funny," Tasha said.

"What is that about?".

"You get very serious when we talk about ourselves," Tasha said. "I have had time after time, some sorrow, but now I have you. This is joy to me. I never thought this possible again. No need for such serious, just joy."

"Well, I never saw this coming. It took a lot to discover you," Jason said still quite serious. "Men with guns and locked doors, crazy mean people all around…" He thought quietly for a moment then continued. "My soul was like a huge flat parking lot that stretched for miles in every direction, all made out of concrete and somewhere near the center is a crack that lets just one flower grow. I never thought it possible but you're that flower … You have no idea how much you mean to me."

Tasha said nothing but looked at Jason intensely, casting aside any concern about his "seriousness." She struggled with allowing the affection for him that was building inside … affection she had learned to bury deep.

They sat quietly a while longer until the need to get working crept into Jason's mood, which meant more coffee. He looked down at his empty cup. and glanced across the room. He could see only a thin line remaining in the pot. "Would you like a little more coffee?" he asked Tasha as a way of announcing the shift to working.

"Sure," Tasha said, knowing Jason's routine very well by now. Jason poured it into her cup and went to make another pot. He sat down as he waited.

Tasha watched the action he took and poured half of her cup into his. "Here, have this until it's done," she said, caving in to her feelings.

"Thanks," he said, taking a sip (he really missed milk). "For now, we're short $300,000. If we have all of the machines and wait two hours instead of six, we could speed some things up. We need about a thousand machines to give us a couple of hundred bucks each. If I pull down today's log, we need to know which machines connect."

"That doesn't make sense," Tasha said.

"I know, I've never done this before," Jason said. "The way we're doing this is really slow. The reason I do the video capture by hand is because it eats the speed of the computer when it saves the file. If we let it go by itself, it might just lead to the entire program being reported to the antivirus agents. If that happens, we might have to start all over."

"I understand, but how will we get so much money?" Tasha noted.

"Yeah, right," Jason said. "There are probably lots of files out on the server. Do you know how to copy them down?"

Tasha shook her head.

"Well, let's do this, I'll pull down what is there and you write an app to look for the email accounts."

"App?" Tasha questions.

"Sorry, 'application,' 'a program'," Jason said. "It means the same thing."

"Okay," Tasha said.

Jason got up and pushed his chair to the machine Tasha used most of the time. He logged into the server and checked how many files: 1,251. He started the process of downloading them to the local shared space so they could be separated. Tasha's new program would take care of that.

"I'm going to need some help with this," Tasha said.

"Not a problem," Jason said.

Jason went back to his laptop. He needed to test the VPN connection some more and write something to let him know the IP address. He settled on a script that kept track of the IP and if it changed, it would email a message to a new Gmail account he created for this purpose.

He connected to the Femtocell box and checked his connections. The guy from yesterday was connected again, along with three other cell phones. Jason refreshed the screen several times to see if they would disconnect before starting to monitor one. The diagnostic mode only worked on one cell phone at a time, probably due to a limitation of the hardware. None of the cells were active in a call. He connected to one at random and waited. Nothing happened for quite a while, so he disconnected. Overall, the box was not very revealing, but might come in handy in the near future.

After a few more reboots, he pulled the plug from the wall, and plugged it back in. It took the script several minutes to send the email, but that was fine. The next challenge would be putting the unit in place.

He thought about sending Anthony an email, but he felt he was an ally— or at least not a threat like Willy. For one, he was smarter and more in control of himself. Jason put on the headset, then took it off and set it on the table. He was already running out of gas.

"We need more coffee, want some?" Jason asked.

"Sure, I can make it," Tasha offered.

But Jason already had a new pot brewing. While waiting for it to drip, he called Anthony at work.

"Law offices," a female voice answered.

"Attorney Jones, please," Jason said.

"One moment, please," came the well-practiced reply.

A second female voice came onto the line. "Hello, how may I assist you?"

"Attorney Jones, please," Jason repeated.

"I'm sorry, but could you please provide me with a case number or your name so I can see who is assigned?" the female voice said. "Or do you have a first name perhaps? We have six attorneys with the last name of Jones."

"Attorney Anthony Jones, does that help?" Jason said.

"One moment please."

A moment later, Anthony answered. "Attorney Jones, may I help you?"

"Hey buddy, how's it going?" Jason said.

"I'm sorry, who am I speaking to?" Anthony said.

"Oh, I'm sorry, we met a while back," Jason joked. "Think you, me and an Irish bar."

"Oh … it's you," Anthony said with mild surprise. "I didn't expect you to call."

"Yeah well, we need to talk," Jason said. "Listen, I never got that birthday gift from you and I have something for you. The walls here are closing in on me so maybe we could take a little road trip and swap."

"Oh, sure," Anthony said struggling to keep up with Jason's coded message.

"Your Aunt mentioned you won a contest," Jason said. "You'll have to tell me all about it."

"I did, I did indeed," Anthony said.

"Any possibility you could stop over and pick me up?" Jason said. "I hate to impose, but my car is in the shop."

"Around 8 p.m. work for you?" Anthony asked.

"Sure, see you then," Jason said and hung up.

Jason took off the headphones and retrieved the coffee pot. He poured some in Tasha's cup and put the pot down. He got right behind her, put his hands on her shoulders, and his head right next to her ear. Then he whispered, "I am going to go somewhere tonight, but I will be back, don't worry, I wouldn't leave you behind."

She turned her body and her head so that her lips could meet his, and they kissed. "Okay," she said, finding reassurance in his eyes.

She then exclaimed as though to cover up their whispering, "I am having problems with this. I looked on the web for help, but I really don't understand."

"Let me see what you have," Jason said. "I see you're doing those list box things. Why not just get the list of files and use it in an array?"

"Oh, I didn't think of that," Tasha said. "The web was showing me this."

"I know, sometimes the answer is simpler than you think," Jason said. "Does it help?"

"Yes, I think so," Tasha said.

Jason took the pot over to his cup and filled it. He wanted to do the reboot test again. Once the box was placed and plugged in, he would not be able to physically get access to it again.

Jason walked under the camera and unplugged it. He tugged on the wire and it fell into his hand. He set the camera on top of one of the computers. If he was right, they weren't watching his every move, now. He moved the laptop with the recording in front of him. When he looked at the screen, it was solid blue with a message that windows had crashed. He restarted the machine.

While he waited, he checked the connection log to the web server. Looking through the log, he saw strange connection attempts from a range of IP addresses. The way he used the connection log in his infected computers would attempt to connect to the server for a file named specifically for each of them. There were many machines that were infected and connecting constantly, each once every six hours since the time that they were last restarted. On over a hundred thousand, that meant a connection from somewhere on the planet every few minutes. What stood out was that whoever was attempting a connection was not someone infected; it was a different string entirely. If he hadn't been watching the logs for another reason, he would have never known this was happening in the background.

The IP address range was all coming from Moscow. A quick check of a number of IP addresses made that part easy. He searched for the strings they were attempting and had no luck. If he were to guess, they were attempting to hack into his web server. Jason really didn't have time for them, so he just blocked the internet connection from Moscow. He also set up a rule so that if anyone else tried using the exact same method they would be blocked immediately.

He tested the penis advertisement on another computer and realized his rule made the advertisement not work. On the third or fourth try, he got what he was looking for.

The Windows machine had finally booted up, so he watched part of the video from the morning's events. The webcam did a good job, even better than the Wi-Fi camera. Jason searched for something to knock down the quality of the video. If he guessed right, he would need only a few minutes of it when the time was right. The process of editing frame by frame would take hours, so he locked the screen.

The door opened and an Asian girl with long black hair came in. She wore the same uniform as all the others. She crossed the room to put the trays on the table. The door stayed open. This time, the big Russian guy was holding the doorknob and staring at Jason. She put the trays down and went back out. The door closed and locked.

Jason wondered what the stare-down was for. Maybe he pissed off Willy with the phone call. That is, if they listened in. There was no way of knowing.

"Do you want water with that? There is a little wine left," Jason said to Tasha.

"I'll have water," Tasha said.

Jason retrieved her cup and his and took them to the bathroom to rinse them out and fill them with water. When he returned, he found Tasha had moved the chairs by the table, put the trays in front of them, and moved the flowers so they were closer to the seats.

Jason put the cup down in front of her and sat.

"I'm making some progress, but it is hard," Tasha said.

"I know you will get there and it will save time later," Jason said.

"I know," Tasha said. "It just takes so long to write something."

"Well, there are lots of computers out there ready to give us their information," Jason said. "If we just let all of them send up their stuff, we would have thousands of bank accounts to go through."

"Is that what you want to do?" Tasha asked.

"No, I never planned on being a thief," Jason said. "Actually, even though these perverts are out there, stealing from them doesn't seem right, either. That reminds me, did I tell you that several people tried to get their money back on PayEasy?"

"No, you didn't," Tasha said.

"I sent them all a note," Jason said. "After we eat, we should take a look at them and see what they are up to."

"Let's take a shower first before getting to work. You have clean clothes in the dresser."

"Thanks, I was going to ask you about that."

"Would you like me to scrub your back after we eat?"

"Huh?"

"I need a shower and so do you," Tasha said, touching his face. "Your face is too rough."

Jason glanced at Tasha in the mirror and could see a red ring around her neck caused by his lovemaking. He rubbed the coarse whiskers on his face. "Point taken," he said.

"Why don't you shave every day?" Tasha asked.

"Well, I used to have a routine, but being here is difficult. I'm usually a very clean person," Jason insisted.

"I have been here for a long time," Tasha said with determination. "I will help you have that routine … should be clean, too."

"I understand," Jason said, accepting her awkward but almost motherly offer. "From now on, I'll shower as soon as we both wake up."

"Okay, I will do that too," Tasha said with a look of accomplishment. She finished her meal and went to the bathroom to run the water. Jason finished his sandwich and got up to follow when he heard the lock click. He turned and Willy was in the doorway. Jason turned to face him.

"I don't know what kind of shit you think you can pull," Willy said.

"What's this about?" Jason asked.

"We pulled out about $4,500 from the bank and it said that the balance was zero," Willy said.

"I put in $7,000," Jason said. "I can put in more. It's not a problem. But something else *is* going on."

"Why are you only putting in such small amounts anyway?" Willy asked.

"Well, if you want I can dump the whole thing in, but then the cops will come," Jason said.

"You would like that, wouldn't you?" Willy said.

"Do you have any idea what the penalty is for hacking in the United States?" Jason asked.

"No," Willy said.

"Let's just say, someone murders someone else and gets caught. They would get less time in prison than I would. Look at this room. If I get caught here, I would never get out of jail, even though you made me do this. The government would give me more years than I would live in three lifetimes. There is no way I want that to happen."

"What is that box about?" Willy said.

"What box?"

"The box you made."

"It's for Anthony," Jason said. "And you really don't want to know. Actually, you don't even want to say you saw it."

"Is it some kind of bomb or something?" Willy asked.

"No, it's not a bomb, but it is used for doing things that are more illegal than you ever want to deal with," Jason said. "He asked for it and he'll be here later to pick it up."

"You're in contact with him?" Willy asked with a look of suspicion and scorn.

"Yeah, but I haven't mentioned your little moneymaking scheme to him," Jason said, returning his scorn. "Should he know?"

Willy stared at Jason and then replied flatly, "You know I'm gonna keep my moneymaker all to myself."

Jason worked to keep the upper hand but knew he must avoid pushing Willy over the edge. "Well, there's no need to tell Anthony anything, I can handle both your request. But he asked me to make this device and to do a few other things for him which take time but keep him off your back." Having offered a workable excuse for his phone call, Jason shifted the focus back onto Anthony, "Did you log into the bank and see why you're short money?" he asked accusingly.

"No," Willy said.

Jason went to the closest computer, which was the one that Tasha was using to write code. He brought up the browser and opened his log file of passwords. He logged into the site, and clicked transactions. A list of transitions appeared. They started out with the initial deposit: a few withdrawals for online purchases and a deposit of $7,000, then a series of ATM withdrawals: $300, $300, $500. Near the bottom was a check for $3,000.

"You wrote a check."

"I didn't write a check."

"Well, someone did," Jason said. "I'll put more money in. I need to check something on that site anyway."

"So who wrote the check?" Willy asked. "Did you?"

"I don't have a checkbook, and why would I need to take money from there? I have money to put in. Is Wanda an inmate?"

"…Fuck!" Willy said. "The fuckin' bitch!"

Willy got up and opened and slammed the door. A second later, it locked again.

Jason left the screens up; he would get to them as soon as the shower was taken care of. He went to the bathroom where Tasha was still tensely anticipating trouble from Willy. She looked at Jason with relief and turned the water back on. They stepped into the shower together and washed off the bad feelings from their latest contact with Willy. As the water reset the mood Jason was aware of how intimate it was to do simple domestic things together. She washed his body and he washed hers. They washed each other's hair. When they were finished, they dried each other. She instructed him to sit on the toilet lid so she could shave him.

Willy left the building in a cold rage. He brought Ivan with him who knew better than to question the often out-of-control actions of his coworker. It was still daylight as they drove onto the grimy street where Big Maurice and Wanda squatted with other junkies in a rundown, abandoned apartment building. Willy passed the building, and they parked much farther down and across the street. They exited the car and walked the two blocks back to the building. It was a dilapidated but quiet scene; it was still early in the day and most junkies were sleeping or just unconscious. Willy and Ivan entered the building and pushed on the door of the first apartment. The presence of Big Maurice usually offered rock-solid security, but Willy had chosen this moment carefully. The door was not locked and swung open without a sound. The interior was large but in ruins with broken furniture, trash and the odor of urine.

There were ancient heavy curtains on the lone window facing the street but a narrow stream of light shone through from the outside. Big Maurice and Wanda were lying, clad only in their underwear, on a mattress on the floor. A skinny, tall youth, fully dressed in jeans, t-shirt and sneakers lay sprawled out on nearby on a couch. All three of them appeared passed out, probably strung out on crack and heroin. Willy put the gun to Wanda's head. He thought for a moment then roughly nudged her awake. Willy was careful to allow her enough time to come to her senses. As she did, her eyes shone wide and terrified as Willy's face came into focus looming above her. She quickly glanced over to Big Maurice. But he was still passed out and more importantly, at some point in the night, he had removed his ever-present shoulder holster and gun. The boy he had ordered to act as lookout had instead injected himself and lay on the couch; a syringe still dangled from a vein in his arm.

Wanda's groggy attention was suddenly jerked back to Willy who shouted, as if to announce a message to the whole seedy collection of addicts in the building, "Nobody takes nothin' from Willy ... not bitches, not nobody!" He glared at Wanda with eyes that bulged with a fierce coldness.

"Willy, I, uh.." Wanda uttered weakly, searching desperately for some excuse for her offense. But before she could find the words, Willy shot her point blank in the forehead. Blood and bits of brain sprayed across the room. By now the others were conscious too and they looked on in horror. Big Maurice attempted to roll from the bed towards his gun but Willy had only to raise his arm slightly to shoot the huge man in the back of the head. Then, while obviously still dazed and completely unarmed, Willy shot the boy on the couch until he gasped in an agony and death. Willy's vengeance was so intense that Ivan held his breath and stood very still, lest he too become a target.

Willy's rampage left the room awash in blood. His large pistol was loud, even more so in the confined apartment. Anywhere else, such noise would bring on excited onlookers and the police. But in this neighborhood, just like the world of the inmates at the hotel, there would be no police, no onlookers, no witnesses. Nonetheless, as he and Ivan slipped out, Willy set the entrance door to lock automatically and pulled it closed with his shirt to avoid leaving fingerprints and to delay others from stumbling onto the bloody scene. They hurried out through the back of the building, now completely deserted by the addicts who had scurried away like so many rats. The back door opened to a lengthy barren backyard, shared with a matching building. They pulled open the rear entrance and cut through the neighboring building back to the street to further deny their presence at the crime scene. However, there was no need for this extra step; the street was abandoned and no one came to the windows of any of the buildings. Fear reigned, as well as a complete surrender to crime and violence. In fact, it would be days before any authorities would arrive … that is, until passersby and even the squatters in the neighboring building could no longer stand the smell of the rotting corpses and gathering rats.

Willy and Ivan returned to the hotel, quickly changed out of their blood-spattered clothes, and then checked on the inmates. Returning to their usual routine, they watched the monitor as Jason and Tasha worked on, unaware of the true extent of Willy's greed and uncontrollable violence. There would be no more unexpected withdrawals from the online account in Wanda's name.

24

Deliver The Package

Jason tried connecting to the VPN again. He tested it one more time before unplugging it. He wanted a final test before delivery. It was connected, but nothing was going on. He logged off and pulled the plug. He picked up the unit, which was very light compared to what it should feel like. It looked exactly as it should; it was just a typical battery backup for a personal computer.

"Come, please," Tasha asked.

"Sure." He moved to see what was on Tasha's screen and looked over her shoulder. "So what's wrong?"

She turned her chair to face him and motioned him to lean over, like she was going to whisper something. Instead, as soon as his face was near, she kissed him and ran her hands behind his neck. She rubbed her face against his cheek. "That's better; you need to stay this smooth."

Jason smiled at her mocking approval then returned to the laptop. The rendering of the video was still not finished, so he logged onto Wanda's PayEasy account, and looked at the resolution center. There were three new ones; one of them was old and for the new ones he sent the same message as before:

> **We are sincerely sorry that you wish to reclaim the money for the four sets of DVDs featuring explicit sex acts with children. We will be happy to return you money. In fact, we will email all of the people in your contact list that you bought this item and perhaps reveal some other habits that they might find questionable. That is, if you still really do want a refund.**
>
> **Please let us know your decision in the next 48 hours.**
>
> **Thank you very much for your business.**
>
> **The grave robber**

Jason clicked a contact to whom he had sent the message earlier. It appeared that Eugene Farmer had decided to play hardball. In utter denial of reality, he claimed he did not order anything, nor would he have.

Jason looked for the files for good old Eugene. First, he updated his program to connect to the web server every 15 minutes and told Eugene's computer to do that update from the web server. He had to wait for the update before he could do anything more. Jason logged into Eugene's email and found something that listed his phone number. Jason looked up the number and saw it was a cell phone. Eugene had sent himself emails from work so Jason knew the email address he used there, too. He pulled up the website at his workplace. The company he worked for marketed enrichment program materials for elementary schools. They offered a complete anti-bullying program and there was a picture of Eugene. He was one of their featured speakers.

Jason checked for the connection for Eugene's computer. There was nothing yet. It could arrive at any time up to six hours from when Jason put the command file on the website. That is, of course, if the machine was currently turned on. He added a notification to the log when that machine fully decided to check in.

Jason downloaded a hard drive scrubber that was a self-booting iso. An iso is a disk image, and this one was designed for CD-rom. If started, it would destroy all hard drive information that the computer contained. It would repeat it over and over. The United States Department of Defense used the same method before releasing hard drives from its secure facilities. It is essentially a "scorched earth" policy for computers.

Jason spent the next two hours making CD-ROM copies—one for each computer in the office. He checked the progress of the video conversion program. It still wasn't done, but the percentage bar moved forward from 23% to 24%. In hindsight, maybe it wasn't too smart to do it on that laptop since they lacked real video cards and were thus not as fast as desktops.

Once again Tasha beckoned him to her.

"What's up?" He asked across the room, unwilling to be tempted.

This time her request was more serious. "I don't understand all the information in these files," she said. "You showed me how to look for email addresses, but where does this information come from? And this—I can't do anything with it, It looks like just many numbers."

Jason instantly realized what was happening. "Sorry Tasha," he explained, "you know what I forgot?"

"No, what?" she replied, surprised that he could forget anything.

"Well, Internet Explorer encrypts the stored information, but leaves the key on the computer," Jason explained. "So we have the key and the encryption data, but I never decrypted them."

Tasha thought a moment and responded, "So the ones that we didn't find anything for might be in these files, and we must go back through all of them?"

The door unlocked, interrupting Tasha's distress. The red-haired girl was back carrying trays.

"No, we don't have to do that," Jason reassured her. "It might be interesting to widen that out a little bit on the videos."

"Must we go back through them?" Tasha said, looking overwhelmed.

The girl put the trays down and picked up the other trays.

"I don't think it's necessary and you know how many we have now," Jason said.

The girl knocked to leave and went out the door. It locked behind her.

"We don't have enough time to do all of the ones we already have," Tasha said.

"Do you want water?" she suddenly offered.

"Sure," Jason said glad to change the topic for a moment.

Tasha took both cups to the bathroom while Jason took the plates off the trays and moved the chairs in front. Tasha came back with the cups and sat down.

"Was the Asian girl new?" Jason asked.

"No, why, what is wrong?" Tasha asked.

"I never saw her before today," Jason responded.

"You think she's pretty?" Tasha asked sharply.

"Well, I think many of the women here are pretty," Jason said. "No, I'm trying to figure how things work here."

"Do you want her instead?" Tasha asked, not distracted from her concern.

"No, don't be silly," Jason said. "I enjoy you for much more than your looks. We haven't known each other that long, but to be truthful, you probably know me better than any of the women I have dated. But, I never tried locking myself in a hotel room with them for a couple weeks to see what would happen. I don't think most people would get along so well."

"I didn't choose to be here though," Tasha said.

"I didn't choose to be here either," Jason said. "You're trapped and so am I. Perhaps it was fate or the alignment of the stars. I don't follow those things, but whatever it was, it led me to you." He paused for a moment and realized Tasha was asking for reassurance. He bent down close to her and whispered. "You are wonderful."

"Thank you," Tasha whispered beaming but looking a little embarrassed. "I really like you," she confided, in spite of feeling she must reveal such things to no one, especially a man. Her defenses toward Jason began to fall aside.

"I don't understand why all of these things happened to me…" Tasha continued, slowly and quietly with tears suddenly welling up in her eyes. " … all of these things."

Jason was surprised by her sudden turn and began to realize that helping her recover from such trauma would require much patience and reassurance. "What's important for you to understand is that it isn't your fault these monsters found you," he offered. "They look for people, they hunt. Whatever they've made you do, it wasn't in any way your decision. It was theirs."

"I am liking you," Tasha offered, her emotion further limiting her English.

Jason took her left hand and put his arm around her. "I really like you, too," he assured her, squeezing her firmly but gently. It occurred to him that she was becoming frantic as the time of his departure was nearing.

"Can you put on the movie thing before you go?" Tasha asked.

"Sure; we're not leaving for a few hours, though," Jason observed. "Maybe we could watch something together or we could play a game."

"Can we play Go?" Tasha asked.

"Sure," Jason offered. Somehow, beating him at Go had become a symbol of comfort – it allowed her a moment of power with a man who did not resent it, but rather encouraged it.

They finished their food and played a couple of games of Go until it was time for Jason to get ready. Jason wore the same pants; fortunately he'd bought an iron for other purposes. He was starting to plug the iron in and Tasha took it from him. "Let me do this," she said. "Boys don't do it right."

Jason found his Cisco product bag and put the UPS inside; it barely fit. He could have used a bigger bag, but this was all he had.

The door unlocked at almost exactly at 8 p.m. and Anthony stood in the doorway. He was wearing a tailored green suit, which looked like it should be in the pages of GQ. "Are you ready to go?" he asked.

Tasha was standing next to Jason when the door opened. She put her head down and stepped backward.

Out of the corner of his eye, Jason watched Tasha shrink away. "Sure, all ready," he said to Anthony, gripping the bag in hand and stepping toward him.

Anthony pulled his cell phone out of his pocket. "Can you put this somewhere? I actually like the phone and don't want to lose it."

Jason paused at the strange request, but took the phone from him and put it inside one of the boxes under the table.

They walked out the door, down the rear stairwell and into the night air. Even in the dark Jason paused for a minute, now unaccustomed to the outdoors, and looked up at the sky. A star or two twinkled innocently. They walked to Anthony's car and got in. Jason put the bag he was carrying out of sight behind the front seat on the floor. Anthony barely waited for him to close the door, driving quickly down the street as if he was as relieved to get away from the hotel as Jason.

"So what's in the bag?" Anthony asked.

"Laundry," Jason replied nonchalantly . "You know I don't get out much."

"D'you like steak?" Anthony asked.

"Yeah … that sounds great," Jason said.

Anthony jumped onto the interstate and drove 30 minutes to the next city. They didn't speak. Instead they listened to the radio tuned a talk station. Jason listened intently as the radio personalities and guests covered a variety of topics that he found new, and revealing about Anthony's character. Finally, they exited the freeway. After a mile or so they pulled in front of a small building surrounded by a large parking lot. Anthony drove up to the valet and handed the attendant his keys.

Before exiting the car he turned to Jason and said, "If anyone asks, just say you're a client."

"Yeah, fine."

They walked into the building, a restaurant, and stopped at the guest podium. A strikingly pretty hostess asked, "Do you have a reservation?"

"No, I…" Anthony started.

A tall man with salt and pepper hair and wearing a in a stylish black suit approached them. "Mr. Jones, how nice to see you, won't you come this way?" he said. The girl politely smiled at them as they were escorted to a table by the window. The table had a white tablecloth and settings for four. The maitre d' was also an attractive woman. She raised her hand in the air and pointed to a short Mexican man. He came over and took the extra plates and silverware while the maitre d' took the napkin from the table and placed it on Anthony's lap. He did the same for Jason.

"I am so happy you found your way back to us," said the maitre d'. "Would you like a drink or perhaps the same wine as you had last time? Or would you like to look at the list?"

"What I had last time is fine," Anthony replied.

"And for you, sir?" the maitre d' said, looking at Jason. "I'm sorry, I do not remember meeting you or perhaps my mind is slipping."

"My name is Jason," Jason said.

"Very good, Mr. Jason," she said. "Would you like sparkling water or spring? And would you like to see our wine list?"

"Tapisfine,andjustyourhousechardwouldbefine,too,"Jasonsaid.

"A fine choice, sir." She left the table and another tall man that looked like he was from Mexico or South America brought over two bottles of water. He poured from the first into Jason's glass and set the bottle on the table. He poured from the second bottle into Anthony's glass and put that bottle on the table and left. A woman appeared with a bottle of wine and displayed it to Jason and Anthony. She opened the bottle and poured a little in Anthony's glass. He swirled it in the glass for a moment, then sniffed it. He turned the glass and put his nose in to smell the bouquet, before putting some in his mouth. It took a second for him to swallow, and he motioned to her that it was acceptable. She filled the glass halfway and then stuck the bottle in a wine chiller.

Jason was not especially fond of red wine nor was he accustomed to such formal treatment. He had been in nice places before, but nothing like this. He had never had a man put a napkin on his lap before. And the patrons matched the setting.   At each table, men wore expensive suits and women the latest fashion in dresses. In the background, a piano offered an air of refinement. It all seemed a bit odd in a building in such a remote, desolate area. Nonetheless, he found himself committing the setting and the sophisticated rituals to memory as if they might come in handy some day. A waitress soon placed Jason's chardonnay in front of him.

"A toast to a new beginning," Anthony offered, raising his wineglass.

Jason responded and they saluted with a distinctive clink of the crystal glasses.

After taking a sip of wine Anthony asked,"So how are things over at the shop?"

"I'm not really sure," Jason said." I've been getting money for him, but Willy didn't follow my instructions. He did something that – "

"That will get his ass into a sling, I would suspect," Anthony interrupted him.

Jason thought about that for a minute. "That sounds about right."

"And we're not going to bail him out this time," Anthony said "I'd advise you to be prepared for any type of eventuality that he creates."

Jason thought quietly a moment on Anthony's words then chose to move on. "I made some headway on your request," he noted.

"That's good," Anthony said. "Oh, hold that thought."

The waiter brought two menus and handed them to Anthony and Jason. He recited the list of specials, and left them to look over the menus.

"Do you know what you're having?" Anthony asked.

"What is couscous?" Jason asked.

"Do you know what grits are?"

"Yes."

"They're similar, but ground finer, and can be quite delectable."

"I see," Jason said. "Maybe I'll get just a steak."

"You haven't been to a place like this before, have you?" Anthony asked.

"No, not like this."

"Let me order something for you, that is, if that's okay," Anthony suggested.

Jason looked carefully at Anthony, "All right,"

"Do you eat asparagus?" Anthony asked.

"Uh, yes," Jason replied realizing that it would not have occurred to him to request that dish.

When the waiter came back, Anthony ordered both dishes. The waiter looked at Jason. "How would you like that prepared?"

"Medium?" Jason said uncertain of what to expect.

"Very good, sir," replied the waiter without hesitation.

"You were saying?" Anthony asked, as the waiter walked away.

Jason returned to his line of thought. "I've assembled a lot of data, but I need to understand who's linked to create enough pressure to forget about other things for a while," Jason said. "What

I've brought in the bag will help locate the links, but you'll need to install it somewhere. It can be anywhere, really. I think it's the same model as the ones your office uses. I saw a couple when I was there."

"I have made some enhancements to your suggestions as well," Anthony said.

Jason was a little surprised by this announcement. "Well, okay," he stated.

"We're here to celebrate a new beginning," Anthony raised his glass to toast again.

Jason didn't really know what they were celebrating, but he did gather that Anthony certainly was in good spirits.

"Have you ever been to the Opera?" Anthony asked.

"No, don't think so," Jason admitted.

"Without a doubt, it will be one of the most inspirational things you can do!" Anthony exclaimed. "When I was in New York, I went to the booth that you sent me to. I purchased front row center for 'Les Misérables'. The clerk handed me tickets for the *Metropolitan Opera* for the next night. They were for another person standing in line and the clerk almost fell out of the booth trying to keep me from moving on with them. No problem, I handed them back, and she set me up with other tickets."

"So I'm in New York City at Times Square in the middle of the afternoon," Anthony continued. "I have no idea where to go or what to do for hours. So I walk around for a little and find myself in a nearby Cuban restaurant for lunch. I sit down at the bar and this white guy sitting next to me says, 'I should have walked away with the Met tickets when I had the chance -- a much better deal.' I ask what he means by that and he explains he was the other customer at the booth picking up the Met tickets for family members. Then he goes on about how the opera is the only art form that has the ability to transform a man's soul. He seemed genuinely inspired, so after lunch, I go back to the booth and buy a ticket for the Met the next night. Les Misérables was wonderful but the next night I went to the Metropolitan Opera and that changed my life. I was so overwhelmed that I wandered around the city for hours afterwards just trying to come to terms with all the feelings it touched in me."

Anthony refilled his glass of wine while he spoke and he looked at Jason. "Would you like some of this? It is much better than…would you?"

Jason was pulled along by Anthony's enthusiasm and nodded his approval. Anthony motioned to a waiter by holding up his glass with one hand and pointing to it with the other. Before he could put his glass down, a waiter was there with an empty glass for Jason. Anthony filled it from his bottle and announced, "Enjoy." He continued his story. "You know, I realized what that man at the bar had tried to tell me. But then it occurred to me what I should do be doing, now and for the remainder of my days."

Anthony reached into his pocket. "Oh, before I forget, take this with you." He put an envelope on the table. Jason picked it up and slid it into his front pocket.

A waiter came and dropped off a small basket of warm bread and rolls for the table. Jason took a roll and put it on his plate. He noticed the butter had the logo of the restaurant pressed neatly into it as he scraped it with his knife to put it on the roll.

"You should go to the opera sometime," Anthony said. "It may change your outlook on life."

"The next time I have a chance," Jason said.

"Do you like the wine?" Anthony asked.

"Yeah, different," Jason noted.

"Yes it is," Anthony said. "You know that if Willy screws up, things might change over there. Are you sure you want to go back over there?"

"Well, I have some things I really need to do," Jason said. "And my laptop is there and…"

Anthony interrupted. "I know about your girlfriend … good for you," he said." But be careful, your 'arrangement' has caused more than a little friction over at the shop."

"What kind of friction?" Jason asked.

"All organizations have politics, even small ones," Anthony said smiling.

The waiter brought the dishes of food. Each looked like it belonged on the cover of some gourmet magazine. On top of Jason's steak was a white sauce that was shaped like a bowtie. He had a bite and the combination of the taste of the steak, crab and béarnaise sauce was incredible.

"Besides you and Peter at your firm, does anyone know what I did for Willy?" Jason asked.

"I only know a little about what you did for Willy," Anthony said. "And I really don't want the details. There is a note in the envelope that will answer some of your questions. How's your steak?"

"It's great," Jason noted. "Best I've ever had."

"This is one of my favorite places." Anthony pointed out with affection.

"Sure, I can see why it would be," Jason said.

"Do you like art?" Anthony asked, continuing his earlier theme.

"I guess," Jason shrugged.

"Take every opportunity to enrich yourself," Anthony said wistfully, "or you'll miss out."

"Miss out with what?" Jason asked.

"Miss out on *life*," Anthony said leaning in. "Enrich your mind by reading and absorbing everything around you. It's the only way to appreciate all that's there. I know you like computers, technology. But there's much more outside of that world than in it. Think of it this way: for every amazing image or work of art that's finds its way into computer space, there's an unlimited number of masterpieces that don't get entered."

"Kind of like the hotel box," Jason said. "What I've witnessed there, just people in a box?"

"I think you are missing my point," Anthony said. "Take look around this room."

Jason took a brief glance.

"Okay, how many of these people are hackers that steal money?" Anthony asked.

"I have no idea, probably none I would guess," Jason said.

"Are you counting yourself? You should be," Anthony said.

"So what's the point?" Jason asked.

"Just like there are other lawyers in here, there are also other thieves. Not everyone steals, but many of them do for the little things. Oh they justify their actions, even if it is a little. Do you know what the world's oldest profession is?"

"Prostitution?" Jason guessed.

"Think about this," Anthony said. "Have you ever seen an animal steal food from another?"

"Sure, I guess," Jason said, becoming a little perplexed by Anthony's questioning.

"Don't you think humans are just as likely to steal too?" Anthony asked. "So why would a woman selling her body be credited as the oldest, when people have been stealing since the stone age, long before money was invented? It's called denial, the cover up that has lasted for as long as humans walked the earth."

"So people steal and always have?" Jason summarized flatly.

"You were forced to steal at some point, but you'll face a new moment of a decision … I just hope that you will make the right decision when the time comes," Anthony said. "That's all."

"I guess I see what you're saying," Jason said, appreciating the sophistication and concern that Anthony was sharing.

The two talked through the first bottle of wine and then another. Finally, Anthony paid the bill and they waited at the doorway for the valet to bring up the Mercedes.

"The box that you have—I guess you mean I should put it in the office when no one is there," Anthony said.

"Uh, that's the idea," Jason said looking at Anthony to acknowledge they were doing something secretive against the Firm.

Anthony paused as if making a decision, and then stated, "Let's go, then." He drove to the office building and parked his car on the street. He opened the trunk and took out a briefcase while Jason took the Cisco bag.

The security guard asked for them to sign on the pad. Anthony signed and handed it to Jason who signed the name, "Jim Longstreet." The guard didn't ask either of them for identification and they were soon on the top floor. The office lights were turned off. Jason walked to the first desk where he saw a UPS, just like the one in the bag. Anthony stood looked on quietly as he swapped the units, plugging the network connection to the computer and to the wall. He inserted the computer monitor and what he guessed was a phone power cord into the box. He put the other unit into his bag.

"Okay, all set," Jason said.

Jason stood up and he and Anthony walked to the elevator. Next to the elevator was a large garbage bin filled with paper cups and garbage.

"Do you really want to carry that to the car? It looks heavy," Anthony said.

"Not really," Jason took the unit out and pressed it into the can, pushing the garbage on top.

They rode the elevator down and had to sign out at the security desk.

"Have a great night," the security guard said.

"You do the same," Anthony returned cordially.

Once in the car, Anthony seemed uncertainly. "You can access that device from anywhere?" he asked.

"Yes," Jason said confidently, which put Anthony at ease.

He drove back to the interstate talking all the while, "Now you have money. The electronic cards I just gave you have enough to get you out and far away from here," he pointed out. Anthony then looked Jason in the eye and asked, "Is the girl really that important...?"

Jason was not prepared for his question but had no doubt

about his answer. "Yeah, the girl is important. She's part of the deal. Can we get her now?" Jason asked.

Anthony shook his head. "No, I can't do that," he said firmly. "If she disappears, what would happen wouldn't be good for me or you."

"Well, take me to a store then," Jason said. "I need to buy some clothes."

"Do you have a way out?" Anthony asked.

"I thought you'd arrange it," Jason said, "but I have another plan ... I'm not positive, but it is worth a try."

Anthony drove to a 24-hour Target store. They entered and Jason went to the women's department and began searching a rack of dresses. Anthony looked on as if he couldn't be less interested in getting involved. However, after a few moments he uttered to Jason, "You're way off ... She is a size 5." He then pointed at another rack. Jason selected a dress and then another. He also collected three different sizes of the same sandals, since they were guessing at her size. They went to the electronics department and got four track phones and a dozen 30 day cards. Finally they went to the register and Anthony paid for all of it with cash. When they got back to the car, Jason pulled one cell phone out and carefully squeezed all the rest of purchases into his bag.

"I will contact you with this one, keep it charged and ready", Jason said.

The rest of the trip back to the hotel they rode in silence. Jason registered the phone with a card and copied the number to a piece of paper and stuffed it into the bag. Anthony parked the car.

"Are you absolutely sure?" Anthony asked.

"It's not a choice anymore ... just a matter of how I'm getting us both out of there" Jason said.

"Remember, my phone is upstairs," Anthony pointed out.

They went into the building and up the stairs to the room. Jason did not see Tasha in the office. He checked the bedroom and found her asleep on the bed. He went to retrieve Anthony's cell phone. As he handed it to Anthony, he saw the Russian guy just outside the door.

"Good work," Anthony said. "You take care of yourself."

"You too, and thanks for dinner," Jason said. "We should do it again soon."

"Yes, we should try that," Anthony replied looking eye-to-eye at Jason then towards the bedroom where Tasha slept, then he turned and left the room. The Russian looked in one last time then pulled the door shut with the familiar click of the lock.

Jason, once again locked up in the hotel, took off his clothes, turned off the light and got into bed with Tasha. She was sound asleep but as soon as his skin touched hers, she moved her head to his chest.

Jason stared at the ceiling for a while. It had been a long day and curious evening. Suddenly Anthony's parting words came to mind: "We should try that." Jason fell asleep with a creeping suspicion that there was a deeper meaning to Anthony's offer.

25

Making The Demand

J ason woke as he felt Tasha get out of bed. He could hear her in the bathroom. He was anxious to use it himself but waited until she finished and returned.

"Good morning," he said to her as she drew closer.

He stood up and Tasha threw her arms around him. He hugged her and they held the embrace for a while. She kissed him on the cheek and breathed him in. "Good morning to you, too. You smell like wine," she muttered sleepily.

He gently guided her towards the bed then turn headed to the bathroom. There, he turned on the shower and relieved himself as he waited for the water to get hot. The intense spray jarred his body awake. Immediately he recalled the previous night's events and the seriousness of his decision. Anthony had offered an easy escape, yet he'd actually chosen to come back to this place. For a moment a small part of him cried, "What an idiot!" Jason stood in the shower until this impulse faded and he could no longer stand the scalding water. He stepped out, now calmed, and began to shave. As if to further remind him why he had returned, he suddenly got a strong whiff of coffee. Tasha was up and her first thought was how to help him. He had made the right decision and chuckled to himself, "It's going to be a strong and bitter morning."

He wasn't quite finished shaving when Tasha came through the door carrying a cup of coffee. She smiled at him and seemed happy.

"You came in late last night," Tasha said.

"Yes, we talked about a lot of things," Jason replied. "He's different."

"What do you mean?" Tasha asked.

"He's intelligent … knows a lot about art and music," Jason said. "I don't think I've ever met someone like him before."

"You like him?" Tasha asked.

"I guess," Jason said, not wanting to seem too impressed. "Why?"

Tasha looked down and away as if she was uncertain about what she was about to say. In a reluctant whisper she uttered, "He likes to make pain." She could not hide the sorrowful expression that made clear her knowledge was from personal experience. She then searched Jason's face for reassurance that her admission, a completely new act of trust for her, was the right thing to do.

"I didn't know," Jason stammered as he struggled to fit this revelation in with his impression of Anthony as somehow different from the other criminals at the Hotel and the Firm.

Jason looked into Tasha's eyes. He could see a pain so deep it remained traumatic and unspeakable for her – and while she had opened the door to him she would not be able to follow through just now. He took her hand and squeezed it. In this simple unspoken gesture he made clear that she was right to confide in him, he would be there for the rest of her story. He would be there for her.

Unable to continue the matter, Tasha struggled to change the mood, "How is your coffee today?" she asked.

Jason tried it and was pleasantly surprised to find it tasted the almost way he preferred,. He smiled enthusiastically and declared, "Wow, just the way I like it!"

"Did you give him his box?" Tasha asked.

"Anthony? Yes, he has it now," Jason said. "Would you like to see what it does?"

"After I take a shower," she offered.

Jason got on with his day. He took his coffee with him while he looked for jeans and a shirt. He made his way through the office and logged into his laptop. While he waited for that, he checked on the holdout Eugene's connection. The computer he was looking for had taken his update and was connecting every two hours now. Jason installed a key logger and told the machine to list all files and directory names and send him the list.

Jason took the side panel off one of the desktop computers sitting on the table. Then under the table and out of view of the watcher's camera, he opened all of the track phones and hooked up their chargers. He put the phones inside the computer and ran the cords to the power outlet so they could charge. He pushed the side panel back on the computer so no one would notice the three new track phones charging.

Jason checked the bank under Wanda's account. It didn't appear that Willy had removed any money lately, but more important, there were no longer any small sums disappearing. He paused for a moment realizing that Willy had no online skills to take on such a problem ... and it couldn't have fixed itself. He shrugged;, the list of things to do was too long to investigate this mystery. At least Willy would have less reason to appear and interrupt his plans.

He checked the connection log on the web server. There were hundreds of thousands of infections, and the number was climbing.

Jason tried his VPN tunnel to the law office. At first, it didn't want to connect. Soon, he realized he had made a typo. After he fixed it, it worked fine. The entire global organization was visible from this single point. He ran his metasploit tool to get connected and the credentials for the Window's server. With that, he could see all of the data in the network. Every hard drive, every printer. This wasn't just local either; he even got a listing of the files on a server in the Middle East. He used the same command many technicians use to see the files on any Windows-based computer, DIR.

He set his laptop to be a bridge so that all of the actions in the room now ran through the law office network. One of the servers was un-patched and old; it was the one their accounting files resided on. Jason remotely compressed all of the spreadsheet files so he could download the entire thing in one shot.

The file named 'office passwords.doc' that he found in that directory were particularly interesting. Apparently someone at that office insisted on knowing everyone's password, so they were kept in a single file on the network. Jason downloaded that and a file called networkdiagram.pdf.

Tasha put her hands on his shoulders as she watched him open the diagram file. It gave the complete diagram for the network including router, usernames and passwords. Jason knew that law firms are famous for not really caring about security, and true to form, there was absolutely no security and documentation. He shook his head and muttered, "Screwy Rabbits…"

"What does that mean?"

Jason replied, "It's just an old expression about people who do things that are ignorant." Then he realized she was pointing at the computer screen. He quickly corrected himself, "Oh … that's a wan connection or a connection at a branch office. That one you are pointing at is their Madrid office. The legs or lines coming out of the circle mean they must have a server and 23, 24, maybe 25 computers."

"Is that the computer name?" Tasha pointed at the diagram.

"Yeah, think so," Jason said. "Let's ping it and see." He opened a command prompt on the Windows server and typed, "ping ma45np1" then hit enter. The machine responded with the same IP address as the diagram stated.

"Let's get working on sending out the notices for the images we created," Jason declared. "I installed a key logger on Eugene's computer. He's the one holding out and wanting a refund for the DVDs we didn't send."

"I don't understand, and I don't think I want to," Tasha said and shook her head. She went back to the computer she normally sat at. "Should I continue with the program or do you want to do some of these?"

"Sure, let's do a special for a $99 deal for 'rape the little girl' DVDs and charge all the ones we got passwords from, that were not the ones I connected to," Jason said.

"We didn't get passwords from any of them," Tasha said. "You said not to."

"Oh…" Jason said. "Well, what do we have?"

"We have the original one that we were doing before," Tasha said.

"You know what, let's get everyone's passwords that we can," Jason said. "Do you know how to do that on the server?"

Tasha replied, "No."

"Okay, go through the email addresses you have and look for things that look like banks,"

"How would I know that?"

"It's in the file right next to the username and password."

"How do I know which are banks?" Tasha asked.

"Do a web search for top banks, then find their URLs in the file," Jason recommended.

"Are you working on something?" Tasha asked.

"I was going to compose an email to them," Jason said.

"Why can't I help with that?"

"You can." Jason went over to where Tasha was sitting. "Let me type."

Tasha moved over, and Jason put his chair in front of the keyboard. She watched Jason type.

"Dear Pathetic Monster,
We have documented your violation of felony law including
that you downloaded and viewed a video of a female (a
child in fact) as she was raped and sodomized. We recorded
your IP address, including details of the computer you were
on and activated the camera on your computer to obtain
clear images of you in the act of viewing the highly illegal
video. We have it in our power to provide this information
to authorities in your jurisdiction or to settle the matter
directly with you. We are reasonable people but will only
make this offer once. You will open an account with the
wire service online. You will then set up the new account
to send money to us. The website will ask you security
questions and other personal information. Keep track of
your answers, as you will need them later. The site will want
you to create a password and follow their instructions. You
will send $2,000 US dollars to a passphrase account.

The passphrase question will be _____ the answer will be _____
. You will respond with an email to this email address _____
_____. The email will include on the subject line: "I complied"
and the body of the email will include the username for the
wire service, the password and the security questions. If you
attempt to tell anyone about this message or you contact
authorities, we will release the documentation described
above to assure you are arrested and charged with violation
of the several felony laws.

Again, if you pay us promptly, you will never hear from us
again. On the other hand, if you fail to do so we will expose
your actions publically and you will most certainly face
significant time in prison where those who commit crimes
towards children are further punished by other inmates.
You have 48 hours to comply."

"What do you think?" Jason asked Tasha when he was done typing.

"Why do you say 'Dear'," she asked with a confused look, "And why do you leave spaces?"

"Yeah, we'll skip the 'Dear'," Jason replied sympathetically. "The spaces are there until I figure out all the details...I think we should create different email addresses for each one and they will have to have unique questions for the wire service," he said. "We should also change IP addresses when we set up each new email address."

"Willy wants only $1,000 for each of them," Tasha pointed out.

"Yeah, but that's hardly enough blackmail for these bastards ... no amount is," Jason explained. "This whole business is sick ... it makes me sick!" Jason continued, his voice becoming strained and louder.

Tasha stepped back, "I just want to help, please don't be angry with me," she pleaded.

Jason realized he had to be more careful in her presence. She couldn't separate his anger at the Firm from the anger that had been directed towards her for years. He worked to reassure her. "I'm not angry with you ... really, I'm not," he said in a calm voice. He looked at her. She looked shrunken and withdrawn. The keepers had so terrified her, he realized. He reached out and hugged her. He held her tight and kissed her cheek softly. He wanted to tell her that he came back just for her—but not while someone might hear on camera.

The door unlocked and they both turned their heads to see the Asian girl come in with trays of eggs and toast. She put them on the table and picked up the old ones and left the room.

Jason got the coffee pot and split the remainder between them, then began to make more.

Tasha had already moved the chairs into position. They sat across from each other and ate their breakfast.

After a few moments Jason asked, "How many days have we known each other?"

"I don't know, I don't count," Tasha said.

Jason replied, "I was trying but I lost track; I don't even remember how long I've been here. Yesterday was Saturday, I think." He paused and got to the point. "Tasha, I think you're really special, do you know that?"

"I think you are special, too," Tasha replied, smiling pleasantly.

Jason leaned in to make his point more clearly, " I could not have gotten this far with anyone else so soon," he noted.

"Why is that?" Tasha asked sensing his seriousness.

"I'm awed by what you're able to do," Jason explained. "I've worked with experienced coders that didn't pick up all the technical stuff as fast as you."

Tasha looked at him soberly, unaccustomed to such appreciation for her intelligence. But she was also confused. Perhaps Jason was saying that he had no feeling for her, just respect for her skill.

Jason read the look on her face and continued, "And, you're the sexiest coder I've ever worked with."

"That's sweet … I think," Tasha said, still uncertain.

Jason became self-conscious and explained, "Maybe I'm trying too hard to tell you this."

"Don't try at all," Tasha reassured him. "I see what is there. Just be yourself. That's good for me."

They finished eating. As a way of saying "back to business," Jason filled Tasha's cup and then his own. They stored their dishes and moved the chairs back in front of a computer.

"Okay, how many do we have, thirty-eight?" Jason asked.

"Forty-one," Tasha answered.

"Let's set up the email accounts from my laptop," Jason said. "We can join TOR. That way, the IP address of the sign-up won't be traceable. We will send the email out using that email address. This way, we'll have a single email account for each transaction. If one gets compromised, the rest will still be okay."

"Maybe we should vary the amounts, too," Tasha suggested.

"Why?" Jason asked.

"Then the systems won't have the same amount to track," Tasha said.

"I like how you think," Jason said. "Smart."

"What do you think the questions should be?"

"Let's do music and musicians."

"What does that mean?"

"Name a song."

"Omul Plajei," Tasha said.

"Hmmm," Jason said. "Maybe that's not such a good idea. How about popes and bishops?"

"No not for this," Tasha shook her head. "What do monsters know about religion?"

Jason and Tasha started the process of creating 41 new email addresses. They started sending each email with a unique amount, a unique question and a unique answer. They even went through the extra step of personalizing each email with the full name of each recipient. They were making good progress with 10 finished and sent. They also sent a sms text message to the people for whom they had the number, instructing them to look at their email.

The door unlocked and the brunette, now recovered from her bruises, came in carrying two trays. She was like the others now, with her head down and completely silent movements. She left the trays on the table, took the old ones and left the room followed by a click of the lock.

"We can finish these after lunch," Jason said.

Tasha got cups and took them to the bathroom for water.

Jason moved the chairs to the table and took the plates off the trays. Today's gourmet lunch was grilled cheese and tomato soup. Nonetheless, Jason offered an air of style and affection holding a chair out for Tasha to sit down.

As they ate he finally said, "I'm really getting tired of the same thing every day," he said.

"You went out, did you eat?" Tasha asked.

"Yes, he took me to an amazing place," Jason noted all the while feeling mixed about conveying any enjoyment with Anthony. He tried to move the subject along, "Do you know how to cook?"

"It has been a while, but I used to love to cook," Tasha said. "Do you like stuffed cabbage?"

"I don't know," Jason said. "I've had something like that—I think with a rice mixture inside?"

"I made it a few times, it was yummy," Tasha said.

"One day you'll have to cook something for me," Jason said.

"I would like that," she said. They both smiled at each other.

"We need some music," Jason said. "Something special you want to hear?"

"Anything is fine," Tasha responded.

Jason got up and logged into Pandora with one of the various free accounts he controlled. The password worked because it was non-secure—one that he used often on sites that he really didn't care about. He put on the Smashing Pumpkins and turned it up so that the watcher could not overhear their conversation.

He sat back down and leaned forward. He motioned Tasha to lean forward, too. "Do you trust me?" he whispered.

Tasha stared into his eyes. "Yes," she said.

"If I left this place, would you want to come with me?" Jason asked.

She looked down so as to hide her surprise from the camera. "Yes," she replied quickly.

"Do you understand that if by some chance you were found by the government here, you would be able to stay in the United States and they would have people to help you?" Jason asked.

"No I didn't know that," Tasha said. "But I want to stay with you. Is it possible that we can leave?"

"Maybe," he whispered. "I have an idea. But I'm not sure if it will work."

"When?" Tasha asked urgently.

"Soon, but we need to finish what we are working on," Jason explained.

They both stood up and held each other.

"Do you feel like lying down?" Tasha asked.

"I do, but we need to get some things done first," Jason said. "For the next few days, we will have to work extra hard."

"Yes," Tasha said, "Day and night, whatever must be done."

"So there are some new things we need to do," Jason stated in a determined voice.

They first went back to setting up email accounts, making up passwords and looking up details about their victims wherever they could.

At account 41 Jason hit "send," paused and turned to Tasha. "Let's do one more," he announced.

"But we did all of them," Tasha said, but intrigued by the rather sly look that came over Jason's expression..

"There's one rich guy that I put aside," Jason said. "We never did his video."

"Why not?" Tasha asked.

Jason put his index finger up across his lips, turned his head and winked at Tasha in a way that it would not appear on the watcher's camera.

"Oh?" she replied and immediately turned away from him and back to her computer to also avoid revealing that they were plotting.

Jason found the file for the 'stockbroker'. He switched laptops in order to use Photoshop. Tasha helped as they made a special image for him. When they were done, they switched back to Jason's computer and the anomaly of the Tor network for creating the email account.

Jason changed his instructions. Instead of a single payment, he asked him for $50,000 in twenty increments of $2,500, and emailed him all the information.

Jason sent the email and followed up with a phone call to the broker's receptionist, Jane, to look at his personal email.

"I hope he doesn't pay," Jason said quietly, not turning to Tasha.

"Why?" she responded also continuing to face her computer.

"Because we're done getting screwed here. We need to make sure at least one of these sick bastards takes real damage and this guy definitely has the money," Jason explained coolly. While he had no expression, Tasha sensed something sinister coming over Jason.

"How about the other one … the one who would not pay?" Tasha asked.

"Oh, yeah, Eugene. Almost forgot that dude," Jason said. "Let's see, we need to download a list of files on his computer."

Jason switched to another computer and downloaded the file that the distant computer had sent. The file listed the name and location of every file on the machine.

Jason searched the file for key words like 'girl,' 'kid,' 'boy' and most important, 'anal.' He got hundreds of hits, mostly for jpg files, a popular extension for picture files on porn sites. Suddenly he stopped … included among his results was a folder titled "baby sex."

Jason had an idea of what he had dug up, but was not sure he wanted to look any further. He found Eugene's home address and pulled up a satellite view of his neighborhood. Then he went to the website of a police department near Eugene. He pulled up the mail address for his employer, the mayor, each of the city councilmen and one councilwoman. He found the newsrooms of every television channel in the area. When he was through, he had well over 50 email addresses. He logged into Eugene's email and sent each of them a similar message, including the list of files on Eugene's computer. Anyone who received the email would see that it came from Eugene's email address, just as if he had sent it himself.

Tasha looked over at his computer as he sent off the email. "Are you more happy now?" she asked, alarmed by his capacity for vengeance, just because the man had not cooperated.

"I'll be happier if he shoots himself," Jason sneered. "He has a permit. It was on one of the sites we were on. We could swat him."

"Swat him?" Tasha asked.

"Actually, that won't serve our purposes. It's a bad idea. I'll explain later," he mumbled, then added more clearly "Maybe we should expose each of them, even if they pay – they have it coming."

The door unlocked and the redhead came in carrying trays. She put them down and picked up the old trays, bowls and plates and left the room. A few seconds later she came back in carrying a vase of flowers and left them on the table next to the trays. She left the room the door locking behind her.

Tasha looked at the flowers and could not resist smiling at Jason.

"Do you want water or wine?" Jason asked.

"Water is fine," she replied, unsure of whether he needed her to work late into the evening.

"Just a few minutes more..." Jason murmured. He stepped over to his laptop and started copying all of the notes and downloads to his laptop. He stood back and seemed to look over all their work with a momentary look of satisfaction.

Then he switched gears and looked for some cups to fill with water.

Tasha moved the chairs around and set the tray in front of the chairs. She moved the flowers closer to the center. This bouquet was exotic and gave off a scent that was new and intoxicating for her.

Jason came back from the bathroom with the water to find a very lovely woman gently inhaling the flowers he had delivered just for her. It was the sort of image that would linger in his mind forever, evoked any time that scent resurfaced. In contrast to the romantic image he put a plastic cup in front of Tasha, now seated at the table.

"Will we do more work after we eat?" Tasha asked.

"No, not really," Jason said confidently.

"So, we can watch a movie?"

"Sure!"

"Pick something that you like this time"

"Sure ... remember though, you may not like it," he said, mockingly.

"I will probably like it," Tasha said. "And if not, it will be my turn to fall asleep first."

"How about a horror movie?" Jason offered.

"No," Tasha said immediately defying her openness.

"So there are things that I can't pick," Jason said.

"I just don't like…" Tasha started.

"No, I'm sorry, I didn't think," Jason said. "I do that from time to time, you know, say something without thinking."

"It's ok; it is my problem, yeah?" Tasha said.

"No!" instated Jason. "There's nothing wrong with you. I just didn't think. You've been through a lot. I just meant…I'm sorry for not thinking of you first, that's all."

"Youshouldn'thavetobesorry,"Tashasaidlookingathimwithregret.

"Look," Jason said softly. "I know there are things you have seen that I can't possibly imagine…things you keep inside. You don't tell me everything, I realize that. But maybe someday you will. In any case, know that I'm trying to understand and we can fit that into what we do together." He reached across the table and took her hands into his. "I plan on being with you for a very long time. I really care about you." He smiled and their eyes locked in a way she had avoided before.

"I care about you, too," Tasha said, tearing up, yet smiling.

"So … how about a romantic movie, something even I haven't seen?" Jason asked.

"Okay, that would be fine," Tasha replied, perking up.

"Wine?" Jason asked.

"Uh-hum!" Tasha replied, still watching as he flew through a list of movie titles.

Jason got up from the table and walked to the refrigerator. Their 'cellar' included a half-full and an untouched bottle.

"I'll wash the cups," Tasha called over to him as she got into the spirit of their little break.

Jason started with the half-bottle and filled their cups. "A toast to each other," he said.

They 'clinked' their plastic cups together, took a hefty drink and laughed still standing in the middle of the room. Then they pulled the mattress down and got the pillows and blankets.

It took Jason a while to find Casablanca online and set a movie up on the computer. Once he did, he opened another webpage and put Bon Jovi on and turned it up a bit. "I need to go to the bathroom, I'll be right back," he said.

Jason took the side panel off the computer that hid the cell phones; he slid them into a bag and took the bag with him to the bathroom.

It took a few minutes to register the three phones. He made sure he could make a call on each of them before returning them to the bag. When he was finished, he flushed the toilet and put the bag under one of the tables.

He stopped the music and started the movie. The two lay on the mattress and watched the move together.

"This is very old," Tasha observed.

"Well, maybe, but it's suppose to be very, very romantic," Jason offered " … we can decide afterwards."

Tasha smiled, though it had been a long time since she had even thought about anything romantic… "How can I tell what is 'romantic'?" she thought as they snuggled on the mattress and watched the movie. Halfway through, they joined the characters in the movie by opening their second bottle for another toast, this time to old loves. Afterwards they sat quietly for a while, enjoying their buzz and each other.

Then Tasha murmured sleepily, "I think he loves the married woman and the policeman … Is that romantic?" Jason chuckled and squeezed her weakly. Within moments they drifted off to sleep.

A Break For It

Anticipation woke Jason an hour ahead of plan, at the very darkest point in the night. The glow of the computer monitors lit the room. He lay for a minute or two listening for any sounds of activity. Beyond the locked door and through the walls, there was stillness. All he could hear was Tasha breathing as she slept with her head on his chest. Realizing there was no chance of falling back to sleep, Jason slowly slid out from under Tasha and placed her head on a pillow. Rising quietly, he headed directly his laptop and logged into the cameras on the Wi-Fi network. He first checked the control room and saw that the guard wearing the familiar cap was, as usual for this hour, sound asleep. Jason moved on to the other cameras, counting as he went. There were people in the cubes; this was prime time for them as they pushed the Firm's perverse product on sleepless customers. Jason could also see their thin guard, his face reflected by the screen of an iPad sitting in front him. His attention appeared completely lost in a video game. Jason sat back. Just as he had planned, with the exception of the room with cubes, everyone else was either sound asleep or had their guard down.

Jason checked the control board and changed the image coming from his room to one of the hallway views. He moved his laptop over by the door and set the video of the guy in the control room to fill its screen – getting past him undetected would be the first hurdle.

Now, Jason had to take advantage of the fact that while the hotel functioned as a prison, the rooms weren't made with prisoners in mind. Since the door opened inward, the pins that allowed the hinge to swing open and shut were on the inside. He grabbed the sturdiest screwdriver from his technician's tool kit and quickly attempted to force the large pin from the centermost hinge. It moved upwards and came out quite easily. Next he tried the top pin, which was harder, but finally loosened. The door came slightly out of alignment so the bottom pin would not budge. Jason knew better than to use a hammer, so he tried to strike the screwdriver and gently coax the pin out. Instead, the screwdriver flew out of his hand and fell to the floor. The sound, though minor, woke Tasha.

Jason picked up the screwdriver and tried again. As Tasha sleepily watched from the mattress on the floor, the pin started to come up out of the hinge.

"Give me a hand!" he whispered to Tasha.

She scrambled off the mattress while Jason pulled out the hinge pins, quietly laying them one by one onto the floor. Jason stuck the screwdriver between the door and the jamb at the back of the door and pried it toward the hinges.

Tasha looked on, "What can I do?" she whispered.

"Hold on just a minute," Jason said. He pulled the screwdriver out of the wood and stuck it back into the door between the door and the jamb and pried. Each time he pried it, the door moved closer to him past the hinges.

It was difficult because of the lock on the other side. They could hear the wood crack a little as Jason pried on the door. Eventually, he was able to get the door past its hinges. Together, they pulled the door back so the lock was cleared of the door jamb.

Jason slowly moved the lock mechanism to the unlocked position. He put the door back on the hinges. "Pick up the pins and put them in," Jason said while holding the door. Tasha picked up the pins and slid them into the hinges. Finally, after wiggling the door to line up the hinges, they were able to replace all the pins and push them down so the door would close more easily and without creaking.

Jason pointed at the laptop screen "Watch him for a minute," he whispered to Tasha, "Let me know if he moves at all."

Tasha caught on quickly and moved to where she could view the monitor.

Jason went back to the table and found the Cisco technician's bag on the floor where he had left it. He pulled out one of the dresses and the three pairs of sandals. While he walked back to Tasha, he handed her the dress and dropped the sandals and the bag onto the mattress. "Here, put these on, and keep watching him," he said.

But Tasha stood motionless and looking at him. Her eyes were getting larger with fear. Jason had not shared his plans with her, to protect her from interrogation and to keep her from being overwhelmed. However, he realized that in spite of her brave face, she was falling into panic as he moved so quickly about the room. So he took her by the arms firmly and whispered into her ear, "We have to go now, get dressed," and forced a smile. He let go of her and walked to the bedroom. From the doorway, he could see as she moved, as if in a trance, to change into the new clothes while keeping her eyes on the laptop sitting on the floor.

Jason found his clothes and struggled into them. By the time he moved back into the office area, Tasha was fully dressed. The dress fit and immediately transformed her from the strange zombie look of the inmates and into a stunning woman. As he walked toward her, Jason grabbed the bag from the mattress and handed it to Tasha. "Gather whatever you think we'll need," he instructed. "Tampons too," he chuckled trying to ease her concerned look. Tasha smiled weakly and took the bag to the other room to collect their few belongings.

Jason put the CD-ROMs into each computer and rebooted them, instructing the machines to start the CD-ROMs. When the last one showed the process running, he went to each monitor and unplugged it from its power source. He turned the laptops to face the wall away from the door. He repeated the process on all the computers in the room except for his laptop and the laptop with the video.

He got a chair and stood on it. He raised the ceiling tile that had the surveillance camera attached to it. The camera had one cable going to an extension cord. He unplugged the camera and broke the tile, attempting to remove the camera from it. The pieces fell to the floor. He stepped back off the chair and put the camera on top of the table. He plugged the power adapter into the camera and moved the camera so it was level on the tabletop. He opened the laptop and started the recorded video of them sleeping together. Then he switched the video to 'full screen' mode so it filled the laptop.

Next, Jason got his laptop and placed it on the table so he could see both screens. He changed the camera view so he could see the image coming from the camera. He adjusted the angle and the zoom so the camera just looked at the computer screen. The problem was that the picture on the screen was upside down, which resulted from the camera being upside down on the table. He stood there for a second. He hadn't anticipated this problem. He started to pick up the camera when he remembered flipping the video upside down by accident on his laptop once.

He tried Ctrl-Alt-Down Arrow on the laptop playing the video. Fortunately, it was an Intel video card and the screen filled upside down on the video. It now looked right for the camera.

Jason logged into the video board in the control room. He found the command to initialize a new disk and erased the disk installed. He didn't want his picture to remain on that system if anyone, such as the police, ever looked at it.

He changed the video to the guy sleeping. He had not moved. Jason grabbed the pad of paper that had his notes scribbled on it. He turned to a new page and started writing. When he finished, he tore the sheet from the pad and stuck it in his pocket.

Jason grabbed his laptop case and a few tools and threw them in the case. He also threw in the notebook. The guy in the control room was still down for the count. Jason turned off his laptop and slid it into the bag. He almost forgot the charger, which lay tangled around the table leg. Revealing his eagerness and nervousness, he scrambled under the table to free the charger, then bumped his head on the table as he attempted to stand.

He stood up in a whirl of stars, but managed to whisper "Let's go!".

"The pictures?" Tasha asked in a low voice.

"Uh right, almost forgot," he replied, still a bit unsteady.

Jason took the bag from her and quickly tossed in the three track phones and a charger, then grabbed his laptop case and threw it over his shoulder and opened the door. He waited as Tasha passed through. They stood in the hallway momentarily and looked at the room. Jason reached in and turned off the light. They closed the door and slowly turned the lock. It turned out that in spite of all his efforts with the door, the heavy lock remained true to form. As he closed the door the lock snapped so loudly that Jim, the guard in the cap, stirred in the observation room. Barely awake, he instinctively looked across his various monitors. He could see Jason and Tasha sleeping and so moved on to the workers in the cubicles. Each cube was filled with a woman with a headset, obviously working to sell product and avoid the harsh consequences of being found slacking off. He could also see the other guards who were for the most part awake and passing time. Everything seemed to be in order; but in spite of the fact he was supposed to be awake and watching throughout the night, it was unusual for him to be awakened at this particular time.

Jason and Tasha made their way as quickly as they could to the back stairway. The door to the stairs had no lock but it was very old and partly stuck. Tasha grasped it and pulled but that was not enough, so Jason placed his hand over hers and they pulled together. It gave way but with a loud creak that was amplified by the stairwell. They paused, wincing at the noise, but went through and began to head down the first staircase as quietly as they could.

Jim was suddenly fully alert. He had worked in the hotel for years and recognized the sound of the stairwell door -- someone was moving through the building. But he had accounted for everyone. Was it someone from outside? He weighed the consequences of waking Willy for nothing versus dealing with Willy in a rage if someone slipped in or out on his watch. Suddenly realizing his own life was at stake, Jim snapped up his cell phone and called Willy.

Willy, jarred from sleep answered with annoyance, "It better fuckin be important, you fat bitch."

Jim got straight to the point. "Somebody's in the stairwell. Can't see 'em, but I heard that big door upstairs. Had to be somebody strong, most of the girls can't handle that door."

"Well count heads, asshole … whadda we fuckin' pay you t'do?" came the now angry response from Willy.

"It's done," Jim replied. "All our people are where they oughtta be"

Before he uttered the last word, Willy bolted to his feet and down the hallway clad only in jeans and sneakers towards the control room, his many gang tattoos, scars and prison-crafted muscles serving as a sort of uniform – the uniform of the most vicious guard in the hotel. Arriving at the monitor room, with a mere turn of the head Willy scanned all the monitors then zeroed in one featuring the sleeping Jason and Tasha. There was something about the feed … nothing that would normally cause concern. But for someone as sickly paranoid as Willy, it was all he had to work with and more than enough to set off his impulsive rage. He turned on his heel and barked at Jim, "Call Ivan on one … it's that tech dude," then thundered down the hallway, making no secret of his pursuit.

Jim stammered something about "but they're sleeping" but his fear of Willy made him speed-dial Ivan, who sat surfing porn in a small room on the first floor.

"What is it you want?" the large man grunted.

Soon, like a lumbering version of Willy he too was out the door and into the hallway. Using his size and brutal mentality, Ivan often didn't need a gun to be lethal. However, he still grabbed his massive Magnum and tucked it into the back of his pants, alongside a huge killing knife.

"Back door just opened; I see a woman and guy walkin' out," Jim reported trying to sound in control.

Jason and Tasha paused on the landing for a second, and went down the next staircase, pausing again to stare forward and listen. Suddenly they could hear people running above them. They quickened their pace only to hear heavy footsteps coming from down stairs.

Jason was behind Tasha and began to pull open a door to floor they were passing.

"No!" said Tasha, grabbing his hand. They descended to the next floor where she flung open the door.

Jason recognized this floor; it was where the cubicles were located and he could hear the sound of the women chatting up potential customers on their headsets.

Tasha led them down a hallway where another exit sign appeared, leading to a stairwell Jason had not seen before.

Before they could get down the hallway, Ivan suddenly burst through the door of the cubicle room, knocking Tasha to the floor. He ignored her, and focused on Jason, who was paralyzed with fear and slowly backing into a wall away from him.

Ivan could easily beat the smaller man to death, but instead he grasped his large killing knife from its usual resting place in the back of his dirty jeans. Its brass knuckles were scuffed and dented from a lifetime of violence but still gleamed in the hallway light.

But Jason had his own resources, not least of which was a deep disrespect for men trying to threaten him, and a quickness in sizing up resources and options in any situation. As the huge man approached, Jason pulled from behind him a large fire extinguisher that had sat on the floor of the hallway. He took one step forward and used his moment to swing the heavy object toward Ivan. It smashed heavily onto Ivan's hand. The brass knuckles on the knife served only to make the strike more devastating and the crunch of bone on metal was loud as the larger man's instant howls of pain. Jason took another step forward, grabbed the raised extinguisher with both hands, and like a battering ram, used the bottom of it to land a blow straight into Ivan's face. Again came the sound of bone on metal, but louder this time. Ivan's nose and mouth exploded in a shower of warm blood, and he staggered backwards along the wall of the hallway, struggling to stay conscious. But blood continued to spray from his head and soon he fell over like a great tree, his huge gun sliding out of its holster and down the hallway, away from them.

Jason dropped the heavy extinguisher with a deep thud and reached for Tasha who was struggling to stand.

Unfortunately, in all the effort and noise, Willy had caught up to the action. He walked from the first stairwell straight towards Jason and Tasha, completely unconcerned about Ivan's bloody hulk lying to the side. He pulled the automatic pistol hanging in the back of his pants, cocked a bullet into the chamber and coolly approached them.

"I knew you was nothin' but trouble ... the both of you," he said, eyeing them both and making it clear he was ready to kill, regardless of the loss to him and his bosses. Then he paused and seemed to think of a more sinister assault. "Naw ... you gotta pay your debts," he said, glaring at Jason. "You still owe me ... and now," he said, tilting his head in Ivan's direction, "now you owe the Firm too." He turned the gun towards Tasha. "So first we gotta break up your little 'thang' ... we gotta get you back to business."

He had barely raised his arm when a deafening gunshot rang out. Willy stumbled forward slightly. Another shot rang out and Willy's eyes glared even brighter, then he fell forward, making no attempt to raise his arms to catch himself. He landed so hard his body seemed to bounce on the granite floor. To their horror, the back of his head was completely blown open and spilled to either side. The rest of his body twitched and he soiled himself, then he lay completely still. Standing behind him was the brunette who had served Jason and Tasha their meals – the one who had been covered in bruises. Now she was covered in her brutalizer's blood. All seemed still. The woman stared for a moment at Willy as if he might move again; then, realizing there was no chance of that, she looked up at Tasha. A faint smile came to her face, revealing broken and missing teeth. They had not seen this before, as she had never raised her head to them, let alone open her mouth.

Tasha took one step towards her and offered, "You will come with us?" The woman looked into Tasha's eyes taking in her compassion. Then her gaze suddenly turned to pain and the smile faded. Before they had any chance to respond, she raised the gun to her head and, without hesitation, pulled the trigger. Her body twisted away from Tasha and fell back into the hallway to join the gory carnage collected on the floor.

Jason was in shock. He could not have ever imagined such a scene. All the while, the sound of footsteps grew louder as Jim and the other guards followed the direction of the gunshots towards them. Jason could not move or look away. It was Tasha who firmly pulled him by the arm, breaking his trance. Her years of trauma had forged a person capable of witnessing and experiencing horror, yet able to continue to function, to survive. She pulled Jason, who kept looking over his shoulder at the bloody corpses. They stumbled into the other stairwell and began to make their way down. It must not have been used for a long time, for it was filled with debris. They arrived at the ground floor only to find the stairwell exit had been completely walled in with heavy lumber and brick. They stood for a moment as their eyes adjusted. Jason then noticed an old coal or laundry chute to one side. He grabbed a piece of debris and began to batter the metal opening of the chute. Tasha found more debris and joined the effort.

Jim followed through Willy's instructions to check other floors. When the shots sounded he joined other guards as they headed to the floor where the cubicles were located. Arriving in a sweat, he could not believe his eyes. Willy, Ivan and the Albanian girl lay in separate bloody heaps. Jim tried to make sense of the situation. He was shocked that the girl had managed to find a gun, and the nerve to avenge herself. He had witnessed Willy torturing the girl and they had been convinced there was no fight left in her – no resistance, no dignity, just slave-like obedience. Suddenly breaking this thought, Jim was distracted by Ivan who grunted and rolled over in great pain, revealing a crushed nose and eyes swollen shut.

When Jim walked nearer, Ivan coughed and murmured "…It's the one with computers … and the Romanian bitch." Jim was stunned. He pulled out his phone and began to call Willy, but the formerly terrifying man lay at his feet in a puddle of blood and brain, eyes still glaring. Jim caught himself and dialed Anthony. The phone rang only once and a calm voice answered.

"What seems to be the problem?"

Jim stuttered slightly and reported, "We got a situation here … Willy's dead and Ivan's busted up …. It's that Albanian girl … no, it's Jason … and that Romanian."

There was silence at the other end of the line. Jim repeated, more clearly this time, "What do you want us to do… I think they're still in the building?"

Anthony thought for a moment and replied "Did you check the roof…? You know Jason is a mountain climber, right?" he lied.

Jim did not waste time responding. He ran back to the stairwell followed by other guards who were on their cell phones, busily redirecting all attention to the roof of the building.

Meanwhile, Jason and Tasha had managed to loosen the rather large door of the chute. Together they pried it with their legs until it suddenly loosed from its decades of rust and flung open wide enough for them to crawl into it. Soon they tumbled into a room just inside the loading dock at the rear of the hotel. The door was locked, but only from the inside. Jason unlocked the lock and held it open for Tasha to pass. After he was outside, he made sure to close the door to further delay any awareness of their escape.

Jason was now back to a space he recognized. He and Anthony had exited from this door a couple of times. However, for Tasha it was the first time in over a year she'd been outside the building. She looked about like an animal adjusting to a completely foreign world, one she had only viewed glimpsed from the filthy windows. Far above them came the sound of people breaking open the roof door and searching for them. Shots rang out as the misled guards began to mistake each other as the escapees.

As they walked quickly away, the air was refreshing but chilly, and it was still dark out with just barely enough light to see. Jason reached into the bag and pulled one of the cell phones as they moved. He turned it on, pulled out a note from his pocket and handed it to Tasha.

She looked at the note. It was a script.

"Read this into the phone," he said ordered firmly looking directly into her eyes. He dialed 911 and handed the phone to Tasha.

The 911 operator answered on the first ring. "911, what is your emergency?"

"Please help me," Tasha said catching on quickly. "Armed men have taken over the hotel and they have shot my husband. I see him bleeding, oh, please help us!"

"Where are you?" The emergency operator asked into the phone.

"It is a hotel at 1147 8th Street!" Tasha said trying to evoke more fearful emotion in her voice to sound like a much weaker, terrified woman.

"Is it East or West 8th Street?" The operator asked into Tasha's phone.

"I don't know..." Tasha said, not expecting to provide more detail. Then she recalled from the few opportunities she had to look out the window. "It is next to McDonald's."

"Just stay on the phone with me, help is on the way," the 911 operator responded into Tasha's ear.

Tasha gave Jason a confused look. He was close enough that he could hear the operator. He reached over and took the phone from her. Without hanging it up, he tossed the phone in a nearby trash can.

That would bring police to their current location. Then, he took her hand and they walked quickly off the dock onto the sidewalk and to the left. When they were a half block away, he pulled out another phone and again called 911. They walked as he talked to the operator.

"911, how can I help you?" the operator answered.

"I hear shooting coming from that hotel on 8th Street," Jason said.

"Thank you, sir, we have units responding," the operator said.

Jason hung up the phone and turned it off.

Jim called Anthony and described the chaos. Two more guards were down, "shot by the escapees," but no Jason or Tasha.

"Well then, you know what to do," said Anthony, having helped in Jason's escape but now covering his tracks so the Firm would not suspect him.

Jim had his own history of brutal crime but had been entirely overshadowed by Willy's ruthlessness. This was his opportunity to finally replace crazy-ass Willy and his grunting Russian gorilla, Ivan. Jim, in fact, was Willy's cousin, but came from the much cooler side of the family known for their more methodical deadliness. Up to that point, Jim had been the bored, slacking underling to Willy, but no more. He was not used to being in charge but with Anthony's say-so, he immediately grabbed the reins of what was left of the guards from the hotel and those now arriving from the Firm. He directed several of them to clear the building of its valuable inmates and essential equipment. Two of the men had the task of torching the building so there was no chance of the fire department gaining enough control to save evidence of the operation. They were also to remove the two corpses so there would be no lingering trail. He then took four additional guards down to the street where they dumped bullet-proof gear, guns and flashlights into black SUVs. They sped off down the street in search of the missing inmates as flames began to engulf the upper floors. At the rear loading dock, shackled women shuffled in the shadows carrying equipment as they were brutally herded into a large cargo truck to be transported to another trafficking site.

Meanwhile, Anthony dialed the number for Zach, a part time security guard and bounty hunter who used the taxi network as his preferred tool. It took several rings for him to answer; it was 4:45 in the morning and he had gone to bed only an hour before.

"Uhh, yeah, what's up?" Zach said into the phone not fully awake.

"This is Anthony. We need you to arrange a pick-up."

"What?" Zach said, sitting up. He had heard the command, he just didn't understand.

"Right now!" Anthony repeated firmly into the phone.

"What the fuck, I'm at home in bed!" Zach protested.

"Get moving," Anthony said calmly, though it was clear that he was giving an order.

Zach then realized who he was speaking to, which snapped him awake. "Uh, yeah man, you bet. Who is it?"

"You'll find a man and a woman on foot. He's around 5'5", brown hair, slim build. She's about the same height, thin, pretty. They shouldn't be that hard to spot -- there can't be too many couples walking near the Hotel at this hour."

"Got it," Zach said. "What do I do with them?" he added having pulled on his clothes and heading for his parking lot.

"I'll decide that when you find them." Anthony said, trying to leave his intentions threatening but unspecific.

"Gotcha," Zach responded as he pulled the door of his apartment open and moved to run down the steps. His cab was just outside; he could radio everyone on night shift to look for the pair. He slid the phone into his front pocket with one hand, and the other fumbled for his keys. His jeans were somewhat tight and with both hands in his pockets, he leaned forward a little too far. He tried to pull out his hand with the keys but instead he became unbalanced on the stairwell. He was four steps from the bottom when he lost his footing. The motion caused him to turn completely backwards, and he hit the hard landing head-first. He saw a bright white flash, and the small hanging lamp attached to a street post before being plunged into darkness.

They were almost six blocks away before they heard the first siren. By seven blocks, they heard even more sirens. It was fortunate that he grew up in this city, so he knew its streets. Eight blocks away they took a sharp left which put them on target for the bus station.

"Where are we going?" Tasha asked.

"We gotta get away from here. We're going to the bus station," Jason replied.

Tasha felt a somewhat-familiar terror, but somehow it was different in the presence of this man. She glanced at him momentarily, then set her eyes forward and worked even harder to keep in step with him.

The station was another eight blocks away.

Though it was still summer, they could see their breath in the cool air. Jason was unaware of the cold. He was slightly in shock, still reeling from what had just happened but yet he was excited. He was free—out of the clutches of those vicious assholes. It began to dawn on him how impossibly lucky they were to have escaped. Then again, maybe it wasn't luck … an unexpected number of people had had a hand in their effort. He'd have to wait until later to take score.

Tasha was still focused forward, trying to regain familiarity with something as routine as walking for any distance. It helped that it was dark and there was no one around – less for her vigilant state to take in as she scanned for possible threats while taking in the unfamiliar sense of freedom.

When they were about two blocks from the station, the black SUV flew past them and down the street.

They continued to walk, heads down, clinging to each other as couples do after a late night out. However, the SUV suddenly skidded to a halt, its rear lights turning the entire street a red glow.

Jason pulled Tasha into the walkway of a brownstone apartment and towards its rusted back gate. Together they shoved it until the latch gave way and they continued into the backyard, over a brick barbeque stove and then down to the alley behind it.

They could hear the SUV screeching as Jim let some men out to follow while he drove around the block.

They came out of the alley as far from the noise as they could get. They continued walking as quickly as they could. Just a block away the bus station came into view, its many lights piercing into the night. Just then, the SUV vaulted into a handicap space in front of the bus station's main doorway. At the same time, the additional guards who had given up looking for them in the alley ran up to the SUV and began to wait.

Around the bus station there were a lot more people on the street, including other couples. The guards from the hotel approached each person and roughly confirmed their identity. Jason and Tasha stood in the shadows of a restaurant street patio, waiting for their luck to turn so they could make their way onto a bus. A half-hour had passed when Jason noticed a taxi stand across the street from the bus station with four cabs, roof lights on, waiting for a fare. The drivers stood in the street arguing sports with each other and sipping coffee purchased at the bus station.

Sticking to the shadows, Jason led Tasha to the first cab in line. He opened the door on the side away from the bus station and the awaiting guards. He and Tasha quietly slid in keeping her head low and turned away from the threat.

"Where to?" the taxi driver asked.

"The bus station in Springfield," Jason replied.

"That's over 50 miles from here." he said, looking them over in the rear view mirror for signs of possible trouble, or just stupidity. "You can take a bus, you know," he said sarcastically.

"We just missed it," Jason pointed out firmly, eyeing the guards standing just yards away. "Get us to Springfield so we can make for our next connection." To remove any additional doubt or unwanted inspection, Jason pulled out his wallet and showed the driver a hundred dollar bill. That was all the driver needed to accept that the couple was serious and would make it worth his while. He put his hack in gear and drove away from the cab stand towards the onramps to the highway.

Less than a minute later, the bounty hunter called Anthony from the station and in a shaky voice tried to recover from his blunder. "I'm at the bus station and they're not here," he said.

Anthony paused. "There are a lot of other ways to leave town besides a bus."

"Yeah, but this is where all the muscle from the Hotel is sittin' ... right out in front," he pointed out. Zach had used his vast network of hack drivers to figure out where the action was at – they served as a form of moving radar and frequently passed the time at night sharing the slightest unusual movements on the streets ... that is, when they were in their hack and paying attention to their radios.

"You still haven't found them, and you probably won't if the guards are keeping them from entering," Anthony replied impatiently.

"I know that," Zach explained, rubbing his three-day stubble thoughtfully. "But I figure you're worryin' about this couple gettin' smoked by the hotel crew ... that ain't happenin' as long as they're sittin' here scratchin' their asses."

Anthony smiled. He couldn't understand why the bounty hunter had chosen this approach to the situation, but he was right. All Anthony wanted was for Jason and the woman to get away; and with every passing moment it was likely that they had made their escape. But he also knew Zach. It wouldn't be long before he would find their trail; he always found his prey.

As the cab sped away from the city, Tasha and Jason sat close to each other, holding hands tightly. Tasha, while unmoved by the violence and death, was overwhelmed by the sight of the outside world; she stared at lights, buildings, and trees with childlike wonder. She thought for a moment of the Albanian woman who had just martyred herself. She had seen her a couple of times but could not remember her name. What was the point of remembering names in a world of bloodthirsty attackers, disposable victims and a world that did not care? But there was an answer to that question. When it became apparent they had driven far out of harm's way, she turned to Jason and asked, "What is your name?"

Jason looked at her perplexed and replied, "You know … 'Jason'."

"No." she continued. "All of your name, the full name."

Jason thought for a moment then leaned in to whisper in her ear. Then he asked, "What's yours?"

There was a serious pause, Tasha had to think carefully as she had memorized so many aliases and "types" that she was required to play. She leaned in and whispered in his ear, as if giving him a gentle kiss. Then they burst into laughter, happy to be alive and discovering they had managed to find someone they could so genuinely. Of course, this good feeling did not extend to the driver and for the most part they sat quietly holding hands, looking out the window at a world that felt new, free.

Jason found Tasha's touch calming and he began to concentrate more fully on the situation. In spite of their escape he felt far from cocky. His plan ended at escaping the Hotel. He had figured out how to escape that trap, but not how to escape his life. He still had a murder to clear up, which meant the police would be looking for him. However, it wasn't likely the cops would associate him with the Hotel. Then again, Tasha had no ID, so crossing into Canada or getting on an airplane would be impossible …There was the cash he had stashed in his wallet and the remainder in the laptop case, which might be enough to get them off the grid. He had heard that in Tijuana you could "buy" identification. That would further cover their trail and offer them both some new options. In Mexico they could rent a car and drive to Brazil. Once there they could approach the Romanian Embassy to arrange travel documents for Tasha. And he would need a passport too. However, after the confinement and the ordeal at the hotel, the challenges before were perhaps minor. Just then and in spite of all his concerns, Jason recalled that Tasha's only desire was to find a beach. That simple goal suddenly captured his imagination and inspired a real plan. Just a few hurdles and they would be on to a new world of possibilities.

Just then the cab driver looked down at a recent group text on his cell phone. "skg blo f & bru m @near pabt $5K no qs" It was from that fool Zach, who made out like some sort of badass bounty hunter. He shook his head, annoyed by the intrusion from the part-timer. "Dude's not legit, his hack not legit," he grumbled to himself, "no papers, no medallion … worse than the fuckin' foreigners in their stolen rides makin' off with my fares." Then again, he had just come from the bus station, the only place to find a fare at this time in the morning. He grew thoughtful and then searched for the time stamp on the text. He blinked in sudden awareness. Then, without moving his head, he allowed his gaze to move slowly upwards to his rear-view mirror to could get a better look at his current fare, whispering intimately in the back.

At the same time, miles behind them, the Hotel, now surrounded by police and fire fighters, burned with unapproachable intensity. As if to reinforce the world's deep denial, the raging flames removed any evidence and witnesses of the global network of slavery and suffering that operated daily without societal outrage or challenge. The Firm, with its shining reputation and powerful clientele, would continue to exploit this dark stain on humanity using technology to better enslave the vulnerable and gratify the vulgar. In less than a week the slaves from the Hotel would be back online in a new location, hidden in plain sight.

The End

Epilog

The dark side of the Internet is closer than you think. The entire world is connected to the outlet that you call your router or modem. Every brothel, psychopath, pedophile, thief and politician is online along with you. The idea that some sort of safety exists is just an illusion sold to us by big and powerful marketing and financial corporations.

After meeting Karen, and retelling her story several times, it became clear that no one I knew really understood this part of the Internet. The very place where you feel safe buying books and movie tickets shares space with the same vermin who trade in humans and use them as points of profit.

The ways to steal money from people are many times more numerous than simply those outlined here. The process of stealing money and injecting advertisements to install malware on popular websites are not new. Criminals have been doing this as long as there have been web pages. You can read it in newspaper headlines; it is all around us.

The following excerpt is from the FBI website

Human sex trafficking is the most common form of modern-day slavery. Estimates place the number of its domestic and international victims in the millions, mostly females and children enslaved in the commercial sex industry for little or no money. The terms human trafficking and sex slavery usually conjure up images of young girls beaten and abused in faraway places, like Eastern Europe, Asia, or Africa. Actually, human sex trafficking and sex slavery happen locally in cities and towns, both large and small, throughout the United States, right in citizens' backyards.

This is how you can be a little safer with a computer:

Step 1: Put tape over the camera on your television and other devices that people could use to watch you.

Step 2: Get a new, cheap computer. This will be your financial computer where you'll never do web searching or social networks. Install an antivirus on it and keep it upgraded. Many of the free antivirus programs that you can down load such as Avast, Avg or Clam (Mac) are more reliable than some of the big name vendors that you buy.

Step 3: Sign up for a new email address from that new computer. Make the new password at least eight characters long. If the site allows it, use a combination of upper and lower case letters, numbers and symbols. Some financial and utility websites don't take security seriously and will not let you use symbols in your password. If you encounter a site like that, make the password as long as you can. Then write down the password on paper so you can remember it.

Step 4: Change all of your financial and utility accounts to the new email address as well as the password; use he best password you can. If they support two-step authentication, sign up for it.

Step 5: Change the security questions of the sites you use. The best security questions will never be repeated. So the best answer on the Internet is a lie. Never give any real information on the net. Just write down your answers so you can remember them. do not save them on a phone or on the internet idiots do things like that.

Only leave the finance computer on when you need to use it. A hacker can't remotely access a box that is powered off or unplugged. Some viruses, however, have code in them to wake the computer from sleep mode to do their dirty work.

www.ingramcontent.com/pod-product-compliance
Lightning Source LLC
Chambersburg PA
CBHW070203120726
47909CB00001B/233